T0357327

Additional praise for **Where Shadows Bloom**

"A magical blend of romance and whimsy, equal parts devastating and hopeful. With a touching, tender slow-burn romance at its core, *Where Shadows Bloom* is a lovely and rich confection of a book."
—AVA REID, #1 *New York Times* bestselling author of
A Study in Drowning

"Gorgeous, lyrical, and incredibly emotional, *Where Shadows Bloom* is a story about love in all its forms—when it's false, when it's real, when it hurts, and when it heals. I cannot recommend this dark daydream of a novel highly enough."
—KAMILAH COLE, bestselling author of *So Let Them Burn*

"*Where Shadows Bloom* is utterly romantic. Every turn of the page brought me deeper into a world that felt like a carefully crafted fairy tale. One filled with sharp shadows, long buried secrets, and stolen glances that set my heart ablaze."
—ANGELA MONTOYA, author of *Sinner's Isle*

"Dark, enchanting, and deeply romantic, *Where Shadows Bloom* is the sapphic teen fantasy I didn't know I wanted! Catherine Bakewell deftly weaves a story filled with monsters and magic, and two brave girls who will remain with you long after you turn the last page."
—TANAZ BHATHENA, award-winning author
of *Hunted by the Sky* and *A Girl Like That*

"The glittering balls of *Bridgerton* meet the dark mystique of magic in this enthralling sapphic love story. Catherine Bakewell's lush and lyrical writing will sweep you away to the exquisite palace of Le Château, where dark shadows lurk just beneath the gilded surface. I was utterly enchanted!"
—LESLIE VEDDER, bestselling author of the Bone Spindle trilogy

"By turns delightful, decadent, and dangerous, *Where Shadows Bloom* is a captivating sapphic fantasy full of heart and hope. I read it in a breathless gallop and was still shocked by the twists at the end."
—JAMIE PACTON, bestselling author of *The Absinthe Underground*

Where Shadows Bloom

Also by Catherine Bakewell

Flowerheart

Where Shadows Bloom

CATHERINE BAKEWELL

HARPER

An Imprint of HarperCollinsPublishers

Library of Congress Control Number: 2024942233

ISBN 978-0-06-335908-6

Typography by Catherine Lee

24 25 26 27 28 LBC 5 4 3 2 1

First Edition

To Lucy,
this story has always been yours.

And to Jordan, Stephanie, and Clare,
brave knights and defenders of books.

1

Ofelia

It was the perfect evening to run away from home.

Mother had locked herself away in her studio and was surely so concentrated on her latest portrait commission that she wouldn't even know I was gone. Until tomorrow, anyway, when she found the note on my pillow explaining my plan to her. If all went well, in less than a week, I would finally be walking the halls of Le Château Enchanté. Not long after, Mother would join me, and she'd soon be happy and carefree, painting the palace gardens.

By my side, exploring that magnificent, gods-blessed place, would be my dearest friend, Lope.

Tonight, though, she would serve as my accomplice and protector.

With a pillowcase full of my belongings slung over my shoulder, I crept down the staircase and hid behind a large marble column. I peeked out and, as I had planned, one of the manor's guards, a young man dressed in a blue coat, was leaving his post. For five whole minutes, the front doors would be unguarded, as the knight who stood vigil swapped places with his replacement so he could have supper. *Perfect.*

I carried my shoes in my hand to soften the sound of my footsteps as I raced to the double doors and whirled through to stand on the terrace, triumphant. My back pressed to the door and my pillowcase clutched tight in my fists, I could hear Mother scolding me in my head. *Don't go outside at twilight. Don't be so moony, Ofelia.* And then, in her loudest, sharpest tone, from just an hour ago, *Never ask me about Le Château again.*

But the palace was the only place in the world where Shadows did not roam. And I could no longer ignore the way my mother's eyes darkened, the way her fear mounted day after day as the Shadows crept closer to our home. We needed someplace safe. If Mother could not overcome her qualms with the palace, then I would take that first step for her.

The lawn was painted orange in the evening light. Our garden was sparse; just a few flowers and some boring boxwoods that were never trimmed. Mother would never pay a gardener for such "frivolities." But I loved it. The azaleas, peonies, and impatiens that grew throughout the garden were meager, but they were mine.

Apart from these and the paintings Mother made just for us, there were not many beautiful things in my world.

The high wall of stone that surrounded the manor was the greatest reminder of this, and of the monsters that lay in wait not far from us.

But the wall also reminded me of a certain knight. And if my clever and hastily concocted scheme was timed as perfectly as I planned, Lope would now be just outside the eastern wall.

Ducking to avoid the windows, I darted through the long shadows painting the manor walls until I reached my destination. An expanse of the gray stone border wall was covered in thick vines and uneven bricks edged out just so, as if it were made for a girl trying to run away from home.

I had practiced the climb before. Just in case this day ever came.

There had at least been a *possibility* before our fight that when I turned seventeen, Mother would come to her senses and allow me to be part of society. Would give me at least a chance to leave the cold, empty rooms of the manor behind and experience all the wonders of Le Château. My heart ticked into a gallop. I longed for the palace more than anything. For a world far bigger than the only one I'd known. A world where I could afford to concern myself not with my safety but with *happiness*. Dances and card games and races through gardens, gardens that flourished. Where nature was not the home of Shadows but simply a place for *beauty*. I was so certain that my heart would be healed and finally, abundantly happy the day I entered those golden gates.

And perhaps I would find not just joy, but *love*, too. A girl who loved me. Loyal, kind, and patient. Tenderhearted but brave enough to follow me on even my wildest adventures.

Well. I wasn't going to have my fairy tale on this side of the wall.

I tied the top of my pillowcase shut to hold all my belongings in, and then, with all my might, tossed it over onto the grass beyond. I heard a gasp and the singing of metal: a sword, drawn from its scabbard. Then, softly, "What on Earth?"

My heart swelled. I'd been right. She was there.

"Lope," I whisper-shouted. "Lope, wait right there!"

With sweaty palms and a thrumming pulse, I grasped on to the thick vines and sturdy brick in front of me and climbed until I could heave myself up onto the wall, sitting astride it like I was on horseback. Below was Lope, shielding her eyes from the dying light, her mouth hung agape.

"My lady!" she croaked. "What are you doing?"

"Going on an adventure," I whispered back. I glanced over my shoulder toward the manor, but thankfully, there was no sign of Mother or any guards. When I looked at Lope again, the distance from her was dizzying. I squeezed my eyes shut and swallowed the knot in my throat. "I—I seem to have forgotten about climbing down."

Lope unbuckled the scabbard from around her hips and tossed it onto my pillow-bag lying in the grass. She approached the wall, holding out her hands for me like I was some cat stuck up in a tree.

"Slide your legs over," she coaxed. "I'll catch you."

I pried one eye open. She and the earth seemed miles and miles below. I wobbled in place and took in a sharp breath, screwing my eyes shut. "Do you promise?" I peeped.

She laughed, soft and shy. "I'll catch you. May the gods strike me down if I'm lying."

In spite of everything, I smiled. Mother said I was too much of a dreamer, that I had an insatiable desire to be in a fairy tale. But with Lope, that never seemed to matter. I was the only person in the world who could make her smile. Practical, focused Lope, who had a near-permanent furrow in her brow and a hand on her sword, but who always listened with relish to my made-up stories of all things marvelous.

What harm did it do, seeing the beauty in the world? Wanting to have a life happier, more beautiful, *safer* than the dull one we lived within this crumbling manor? Seeing Lope now just reaffirmed that I was making the right decision. For all of us.

I slipped over the wall, and just as she'd promised, Lope's arms anchored around me. I was in the warmth of her hold for just a moment before she delicately stood me upright. I dug my boots into the dirt, grateful to be earthbound once more. I gazed up at my dearest friend, taking in the face that was as familiar to me as the ground beneath my feet: pale, marked with faint white scars, her long, elegant nose, the notch in her brow when she frowned. The eyes that could be as bright as silver were dark as storm clouds today, and rimmed with red.

"You shouldn't cry on your birthday," I said softly.

She turned from me and scrubbed the heel of her hand against her eyes. "You're right. Forgive me. And happy birthday to you, too."

I always found it the most charming, magical thing that the two of us were born on the very same day, under the very same star. It was as if we were fated to be friends.

But despite the happy occasion, I could tell something was amiss. Her short words, her weak tone, the way she kept glancing to the horizon—some very special days, Lope would share her worries, her fears, her pain with me. Other times, like this evening, I knew that she was not ready for me to ask about her heartache.

"I brought you a gift!" I chirped instead, scooping up my pillow. Lope's sword rolled aside into the grass.

"You needn't have done that, my lady." Lope surveyed the countryside, orange and gold as candle flames, with the plains cast in amber. "It's getting late. You—you shouldn't be out."

"I know. But this is my chance." From my bag, I procured a book bound in red leather with a rose etched onto its cover.

Lope's eyes widened as I placed it in her hands, her lips

tilting into a wondrous smile. "Such a beautiful journal, my lady." She touched the cover so delicately, so reverently. "This is . . . this is more than I could have dreamed of." When her eyes met mine, my heart fluttered, perhaps from the sheer delight of choosing such a perfect gift for her. "Forgive me, I do not have a gift for you here—"

"There's something you can do for me!" I interjected, folding my hands penitently and offering the loveliest, most innocent smile I could muster. "Something that could inspire you to write a hundred new poems!"

As I batted my lashes, she glanced from me to my bag to the wall and then back at me. Her smile slowly began to fade into something like suspicion. "My lady . . . what did you mean when you said you were going on an adventure?"

I took a deep breath. My speech would go much better the second time. "Since I am seventeen now, I've decided the best thing for myself, *and* for my mother, is to go to Le Château and petition His Majesty to let us stay in his courts." Already Lope was opening her mouth, her brow furrowed, but I kept speaking with fervor. "The stories say there is only one place in the world safe from the Shadows, and that's Le Château. We *must* go. You told me just last night that more and more Shadows are appearing, just in the past few days!"

Lope grimaced. "Yes, but—"

"So it's more dangerous than ever out here! And what sort of future am I meant to have in this manor?" I asked, a tremor shaking my voice. "Am I meant to rot away inside, embroidering and reading, isolated from the rest of the world forevermore?

"And"—I hesitated but pushed on—"Mother is *miserable*; she's so lonely, and she worries daily about the Shadows, but she won't do anything about it because she thinks I am too young and too naïve to live at the palace!" I jabbed my thumb at my chest. "I'll prove to her that I'm mature. I will go and make a place for us. I'll show her that I'm capable enough for court life, and I'll take care of everything. I'll have a royal carriage fetch her and bring her safely to the palace. None of us will have to fear the Shadows again."

"Your Ladyship—"

"Ofelia. Please, call me Ofelia." Lope never listened to me when I told her this, but I'd never given up trying, either. We'd known each other for five years now, since she first came here as a knight-in-training. Part of me wished she would set aside the differences in our stations and just call me by my name, but a smaller part of me felt a thrill each time, at the unending chivalry Lope extended to me, just as a knight in my fairy tales.

A blush rose up on her face, beautiful as a sunset, and she tucked a lock of black-and-silver hair behind her ear without meeting my eyes. "My lady, what happened? What brought this on?"

My throat was still raw from the shouting I'd done. And

my heart still trembled as I thought of the fear in Mother's eyes when she'd said, *Put this dream of yours to bed. You are safe here.*

Safe. Safe, while monsters crept closer to our walls every day.

"It's three days to the palace by carriage alone," Lope murmured into my silence, worry making the little wrinkle between her brows deepen. A part of me longed to press my thumb against it, smooth it out so she could smile again. "Do you mean to travel on foot?"

"It's not a far walk to the next town, and I can hire a coach there." I gave the bag over my shoulder a little shake. "I brought enough money to get by."

"But . . . through the night? What about the Shadows?"

I smiled up at her. She looked as she always did: a knight from an old storybook come to life, noble and handsome, with her broad shoulders and her shining breastplate. My heart quivered at the thought that she would be a part of my story. "That is where I need your expertise," I said.

But there was darkness in her eyes. Sadness. The same sort my mother had whenever I asked her about Le Château.

"The journey is not safe," she whispered. "Trust me."

I shivered at her words. She knew those Shadows well. Sometimes, on a very hot day, she would unwind the cravat that she always kept around her throat. Her neck was long and slender but covered with bruises and scars and scratches. Claw marks.

"You are too skillful a knight," I said, shaking away the memory. "You would not let a Shadow even steal a glance at me."

Her full lips pressed into a thin, pale line. In a blink, her eyes had grown glassy. She breathed, squared her shoulders, and then the strange shimmer was gone. "I'm sorry. I can't. I can't risk anything happening to you—"

"Nothing will happen to me. You'll protect me," I cooed. Inside, my pulse raced; I could feel my beautiful future slipping through my fingers like stardust. "Please, Lope, I'm willing to brave the journey. It is worth the cost. The palace is my heart's greatest dream. My mother and I . . . we need it. Le Château Enchanté is a place blessed by the *gods*. It could be our sanctuary."

There was a book I liked to steal from the highest shelf in our library, a book that told the story of our king. In it, King Léo was crowned with a laurel by six of the gods, clouds artfully shielding their faces even in the illustration. The gods were too far beyond us, too good for us to know their appearances. But they were so pleased with the king that they *blessed* him.

On the next page was a sprawling depiction of the palace itself. It was surrounded by a beautiful garden filled with statues and hedges and flowers, all drawn in shades of black, white, and gray. The very gates, the book claimed, were covered in gold. I could imagine it, a whole palace surrounded by brilliant light, like the rays of the sun.

It seemed fantastical, too good to be true, but my mother *had* lived there. She was proof that this place, this story, was *real*.

Mother could have that fairy tale again, with me by her side. I could change everything. And she'd be happy at last.

"Think of it," I whispered. "Together we'd dance in the ballroom and ride gondolas on the canal in the gardens . . . and you wouldn't need to fight Shadows anymore." I tugged on her hand imploringly. "You *must* come with me. You must see a world beyond this wall. Think of all you could write about! I cannot bear to see such beauty without you. And also, I'm horrible at reading maps, so I would be quite lost without you."

At this, she let out a bark of a laugh, and a slow, relenting smile dawned on her face. "Very well. I'll be your knight."

I gasped in delight. "Oh, I hoped you would say yes! It's going to be a dream, I promise; we'll dress in violet and dance all night and try foods we've never dreamed of!"

With a twirl, I faced the horizon, the world sweet as sparkling wine and ours for the taking. There was a forest far off, like a low storm cloud. And then, near the edge of the hazy gray woods was a dark silhouette, a tall person standing afar, their head cocked at a strange angle.

Lope stood by my side. Her eyes narrowed into slits.

"It couldn't be," she whispered. "It's too early."

11

"Too early?"

The silhouette seemed to stand taller. Its edges were fuzzy, as if a trick of the fading light. And in the next blink, it had collapsed, melting into the ground. In its place, a vast, black Shadow sped across the grass, like some great bird was flying overhead.

Flying right toward us.

Fear and memories clenched my heart in a cold grasp—*I have seen this before*, I thought.

Lope swore and dove for the sword discarded in the grass. I whirled back toward the space where the Shadow had been, but—

Sharp claws anchored in my hair, scraping against my scalp before wrenching me backward. I felt the world tilt as I hit the grass with no time even to scream before the breath was knocked from my lungs. Directly above me was a shape that bore only the faintest memory of what a human looked like. Its face was swirling, black smoke, completely featureless. In the void where its mouth ought to have been, jaws slowly unhinged, down, down, far past what should have been possible.

Suddenly, I was seven years old again, as helpless as I had been the night I had first seen a Shadow. It made the same horrible, rattling growl, the sound that lingered in the back of my mind during the darkest nights.

A scream tore out of my throat, my entire body going

cold. *I'm going to die I'm going to die I'm going to—*

The creature howled as it was wrenched away from me by some unseen force. In that moment of freedom, I scrambled up to my feet, just long enough to see Lope atop the Shadow. With one hand, she pressed upon its neck, forcing it down even as it hissed and writhed and snapped its toothless jaws at her. With a jerk of her arm, she held her sword high before she rammed the blade through its head.

It seized and wailed, and then it was gone. Fizzled away into bits of smoke and shadow that melted into the earth like rain.

Lope's chest heaved. She yanked her sword out from where it was now plunged into the dirt. Aside from the remnants of dark soil against the steel, the blade was unstained. Shadows had no blood.

My trembling legs failed me, and I fell back onto the grass, shielding my head with my arms. Weak, childlike sobs broke from my lips. I was two places at once: I was a little girl in the garden, and Mother was lifting me out of a Shadow's grasp, her arms weeping blood; I was lying in the field just beyond the wall, breathless with tears.

An urgent voice came from above, from the waning sunlight itself. "My lady, are you harmed?"

The fearless knight, the knight from my storybooks. Lope looked me over with frantic eyes, even as she held steadily to her sword. I could barely fathom how she was so calm.

But Lope had faced such creatures every night since she was twelve years old. Not just one. *Hundreds*, she said. Dozens at a time, always in the darkest part of the night. That was a Shadow's domain. They never ever appeared during the daytime—but the faintest bit of daylight still lit the sky a pale, mournful pink.

"I'm going to carry you," she said, and I blinked past the evening light, focusing on the gray of her eyes. "Keep your arms around my neck."

The Shadow was gone now; we were *safe* now, but all I wanted to do was bury my head against her heart and weep. Why could I not stop shaking?

I held on to her like she told me to, but my pulse thundered with her every step. My mind was slowly, desperately trying to catch up with all that had happened. *I was going to die. She saved my life. She saved me.*

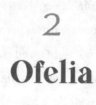

2

Ofelia

When I was seven years old, the night after I had first seen and survived a Shadow's claws, Mother held me and hushed me to sleep, even though her arms were raw and covered in fresh sutures. She sang to me and comforted me.

There had been no wall back then. Back then, I was obedient and innocent and good. I had not tempted the Shadows by crossing into their domain.

Now, Mother sat in the parlor, her face pale and horribly blank. She had cried more when I was younger. Her stillness was worse.

I sat across from Mother, a knitted blanket wrapped around me in an effort to stop my trembling. Tears still clung to my cheeks. Lope reached into the pocket of her breeches and silently offered me a handkerchief. The one I had decorated for her with a messy embroidered *L*. I thanked her under my breath as I cleaned my face.

"You could have died," Mother said, her voice faint, broken in two.

"Lope was there to protect me, Mother, she—"

"And what if she hadn't been?" Her blue eyes narrowed. "I nearly lost you to those creatures before. I built this wall to shield us, I hired a dozen knights, and still you have the *gall* to ignore your safety to, what, go on a nighttime stroll?"

"It was still light outside," I whispered, but with my weak voice it was hardly convincing.

"That makes things worse," she said, her voice delicate but quaking with rage. Her gaze flitted to Lope, who stood stock-still, her posture tall and noble as a suit of armor. "Caballera de la Rosa, have you ever seen anything like this before? Shadows out before nightfall?"

Lope shook her head. "No, Your Ladyship. But there have been more of them each night. We try our best to keep count of the monsters that assail the manor."

"More of them," Mother whispered. She leaned forward over the tea table, pressing her hands against her eyes. "Gods above. Ofelia, what were you doing beyond the wall? What did you think would happen? A knight your age just *died* at that wall."

Memory struck me. She was right. A boy a little older than me. Carlos. Lope's friend. No wonder she was crying before. I glanced at her, but her face was stony.

"Did you think the Shadows would just ignore you?"

Mother continued. "Did you *wish* to be harmed?"

I flinched at each accusation.

"Your Ladyship," Lope said softly, "I'm the one to blame. I should have been more alert. And Lady Ofelia only wanted to be outside to meet with me. It's my fault she was out."

Of course she'd try to save me, even from my own mistakes.

"Nonsense," said Mother. "She's only alive *because* you were there." She wiped her eyes and shook her head. "Thank you for saving my daughter, Caballera de la Rosa. I will reward you for your valor. For now, please—please let me have a word with Ofelia in private."

My stomach sank. Lope hesitated for just a moment, head turning toward me, before she bowed to my mother and then to me. I watched helplessly as she slipped through the double doors of the parlor and shut them.

The clock on the nearby table ticked a frantic little heartbeat. Mother sighed. The sheen of her tears made the candles' flames flicker in her eyes. "How could you do something so heartless?"

The word was a blade in my chest. *Heartless,* as if she herself hadn't listened to me pour my heart out hours ago and rejected all my pleas. *Heartless,* as if I could sit silently at home while her sadness grew daily.

Rage bloomed inside me, and I cried, "Mother, I did this for you! You have been so unhappy and so frightened

17

and—and you've shut yourself away on *my* behalf. But you don't have to! We would thrive at Le Château, I know it. We could all be happy there! So I decided to go to Le Château so that I may ask the king for refuge."

"Ofelia, don't—" Mother did not even let herself finish her own sentence. She wrapped her arms around herself tightly, like she needed an embrace but didn't have the strength to ask for one. My heart twisted. Even after all our quarrels, seeing her hurt made me feel like I'd swallowed poison. I crossed the carpet and sat beside her on the sofa. Suddenly, her arms were around me.

At the soft touch, it was like a barrier I had put in place crumbled away, and the memories and the fear of the last hour rushed back in. My memories flickered between my childhood terror and the one I had met just minutes ago.

I leaned into her embrace, sobbing. No matter how I tried, I couldn't stop shaking. The scene played itself over and over against my eyelids, the creature lunging, its empty eyes, its jaws, widening, widening, widening . . .

"I'm so glad you're safe," Mother whispered, covering my head in kisses.

"I'm sorry," I said, my voice smothered against her gray gown. Her lilac perfume embraced me as she did.

Mother sniffled as she rubbed her hands against my back. "My sweet girl," she murmured. "I am here to protect *you*. You should not feel burdened with my fears. I wish I could just keep you locked away, keep you safe from all this trouble."

When I finally caught my breath, I lifted my head and began to brush the tears from her own cheeks. It was rare to see Mother show her emotions so plainly. It made me forget my own fears and only long to tend to her own. "We'll be fine," I told her. "We have the knights to protect us."

She shook her head. "No, I—I had thought so, too. But every day things get worse. And now we cannot even rely on the sun for safety."

Mother pulled away from me, a distant look in her eyes as she drifted toward her gallery wall, past one painting, then another. She paused at the first portrait she'd made of the two of us, me as a little girl with my arms around her neck. Mother had spent months on it. She had liked it so much she commissioned it to be painted in miniature. The tiny portrait of myself at age six was tucked into the golden locket that she always wore: the one she twirled when she was anxious, as she did now.

Mother always seemed drawn toward the past when she was upset. As the silence stretched, I knew which painting she'd turn to next: the portrait of my father, hung in a chipped gold frame on the wall. Long dark hair, blue eyes, thin lips. I took after my mother, mostly, though my father had a smile similar to mine. His pure white cravat and his red brocade coat spoke of his title, Comte Luc de Bouchillon. According to Mother's stories, they first met when he commissioned a portrait from her.

I joined my mother by the painting as she brushed her fingertips against his painted hand, resting on a saber at his hip.

"Did he ever fight any Shadows?" I asked.

"No. He courted me at Le Château Enchanté. There were no Shadows there."

A thrill zipped through me like a bird flitting through open air. Mother had many rules; the most important being that I was to never *ever* speak of Le Château or her time there. Sometimes she would let slip some detail about the marvelous gardens, the grand canal, the fountains. But if I asked her too much, her eyes would turn cold and hard.

"I—I had heard stories about such things in the town market," I murmured. "It's true, then?" I touched the topic so carefully, just brushing against it. I knew if I said the wrong word, she'd never speak of it again.

Mother nodded with a far-off look. "The gods built Le Château for His Majesty. The ground it's built on is blessed. The walls, the statues, the gardens, every inch of it is sacred, they say."

They say.

"Is it not so?" I asked.

"I'm not sure what I believe." She shivered from some wind I could not feel. A memory perhaps, cold and invisible. Once more, she turned her gaze to the painting of Father. "There are no Shadows at Le Château. That I know; I lived there in safety."

In my smallest voice, I said, "We could *both* live there in safety."

Mother shut her eyes, a tear dripping onto her cheek. "You're just a child," she whispered.

"I'm seventeen now. I—I think I'd flourish at court, actually." I fidgeted with my dress; I shifted back and forth on my heels, my heart pattering, hoping, *desperate* for this chance. "You know Le Château well; it's not as if it's a whole new world. And you could find me a tutor there instead of having to teach me yourself. Think of all you could paint there. I could sit out in the sunshine, and you wouldn't have to fret over me, and I would—" *Be happy* was at the tip of my tongue, and I only just choked it back. "*It* would be good for me. I could meet other people. I could learn about the court, and I'd become more independent. And perhaps . . . well, you met Father there, perhaps I could . . . find someone, too."

"Ofelia."

I bit down on my tongue, feeling an ache already unfolding in my chest. She'd never approve of it. I'd stay in this manor, alone, bereft of all beauty and romance and intrigue, until I was old and gray.

Mother bent close, resting her hands gently on my cheeks. She took a long, shaky breath. "We no longer have a choice. It is the only safe place in the kingdom," she said. She gave a grim nod. "In the morning, I shall go to petition the king."

My heart was overflowing. I was made up of a million brilliant butterflies, finally about to be set free. I squealed with delight and wrapped her in a crushing hug.

"Oh, Mother, Le Château! I can't wait to see it! Is it really true that the grand canal is so big the king has galleons sail on it *for fun* and that you can borrow a gondola and—"

She pressed her finger to my lips, a stern furrow in her pale brow. "I will go first. Alone. It's too dangerous a journey for you to take. I'll hire a carriage, and once I arrive at Le Château, I will ask His Majesty for a place for us. Then I'll return for you with his knights and a royal coach."

I groaned. "Mother, I can brave the journey! I should come with you, introduce myself to the king—"

"No." The ferocity in my mother's usually gentle voice shook me. I blinked, as startled as if she'd struck me. With delicate fingers, she brushed baby hairs from my brow. "It'll only be a few days. A week at the very most." She pressed her locket against her heart. "I will be fine. I'll have you with me."

"So you don't forget what I look like?" I asked with a grin.

Mother kissed the crown of my head. "For luck." Her lovely blue eyes were as hard and flat as turquoise. "Ofelia, some things will be different once we start our new lives at the palace. I tried all my life to keep you from having to go to a place like that, a place with such—" My mother's voice caught, and she took a deep breath before continuing more calmly. "You must stay by my side always."

The idea made me squirm. It was too much like how things already were. "Mother, you needn't fasten yourself to me all day—"

"If we go to Le Château," she said, the sweetness in her voice giving way to cold finality, "you have to do what I say." Her fingers trembled as she tucked a curl behind my ear. "It's the only way to keep you safe. Do you understand?"

So it was a bargain she proposed: I could go to the palace but only on her leash.

"What are you keeping me safe from?" I murmured. "You said there were no monsters there."

"There are no Shadows. But monstrous people? They are not hard to find in that place."

I did not have the same wiles that one might gain from spending their whole life at court. But I had read hundreds of novels about it. I was quite adept at detecting the emotions of others; even Lope had told me so. I knew a great deal when it came to people, and my heart was a compass: I was sure it would easily determine whether those I spoke to had good or bad intentions.

Now I could finally prove this to my mother.

There was just one important character missing from this beautiful fairy tale unfolding.

"Maybe Lope could join us?" I asked.

The look my mother gave me was tinged with something—fond exasperation, perhaps? I flushed.

"Yes, if she wants. She could help me keep watch over you." She gave one of my curls a light little tug. "Gods know I'll need it. You must promise to be diligent and obedient and virtuous, if you really mean to live in that place."

Obedient and virtuous. I almost shuddered. Those words sounded terribly boring, but for the palace, and with Lope at my side, I could make such sacrifices. "I'll do exactly as you say," I told her.

She nodded, unsmiling. "Then I'll leave in the morning."

I took a steadying breath. I was so close. So close to my heart's dearest dream finally coming true. And a whole week to wait, while my mother traveled to Le Château and back . . . I could hardly bear it.

When I stood in the drive the next morning, blowing her kisses as her hired carriage pulled away, my head was filled with beautiful, painted-gold dreams of the balls we'd attend. The people we'd meet. The life we'd live.

I spent the entirety of the first day packing all my things into various trunks, debating which gown would be the best for making a first impression at court.

The second day I spent cleaning the house with more vigor than I ever had before. When Mother returned home, she would see how diligent and responsible and *good* I was. That I was grateful for this gift of a new life.

Mother was due to arrive at Le Château on the third day, and in her honor, I requested the cook prepare a cake, and I drank the sweet wine that Mother and I loved the most. I giddily imagined Mother meeting with the king and his enthusiastic greeting; how he would beg her to go fetch her charming daughter. How she would see it was the perfect place for us.

After the fourth day, she was on the journey back to me. Every evening, with Lope to guard me, I waited on the terrace, breathless with the hope that each night would be the one when she returned. I felt silly, at first; surely she could not leave the palace and arrive home to me in the blink of an eye.

It was strange how much I already missed her. She had always been with me. Every single day. Even on days when she preferred to be alone, I could press my ear to the door to her studio and hear her murmuring to herself or the clinking sound of brushes being cleaned.

By the sixth night, the ache in my heart led me to sleep in her studio. She'd left her shawl there, and it still smelled of her: lilac and linseed oil. When dawn broke, I woke to see her great works all around me. Her current project was a portrait of a little boy, the mayor's grandson. There was a blank spot on the canvas where his hand ought to have been, and when I stood near, I could see the lines of her pencil outlining the hand holding a ball.

I couldn't help but laugh at the section she had left for last. She made her art seem so effortless, but I knew her better than that.

"Gods," she'd always said, "I'd be a happy woman if I never had to draw hands again."

I smiled at the memory, my finger gently tracing her signature on the painting, a simple curling *M*.

There was a wound in my heart where she ought to have been, but surrounded by her art, I felt close to her again.

"Soon," I told myself. "She'll be home soon."

But one night passed, and then another.

I waited at the gate until the knights insisted I return inside. Even then, I sat by my bedroom window, watching the horizon.

She had said her journey would take a week. I promised myself not to worry until it had been more than a week.

An eighth day.

A ninth day.

A tenth.

My mind was racing. Because this wasn't right. In the fairy tale I was writing, she was supposed to come back.

Was she lying somewhere, injured, in pain? Had she been attacked by brigands?

Was she in a field somewhere, a Shadow's claws pinning her down, its rattling gasp filling her ears, the breath torn from her body until—

No. No, I couldn't bear to think like that.

And if something awful had befallen her, if she'd been attacked by Shadows or waylaid by the court—that wasn't a tale suited for someone like me.

In the evening, as I stood on the drive, I looked to Lope, her eyes fixed hawklike on the twilit horizon.

It was a story suited for a knight.

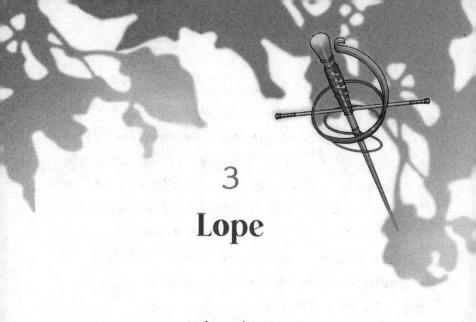

3

Lope

A whispered name,
A whispered plea,
A blade plunged through shadow—
Two gone up in smoke.

In the dim light of the countess's guest room, I sat at the desk and wrote down last evening's nightmare. I did so in fragments on pieces of letter paper, in my smallest writing.

The freckle-faced boy
Skin from red to blue
Eyes from blue to white
A desperate—

I sighed. I hated the words and hated the images. I folded the paper, watching the flame dancing in the candlestick.

"To any divinity who will listen," I murmured. They had not been on friendly terms with me lately. But speaking to the gods was like dancing with a partner you could not see. I had to trust that if I took one step, the gods would respond with another. At least, they were supposed to. These days, it more often felt like I was dancing by myself. Looking like a fool.

Perhaps I was. Perhaps I was arrogant to think I was worthy to be heard by any of the hundredfold nameless gods. No matter how many offerings I presented to them.

And still I let the flame devour my words.

"For pity's sake," I murmured. "Help me end these monsters for good."

Wouldn't the gods want that, too? Wouldn't they approve of my quest, dispelling the monsters created by the dark god they had cast into the Underworld? Couldn't they see how desperately I wanted to serve them?

The foul smoke rose from the candlestick and into my lungs as the paper curled in on itself. Black husks. Like the bodies of the Shadows, withering beneath my fingers as I screamed, blood rolling down my face, and Carlos lying motionless beside me—

I breathed. The wrong thought, the wrong memory, the wrong *smell*, and my stomach would tighten, my chest would ache, the world would spin, and I would be back *there*. As if that final day were playing out all around me. As if it hadn't been twenty-six days ago.

Sighing, I massaged my eyes until red spots danced through the darkness of my vision. I wished I could erase the nightmares, erase the memories, burn them up in little pieces until I was back to what I'd been twenty-six days ago.

Twenty-six days. A thousand years ago and a moment ago, all at once. The wound still felt so fresh.

I had many scars; every knight did. Faint silver lines down my throat, rough scrapes down my arms and legs, calluses and nicks littering my hands. They proved that I had endured much and had lived, had fought against monsters and come away with my life. But I hated that this gaping wound was on my brain, unseen, invisible, pulsing, begging to be remembered.

Seeing that Shadow lunge for Ofelia . . . it had dragged me back through time, had made me stare once more into the face of my dying friend. It painted blood on the backs of my eyelids and whispered fiercely to me, *Remember*.

I dipped my quill in ink and pulled my new journal toward me.

Every book I owned, every journal, they were all from her. Even my words I owed to her. She was the one who taught me to write in the first place.

I had only just arrived as a new recruit at the manor. The moment she saw me at the wall, that very first day, she decided I'd be her friend. Despite my severe expression, she sought me out, asked me dozens of questions until my heart cracked open just for her. And when our little chats weren't enough for her, she showed me how to write just so that we could exchange letters.

Why would we write letters? I'm not far, my lady, I'd said. *I live just at the edge of the wall.*

Her laugh, bright as silver, had rung through the courtyard. *But it's so romantic to write them, don't you think?*

Thanks to her, I had learned to wield a new weapon. I learned the beauty and the magic of words, the power in collecting them, piecing them together. My journal was filled with ink, with broken lines and words and phrases that could sometimes be stitched together into a poem. I shared with Ofelia only those that I was truly proud of. Little shards of beauty that I had gathered: a description or a couplet. She would marvel at my words like I was something great, and my heart would flutter in my chest like it had grown wings.

Carlos was the only other person who had coaxed me into sharing my poems. From the day we met, he had teased me like the other soldiers had for having my head in the clouds, but once I read that first poem to him, he smiled at me and called me an artist, and he meant it.

I sighed and set aside the paper. Even *writing* made me ache.

I granted myself one luxury to placate my writhing heart. A sweet daydream I often turned to, letting it rest within me like capturing a firefly within the cage of my hands. I imagined myself on horseback with Ofelia's arms around me, and we would ride off, the two of us, to someplace better. To a

30

place with no monsters. Where she would be safe, and I could write poems. Where I wouldn't have to fight anymore.

Where I wouldn't have to watch a friend die. Where death didn't exist at all.

It was all so clear: her reddish curls streaming in the wind, the rose-petal perfume of her, her soft cheek against my neck—

I pushed away from my desk, breathing out, letting the firefly-dream drift away.

This world was different. This world was full of Shadows. This world decided that one girl was born the daughter of a countess and another was born to fight monsters. A world in which children lost their parents, where children sought freedom and revenge by learning to fight; a world in which death was called *the noble final sacrifice of every knight*.

I swept up the notes I'd kept on the desk, where I had recounted the movements of these monsters for the past few weeks.

> *July 4—From the northeast. Thirty Shadows.*
> *July 5—From the north. Thirty-one Shadows.*
> *July 6—From the north. Twenty-seven Shadows.*
> *July 7—From the east. Forty Shadows.*

I swore and stood up from the desk and began pacing. Forty. There'd been forty, and Carlos had been by my side, and I'd cut down the beasts, one and then two, and then I felt his scream ripping through me.

I gripped the bedpost to steady myself as sorrow clenched around my heart like an ice-cold fist.

We were so helpless. We'd known nothing of these creatures when they first appeared, and we knew even less now. They had begun to appear only around thirty years ago, and never in such numbers. How could it be? How could anyone have ever lived in a world where monsters only existed in fairy tales?

Desperate and enshrouded in a fog of anger and misery, I stumbled back to the table and unrolled a map of the kingdom. I muttered prayers of supplication and marked with my quill the number and the direction of the monsters in the past thirty days. North and east. Always, always north and east.

Perhaps they fled to the sea? Or hid away in the forests? My fingers traced northeast, through a forest, through a town, up to the coast—but no, there was something more significant before that. On that path was another landmark, its name written in beautiful, curling text. *Le Château Enchanté*.

There are no monsters at Le Château, the countess had said.

And yet they always seemed to make their way there. And yet Her Ladyship hadn't returned.

Was this claim about the safety of the palace another fairy tale? A story the king wove to sate his anxious people?

Someone rapped their fist against my door, making me

jump and grasp the penknife resting beside the candle.

"Lope?" Ofelia's voice was soft and sweet with a small, frightened quiver to it.

My heart nearly leapt out of my breast.

The knife clattered on the desk as I set it aside and scrambled to unlock the door. This was the exact reason she had asked me to sleep in the house and not in the barracks. So I could keep watch over her in her mother's absence and for nights like these, when she was fitful and needed solace.

She stood in the doorway, a ray of starlight dressed in a pure white shift. Her eyes were the very color of the dark walnut of her jewelry box. Upon seeing her—the freckles peppered generously across her rosy cheeks, the way her auburn hair was hanging in loose, riotous curls before bed—I had to suppress a moonstruck grin.

"May I come in?" she asked.

I stepped aside, and in an instant, she whirled into the bedroom, shutting the door. Fear was written in her eyes.

"I need your help," she said.

At this hour? My brows rose. "Anything, my lady."

She shook her head. "I doubt you will be so enthusiastic when you hear what I plan to do."

What she planned to do. Gods, I loved her mind, her scheming, her imagination; but it was a fearsome thing, too. Her brush with death days ago was proof of this.

"Mother's been gone too long," she said, gliding past me

to pace across the plush, ornate rug. "Either something's happened to her on the road to Le Château, or—or maybe she's still at the palace. Maybe she fell ill. Or maybe the king thought her request to stay was so foolish, he's thrown her in a dungeon!"

"My lady," I said, "I'm certain everything's—" I stopped myself, looking at her. At the anguish gleaming in her dark eyes. Tears rolled down her cheeks, and I balled my fists to stave off the urge to brush them aside.

"Don't tell me I'm foolish for worrying so," Ofelia whispered. She laughed, harsh and joyless. "I've tried to be practical. I know it's too dangerous for me to go after her. I know that I could be fretting over nothing. Mother could walk through the entryway any day now. But"—she shook her head, her pale hand pressed against her heart—"something is wrong. I *know* it. I—"

She could speak no more. Ofelia inhaled shakily, her lip trembling, her fists tightened, as if she could will away her tears. Each one was like an arrow piercing my ribs.

I took a step nearer, and she embraced me, the last vestiges of her resolve melting away into loud sobs. I held her in turn, so grateful, and so sorry, to have her heart pressed close to mine.

Standing there with her in my arms, as the fear and the grief weighed her body down, my choice felt clearer than ever. She was *light*, laughter and kindness and curiosity and joy, the sun itself. She did not deserve to live in a world where such monsters roamed free. Carlos did not deserve such a fate, either. No one did.

I would seek out her mother. And I would find a way to destroy these beasts.

"I'll go," I said.

She sniffled against my waistcoat. "What?"

"I'll go to Le Château. I'll find your mother."

Ofelia lifted her eyes to mine.

Heavens.

Up close, I could count the freckles dotting her cheeks and nose, see the streaks of auburn in her dark eyebrows, watch her long lashes brush against her eyelids as she gazed wide-eyed at me. If I believed in such things, I'd think she was a changeling. Some fairy-creature and not just a person.

"I'm coming with you," she said.

All I could see was that Shadow barreling toward her, the startled scream she'd let out, and Carlos, knocked to the ground, his face white as bone as his breath was torn from his lungs—

"*No!*"

She startled, and I staggered back, alarmed by the ferocity of my tone. I spoke like that to the other soldiers when they were being reckless and foolish but never to her.

"I—I'm sorry, my lady," I mumbled, keeping my gaze from hers. "I simply meant that I cannot put you in danger.

It's a few days' journey to Le Château. I'd be traveling both day and night, traveling in the midst of Shadows. It's not safe for you."

Her hand slipped into mine, her soft skin making shocks zip up my arm.

"You will keep me safe," she said. She swept her thumb back and forth against my hand. "You always have."

"By—by the wall, my lady, you nearly—"

"You saved me then." Her eyes became sad, then, and serious—a look that was eerily unlike her. "Lope, this is for my *mother*. I would walk into the Underworld itself if it meant getting her back. If you do not come with me, I'll just go on my own. You know I will."

She pulled back from me, wiping the tears from her eyes. "But Lo," she whispered, that dear name making my heart-strings pull taut, "there is no one else in the world I'd want to go on this journey with. The choice is yours, but . . . I hope you'll say yes."

Deep down, a wiser side of me knew this was a terrible idea. To travel, just the two of us, all the way to Le Château, on a road where Shadows prowled . . . What could lie before us but peril?

The sincerity and hope in her eyes made any protest die within me. The way she spoke of it all seemed so logical, so certain. We *would* make it to the palace, the two of us. And besides, she was my charge. I was instructed to protect her, no matter what road she chose. All this time, this was what I had wanted. For her to depend on me, for me to be of use to her, for me to be her knight. Perhaps at the palace, we could be—

I quickly dismissed that thought.

I was not made for love or for courtship. I had been trained to be a knight. I was made for killing Shadows. So when we arrived there, she could reunite with her mother—and my search for answers about the monsters who haunted our lives could begin in earnest.

I would find their origin and destroy it; keep these creatures from entering our world ever again. No more children would die at the hands of monsters.

Ofelia's journey would be for love. This quest of mine would be for justice.

"What must we do?" I asked.

4

Lope

Darkness awaits us in a day's time,
And I will follow her within.

Since the guards were commanded to keep Lady Ofelia in the house after nightfall, as soon as morning came, she expertly crafted our lie. She told the captain of the guard, Chevaleresse Beautemps, that the best way to ease her anxieties over her mother was to go into town and buy as many things as her heart desired. So she and I ended up with a wagon, two horses, and no questions.

She sat beside me on the driver's bench, glancing over her shoulder at the manor, white as snow in the morning sun.

"If—when—when we find Mother, we're going to stay there at Le Château. We'll never see this place again," Ofelia said.

It was true. This estate was my only home, besides an

orphanage and a camp where knights like me were trained. The manor housed all my fondest memories. And the wall, my most horrid ones.

"Will you miss it there?" she asked me.

"No." I flinched at the sound of my own voice; that I could so easily cast aside my old life, and that I could speak so harshly before Ofelia. But when I glanced at her, I found her watching me intently, her eyes alert and sunlit as they always seemed to be.

"This feels . . . like the beginning of something," I murmured. "Like I've turned the page of a book and a new chapter is about to begin. I've never even seen beyond the nearest town before today."

I searched the horizon, a sea of golden-green hills. We would follow the road north, where we'd eventually find the palace and whatever awaited us there. *Possibility* lay before me. A world where I could do anything, *be* anything. The kind of world I dreamed of. The kind of world I longed to write about. *A world as ripe and delicious as a crisp apple, begging for me to pick it and taste it for myself.*

My sweetest dreams looked so much like that morning. Ofelia was at my side. For just a moment, I wasn't a knight. Only her dearest friend.

Now that I was alone, now that the sun shone boldly and I did not have to take on the mantle of a knight, I felt that I could *breathe*.

"May I drive?" Ofelia asked brightly, holding out her hands as she sat beside me on the driver's bench.

"Oh—you don't need to trouble yourself with that, my lady."

Her eyes became little crescent moons. "I want to. And besides, I can just *tell* you want to write. You have that tiny smile creeping on the corner of your mouth, the one you get when you're inspired."

It was sweet and startling all at once to be known so well. My gaze whipped hastily from her back to the road, and I tried in vain to suppress that smile. I was her protector, not a poet.

She reached into the bag between us and procured my red leather notebook with the pencil tucked inside. For a split second, seeing her touch that journal made my heart jolt as I imagined her flipping through the moony love poems I'd *already* written for her.

"It's just holding the reins, isn't it?" With her free hand, she pointed at the road before us, straight and unending. "I can hold them for a half hour." Ofelia batted her lashes at me like she was begging her mother for new books.

I relented and passed her the reins. She grinned and exchanged them for my notebook. Drawing the bloodred journal close to my chest felt like I was bringing my heart back to its home.

A smile dawned on my face as I took the pencil and looked

up, not as a navigator but as an *artist*.

Beyond this was the world, all of it, bathed in golden sunlight, rolling hills of yellow rapeseed. I wanted to pluck the horizon and wear it like a cloak; or drink it like a flood of gold, to let my body, all of me, become so bright and *beautiful*.

I laughed. Poetry. Rushing toward me, words, words that I loved, came so easily in this brilliant light.

As fast as I could, I scribbled in my journal each beautiful, fleeting thought, and I realized, *This is just the barest fraction of what could be.*

More lay beyond. A palace. Cities. Other kingdoms. Valleys, mountains, caverns—oceans. Places I could see, places I could enjoy, not as a knight but just as a girl. Like Ofelia.

Ofelia, with her eyes bright as starlight.

As I touched the graphite pencil to the page, the words flowed from me like a burst dam.

And you! My daylight,
I cannot gather up the words I want to give to you.
I want to weave them into a crown
And softly place it on your brow.
Standing in your radiance,
Each word a kiss—

"Lope!"

Ofelia's lilting voice struck me, and to my horror, I

41

remembered that she was sitting right beside me on the driver's bench. I slammed the notebook shut, my face aflame.

Enough, I chastised myself, *you cannot protect her when you lose yourself like this.*

My cheeks burned, my heart thrummed against my breast, and I *hated* it. Yes, without a heart, I'd be a sore poet, but with one . . . well. A tender heart was an easy target.

The sun gilded Ofelia's curls as she turned toward me on the bench. "Have you found some inspiration?"

Ah. There was my heart again.

"Oh, um—a little bit. I've not written anything good yet."

Ofelia smiled at the world shining before us. "I bet the palace will inspire you." She squeezed her hands together like she was praying. "I cannot wait to see it. I hope it's as magnificent as I've dreamed." The light dimmed in her eyes somewhat as she added, "And—and Mother will be there, I know it. She'll show us around. She'll teach us the ways of the court."

She took a shaky breath and pasted on a hopeful grin. "It sounds so splendid. Mother once said they change gowns at Le Château several times a day. And that for parties, all the courtiers dress in the same color, whatever the king chooses. She once told me about dancing at one of those balls with my father. . . ."

The way she was staring so distantly out at the road, the

way she wrapped herself in stories like a warm, soothing blanket—I could tell how worried she was for her mother. She kept her fear tucked aside, as I did. Yet I did so out of duty, as her knight. Why did she keep her heart guarded now?

"My lady?" I murmured.

She blinked rapidly, waking herself from her reverie. Her brown eyes flitted up my body and back down again, glimmering with mischief. "You know, I don't think I've ever seen you in a gown."

Heat flooded my cheeks. "It—it has never been necessary."

"It soon *shall* be necessary! When you're at the palace with me, you'll have to be dressed up as wonderfully as the rest of us." She beamed. "You'll have to wear your hair down like I do. Can I see it?"

My eyes grew wide. "My hair?"

"Yes," she said. She tossed me the reins, leaving me scrambling to grasp them as she reached across the driver's bench. She unwound the ribbon I'd kept my queue in. My hair tumbled down my shoulders, nearly to the small of my back. My whole body went hot as liquid metal. My breath sat tight in my chest. Her fingers softly combed through the knots and tangles, and I imagined her counting each and every silver hair. Instead, she said, "Oh, how beautiful!"

"It—it's a mess. It gets in the way," I muttered. "It's best to keep it tied. It could get in my eyes in a fight—"

"There won't be any fights at Le Château," she said. As I stared ahead at the road, her fingers grazed across my scalp, and she tenderly swept my hair into three sections, winding them slowly into a plait over my shoulder. "Do you think it's true? That there aren't any Shadows there?"

Such a world would be better than any dream. Then again, I felt quite certain that I was in a dream right then, her soft rose perfume curling around me, flooding my senses. Chills danced down my neck as she swept her fingers through my hair.

"It—it couldn't be," I murmured. "There are Shadows everywhere."

"Yes, but the palace isn't like everywhere else." Her fingers tenderly tied off the plait she had fashioned in my hair by securing the end with my ribbon. "Perfect."

Her hands returned to her lap, and I felt something like homesickness at the absence of her touch.

"Thank you again," said Ofelia softly. "I didn't ask you to come because you are my knight but because you're *you*. Leaving everything behind, going on this mission with me . . . it is a lot to ask. Especially given the danger. You're my dearest friend. But what kind of friend am I to put you at risk?"

Some distant, logical part of myself understood that the two of us were close, that we were friendly—yet joy still spread like a hearth fire within me at her words. She enjoyed me. She preferred my company.

"I do not fear the Shadows," I assured her. "I will gladly slay them. I'll do whatever I can to protect you. As you said, not because I am your knight but because I—" Emotion made the words snag inside of my throat. "Because I could not bear it if you were in danger."

"Thank you," she said again. Her eyes, the bright color of amber in the sunlight, met with mine. "What about tonight? We—we should not risk traveling at dusk."

Ofelia was right—as the Shadows grew more powerful, being out at night became a near death sentence. Yet it might be inevitable for us. I passed her back the reins to reach into my leather satchel. I unfolded a map for her, pointing to where we were. "We'll reach a small town just before sunset," I told her. "We can spend the night there. But when night falls and we have yet to return from our "shopping," the other knights will doubtlessly assume we're on our way to Le Château. They'll pursue us and probably send us back to the manor as your mother ordered, if we're caught."

Ofelia bit her lip. "So to get to Mother first . . . we'll *have* to travel by night."

I sighed. "Unfortunately so, my lady."

Across my body, like a king would wear a riband, I wore a leather belt with two sheathed knives. I removed one blade, sheath and all, and held it out to Lady Ofelia. She accepted the gift with a slight frown.

"I promise to keep you safe," I told her softly. "I promise to kill as many as I can. But if something happens, I want you armed as well."

Ofelia gazed down at the knife, her brow knitting with concentration. She carefully withdrew it from its sheath, watching the steel glimmer in the sun. "Perhaps I'm a fool. Risking so much when Mother could be fine."

"You're not a fool. You love her. You'd do anything for her."

Her gaze met with mine, and in the silence, my own words seemed to echo back to me, seemed to turn a mirror toward me. The way she looked at me, like she understood something, like she saw something in me that I did not—it made me burn.

For her, I would gladly let myself turn to ash.

5

Ofelia

We spent one night in an inn, where Lope insisted upon sleeping on the floor so that I could have the bed to myself. I knew she would ignore any of my protests, so I let her have her stubborn chivalry. This was our one night when we would be sheltered and safe. I savored every minute of it. We whispered to each other in the darkness until I was enfolded in sleep.

The next day, we traveled as fast as the horses would allow. And the journey was marvelous. Rolling hills and sunflower fields passed us, great pastures of green and yellow, hushed forests with winding paths carved through. Little veins leading to the beating heart of Le Château. My own pulse quickened as we inched closer. I imagined a string pulling on my chest, pulling me home, to Mother.

But night fell.

Lope was right. There weren't any cities nearby; none that

I could see, even when I squinted at the horizon. No steeples, no towers, no silos, no hovels. Just the dark, cloudlike wisps of trees in the distance.

I sat beside Lope on the driver's bench, her cloak wrapped tight around me like a blanket. I kept my gaze affixed to the horizon, waiting, *longing* for the palace to appear. The night dragged on, every minute torturous, filled with the fear that a monster lurked nearby. I watched the sky darken and then turn a deep dusty blue with the pearl-white moon faint and low in the sky.

"Should we find shelter?" I whispered, my voice and my body drooping with fatigue.

"We'll reach Le Château soon, my lady," she said, "but until then, we cannot stop." I held on to her words like an anthem, one that tolled in my head again and again and brought me hope.

Then, gloriously, wonderfully, I saw a small shape in the distance. Rounded at the top like the dome of a building.

No, smaller. A slender neck and shoulders. It was a person. No.

Lope glared at the shape like it had offended her. Then she held tight to my wrist.

"Shadows," she whispered.

My heart ricocheted just at their name. "What should we do?"

"Hold on to your knife."

I gripped the dagger, covered in its sheath. My heart throbbed in my throat. Could I, a girl who'd only ever wielded an embroidery needle, face down and kill a *Shadow*? Especially after the last time?

"We're going to try to outrun it," she said.

At her command, I held tight to the little wooden railing on the right of the bench. She lashed the reins of the horses. They lurched forward, picking up into as much of a gallop as they could, bearing the weight of the wagon. The messenger bag and the crates in the back jostled and slid about as we raced forward.

In the distance, the Shadow began to shrink, like it was melting into the earth.

Over the clamor of hooves and the shaking of the wagon, I cried, "I think it fled!"

As soon as the words left my lips, some great force slammed into the wagon, turning the bench on its axis and sending me careening.

I was pitched out of the wagon, tumbling forward and crashing to the grass, landing on my back. All the breath was kicked out of my lungs. Looking up, the stars spun around in the sky.

"My lady!" Lope's voice bounced around in my head, sharp and full of panic. I wobbled into sitting, the back of my head throbbing, and looked around.

The wagon was tilted over, and our horses were thrashing

about on their sides, trying and failing to stand—and each was held down by a creature as big as I was, black as the sky, with large, cavernous mouths hanging open over the horses' faces.

When I shut my eyes to blink, memories spun around me, unstoppable as a dance. The evening in the garden. The day at the wall. Mother. A scream. An endless, hungry mouth. Falling. Breath. Arms. Blood.

I frantically patted the grass around me, reaching before I even remembered what for. *A knife*, I recalled, *I need my knife*.

My hand shook violently as I found it a few feet away, rolling to my feet as I tore it from its sheath. Dim moonlight bounced against it, pure white against the darkening world around me.

Something grabbed hold of my neck, throwing me back onto the earth. Above me, there was an open mouth, a void, and a horrible, groaning, hissing sound—

"My lady!" cried Lope.

I thrust the dagger above my head, stabbing madly but missing. The creature withdrew from me, scuttling backward on clawed feet.

Leaping out from behind the wagon, Lope tackled the creature, her sword drawn and plunging straight through the monster's head. In only a second, it went limp and then disappeared into black smoke.

"Aim for the head," she said, her chest heaving as she

jerked the sword out of the ground she'd planted it in. She waved me close, and I ran to her side, my free hand tangling with hers.

That's when I saw them.

Aside from the Shadows atop the horses, there were at least ten others. Four or five climbing the wagon, their eyeless, blank faces swiveled toward us. To my right, another six or more, like a crowd of people, watching me.

Lope squeezed my hand.

I looked into her eyes, and for just a second, the world paused. Her eyes shone bright as steel, and my heart ached at the devotion, the ferocity, the bravery painted so clearly across her face.

"I'll protect you," she whispered. "Don't move."

I'd obey her every order. I'd trust her with my life. Always.

A Shadow jumped forward, clawed hands reaching for Lope's throat. In one swift move, she pierced her sword through its head. It crumpled to the ground and then dissolved into the air. With her other hand, she took a knife from the strap around her chest and ran in front of me toward the mass of Shadows. Yet to my horror, the monsters melded together, becoming one creature with many heads, a towering wave of darkness looming over Lope.

Another, smaller Shadow darted across my vision, as if chasing the horde of Shadows toward Lope. Before it could get any farther, I cried out, "Stop!"

The sound of my voice was enough to make the smaller Shadow swivel its body. It hissed, and then in a blink, it was bounding toward me on all fours.

Fear pierced my heart, but more than that, rage, rage at the thought that this beast would go after Lope. I sprinted toward the monster, anger flaring inside me like a lit furnace. It flung itself onto me and pinned me to the earth. The pain of the impact was interrupted by the pressure of the Shadow kneeling atop me, its jaws agape. I plunged my knife forward through its mouth, my fist going through the strange, swirling darkness of its body, wispy and cold like fog, and then out the back of its head. The Shadow fizzled into nothingness.

Just like that.

Just like that, I'd killed my own nightmare.

There was a retching, choking sound to my left.

Lope.

Plumes of what looked like black smoke floated around her ankles and seeped into the ground, remnants of the Shadows she had already destroyed. But it was not enough.

The monstrous, many-headed Shadow had one set of hands wound around her throat; another dug its claws into her wrist, making her drop her sword and let out a weak, strangled cry. She thrashed her other arm, wrestling to get the knife into the skull of one of the Shadow's heads.

The creature split into two as it pulled her backward

onto the grass. The head behind her opened its mouth above her; the one in front of her gripped tighter to her throat and seemed to grin as she screamed in fury.

They could not have her. They could not *touch* her.

The world was shifting, sliding, turning as I cried out for her, racing across the grass. I flung myself at the Shadow astride her, knocking it away, my arms around its neck. It bucked like our startled horses had; it grasped and scratched at my arms, even as I tried to plunge my knife through its skull.

I rolled with the monster until I could hold its head down with one hand. It howled at me. Fueled by the blaze of my own anger, I bore my knife into its head. Like with the others, that was enough—it disappeared, a storm cloud evanescing away.

My heart punched against my chest as I glanced back toward Lope. The part of me that knew her to be unstoppable expected her to be standing tall behind me.

But she lay there, paler than moonlight as the Shadow crouched over her and devoured her breath. It tipped back its head, like it enjoyed the taste of it.

And she wasn't fighting back.

My body moved before my mind could make sense of it. I was atop the second monster, screaming at it so loud my throat tore. I jammed my knife into where its eye would be, again and again, even when I was doing nothing at all, only plunging the blade into the dirt.

The sounds of my heaving breath and pounding heart began to fade, and the more I breathed, the more I was able to come back to myself. I was in a field. On my way to Le Château. And Lope, Lope, she'd saved me a dozen times—

She was lying there. Unmoving.

I crawled across the grass and sat at her side, lifting up her head. Her eyes were shut. Her face was still and white as marble, half of it covered in dark blood. Her lips were parted and pale, nearly blue.

"Lope," I whispered, urgent and sharp. Still she did not stir.

I shook her shoulders; her head slumped backward, exposing her silvery throat, covered in long red scratches from where the Shadows had held her down. I gasped and pressed my ear to her chest. The galloping heartbeat I heard—was that my own?

Again, I shook Lope by the shoulders, as if it would wake her. My face felt stiff and damp; my brain rattled about in my skull, making the world spin like when the wagon had toppled over.

A voice in my head remained calm and steady, the voice of someone wiser, a voice like Lope's, saying, *She's dead, and you need to think about what to do now.*

A life where Lope did not exist—the very idea felt like a clawed hand had reached into my chest and carved out my heart.

She had been my constant companion for five years, and even that didn't feel like enough. I wanted every moment. Every laugh, every tear, and every part of her heart I had yet to discover. It wasn't enough time.

The truth was like an arrow through my chest: *This is the kind of love the poets write about*. And I had realized it too late.

I wept. My hands fisted around the sweat-slicked sleeve of her chemise, and I pressed my forehead to her chest, letting her waistcoat absorb my tears. "Come back," I begged her at a whisper. And then, desperately, to the gods I hissed, "Bring her back, *please*."

My name drifted through the air, whispered and faint.

I lifted my head.

Lope's eyes were open. Red veins bloomed across the whites of her eyes. She blinked.

I threw my arms around her neck, my laughter delirious and high-pitched.

"You're alive!" I squeaked.

"I'm sorry." Even her whisper was hoarse, broken from the damage the Shadows had done to her throat.

"Why are you apologizing?" I asked through my tears, leaning back to scowl at her—but she looked so frail. Her eyes were steadfast upon me, but her lips barely moved. Her eyelids continued to droop, like she was about to fall into a long, deep sleep. I pushed damp strands of graying hair from her blood-soaked temple. My heart was learning a new rhythm, *I am in love with her.*

"We need to get help," I whispered.

"Go on." She clenched her eyes shut and gritted her teeth. Sweat beaded on her brow and she pulled herself up half an inch before collapsing back onto the ground. Her chest rose and fell like a bellows desperately trying to make a fire grow. "Go—go on to Le Château without me."

"Are you mad?" I cried. "I can't leave you, not in the state you're in!"

Of all things, her full lips curved into the slightest smile. "You don't need me," she whispered. "I saw you . . . I saw you kill those Shadows."

I shook my head furiously, my hands trembling against her ice-cold cheek. "Don't say that. I need you. I'll always need you." Tears made my eyelashes clump together. "I won't leave you behind. We must find help. Can you stand?"

She furrowed her brow and bobbed her head in a sluggish nod. "It's perfectly normal to be tired after . . . after one of those attacks. I'll just need to rest for a bit once we find shelter."

Taking both her hands, I pulled her onto her feet. She abruptly slumped against my shoulder, her breath loud in my ear.

"Forgive me, my lady," she mumbled.

She had nearly died saving me from those creatures, and still she apologized; still she maintained decorum and treated me like I was the most important girl in the world. I sighed even as my heart ached, wrapping my arm around her middle to let her use me as a crutch.

A few paces from us, our horses lay on their sides in the grass, their eyes glassy, the breath stolen from their lungs.

I led her to the toppled wagon and let her sit beside it for a moment. Our belongings had fallen from the wagon, but not too far. I found my trunk and ignored the pretty gown I'd packed. We needed to survive. We needed only what was necessary. I dug my velvet coin purse from where I'd buried it beneath my gown. I found Lope's knapsack and slung it about me. I swept up the traveling cloak and settled it around Lope's shoulders. A few feet from where she lay with her head tipped back against the bottom of the wagon, Lope's sword still rested in the grass. I fetched it, carefully placing it across her lap.

"I won't ask you to fight," I said. "Never again. No matter what you say your duty to me is." I nodded to her, to the sword. "But I scarcely recognize you without that blade, so it's only right that it should be returned to its mistress."

Lope showed me a meager smile as she fit the blade back into its scabbard.

"Can you walk very far?" I asked softly.

She nodded and slowly, achingly, pulled herself to her feet. Her head drooped in a sort-of bow. "Yes, my lady."

"Call me Ofelia," I said. "Always Ofelia."

I slipped my arm around her, holding her up. Side by side,

57

we began to amble down the winding road before us.

Then, as we passed through the edge of the forest, parting like a curtain before us, we saw it. A collection of lights hovering in the distance. A city. My shoulders slumped with relief. Even in her exhaustion, Lope managed a smile.

"We're almost safe," I said.

She bobbed her head. "Just a few more steps."

The farther we walked, the harder it became. My shoes squelched as I pulled them out of the slick earth with every step. The air was thick and eerily still, eerily quiet. All the same, I did not let my gaze waver from the lights, starlike beacons calling us home.

I defeated monsters and lived. I fought beside her. I did not perish. And I will not stop here.

As we neared the lights, they became more defined. They were not simply flames hanging in midair, but dozens of lamps lighting up walls of brick and limestone. They seemed to stretch the whole horizon, but the walls they illuminated were all connected, like arms attached to the body of a marble-columned hall in the middle.

My heart stopped.

This wasn't a city. It was one building. A palace.

"Lope," I whispered. "Lope, Lope, it's Le Château Enchanté!"

The lights looked even lovelier reflected in her eyes. Her arm loosened around my waist. "It's beautiful," she said.

A long paved road led us closer to Le Château. We stumbled faster and faster toward it. Behind it, the sun was rising, magnificent and splendid, illuminating the palace and its entrance. Every bit of the gates, from the bars to the decorative suns crowning the top, was aglow, covered in pure gold. As we finally stood before them, I understood all the stories that said this place had been crafted by the gods.

Mother had to be inside. Who would want to leave such a place?

"Who goes there?" came a voice, low and rumbling like thunder.

I yelped and held tight to Lope as a man in a golden breastplate appeared behind the gate. He glared at us, but his look softened after a moment.

"Gods above," he muttered. "You're just children."

I curled my hand around one of the bars of the gate. "I've come looking for my mother," I said softly. "My name is Ofelia, and I—"

As I spoke, his thick brows pushed together. He pointed to Lope—her bloodied face and throat and the way she could hardly stand on her own. "What happened?"

"We were attacked by Shadows—"

"Robbers," he said.

I shook my head. "No, sir, there was a swarm of Shadows not far from here—"

"We do not speak of those creatures in this place," the

guard replied, his voice low and utterly serious.

I glared. "What are you talking about? Just look at my friend, look at her *blood*—please, she's injured. Just let us inside!"

The guard leveled a severe gaze at both of us. "To speak of Shadows is to speak against His Majesty."

"We—we're telling the truth," croaked Lope.

He did not move. His eyes bore into me. "If you wish to enter these gates," he said firmly, "you will never speak of those beasts. Do you understand?"

Part of me longed to shout at him, to call him a fool for ignoring the existence of such monsters when a girl stood wounded before him. Would we be turned away after we'd come so far? I had no choice but to deny reality to save the girl I loved. "Whatever you say. Please, just let us in!" I said, my voice fraying with desperation. Lope's head had started to droop against my shoulder again. "Please, sir, I'll do anything."

He pressed his lips together. "There is a registration process for the nobility, but the fastest way in is to pay—"

Before he could give an amount, I drew the velvet pouch of coins from my pocket and placed the entire thing in his hand.

Something about the look in my eyes silenced him. He nodded and pocketed the coins. "I'll get you a room and send you a physician."

As relief swept through me, the knight backed away from the fence, tipping his face upward to the guard tower. The farther he stepped, the more my heart sank—was he playing us the fool? Was he just going to run off with my money, leaving us hopeless, helpless?

He lifted a hand to the brilliant, sunrise-painted sky . . .

At his signal, the massive golden gates soundlessly swung open.

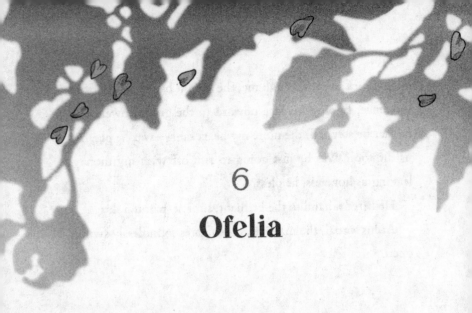

6

Ofelia

The guard shepherded us through the gate—but only after confiscating any weapons he could find in our possession. Lope was too fatigued to even remark on this, but I was certain it would grieve her greatly in a few hours' time.

A maid escorted us into the palace. Painted ceilings and marble floors and walls lined with golden paper blurred together. My arm was firm around Lope's waist, and though she could still walk, her head was starting to fall like a wilting flower. Finally, we reached a small room with a bed wide enough for two, a chair, a window, and a washbasin. The maid mentioned something about a doctor before flitting out of the room.

Ever so gently, I helped Lope sit upon the bed. My arms and shoulders ached from supporting her for so long, yet I barely registered the pain. I untied her cloak and tossed it to the floor. Then, with my hand upon her cheek and some fervent whispering, I finally coaxed her into laying her head down. Her dark hair spilled upon the pillowcase like a pot of mother's expensive paints. I could match the color perfectly—ivory black.

"My lady, I'm fine," Lope mumbled. By the sunrise pouring through the window, I could see her much better. Her neck and the left side of her face were stained bright scarlet.

"Stay there," I said, with as much strength in my voice as I could muster. It sounded more like a plea than a command.

She did as I told her. I pulled her knapsack over my head and let it slouch against the floor. Each step was heavy and sore as I shut the painted-white door and then stumbled over to the washbasin. There were some folded linens, the plainest things I'd seen in this palace so far, and a pitcher full of tepid water. It looked clean, at least. I couldn't do as much good as a doctor could, but I couldn't sit by and do nothing.

Scarcely an hour ago, Lope had been so weak. Her eyes had been so dull. The fluttering, hopeful, and steady thrum of her heart I knew so well had gone so quiet.

I sat beside her on the bed, pouring water onto the linens with a shaky hand. "You mustn't scare me like that again," I murmured, my throat thick with tears.

"It's just a few scratches," she whispered. Her eyelids, delicate and blue as iris petals, began to fall shut.

I lightly pressed the damp cloth against her cheek, cleaning away sweat and dirt and blood. A large, deep gash carved from her cheekbone to her jaw. One of my tears dropped onto her cheek, and I brushed it aside with my thumb.

"You nearly died," I said. My heart ached as I imagined it. If her story were to have a different ending. If the beauty, the bravery, the *light* that was Lope had been extinguished.

Was this how Mother had felt, that day in the garden? The moment, the *second*, when she snatched me out of the arms of certain doom?

"It is my duty," said Lope, her voice fainter than an echo.

"What is, Lo?"

"To give my life. If you ask me to."

I shook my head at her, cradling her face in my hands. She was so pale, so frail, like she was a drawing fading under sunlight.

"I want you to stay with me," I said, a quaver in my voice.

A slow, sleepy smile crossed her face. "As you wish."

She tried and failed to keep her eyes open, and in a moment, her head lolled against the pillow.

Beside the bed, I'd cast aside her knapsack. Perhaps there were more useful supplies among her things, something I'd forgotten. I unwound the little knot keeping the bag shut and set aside items one by one. Extra stockings and a chemise. The flask of water we shared. Then, a journal. Deep red, with the shape of a rose stitched into the leather. I'd given it to her a few days ago.

I cast one quick glance back to her. Her chest rose and fell in loud, slow breaths.

She was smarter than I was. She knew more about the world, about survival. Perhaps among her poems she'd penned down some of her other, more practical thoughts. Gods willing, she'd written *something* about wound care. I laid the book open upon my lap and flipped through its pages, filled with as much spidery text as could be crammed onto each page. With a smile, I remembered teaching her how to write. My hand upon hers, gently correcting the way she held the quill-pen. The first word I taught her was *sun*, in both the southern and northern tongues, sol and soleil. And she had looped the word together over and over across the page, a rare smile growing across her face the more graceful the strokes became.

I pushed back another page and found the words aligned differently. Little phrases, almost like a list.

In my head, I could compose for her
A thousand lovely sonnets;
Strung together like diamonds and pearls,
Perfect couplets and rhymes,
But my words run dry before her.
I wish above all earthly things
That I could speak to her
And share with her completely
All manner of my heart's musings.

In an instant I slammed the book shut, my eyes round as dinner plates.

Her poetry, her *sacred* poetry.

About a *girl*.

I hesitantly flipped the book open once more onto a random page and came across another line.

The one I love with flowers in her hair
Blooming under sunlight—

"Good *gods*," I whispered, closing the book and pressing it to my chest.

Love poems. All these years, she'd never spoken of such things, despite my musing about romance and true love and all that I had read about in storybooks. She had always listened carefully, but never contributed anything; if she found anyone handsome, she didn't tell me so. I thought that perhaps romance was simply something she did not care for. I would have supported her if this had been the case. But she'd never had anything to say on the matter.

She kept her heart hidden so deeply, her eyes stony and stoic, but I always knew that beneath her severe, knightly face lay a churning storm of emotions.

This, though. These words. They spoke of *love*.

I wondered for a moment who the girl she wrote about could be—who she knew well enough to love in the barracks. Except for that boy, Carlos, I hadn't a clue as to who her friends were.

Besides myself.

At the thought, my heart ached. A lump formed in my throat. Could I be—? What if that girl was *me*? Could I dare to hope that girl she called beautiful, that girl she felt so shy before, who she longed to recite poetry to, who she *loved*— was me?

There was a knock at the door.

My stomach dropped and I hastened to tuck the book back into the bag. A blush scalded my cheeks. I glanced over my shoulder—thankfully, Lope hadn't stirred and hadn't spotted me rifling through her things. How would she react, knowing that I'd read her private poems and learned this secret? It could crush any budding confidence in herself, in her words. It could topple the years of friendship that had been built between us.

I scurried to the door and found a man dressed in plain, brown clothing with a dark apron over his suit and a leather bag in his hand. For an instant, I was back at the manor, watching an almost identical man suture up the flayed flesh of my mother's arms. The smell of blood and chemicals I had no names for, her cries of pain muffled by a sponge.

"Mademoiselle," said the physician with a bow. "I was told there was someone injured?"

"Yes," I said, unmoving in the doorway. "I entreat you, please be very careful with her."

His lips quirked in the vaguest idea of a smile. "I will do my best."

I stepped aside, letting him enter. From behind his spectacles, his eyes widened at the bloody cloths I'd hastily set at the foot of the bed. At this angle, he couldn't see the injured half of her face—but a few steps more and he hissed, like he was in pain himself.

"I tended to it as best as I could," I piped up. "I—I just wanted to clean the blood from her face."

He set up a chair at her bedside. "Young lady?" he asked. "Can you hear me?"

Lope's eyes stayed shut, even as she sluggishly swiveled her head toward him. Before she could say anything, he was grabbing at her face, peering first at the gash on the left side. Then he began prying open her eyelids.

Lope moved quick as a striking snake—her right arm sweeping his hands away and her left hand suddenly upon the man's throat. "Don't touch me," she snarled.

I grabbed the man by the back of his coat and jerked him out of Lope's hold. He gasped for air and threw her a glare.

"I'm sorry," I murmured, keeping my voice cool and sweet to coax him to stay. "She's only frightened. We just escaped an attack from a horde of Shadows."

As he rubbed at his throat, the doctor shook his head. "No, you didn't."

My simpering mask cracked just a little bit. "I can assure you my memory is quite clear."

"It's simply not possible," said the man matter-of-factly.

"Such creatures do not dwell anywhere near this palace. It is holy ground."

"Then what in the bloody Underworld is *this*?" Lope asked, her voice raspy as she pointed to her newest wound.

"Judging by your temperament, I daresay it could be a prize won from a duel," the doctor said primly, distaste plain. He turned back to me, looking me up and down. "What is she to you? Your servant?"

My protector. My confidant. My dearest friend. My savior. And, when I glanced at her, her soft, silver eyes meeting mine, the way my heart fluttered assured me that there was some other word for her altogether.

"La Caballera de la Rosa is my sworn knight," I said softly. "It's thanks to her valor that we arrived here safely. Deny the monsters we fought, if it helps you sleep well. Set that aside. I only want to know that she will be well."

"I think she means to bite me if I continue my inspection, mademoiselle." He sniffed and pushed his glasses farther up his nose. "A bit of sleep will tend to that spirit of hers. Her color is a bit pale, but a turn in the garden will do her well. As for that wound . . . let it rest. Her body is getting rid of her bad humors through her blood. She will heal with time."

What an utter waste.

I thanked him profusely and kept a smile pasted on my face until I could shut the door behind him. I sighed. "Forgive me, Lope, I didn't think he'd be so intrusive."

She sleepily smiled at me from the bed, utterly relaxed again now that it was just the two of us. "You did nothing wrong."

My pulse leapt at this, for I had *indeed* done something very wicked moments ago, peering through her journal and into her heart. I bit on my lip to keep my calm facade from falling.

"The surgeons here likely only know how to treat broken nails or ankles twisted while dancing," said Lope. She took a deep, labored breath. "I know plenty about Shadow attacks. I just need air. And sleep."

Without another thought, I dashed to the window, unlatching the two panels so they would swing inside, letting in a rush of warm, end-of-summer air. Blinking back sunlight, I stepped forward, craning my neck out the window.

Before me was a sprawling, seemingly endless garden, all the plants gilded by the morning sunshine. Bushes were carved into perfect cones and swirls, and between them, golden-pink flowers were planted in an arrangement so vast they made a flowerbed seem like just that—a giant bed upon which I could easily fall asleep.

"Lope," I said in a hallowed whisper, "it looks like a dream."

She made a little murmur of agreement, the same sound she'd make when it was late at night and I had chatted her ear off, even while she was half asleep.

"Describe it to me," she said from the bed, her words drawn out and slow.

I was no poet. Not compared to her. I knew myself well enough to take pride in my storytelling, the way I could unfold a tale in delicious, captivating ways. The words themselves, though? Lope was the true master there. When I gave her a book to keep, I'd even see her taking notes inside it, circling individual words, like little gems to collect.

And—my heart stuttered—if I was right, what pretty words she'd chosen for me in her journal.

I cleared my throat and focused on the gardens beyond. The sweet perfume of flowers wafted inside, and faintly, I could hear robins greeting one another. "There are so many flowers. Like a meadow. Petunias, I think," I said. "They're all matted together, almost like they're forming a great quilt made of petals. What a lovely bed that'd be. How soft it would feel."

The exhaustion and the fear that had coiled up in my body seemed to pull at me as I described what I could see of the garden, reminding me that I, too, was overdue for rest. I yawned and turned back to her—as I'd hoped, she was already fast asleep, with one hand in a loose fist against her heart.

It was so plain to me now. How beautiful she was . . . and how my heart longed for her.

I curled up in the far corner of the room, watching her and counting her every breath. My stomach ached, and I suddenly, desperately missed my mother. I wanted to ask her, *Is this what love feels like?* I wanted to hug her tight and to ask her what she'd do in my place. I wanted to assure her that I was well and safe. I just wanted to be in her arms again, swept away from darkness like she'd always kept me.

The anxious thoughts rang in my head, echoing like lightning and thunder—a bright, sharp pang of concern for Lope, her weakened state, and her tender heart. Then the worries, rumbling inside me, *Is Mother in this palace? Is she hurt? Is she even alive?*

My worries swirled around and around like Mother mixing linseed oil and pigment. The smell of her studio, sweetened with flowers, soured by oils. The graceful movement of her palette knife arcing across the canvas. The soft tap of her brush against her palette. Exhaustion and memory finally swept me away, making the world grow dark.

Someone knocked at a distant door.

I lurched awake, alarmed by my hard pillow, by the ache in my neck, by the fact I was sleeping on a chair—but felt a measure of steadiness again when I saw Lope already on her feet, facing away from me. A woman about my mother's age stood in the doorway. She wore a deep gray gown with an apron about her waist. In her chapped hands was a large ring of keys.

"Where's my sword?" Lope hissed at the lady.

She frowned at Lope and then at me. "Every courtier's weapons are confiscated upon entry to Le Château," she said. She curtsied to each of us. "The day's fête begins in a few short hours. As residents here, it is mandatory that everyone attend."

Though my heart thrilled at the thought of a party, a *real* one here at Le Château Enchanté, my body and my spinning head protested the idea of any sudden movement. But I clung to another word: *everyone*.

My mother would be there.

"I've come here looking for someone," I told the maid. "My mother, la Condesa Mirabelle de Bouchillon? Will she be there?"

Behind her eyes, I could detect a flicker of annoyance. "My lady, there are hundreds of nobles in this palace. I could not account for each one. But if she is at this palace, she will be at the fête tonight."

I glanced back at Lope, at the dark rings under her eyes, at the red cut along her face, at the way her shoulders slouched.

"We—we have traveled quite a long way," I told the woman. "My friend is recovering from . . . our journey. Perhaps she could stay here while I—"

"I'll come with you," said Lope.

I twisted the fabric of my skirts in my fists. "You don't need to—"

"Yes, I do." She stood at my side, and her presence alone made my heartbeat settle and then quicken again.

The maid smiled stiffly at us both. "If you'll follow me, I'll take you both to your chambers. We'll get you looking your best for the party."

I raised an eyebrow. "I thought . . . I thought this *was* our chamber."

She guffawed loudly and then covered her mouth with her hand. The maid cleared her throat to try to tamp down the offense. "No, my lady, this is just a place for footmen to clean their boots and get new cloaks." She tipped her head toward the hallway. "Come, come."

Lope picked up her cloak and slung the bag over her shoulder with a stormy look. Her gaze softened when it fell upon me. Her skin was clean of all the blood from before, leaving only the deep cut from the Shadows tracing down her left profile.

Now that I'd read her poems, now that I understood my own feelings, every time I looked at her, I saw someone a little different from who I once imagined. It was like her secret was painted across her face, and I had to pretend I couldn't see it.

If I said anything, I'd only shred this beautiful, golden veil between us, this peace and trust and love that was so precious.

I did not want to tarnish what was already so marvelous. I resolved to keep her secret close to my heart until she was ready to share it unbidden.

For my own sake, to hide my own blushing, I broke our

gaze and swept into the hallway, following fast behind the maid.

She led us to a large room that may have well been lifted from my dreams. The walls were the color of cream but lined in gold. The only gold in our home was inside Mother's jewelry box. Hanging from the ceiling was a sparkling chandelier, laden with crystals like a tree with fruit ready to be picked. There were two privacy screens, each painted with springtime blossoms, a wash basin, a wardrobe, a vanity, a daybed, another breathtaking view into the gardens . . . and a large, white bed, with bed curtains embroidered with more flowers.

My attention snapped from the fairy-tale bed to the young women standing by it, carefully laying out matching bodices and skirts in midnight blue.

"Virginie and Carmen will prepare you both for the fête." Our guide curtsied to us and then slipped out of the room, the oak door clicking shut behind her.

As if the closing door was a command in itself, the two women, a little older than us, swept to our sides. The red-headed maid took Lope's bag, ignoring her protests, and then pulled her by the hand behind a privacy screen. Before I could even think, the blond maid had done the same to me. The way we were positioned, we would have been face-to-face were it not for the two screens in our way.

At the manor, we had no maids, just a cook and one

servant to help us keep the place clean—otherwise, all our funds went to protecting ourselves. Mother and I would help each other dress when it was needed. Sometimes she would have dinner with a wealthy benefactor or a prospective customer and would wear her best gowns: rich silks that must have come from her time at Le Château. I often begged to try on such fine clothes, but she refused and kept the gowns locked away.

Now my maid, Virginie, slipped a buttery silk skirt over my head and tied its strings at my lower back. I held the fabric in a loose fist, watching the silk shimmer in the sunlight.

I had dreamed of this for so long.

I had hoped my mother would be there, too. Safe and happy. Without a single thought about the Shadows. But she was gone. Missing. What if she hadn't made it here? What if something happened to her?

Something slowly wrapped around my throat.

I gasped, grabbing at it; I could almost *feel* the cold breath of the Shadow upon my neck.

It was a strand of pearls.

Virginie tied the ribbon of the necklace and then gave my bare shoulder a little tap. "Come to the vanity, mademoiselle."

With the haze of sleepiness and fear still clouding around me, I settled on the velvet stool before the table and mirror. I couldn't help but laugh at my own reflection. My matted curls, a bit of grass hidden within; my pink, sleepy eyes; the utter lack of color in my face.

Virginie, too, seemed overwhelmed by the task before her. She sighed heavily and took a brush to my hair with great fervor. I was immune to the way she tugged at my hair; Mother had been ruthless when it came to brushing my curls.

I couldn't think about her. Not then.

I took a deep breath and imagined unpinning myself from the tangled threads of the past few days. Instead, I was simply a girl, the luckiest in the world, at the world's most splendid palace with her dearest . . . her dearest friend.

"Are you well, Lope?" I called.

"As well as can be, my lady," she replied, her voice taut and forced.

It would all be worth it. "You'll look just like I imagined," I cooed. "In a ballgown and everything! And with your hair curled and pinned and decorated . . . you'll look like a princess!"

There was a long silence. "I suppose anything's possible."

Virginie gave me large pearl earrings, and as I put them on, I said, "Where did such fineries come from? Lope and I brought precious little with us."

"Directly from His Majesty," said Virginie. "The king likes the court looking their best for his parties. Even the color of dress is decided by the king."

One by one, like placing stars in the sky, she tucked my

curls away with pearl-tipped pins. She let one lock of hair fall gracefully over my shoulder. I was looking more and more like . . .

Like my mother.

No. Not now. All will be well. She will be fine.

"Will—will we see the king at the party?" I asked.

"He is traveling tonight, but he will be back soon."

I frowned. "Then what is the occasion for the fête?"

"Every day we celebrate His Majesty," said Virginie with a smile. "He shares the blessings of the gods with us all. This palace is our sanctuary. Everything we have, it's all thanks to him."

It was all quite odd, I thought, having parties by royal command. But then again, our world was so dark, so cruel. Monsters lingered not too far from the palace gates. If Le Château was truly the one place where Shadows dared not go, why not rejoice in that fact? After all, we celebrated our grandest holy feasts every year during the bleakest winters. A little bit of hope and delight to shield us from the world beyond.

I longed for that. A beautiful, golden bubble to keep me safe from nightmares.

Virginie painted my lips red and daubed rouge on my cheeks and helped me into my matching blue bodice, lacing the back with nimble hands. Then she slipped on new stockings, bright yellow, with red ribbons holding them in place, and white shoes with crimson heels. I could barely believe that these were all real and for me—but I forgot about myself entirely when Lope emerged from her corner of the room.

She strode toward me with the elegance and control of a true noblewoman. Her broad shoulders were pulled back and her head was held high, exposing the long, graceful arc of her neck. A long black lovelock rested over her heart. Beneath her voluminous, sapphire sleeves, her pale forearms were also bare, covered in faint, silvery scars in the shape of claw marks.

My throat had gone dry. It had not occurred to me how she always kept herself so covered up. A soldier's breastplate over a coat and breeches, a cravat at her throat, her hands often protected by leather gloves. Now I felt as if the pale touches of skin at her arms and shoulders would make my heart leap right out of my breast.

"Thank you, ladies," I told both maids, and quietly dismissed them. They looked to each other, as if they had more to say or do, but deferred to my request, slipping out of the room.

"I'm sorry," said Lope.

I coughed a laugh. "Gods, what for?"

"I—I am unused to this way of things. I am unused to . . . all of this." She gestured to the chandelier, the furniture, the gowns. The painted-on blush on her cheeks was quickly overtaken by her skin flushing a true red. She bowed her head to me. "Forgive me. I'll endeavor to adapt as quickly as I can."

I swept her hands in mine. "You look like a *queen*, Lope. You look so very beautiful—I can scarcely put it to words."

She forced a smile. "Thank you."

I could feel the discomfort emanating off her. She was so *lovely*. Yet it was as if someone had painted over a portrait of the girl I adored.

"Here," I said, dampening a handkerchief with a pitcher of water. I carefully pressed it to her soft lips, brushing away as much of the paint as I could. Her lips were left a little redder, but at least she looked like herself again. Nearly.

"Perhaps I can take those pins out of your hair," I said.

Light entered her gray eyes. Her whole face was the color of the azaleas in my garden. "If—if you'd like, my lady."

I shook my head with a smile. "What would *you* like?"

She blinked rapidly, like I'd said something truly alarming. "I prefer my hair pulled back," she said softly. "It makes me feel like myself."

I urged her into the seat before the mirror. She frowned at her reflection. But she tipped her head, looking at the pearl earrings they'd given her. "I don't mind these, though," she said.

With a grin, I smoothed back her hair. "That makes me think of that night I pierced your ears. You were so brave. And *I* nearly swooned from the blood."

"I had to pierce my other ear myself," she said, shaking

her head. Her gray eyes crinkled as she smiled. "I wanted to match you."

Back at the manor, when we spent time together, sitting and reading, I'd let her wear any of my earrings she liked.

They make me look like a pirate, she had said.

Smiling fondly, I plucked pins from her hair like I would have picked clovers as a child. As I swept her hair into its usual chignon, I asked, "Do you remember when I'd gather clovers for you in the garden?"

Her reflection smiled. But she kept her gaze averted from the glass. "I kept them in a jar at the barracks."

My eyes widened. "You kept them?"

"For good luck, you said."

What a marvel she was. Gentle and poetic and fierce and brave. The bane of any monster. But before us lay the court that Mother had always warned me about. A cruel, selfish place, she had said, a place that preferred fame and riches to kindness or truth.

Could my knight defend me from monstrous men?

Or was it my turn to protect her?

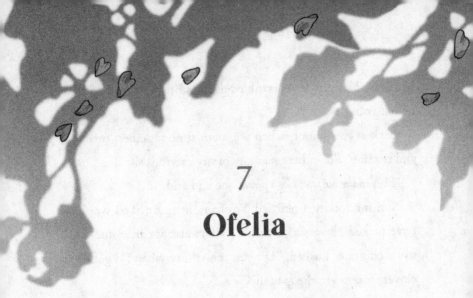

7

Ofelia

Dressed in our finery, Lope and I breathlessly stood in a queue of courtiers entering the ballroom. My heart was fluttering like a butterfly trapped in my chest.

I curled my fingers tighter into the hard muscle of Lope's arm. With her other hand, her thumb grazed against my knuckles. All the warmth in my body rushed into my cheeks as I met her gaze. Could she tell by looking at me how tender my heart was toward her? Or that I knew about the beautiful words she'd written—possibly about me?

"I'll be beside you all night, I promise," she said.

Relief washed over me. She was the steady ground I could rely upon, always.

We had survived the Shadows. A party would be a trifle.

We entered into a hurricane: dancers spinning in skirts of blue silk like crashing waves, their sapphire-suited partners whirling them around and around in the storm. Above it all soared beautiful music, light and chirping, fifty times louder and fuller and lovelier than the lone harpsichord my mother played at our manor.

The thought of my mother stung me, and I breathed steadily through it. I couldn't be afraid now. I had to find her.

Mother will be just around the corner, I tried to tell myself. *We will find her, and everything will be back to normal.*

I carefully removed my hand from Lope's arm to smooth my skirts. Just like the others did, I held my shoulders back and my head high and confident. I dove into the current of courtiers standing at the edge of the dance floor.

"Excuse me," I said, locking my gaze with the first person who looked in my direction—a lady about my mother's age with golden paint on her eyelids. "Excuse me, madame, I'm looking for my mother, Mirabelle de Bouchillon? She looks like me. She's a little taller than I am. . . ."

The woman turned away and carried on her previous conversation.

I asked another stranger and another. When I said Mother's name, the partygoers gave me the same confused stare. Even Lope, who'd rather fight monsters than attend a party, was willing to ask a courtier or two whether they'd heard of Mirabelle de Bouchillon.

"Her Ladyship arrived only a few days ago, we believe," said Lope to a viscount in a cerulean suit.

The viscount shrugged helplessly. "I'm sorry, mademoiselle. A new arrival like yourself always brings new gossip to the court. I'd certainly know if she had arrived." He pointed behind us, past the dancers and past tables stacked high with fresh fruit and pastries. "The salon des jeux is that way. Ask at the gambling tables. If there's any news, they'll have it."

We thanked him profusely and tore through the ballroom. In our mad dash, I caught a quick glance of extraordinary beauty—the ballroom's ceiling, a massive painting of the thousandfold gods in their finery, each with their face turned from the dancers swirling on the parquet below.

Please look at me just this once, I begged the divinities. *Help me find her. I'll be the most obedient daughter, I promise.*

The adjoining chamber was more intimate. There were a dozen tables with a dozen different games, and courtiers all around, laughing and shouting and clinking their bags full of coins. The faint haze of pipe smoke swirled around us. That and the perfume and the cologne and the sweat and the spice-filled pomanders made my senses reel.

"You there!"

I started and whirled on my heel toward the voice. Quickly, I scanned each of the gamblers, looking for the chestnut brown of Mother's hair or her turned-up nose or the way she'd tilt her head when calling to me. . . .

"Coucou! Mesdemoiselles!" called the lady with her hand aloft. She had sapphires and diamonds placed delicately among her scarlet curls. "Come here, come here!"

Hand in hand, Lope and I drifted toward the noblewoman and her friends.

At the center of their table was a heap of pastries, covered in melted chocolate and ripe, bursting fruit, all sprinkled with flakes of gold. And all around the pastries were stacks of gold coins, diamond rings, pearl earrings, hands of cards, wooden fans set aside, and a dozen glasses of wine.

"New arrivals!" shouted the woman who had called us with her swooping, musical voice. I glanced down at her, sitting far back in her chair while a young man languorously pressed kisses along her arm. In her other hand, she waved her cards back and forth like they were a fan. "*Very* new arrivals in*deed*! I've not seen these faces here before."

"I daresay I'd remember that face," remarked a man with blue ribbons tied into his long dark curls. He pointed at Lope. He pointed at her wound; the scar that looked like a tear had seared its way down her cheek.

Hot fury boiled in my middle. I opened my mouth, ready to scold him for drawing mocking attention to this sign of Lope's bravery, before I remembered: people at this court did not seem to like speaking about the Shadows. And I needed to ingratiate myself with these nobles as much as possible if I wanted to find my mother. I breathed out the anger and tried to be as cool and unflappable as Lope.

"Yes, sir, we are new," I said, my voice small. All my life I'd yearned for this, and now that I was here, in this moment, it all seemed so big and so *much*. Days ago I'd been full of such hope for this place. But this reality had never been my dream.

"We arrived here at dawn."

"How fascinating!" remarked a man with dark brown skin, setting down his cards and leaning his hand on his cheek. "Where did you come from, then?"

"The countryside," I said. "The nearest town is Bosque de las Encinas—"

"The countryside?" exclaimed a girl, leaning forward onto the card table. "How curious! So how does a little country bumpkin find herself *here*?"

"W-we are seeking My Ladyship's mother," Lope intervened. "She is la Condesa de Bouchillon. We suspect she came here recently."

The lady with the sapphire-studded coiffure gave her head a very small shake. "I've never heard of her."

"And she would have," volunteered the man who'd been kissing her. He gave her a reverent look as he said, "Emilia remembers everyone."

The possibility had started to take root in my heart—that Mother really *hadn't* arrived. She'd never made it here. My heart felt like it had floated outside my chest, like I was no longer in my body at all. Each breath was slow, crawling its way in and out of my lungs.

Lope bent close, a loose lock of her hair tickling my ear. "Should we leave?" she asked.

I wanted to. I wanted to be a child and curl up and hide. I wanted this to be like that day at the market, when I had lost Mother for only a few minutes before she had found me, scooping me up in an embrace while I collapsed into a puddle of tears.

Just breathe, I told myself. I clung to Lope's hand. I felt the steady, plush carpet beneath my shoes. Inhaled the sweet perfume and the sour sting of smoke in the air. All these years I had wished to jump inside a fairy tale, and all around me was a world just like those illustrated in my storybooks. A room sparkling with diamonds and gold. Music I'd never heard before, beauty I'd never seen. Glamorous people, laughing and carefree.

To uncover the truth, I had to become one of them.

Imagining what a confident, fearless noblewoman would do, I boldly took a chair from another table and placed myself beside Señora Emilia. Without even looking, I could feel Lope standing behind me, watching over me, just in case.

"Forgive my eagerness," I said to the scarlet-haired lady. "If it's true you know everyone at court . . . I take it you know the best gossip, then?"

Emilia set down her hand of cards with a loud slap. She showed me a wide grin. "Oh, thank the *gods*. I was hoping you'd ask. The past few weeks have been absolutely mad. And you're completely new here? Searching for your mother, too? Come, come, tell me everything." Her bracelets jingled as she raised a hand in the air, snapping her fingers. "More wine for the table!"

Emilia turned back to me with her green eyes alight. "What is your name, my pet?"

"Ofelia de Bouchillon, señora." Over my shoulder, I smiled at Lope, who curtsied as I introduced her as "My knight, la Caballera Lope de la Rosa."

Emilia smiled at the two of us. "Enchantée—or, judging by your accent, encantada. Your family must come from the south, like mine." Emilia glanced from where I sat to Lope, standing behind me. "Well, if you were looking for gossip, you've come to the right place at just the right time. Only a few days ago, we had a strange little miracle unfold at the palace."

My brows furrowed. "A miracle?"

"A mystery!" said the man with ribbons in his hair.

Emilia shot him a quick glare, as if annoyed she'd been interrupted. "Yes, indeed, a mystery. You see, it was very recent; it's the talk of the court. A new room, a new *hall*, appeared in the palace overnight."

"A . . . an entire hall, my lady?" Lope asked.

"An entire hall," said Emilia, her eyes only upon me. "There were no workers, no sounds of construction, no announcements that it would come to be or that it was planned. . . . We all woke up and found a strange black-and-golden door in the west wing of the palace."

I leaned forward, as enraptured as if I were reading a novel. "And what lies behind that door?"

Emilia's grin sparkled in the candlelight. "*No one knows.* The king won't allow anyone in. He says it's still in progress. It's so strange; we can see from the edifice of the palace that it is truly a room and not just a door with an empty wall. But whatever's behind that door . . . none of us knows. No matter how we beg and plead with His Majesty." Emilia pointed her fan at a young girl in green. "You should have seen how Camille was batting her eyes, asking for a chance to look upon this new divine miracle the gods had given the king. . . ."

Camille huffed. "He just said the hall wasn't open to the public yet. Now they've got guards watching over it day and night."

"Do you really think there's just . . . scaffolding and dust in there?" Lope asked me softly.

I echoed her question, since I knew she did not wish to say it aloud.

Emilia shrugged. "Who knows. The gods gave the king this beautiful palace, every inch of it, the ballroom, the gardens, the canal, the rooms, the theater, all of it, from floor to painted ceiling."

A young man smiled and touched Emilia's arm. "Gifts are much better when anticipation is built, you know. I'm sure the king is going to dazzle us with something grand in a few months' time."

Camille leaned forward in her seat. "I will mention one

thing—when the king spoke of the room, he called it 'the Hall of Illusions.'"

"How intriguing!" said Emilia.

I wondered what sort of illusions could be inside—how such a thing could be captured and put into a room. But something else confused me. "Why would a gift from the gods need renovations?"

My words were greeted with thick silence. Shame washed over me, though I didn't quite know what I'd done to offend.

Emilia cleared her throat, smiling. "So, mi linda, why is it that you brought your knight *here*? To the safest place in the world?"

It was simple: because she and I were not to be parted.

"Lope and I traveled alone, all the way from the countryside," I said. "It was imperative that I come here, that I find my mother, even if we faced monsters on the—"

The gamblers gasped and hushed and whispered. A young woman's fan clicked rapidly as she fluttered it. A man clutched at his heart. Emilia waved a hand at me.

"Enough of that," she said. "You're new here; you do not understand. The king loathes such talk. He'd have you thrown from the palace if he knew you spoke of those . . . *things*."

I frowned. "But His Majesty is not here."

Emilia lifted her own fan, white and covered with flowers. She hid her mouth as she said, "One can never be too careful, my dear." With a flourish, she shut her fan and tapped the back of my hand. "How curious it is, that a noblewoman would be raised in the countryside. You are nearly a woman. You should have been *here*, finding yourself a match, not languishing out in the middle of nowhere."

Yes. Yes, she understood. That had been all my heart had wanted. Mother and Lope and I, tucked safe within the pages of the story of this beautiful, blessed palace. A story where I was independent and bold and in love. In love with a stormy-eyed girl, spinning in a ballroom . . .

"Who is your father, dear?"

I blinked, awaking from the reverie. "My father?"

Someone at the table giggled and then hastily tried to disguise it with a cough.

"Yes, love. If he was a count, he must have lived at Le Château, mustn't he?"

Mother rarely spoke of him. A few paintings of him were among the many portraits lining the halls of the manor. I had always assumed that stories of him, like stories about Le Château, were simply too painful for her.

"I—I know little about him," I admitted. "He was Comte Luc de Bouchillon, and Mother fell in love with him when she was commissioned to paint his portrait. He and Mother both lived at Le Château before I was born."

"Another clue!" said Emilia. "How long ago was that, dear?"

My heart quickened. Perhaps she remembered. Perhaps the tiles of this strange, muddled mosaic were coming together. "I just turned seventeen, señora."

"Seventeen years ago . . . I was a little younger than you are now." She looked heavenward as though trying to remember something. "So your mother was a painter. That does not help our mystery, I'm afraid. The king loves to collect artists." Emilia fluttered her hand in the air to every wall. "As you can see."

My eyes flitted from one canvas to another. Vistas I'd never seen, great boats amid violent storms, castles and manors, and snowcapped peaks.

If one of her paintings had been on these walls . . . if some trace of her remained in this very room . . .

"Excuse me—!" I cried as I leapt from my chair and moved toward the gallery walls. I knew her style so well. She preferred simple, realistic settings, pastoral and sweet. Her favorite part of painting, she'd said, was trying to capture how the light would play against the features of her subjects.

Weaving through the tables, I glanced from one painting to the next. A portrait of an old woman—no, it was painted indoors, which Mother didn't care for. I looked past every landscape, every dull painting of a bowl of fruit or a stack of books.

"My lady!" I heard behind me.

I called back to Lope, "Maybe Mother painted one of

these!" and dove back into the crowd. There was a smaller portrait, the size of my hand, hanging beside a window, similar to what Mother would have painted. But the artist's signature in the corner was a *J* and a scribble—nothing like Mother's at all.

It was a useless hunt. One fueled by desperation and fatigue. We had journeyed for *days* and had been whisked into this room like leaves blown by storm winds. My head was addled, I was losing my—

Across from me, among a thousand other paintings, one captured my eye. It was no bigger than one of the history books in our library. A small window without any panes.

In the painting, bushes overflowed with scarlet roses, and spraying fountains were placed along a dirt walkway into the vanishing point of the painting. The bright sky with the softest brushstrokes of clouds was so realistic that I could imagine the sun shining warm upon my face.

Two statues were rendered delicately, tenderly, within the painting. A marble statue of a man was on the left side, dressed in robes like he was from a thousand years ago. His hand was upon his hip, where a sword was kept. His head was turned toward the right side of the canvas—toward his companion statue, a woman. Though made of stone, her full figure appeared soft and graceful beneath carefully draped fabric, carved in marble. She looked fondly at the other statue—and cold seeped into my stomach as I looked at her.

The shape of her nose. The dimple in her smile. The

paintbrush hidden within the crown of laurels in her hair. The statue of the woman—my mother?—gazed so intently at the statue of the man. If she was real . . . who was he? This man looked nothing like the painting of my father hanging in our manor.

I stumbled closer, my eyes darting to the bottom-right corner of the canvas. Among boughs of ivy was a single letter painted in white—*M*. The same curves and flourishes of Mother's signature.

"My lady," said Lope, just behind me, her words punctuated with frantic breaths, "forgive me; you move too fast—"

"She really did live here once," I whispered. I longed to touch the canvas—instead I stood as close as I could, examining each glob of paint and trace of the swirling of her brush.

"That—that painting, it looks—"

I pointed to the *M* in the corner. With a proud, pained smile, I turned back to Lope. "I'm not dreaming," I said. "She *was* here. She painted here. She lived here. This is proof."

Without a second's thought, I scurried back to the card-players, who had become distracted by the wine that had just been served. When I touched Señora Emilia's arm, she jumped in her chair and let out a nervous little laugh.

"I've found the painting," I said.

"Mademoiselle, I'm in the middle of a game!" She grinned back at her fellow cardplayers. "Poor dear didn't learn manners in the countryside, did she?"

Desperate for her help, I took the barb she'd meant to hurt me and twisted it into a tool of my own. "I have a great deal to learn," I said, my gaze respectfully low and demure. "All I want is to be a part of the magnificent story of this palace, this marvelous tale you've woven. I believe there is more still to learn about myself. About my mother. Could I impose upon your kindness just once more?"

"Darling thing," cooed a blond noblewoman.

Emilia heaved a sigh. "Very well—which painting was it, my love?"

I pointed to it. "The one of the two statues in the garden."

The table erupted into gasps and whispers and laughter. My confident, charming smile faded; a great chill swept through me. I had heard this sort of laughter from the gossiping market-goers back home. Mirthless and cruel.

"*That* painting has an absolutely delicious story," Emilia said with relish. "Sit, sit!"

Lope and I took our places again, but this time, I reached for her hand. Each callus and scar was so familiar to me. So faintly I thought I'd imagined it, I felt her thumb brushing against my knuckle.

"That painting was done by la Comtesse Marisol de Forestier. The king's favorite painter. And his *favorite*."

As the others snickered, I threw a confused glance to Lope, who always knew more than I did—but her brow was furrowed, too.

"My—my mother's name is Mirabelle," I said weakly. "I've seen her sign it—"

"That may very well be her name *now*, but when she was at court, it was Marisol." Emilia lifted the fan from where it hung on her wrist, covering her mouth once more. The glee in her eyes, however, was undisguised. "So she changed her name, ran off to the countryside, and had *you*. . . ."

"Señora," interjected Lope, anger glinting in her eyes, "please—speak plainly."

"Yes, yes, tell the story," said the man with a flock of ribbons in his hair. "No interruptions from *anyone*, agreed?"

The table nodded solemnly. I pressed my hand to my hammering heart, as if I could silence its beating.

"Yes, yes, dear. Once upon a time," Emilia began, "there was a young countess. She was considered one of the great beauties of the court, and His Majesty himself spotted her. During a ball, he plucked her out from the dancers, and she danced just for him. The two of them, they were like the sun and the moon. Resplendent and glorious. They were captivated by each other at once."

My throat had gone dry as sand. All Mother had ever said was that she had met the king once or twice. And even then, she'd say precious little about him, no matter how I pestered her. "Are you saying that my m—that Marisol was in love with the king?"

The others at the table tittered behind their fans. Was my question *that* ridiculous?

"Oh, my sweet girl," said Emilia with a twinkle in her eye. "You know so little about the ways of the court." She poked my arm with her fan. "Whether or not true love bloomed between them, one tiny problem remained. The countess already had a husband, and he was no fool. Well, in some aspects he was. He was jealous, too jealous."

Emilia shook her head, her red curls wagging like the ears of a dog. "The count was so angry, hearing rumors that he was made the cuckold, that he fetched a horse and rode off to be a soldier in His Majesty's army at once." She jabbed her finger against the tablecloth, making it ripple like she'd dropped a lump of sugar into a cup of milk. "He preferred to die rather than see his wife shame him so. They say that before he threw himself in front of a cannon, he shouted, 'I curse my wife and her lover!'"

"No!" I cried.

I blinked, reacquainting myself with my surroundings. Everyone around the table, even Lope, had turned to gape at me.

The gamblers. The music. The laughter. A moment ago I was on a battlefield, watching an innocent man fling himself into the arms of Death.

Was any of this true? Was my mother this same woman? It seemed impossible to believe. This *Marisol* they described was so bold and careless, so easily swayed by the pleasures of the court—the kind of woman my mother feared I'd become.

My thoughts were a tide quickly sweeping over me. My

mother had rarely spoken of my father. She had never spoken of the king. She avoided talk of Le Château. . . . All these years, could she have done so out of *shame*? Had she left behind an old life, an old name, and all memories of the husband she had betrayed?

The faces around me swirled, morphing in my tear-spotted vision, looking more like twisted masks than faces at all. Emilia said something I couldn't understand, and the courtiers around the table laughed—laughed at me. I thought of Shadows grasping at my throat, and the way their faces split, almost like a smile. How Mother had saved me in the garden. Mother. Mother. Mother, who I knew, who I loved, who had been a *lie*?

I left behind the ballroom. I left behind the beauty and the dreams, staggering about in the dark hallways until Lope finally found me. She rescued me, yet again, as I clung to her, sobbing.

8

Lope

I loved her in the darkness,
When the warmth of her body
And the sweet push and pull of her breath
Was the entirety of my world.

As I lay in the daybed, I counted Ofelia's breaths. She had stopped crying hours ago and had finally fallen asleep. Each breath I counted was supposed to assure me that she was well. That she was alive. It was supposed to lull me into sleeping, too.

But when I closed my eyes, the world grew dark, and I was no longer alert. And she'd no longer be safe.

I remembered being a child, arriving at the barracks at the edge of the manor. Those first few hours—Carlos, a year my senior, introduced himself and explained to me that I would be sleeping during the daylight hours from then on. I couldn't fall asleep then, either.

"I cannot listen to you tossing and turning one more minute!" he had said with a dramatic sigh. And as sunlight had gleamed in a small beam through our shutters, he sat on the floor across from me and taught me to play chess.

Cradled in the warm embrace of the palace daybed, for a moment, I could still feel the smooth wood of the rook beneath my fingers. Hear the triumphant click as Carlos knocked down my king and then laughed at me.

"Another round," I'd said.

And he'd said my name, my old name, *Luisa*, the name that didn't suit me. "This is supposed to bore you to sleep."

"I want to learn," I had whispered, while the world was awake beyond our window.

His eyes, green like crisp apples, had twinkled at me. "You're stubborn. You will make a good knight."

What good knight allowed their mentor to die?

I clawed my way out of my memories and sat up in the bed, rubbing my eyes. My gaze fixed once more upon Ofelia, lying on her side in her bed, her hands tucked beneath her cheek.

She looked like a painting. Not like the ones here, in dark tones with ostentatious gold frames. She was softer, sweeter. Something painted not for the need of lavish decor, but because such beauty *needed* to exist.

I sat on the daybed, my breath held tight in my chest.

I failed Carlos. I cannot fail her.

My hands trembled. I had no more weapons. And at this

court, they did not fight with blades. They wielded stories, and the story of Ofelia's mother had been like a dagger to her heart.

With such cruelty within these walls, I needed to be stronger, strong enough to protect Ofelia.

I needed the strength of the gods. Any god, any that would listen to my fervent prayer.

I crept toward the nightstand beside Ofelia's large bed. Silently, I drew open the drawer and selected a single yellow candle, and then lit it with the flint from my tinderbox. I placed the burning candle in a brass candlestick before the vanity and frowned at the faint, white blur of my reflection in the dim light. A moment later, I threw my bedsheet over the mirror.

From my rucksack, I procured the journal Ofelia had given me, filling up fast. Poem after poem, verse after verse. All of the nonsense I could not keep trapped in my mind. By the flickering, golden light, I wrote down a few verses. They were all I could give.

You are attached to my heart,
If I am a tree, you are all of my roots,
You bring me life, you hold me,
You turn me toward the sun

I paused, imagining my small, stumbling voice as I'd read this to her. But I could never dare to do such a thing. My metaphors were poor, my words were so weak. She deserved perfection. And she certainly didn't deserve the paltry affection of a common knight.

I sighed and massaged my eyes. "Gods above, numerous and unknowable, please give me the strength to keep her safe."

Even if this ritual was useless, I had to carry it out. The orphanage that raised me taught me to be devout, and a part of me clung desperately to the constancy of the faith I had found there. Even if my cries were to fall on ears that did not care to hear . . . I had to try.

I carefully fed the poem into the flame. Ashes crumbled into the candlestick. I waited. I watched the smoke rise.

When I prayed, sometimes I thought I could hear a voice. I could remember the sound, remember the tone, but whatever that voice had said, I could never remember.

Maybe that would be the only sign of holiness I'd ever receive.

Maybe I was only calling into empty darkness.

"Lope?"

I turned. I had been so ensnared by my own worries and prayers that I hadn't noticed Ofelia stirring. She was sitting in her bed now, rubbing her eyes. Her hair was an artful mess of copper curls.

"Yes, my lady?" I replied. I dug my nails into my hand to suppress the foolish, lovesick smile building within me from just looking at her.

She blinked slowly and sleepily. Her shoulders were slumped, as if the night's slumber hadn't been restorative enough. "I thought this place would be a dream," she mumbled, her words slow as the fog of sleep lifted. "I thought we'd find Mother and that we could live here and be happy, but . . . I feel more confused than ever. More hopeless than ever." She bunched the embroidered sheets in her fists. "All those things that lady said last night. It feels as if I don't really know my mother. I . . . I almost wonder if she isn't coming at all. If she abandoned me. Like she abandoned her old life. I worry those stories about my mother were true."

I could see the storm clouds in her eyes. My heart fractured. She did not deserve to live in a world with dreary skies.

"I'm sure that isn't so, my lady," I said. "They like stories and rumors around here. And a good story is always exaggerated." I slowly crossed the room and held out my hand for hers. "Your mother would never abandon you. I'm certain she will arrive at the palace in a day or so."

I did not fully believe my own words, but the hope dawning on Ofelia's face made me want to.

"Come," I said, pulling her up gently, "we've come all this way, and you have yet to show me those beautiful gardens you always read about. Perhaps the sun on your skin will lift your spirits."

Her hand squeezed mine. "A walk would be nice."

I nodded. "We will continue to investigate. Ask everyone

we meet if they've seen your mother. And we shall stay at the palace until she arrives."

Ofelia smiled. "No one knows how to make my heart glad like you do, Lope."

My face burned. Her smile widened into a grin, and she slipped out of her bed. She approached one of her windows, parting the latched doors of the shutters. Beyond lay vast gardens with fountains spraying mist like rain high into the air, glimmering with rainbows.

"Oh my," she said breathlessly. The sun glowed yellow upon her freckled skin. She was a daisy, blooming in the dawn.

The second we pushed open the doors leading outside, we were overtaken by a flood of bright sunshine. I blinked back stars, disoriented and dizzy—and then the world came into focus.

Before us, the sky was an endless blue canvas, without a single cloud. White gravel walkways extended before us far into the distance, interrupted by terraces with boxwoods and rows upon rows of flowers, kept in tidy, colorful beds.

Ofelia cried out in delight and barreled toward the nearest flower bed, bending as low as she could to smell the lavender and freesias. She knelt down on the gravel and practically embraced the flowers. "Lope, come smell them!" she called.

I laughed and joined her, kneeling in the dusty pathway,

the rocks pressing against my knees through my stockings and breeches. The delicate, beautiful scents washed around me.

Her fingers brushed each leaf and petal so gently, so lovingly. When I closed my eyes, I could almost see her caressing my cheek with that same fond look upon her face.

I woke from my reverie when I heard a small gaggle of people laughing not too far away. My eyes flew open, and to our left, a group of courtiers tittered as they looked our way, at the two girls kneeling in the dirt.

Ofelia leapt to her feet and dusted off her skirts, her cheeks flaming the bright pink of a sunrise.

"Let's walk on," she said softly.

I followed in her shadow, until she slowed, shifting slightly, so that we walked side by side. If I wasn't careful, our hands would nearly touch.

She took my arm, and we walked onward, this time toward a long corridor made of hedges that climbed all the way up to the sky. The garden was beautiful, fragrant, and sunlit. But being outdoors, even on the brightest day, set me on edge. Nature, the subject of so much poetry—it was also the Shadows' domain.

Ofelia grinned as we rounded a corner and found another long hedgerow before us. "The king's labyrinth!" She eagerly tugged at my arm. "Oh, it's just like a storybook! Perhaps a secret is hidden here. Where else would someone hide a treasure?"

Or a monster, I thought, recalling one of the stories she'd read me by candlelight.

The farther we walked, the darker the world became, with the shade of the hedgerows blocking the morning light. The growing darkness made the hair on my neck stand on end. We had seen a Shadow attack us while the sun was still in the sky. The dimming light still made me anxious. This kind of thick, heavy shade was a Shadow's chosen battleground. If any creatures were lurking about these grounds, they'd be hiding here.

"Follow me," said Ofelia, walking faster.

I raised my brows. "Do you know which way you're going, my lady? This . . . this labyrinth seems quite vast."

She walked backward, smiling impishly at me. "I read the book about Le Château so many times I've practically memorized the garden. At night, before I fell asleep, I used to imagine what it would be like to walk these allées." She twirled in place, her skirts blossoming around her. "And we're *here*!" Ofelia's smile faltered the smallest bit. "Mother must be here, too. She . . . she surely wouldn't have gotten lost. She hired a coachman to bring her here. She must be here already, and we just haven't found each other yet."

I hoped that was so.

She turned a corner, and we entered an area surrounded by a round wall of hedges. A large fountain was in the middle of the space, with the statue of a woman draped in cloth that seemed thin as paper, even when carved from marble. Her arms were outstretched, as if asking for an embrace—but the flat, blank surface of her face was a reminder that she was a goddess. We mortals were not worthy of knowing whatever beauty she held.

As we walked into this little pocket of the labyrinth, we approached the fountain. At its base was a massive pile of offerings, red roses, letters sealed with kisses, locks of hair, books of love poems. Candles flickered and the smell of freesias was thick in the air. In a few days, this would all be burned in a passionate, desperate gift to the goddess, casting all the prayers from Le Château into that invisible palace where the gods were said to live.

"Le Bosquet du Temple de l'Amour," Ofelia noted. She smiled up at the goddess of love as if she were an old friend.

When I looked to the goddess of love, my stomach clenched. It felt too bold of me, too wrong, too foolish to ever even attempt to pray for love. My pulse always raced for Ofelia, but even I knew that the flutterings of my heart were pathetic, terrestrial things. My feelings were true, certainly—but surely not important enough to ask for the aid of a goddess.

"You could write such beautiful poetry about this place," Ofelia mentioned. How sweet it was that her mind never strayed close to the darkness. I wished often that I could mold my mind to be like hers. That my eyes would see beauty like hers did, instead of danger. Basking in her light was the closest I could come to viewing the world like she did.

"I hope I'll get the chance to, my lady." She was so near to me, her cheek almost brushing the shoulder of my coat. I had to catch my breath. "You gave me a great gift when you taught me how to write. It was like teaching me how to see the world in new colors."

"Even when you talk about poetry it's like poetry," she beamed.

I laughed, bowing my head and praying she didn't notice the red in my cheeks.

Ofelia pointed at a small green book in the offerings pile, *Grandes Obras Poéticas*, and said, "Oh, you have that one!"

I smiled—it, like every book I owned, had been a gift from her. "I've read that one so many times the binding is holding on by a thread."

"Oh, I shall have to buy you another one as soon as I can." She turned on her heel and began to walk out of the bosquet, her hands behind her back, like this was some ordinary morning stroll. Like she belonged here. "So which one is your favorite poem?"

"There's a poem I like," I said. "The writer says that he knows that one day his lover will pass away. That one day *he* will pass away. But he writes that death cannot erase the love they had. It exists outside of time, outside of flesh. He says even when they are dust, they will be enamored dust."

Ofelia let out a delicate sigh. "Oh, how romantic!"

The inevitability and the strength of death did not strike her as it had me when I'd read the poem for the first time. She gleaned immediately what took me months to understand. The beauty of love so deep it could not be separated even from one's own ashes.

Part of me wanted her to keep looking at me like that, swoony and fond, and part of me wanted to turn invisible at once, so I could run away and stop making a fool of myself in front of her. What was I doing? Knights didn't recite *poetry* to those they were sworn to protect!

"Do you believe that?"

I blinked, leaving my cloudy thoughts behind. "Believe what, my lady?"

"That love is something immortal."

I stared down at my feet as we walked, watching the gravel turn the toes of my boots white. *The poets always said love is immortal . . . but is it?* I had loved only two people in my life. And one I could still see behind my lids. Carlos's face, so still in death, and then wrapped forever away in a sheet, his freckled face a blank, nameless skull.

Love was not only some romantic thing, not just something bright and pure like the illustrations of knights and princesses. It was strong and angry and resilient and most of all, painful—viciously so. I looked at Ofelia, and my heart ached for a future that could never be. I thought of Carlos, whose memory still wounded me, even after he was gone.

"Yes," I said to her. "Love outlives everything."

The two of us entered another bosquet, with orange trees planted in a circle around us, their perfume thick and sweet in the air. Bushes with berries and patches of vegetables all surrounded the fountain in the center. A marble statue of a deity with a bird on their shoulder, a lamb in their arms, vines crawling along their robes, and a crown of abundant flowers.

"Le Bosquet du Jardin de la Vie," said Ofelia. "To the deity of life."

We stood, wordless, listening to the rush of water and the wind breezing through the orange trees. I gazed up at the statue, at the bird on its shoulder, and my forehead wrinkled. I hadn't heard any birds, not in the whole garden. I looked to the sky to see if I could catch any flitting by.

"What is it?" Ofelia asked.

"Birds go quiet when Shadows are near," I said softly.

Ofelia's hand took mine, and she slowly led me out of the bosquet. "There are no Shadows here—we're safe now."

Still I listened; still I looked to the skies. "We saw Shadows just beyond the palace gates."

"Yes, but we are within the palace grounds now." She gestured behind her back to the bosquet. "This whole place is blessed. It honors the gods. Surely no monsters could come into a place like this."

How sweet her words sounded. How much I longed to believe them.

Yet as we walked, something within me, something trained but unnamable, continued to feel ill at ease. The hairs on the back of my neck stood on end. There was a tingling in my spine, that strange, invisible sense of someone watching me. I glanced behind me—but there was only a sunlit garden.

Ofelia's hand petted my arm. "It's all right," she promised. Like I was some child having a nightmare.

Perhaps I *was* imagining things. Years on the wall, being trained to be nothing but vigilant . . . it could have addled my mind.

But no birds sang.

I kept my eyes upon the vast, black shadows the hedges cast onto the gravel.

Ofelia guided us into a new area—but instead of an open space, there was a large iron grate between the two walls of hedges. She approached the grate, frowning, her fingers curling around the little diamonds formed between the lattice grate. "I don't remember this area on the map," she remarked.

I stepped closer, peering through. This bosquet was a large circle, like the others, lined with white gravel. But there were no plants, no fountains. Only a white, domed pavilion. At its center was a black door with a golden handle—it stood alone, attached to nothing but the marble floor.

"Each bosquet honors a god," I said softly. "Who could this be for?"

Ofelia's eyes had a little twinkle in them as they flicked toward me. "The deity of doors, perhaps?"

We frowned at that strange door.

"Or maybe it's some sort of artwork?" Ofelia murmured.

I kept my fingers curled against the cool iron. The feeling from before—that Shadows were close by—it didn't abate. The hissing sound I heard—was it the water from the fountains? Was it the wind through the trees? Or could it be the monsters that had followed me throughout my entire life?

I watched our silhouettes on the gravel drive, mine tall and angled, hers short and round, and then—suddenly, a large shadow swallowed both of our figures.

In an instant, I withdrew the knife hidden in my boot— the only weapon the palace hadn't taken from me. I whirled around, pushing Ofelia behind me, and in a second, I had my dagger pointed—but not at a Shadow. It touched the silvery throat of a soldier's armor. He wore a breastplate and gorget over the deep blue coat of the king's guard. He had a halberd leaning against his shoulder as he glared down at us with icy eyes.

The soldier grabbed me by the lapels of my coat. "Who do you think you are, assaulting one of the king's knights?"

Ofelia darted close, and with her so near, I lowered my blade.

"Sir, this lady is my personal guard," she said. "She was only protecting me; you startled us. Now, please, enough of this roughness. Let her go."

He shoved me back a pace. I kept my hand around the

handle of the blade, and even though I knew that this man wasn't the enemy, I remained on my guard.

The soldier gave me a hard look. "Courtiers are not permitted to have weapons, señorita."

"Caballera," I corrected. "It is my duty to protect Lady Ofelia against the Shadows, and I will not do so unarmed."

His lip curled. "There are no Shadows at Le Château."

"I've seen them just beyond the gates!" I cried, incensed that a fellow soldier would enforce this lie. "They could slip under the walls or into this garden in an instant!"

He stepped even closer to me, his eyes blazing. "We do not welcome troublemakers in this palace. Perhaps you and your mistress would like to cut your stay here short?"

"No!" yelped Ofelia, grabbing my arm. Her eyes shone imploringly at me. "Lope, please." She glanced up at the soldier. "Please, sir, she means no harm. We were only taking a walk. We've traveled so far, and I'm searching everywhere for my mother. She was supposed to arrive here and—I'm looking everywhere for her." She slowly pushed me behind her. Her voice wobbled as she spoke. "You're a king's guard, sir. Would you know if she arrived? Her name is Mira—" She paused. "Her name is Marisol de Forestier."

The soldier's posture eased. It was like some magic Ofelia possessed, being able to calm people, to get them to listen to her and want to help her. It worked on me, certainly.

"I do not know every soul who's come through the gates,"

said the soldier. "But a ledger of all guests who enter and exit Le Château is kept in the library, along with all other records."

Hope made her eyes sparkle. "A ledger! Oh, excellent. Thank you, sir!" She turned to me, squeezing my arm. "Let's go to the library. They ought to have some proof if Mother arrived here safely."

She curtsied to the soldier and started to leave, but I lingered for a moment.

"Why did you approach us?" I asked him coldly.

"This bosquet is not open to the public," he said simply.

My brow furrowed. "Why would that be?"

"The king's order." The soldier held out a gloved hand. "Now, your knife, señorita. Unless you wish to leave the palace alongside it."

As I placed it in his hand, my heart plummeted. They wanted us defenseless here. *Why?*

He nodded his head. "Be on your way."

Ofelia grabbed my arm and pulled me away from the bosquet, back into the brightly lit allée. Her hand slid down my arm, her fingers entwining with mine. It made the heat of my anger and confusion melt into something sweet and warm.

"Let's go back to the palace and find this library, like he said," Ofelia told me as we walked side by side.

I glanced back over my shoulder. The soldier lingered in the shadows of the bosquet entrance, his halberd held in his fist. "Why would he concern himself with us?" I murmured. "The place was gated off, anyhow. . . ."

"He probably just has a temper."

Her thumb brushed against mine, the only thing that could make me tear my eyes from the soldier and that little alcove.

"Something's hidden there," I murmured. "Something we got too close to."

She let out a soft sigh through her nose, her gaze firmly upon the palace in the distance. "Lope, I don't want a mystery," she said, small and defeated. "I want my mother back."

Her eyes looked like sunlit water. My heart twinged. I was letting my ambition take charge. My knightly need for duty and honor and defeating evil.

Now Ofelia didn't need me to fight her monsters. She needed me to guide her someplace safe.

I clenched her hand to ground me. To turn my thoughts from myself to her—her and her mother.

Yet when I looked at the palace before us, golden in the morning light, something unsettled me. That ethereal, splendid beauty. It reminded me of the divine stories the pious caretakers would tell in the orphanage. That if the gods were to visit us, they would be too resplendent. That blood would seep from our eyes.

Beauty so brilliant it was deadly.

9

Lope

Within the pages of a book,
I wrap myself in solitude and solace.
Words from long-gone poets, friends I'll never know,
Curl around my heart like loving hands.

Inside the palace, vast corridors extended before us, lined with columns of red marble. Golden candelabras dotted the hallways, and each candlestick bore crystals that resembled long fangs. Every wall, even here in an inconsequential corridor, was crowned with carved leaves and fruits painted gold.

It was beautiful, I could admit. Far too ostentatious for my liking, but perhaps fitting for the gods that had created this palace. It was said that *they* answered the king's prayers, if not those of a peasant girl turned lovelorn knight. What had the king done to deserve such a gift, while so many who had done nothing wrong suffered?

Ofelia's fingers curled against the sleeve of my coat. I looked down at her as she gaped at her surroundings. The wonder in her eyes was far lovelier than anything I'd seen in this palace.

"It's just like I dreamed," she whispered. She gave her head a tiny shake. "Why did Mother want to keep me from this place?"

The countess was strict, and though Ofelia always bemoaned her mother's harsh rules, in truth, I respected them. Her Ladyship carried herself with the carefulness of someone who has had to live in fear. Of someone who wants to protect her daughter from that same fear. Which convinced me further that some unspoken danger lay hidden in these walls, covered up with gold and lies.

Before I could say anything, Ofelia grabbed my hand. My heart swung back and forth between finding the gesture familiar and thrilling. We had always touched each other like this, but now each gentle brush had me foolishly imagining that the contact might be because she was fond of me, fond in the way I was fond of her.

She declared, "Let's find the library!" and began tugging me forward in her wake, and suddenly we were running, whirling like petals tossed to the wind.

Down one corridor, then another. Past tapestries showing ancient battles. Past épées and rapiers and beautiful ruby-encrusted daggers hidden within locked cabinets. I lingered near those for an extra second, longing for my own rapier, before Ofelia pulled me away again.

Even though this place was new and strange, and even though we had yet to find her mother, she somehow found it within her to laugh as we ran faster and faster. She glanced back at me, slipping her hand out of my grasp. Her nose was wrinkled playfully as she teased, "Catch me!"

She scampered off, taking a sharp turn down the hallway to the right. My heart was like a horse at full gallop. This joy of hers, this light that glimmered even in the darkest times of her life, I loved it so, even if I couldn't always understand it.

Poetry drifted through my mind, *I seek her with the desperation and reverence of a moth to candlelight.*

A laugh broke from my lips, even though my ribs were sore, even though my throat ached from the Shadows' attack. Her giggle bouncing through the marble halls was like birdsong after a long night.

I had been trained my whole life to be strong, to be quick. I caught up with her in no time, looping my arms around her waist and pulling her gently into the air before settling to a stop.

Ofelia beamed up at me. In the warm afternoon light, her skin was like gold, her eyes glimmering like the crystals of the chandeliers; her hair was the same mahogany as the trim along the lintels. She *belonged* here.

"What are you thinking about?" she asked me.

It was a simple question, I knew, but I stammered. She couldn't know. She couldn't know how I adored her. That wasn't how her storybooks went. It wasn't how *reality* went. A noblewoman like her, she would marry a duchess or a viscount or a marquis—not a servant.

Desperate, I looked away from her, gazing at the gold-and-black door at the end of the corridor. It was flanked on either side with guards in shining black armor, like they were crafted from obsidian. If it weren't for the gold glinting on their armor and the halberds in their hands, I might have mistaken them for Shadows.

"That door," I murmured. "Black and gold . . . like that lady mentioned in the salon des jeux."

Ofelia's eyes gleamed. "The Hall of Illusions!"

Without another second to assess the situation, she marched up to the two guards, her pale pink skirts fluttering about her like rose petals. "Good afternoon, gentlemen," she said brightly. "What's behind this door?"

"Move along, please, mademoiselle," said the deep-voiced guard on the left.

The one on the right tipped his head, faceless beneath his visor. "You don't know? You must be new here."

I joined her by the door, carefully placing myself between her and the men with their halberds. "We're only curious, sirs," I said.

The guard on the left shrugged. "The king requests this hall remain closed while it undergoes repairs. Nothing more."

I did not consider myself very shrewd, but even I knew well enough that this was a lie.

"Can't we take a peek?" begged Ofelia.

"No," the guards said in unison. "By order of the king."

"You don't understand," she said, "my mother is missing. She's somewhere in this palace, I'm sure of it. I think there's just been some mistake. Her name is Marisol de Forestier?"

"She wouldn't be in *this* room," said the deeper-voiced soldier.

Ofelia huffed, an auburn curl fluttering in front of her eyes. "Very well. Could you at least tell us where to find the library? Perhaps we'll find her there."

A guard pointed us in the correct direction, and we finally acquiesced and returned on our path to the library.

Ofelia smiled mischievously as she looked back at the door. "If there are all these guards and all this secrecy, whatever is in that hall *must* be something very important."

"Something horrible," I murmured.

"Something wonderful," said Ofelia, her voice soft and dreamlike.

After a few minutes of walking through the splendorous halls, Ofelia and I stood before a massive set of golden doors. They were carved with leaves and flowers and fruits and vegetables—boasting the abundance of knowledge we would be sure to find inside. I started to pull on one door's handle, but Ofelia's hand quickly touched mine, then drew back. My pulse ricocheted.

"Oh! I forgot to tell you something," she said.

I turned to her, my fingers still curled around the door handle. "Yes, my lady?"

"You look beautiful today."

My breath faltered as I turned to look at her. With Ofelia's encouragement, I had asked the maids to change my wardrobe a bit, so they'd finally given me a pair of breeches and a waistcoat, simple and cream. They were practical, comfortable. *Beautiful* was the word I would have reserved for her—her copper curls tucked back with a fabric rose, and the pale pink of her gown making all the freckles on her shoulders all the more prominent. For a fraction of a second, my thoughts veered into daydreams. Into kissing her shoulder, kissing each freckle, and then I cleared my throat and said, "My lady, you don't need to—"

"I mean it. You were lovely in a gown, and you look beautiful in a suit." She smiled like her words weren't in danger of stopping my heart.

I didn't know what to say to her remark. Instead, I stiffly pulled open the door for her, and she stepped across the stoop. She let out an excited gasp. I hastily joined her inside the library.

My mouth fell open. I had never seen so many books in

my life. Every wall from top to bottom was filled with them. It was almost obscene; no one man could possibly read so many books, surely! But even the deepest, most cynical part of myself could shut up long enough for me to recognize the library for what it was: a jewel. The spines of the books shone gold in the sunlight from a large, circular window. The books looked like gems lining the walls, every color of a prism.

The task of choosing only one to focus on seemed impossible. Then I saw that word, my favorite word both in meaning and in sound, *poetry*, and reached out to touch the spine of the book in front of me.

Something touched my shoulder, startling me. An old instinct was ready to claw and fight back—but it was Ofelia, her dark eyes glimmering in the sunshine. Without a word, she took my hand and pulled me down the aisle of bookcases.

The library was vast, with a ceiling that seemed as wide as a field, painted to show the heroes from different ballads and fairy tales. My neck ached trying to take in the immensity of the painting, and I felt a pang of unease for the poor painter who had to lie on their back creating such a wonder.

Among the shelves was nestled the occasional chair or desk, but none were occupied. I'd heard whispers long ago of how the palace was so large it housed a population the size of a city, and after the vast crowds I'd seen last night, I believed it. But it seemed absurd to me that they weren't *here*.

Ofelia halted in her stride through the library, her hand

still curled tightly around mine.

Ahead of her was a desk covered in pages. A lady with grayish hair sat at the desk, her head slumped atop a stack of books. For a split second, my heart clenched painfully at her too-still posture, but Ofelia confidently strode forward, saying, "Madame?"

The woman jolted in her seat, looking up from behind round spectacles. Her hair, the faded yellow of tarnished silver, was all in disarray, and her pale cheeks had grown pink with surprise. "Gods! I didn't see you. I—Can I help you?"

I followed close behind Ofelia, my fingers itching for my sword or my dagger. Any stranger could be a threat, just as any silhouette could be a Shadow.

"We're looking for a ledger of all the people who've come and gone to the palace in the past few weeks," said Ofelia. "Could you help us find it?"

The woman smiled, kindness etched in the lines of her face. "I should hope so. I'm the king's librarian and registrar." She rose to her feet, which did not do much to improve her stature; she was shorter than the already small Ofelia. But this was not as remarkable to me as her clothing. She was dressed as ornately as the rest of the court: a gown of shimmering silver fabric, with sleeves and skirts like full moons. It hardly seemed practical for a librarian.

"It's nice to meet you, Madame—"

"Call me Eglantine, please. There should be no courtesy

or stations in a room full of books—at least, that's what I think."

I liked her already.

Ofelia curtsied nonetheless and introduced herself. When I told the librarian my name, her eyes twinkled.

"You share the name of one of the great poets and play-wrights from the south," she noted.

My mouth popped open in amazement. The people I consorted with rarely made the connection.

"Lope named herself after him," Ofelia said, her voice strangely gilded with pride.

I nodded to Eglantine. "That's correct. I . . . I thought the name suited me better than my old one."

Her smile brightened. "My mother did the same thing, in fact. She renamed herself *Sagesse*—she named herself after wisdom. There is great power in claiming a name of your own."

Eglantine sorted through the pile of documents and books surrounding her. "So, what name is it you're looking for, my ladies?"

In a small, uncertain voice, Ofelia said, "Marisol de Forestier."

Eglantine hummed and sorted through the stack of books before her. "That name *does* sound familiar."

Among the books and the papers, something gold twinkled in the sunlight. A small, thin penknife. My breath caught. They'd taken away all my blades. They'd taken away the clothes I could run in. They said there were no Shadows here, but . . . we had believed we'd been safe before.

"You know her name?" Ofelia cried, dragging my attention away from the knife. "Did you see her? Did you ever know her? Were you here at the palace about twenty years ago?"

"Just a moment, child." She flipped open a large, leather-bound volume as long as my forearm. After flipping through the pages, she dragged her finger down a column of names. She jabbed one with her index finger. "Yes, she arrived five days ago!"

Ofelia let out a squeal of delight and hopped up and down, and suddenly she was embracing me as tight as she could. "I knew it! I knew she'd be all right!"

"And there's no indication that she left the palace," said Eglantine.

"So she's here? On the grounds somewhere?"

"It appears so." Eglantine held up a finger and then flipped through another book, pushing back pages with a furrowed brow. After a minute, her frown deepened.

"What?" asked Ofelia. "What is it?"

Eglantine tapped the book. "I can't find a record of her being assigned any rooms."

Ofelia's arms loosened around me, and my heart fell an inch. "What does that mean?" she asked.

"I—I'm not sure." She stared down at the words like they would whisper some secrets to her if she glared hard enough. "Where are your parents, Mademoiselle Ofelia? Have they provided you with no answers about this missing woman?"

"My—my mother *is* that woman," she said meekly. Her fingers trembled. She picked at her nails until I stilled her hand. "And . . . and my father died before I was born. I have no other family."

Eglantine shrank back into her chair, her skin grown ashen. "My apologies, dear. I . . . I know what that's like."

Ofelia's complexion was growing very pale again. Her hand clung to mine, her skin clammy and cold.

"Perhaps," I said, "perhaps there is some record about her father? And his family who might be here?"

Ofelia nodded eagerly. "Yes! He was Comte Luc de Bouchillon. . . . He served in the king's army about twenty years ago, Mother said."

Eglantine tilted her head, like Ofelia had said something amiss. "He was a count, you said?"

Though she bit her lip, Eglantine rose from her seat and walked toward the massive forest of bookshelves. "Follow me," she called. "We have records of all of His Majesty's military victories. Your father's name will be on there, as well as more information about his family. Perhaps your relatives have some quarters here or a summer home not far away. Anything is possible. . . ."

Ofelia's hand pulsed against mine, gently letting go. She wordlessly followed in the librarian's footsteps.

I lingered for only a few seconds. I'd been trained to strike fast, to move quietly. In a blink, I had grabbed the penknife and tucked it in the pocket of my breeches.

Ofelia would scold me for stealing or perhaps for being so overly worried. It couldn't be helped. As it was a Shadow's instinct to consume the breaths of the living, I was driven and desperate to wield a blade.

I joined the librarian and Ofelia before an oak bookshelf filled to bursting with identical gold-spined tomes. Eglantine gestured to them. "Just a fraction of the glorious victories of our king."

Ofelia looked at the ranges of dates carved on the spines, drifting toward the time her father would have been here.

I asked, "Are only his victories recorded, madam?"

The librarian blinked. "His Majesty never fails, my lady." An odd, sloppy smile formed on her painted-red lips. "It would be silly to have a blank book on the shelves, wouldn't it?"

And yet his own people were tormented by monsters. I managed the one-beat chuckle that I always gave when some superior expected a laugh. "Quite, madam. Excuse me."

Following Ofelia's suit, I piled up several golden tomes and carried them over to the large table where she'd splayed out hers. Eglantine settled at a nearby table with a tome of her own, and Ofelia sat close to me in a painted-gold chair, running her finger down a column of text. The way her forehead scrunched together reminded me of bunched satin, and I found it terribly lovely.

I turned my attention forcibly to the page of the records in front of me, detailing the strategy the king had devised himself as he prepared to sack some vast, foreign city. But my gaze was pulled to a watercolor painting on the following page, one so vivid, so detailed, it was like a window had been placed between the pages of the book.

The sky was a soft robin's-egg blue, with fat, fluffy clouds shrinking and pulling apart on the horizon. Beneath the sky, in a perfectly straight line, was a massive body of water, shimmering in the sunshine, stretching from the left page to the right. Beneath this was sand, a strange, pale shade of pink, like it was made of petals. A line of text was written beneath, "The southern shores were claimed and now belong to His Majesty's blessed kingdom."

This was the ocean.

Carlos had longed to see this place. I had thought him mad for wanting it. For thinking it was possible to ever go to such a beautiful, perfect, faraway place. A place set aside for kings.

And here I was, looking at it.

I pressed my fingertips to the page, feeling dried ink and not the wet, shifting surface of the ocean like I imagined.

Before I could drown in my thoughts again, I shut the

book and took a deep breath. I turned my gaze to Ofelia. Ofelia, whose heart I would rather fear for than my own.

She glowered down at the book before her. Her cheeks were flaming a deeper and deeper red, and when she blinked, looking to me, her eyebrows were furrowed and her brown eyes glimmered. "Maybe I'm mistaken," she said. "The—the date, it doesn't make sense."

I frowned. "My lady, I don't understa—"

She rose from her chair, lifting the book with trembling hands. She heaved a deep breath and dropped the book onto the table before me with a coarse thud, pointing to a line in the text. She leaned over my shoulder, her lovelock tickling my bare skin as she read, "Of the number who happily gave their lives in the foreign lands for the service of our blessed king, whose campaign began in the year sixteen hundred and forty-two, on the day of the twenty-fifth of May—"

She interrupted herself and moved her finger to point at a name near the bottom of the list of the dead: "Luc de Bouchillon, July 1642."

"Eglantine," called Ofelia, her voice crumbling, "there's a mistake in this book. It—it says that my father died in the summer of 1642, but that couldn't be. That couldn't be, because I was born in . . . I was born in . . ."

Her lips moved, but no more sound came forth. But I knew the date well. We shared the exact same birthday: August 1, 1643.

More than twelve months after Ofelia's father's death.

My blood went cold at the insinuation. I tried my best to keep my expression stony for Ofelia. All the while, I thought, *Who, then, is her father?*

Eglantine's eyes grew wide, and she glanced from Ofelia to the book. "Count Luc de Bouchillon," she mumbled to herself. She snapped her fingers, pointing. "His—his wife, she was a—a composer? A singer?"

"A painter," said Ofelia. "I don't understand. If Father died a year before I was born . . ."

Ofelia brushed tears from her eyes, though I longed to do it for her myself. I hastily passed her a handkerchief, and when Eglantine touched a hand to her shoulder, she began sobbing in earnest.

"Perhaps there is a mistake," Eglantine said softly. "But . . . you did not even know this man. Whether or not he is your father does not matter—"

"Mother told me!" she snapped, her left hand curling into a fist on the tabletop. "They were married. They were in love; they fell in love *here*. How could—" She cut herself off.

Yet according to the gossipers' stories . . . Marisol had fallen in love with another.

A mosaic of facts was piecing itself together in my head.

The countess. The king. A baby, raised as far from the palace as possible.

Ofelia's hand covered her mouth, as if the realization had

struck us both at the same time. She looked to me, desperate, frightened. My heart beat against my breast, wanting to fly to her, to comfort her.

The deep clanging of bells sounded in the distance. I turned to the sound—near the palace gates.

"His Majesty has returned," Eglantine said. She looked to us, her brow wrinkling almost apologetically. "We'll all be expected to attend his homecoming celebration."

Ofelia slowly wobbled to her feet, her cheeks still red and tearstained. "I need to speak to him."

Eglantine's eyes widened behind their spectacles. "You mean to approach His Majesty?"

My mind plunged into disaster. I could so easily picture sweet Ofelia standing before him, declaring him to be her father, and how he'd have her imprisoned with a flick of his hand. "My lady," I said, "I do not think it would be wise to speak so publicly about any of . . . *this* in front of the king, with the whole court watching—"

"Then I'll speak to him privately." She leveled a stare at me, arresting me with the determination blazing in her eyes. "You cannot dissuade me from this, Lope. If anyone knows where Mother is, it'll be him."

When she strode out of the library, I followed her, even though my pulse was crashing madly. Even though my heart was screaming how dangerous this was.

"Wait!" called Eglantine. "My ladies, please wait!"

We turned, and the librarian met us in the hallway, her lips pressed into a thin, grave line.

She touched each of us on the arm. "I know that you are new here, so please, might I offer you some words of caution? Please, I will not be able to rest easy if I do not speak plainly with you."

Ofelia's gaze met mine. We nodded at the same time.

Already, courtiers in their bright gowns and suits trickled down the honey-colored halls to see the king. Eglantine pulled us into a quiet alcove.

"It is forbidden to go to the gardens after sunset," said Eglantine softly. "Furthermore, though the whole palace is at your disposal, you must not travel alone. The two of you— you must stay side by side at all times."

The request was unnecessary. It was as though she were instructing me to breathe. I would never leave Ofelia alone.

Yet Ofelia's head tilted. "Well . . . well, yes, madame, I never walk without Lope by my side. But why do you give us such a warning? This palace is a safe and blessed place."

Eglantine squeezed her hand against Ofelia's arm. "Yes, dear," she said softly. "It is safe and blessed." Her eyes met mine, serious and cold. "That does not change certain facts. Your mother's disappearance, for one. I pray she is on her way to you, but . . . it concerns me. Not a month ago, a singer in the royal opera, a young lady of only twenty years, vanished. If your mother is the—" She cut herself off abruptly before seeming to choose her words carefully. "If she's the second in a series of women vanishing from this palace . . . I only ask that you stay together. Please."

My eyes narrowed. "An opera singer? How could she have disappeared? Was she not well-known among the court if she was a performer?"

"She was well-known, yes. Her name was Françoise de la Valliere. A soprano. The court loved her." Eglantine retracted her hand, folding her arms as if she had a chill. "But she is gone now, and no one speaks of her anymore." The librarian nodded and then glanced back at the flood of nobles excitedly walking—and even running—to the courtyard. "That's all I know about her. No matter how loved she was, she wasn't safe from . . . whatever it is that happened to her."

I stood in front of Ofelia. "Speak plainly, madam. Do you think there is some kind of danger at this palace?"

She gazed at me, unblinking. "Gracious, no, I'd never suggest such a thing. The king watches over us all." The librarian offered me a stiff smile and a curtsy. "You know where to find me, mesdemoiselles." And with that, she turned and swam along with the current of lords and ladies streaming to the palace gates.

Ofelia clung to my arm. "If there *is* some sort of danger," she murmured. "If I see the king, if I tell him that I am his . . . that I am his *daughter* . . . he would keep us safe. You and me and Mother. Wherever she is."

Her body was rigid, her fingers upon my arm as firm as claws. Fear shone in her amber eyes.

"All will be well," I told her in a soft voice. It was not a lie, not really. It was my own hope, desperate and frail. But I would gladly give her any strength within my own heart if it meant she would smile again.

Just as I'd wished, a small, faint smile graced her lips. Her hand squeezed into my arm, as if to say, *Thank you*. And she led us on.

While I walked by her side, I kept my gaze forward and my focus solely on the knife at my hip.

10

Ofelia

There were so many courtiers crowding the view of the courtyard that we were not even able to see the king. I found this to be a relief, in some way. My stomach was all tied in knots, and my thoughts were like a river cluttered with twigs and leaves, about mother, about the king, about *my father*, whoever he might be.

Yet my chance to see the king came all too quickly that evening, when all were called to the Hall of Ceremonies. This chamber was grander and more decadent than any room thus far. The vast ceiling portrayed a morning sky fading from day into night and then back into sunrise, like one could spend an entire day just walking the length of the room. One wall was covered entirely with large windows, proudly displaying the sunlit gardens. Fading sunshine spilled through the room, turning the parquet floors gold.

To celebrate the king's return, all courtiers were to wear

silver clothing that day. The maids had given us new gowns and shoes, the color of moonlight. My hair was adorned with pearls like twinkling stars, but at my request, they left Lope's alone and found her a silver coat and breeches. She'd kept her hair in a plait, and seeing her look like herself again—well, it gave me a bit more courage.

We were crammed into a room full of people in their silver costumes, all of us pointed toward a set of golden double doors. Courtiers craned their necks, murmuring eagerly to themselves.

Any moment now, the king would walk through. That alone was terrifying, to see the man whom the gods had favored. But . . . the thought that I could be meeting my father. The thought that perhaps he knew where my mother was now.

I clung to Lope's arm. She was steady, she was never-changing. And I needed all her steadfastness in this moment.

"What if I make a fool of myself?" I whispered to her. "What if he laughs me out of the palace? What if our search leads us nowhere?"

Her thumb gently swept against the back of my hand. I looked up to meet her gaze. For a split second, the world was still and peaceful, and all I could see were her dove-gray eyes. They were so full, so easy for me to read. *Love*, I thought. *This has to be love. It has to be me.*

Please, my desperate heart whispered as if she might hear it. *Please say it's me.*

"My lady," she said, "I know you. You are not quick to give up under any circumstances. I don't think anything, even a king, will be enough to stop you from finding your mother."

I wished I was as strong as she thought me to be.

Trumpets sounded, ringing through the hall. At their music, the hundredfold nobles fell silent. Standing on my tip-toes, I could see a soldier on either side of the doors, each dressed in the finery of a courtier, except for the silver breast-plates over their blue uniforms.

The first soldier beat the staff of his halberd against the floor. "Vive le roi!"

"Long live the king!" we replied.

The second soldier repeated the gesture, the boom of the halberd like a clap of thunder. "¡Que viva el rey!"

"Long live the king!" we repeated.

As the doors opened, the world grew silent, like every-one in the room was holding their breath at once. I stood as tall as I could and tried to nudge people aside so that I could see *him*.

Suddenly, like the crowd was one great wave, they moved as one, bowing and curtsying. I followed along, and when I stood, I turned my attention, like all the others, toward a wall covered in jewel-toned tapestries.

"Friends!" came the voice of a man. Warm and welcom-ing. "How glad I am to be with you again. Please, dance, enjoy yourselves. I am happiest when I see you rejoicing in the pleasures of my court. Carry on!"

At the sound of his command, the courtiers scattered, some admiring the gardens, some sampling the wines carried on trays by servants, others lining up in the middle of the room for a minuet.

Musicians started up a joyful melody, with strings and harpsichord and a strumming lute.

The courtiers began to dance, arms raised in perfect arcs, sweeping their legs, twirling, leaping, bowing. With Lope by my side, I walked around the group of dancers, trying desperately to catch a glance of him.

There—past the sea of silver dancers, a strange flash of gold. I could think of only one person who'd be allowed to stand out in this crowd.

With Lope's hand in mine, I wove through the throng of onlookers, inching closer and closer to the king. My breath was whirling and tight as a storm in my chest. Again and again, I prepared my words in my mind as I focused on the gleam of gold ahead of me. The king. My father.

Your Majesty, I'd say, bowing, *my mother is Marisol de Forestier.* What would come next would be either a fairy tale or a nightmare.

The nobles grumbled and gasped as I pushed past them, each of them also craning their neck to catch their own glimpse at His Majesty. With each person I bumped aside, I could see more and more of the man in gold.

Until there he was.

He sat in a golden throne, watching the dancers serenely from atop a dais. On either side, he was flanked with guards, their hands against their rapiers.

Between the current of dancers, the spectators, and the throne, the floor was empty, like there was some invisible wall keeping the courtiers from coming too near to the king. Some were so brave as to extend their hands, to wave, to blow a kiss—but no one dared enter that sacred space surrounding this gods-blessed man.

I took one final look at the soldiers and their rapiers, twinkling in the light. Crammed in among the crowd of nobility, I turned to Lope, both of us pressed up against each other. She gripped tight to my arms, as if to keep me from falling over.

"You don't have to speak to him," she said. "We can just . . . enjoy the party. Or write him a note."

I knew it was foolish. I knew it was dangerous. I didn't think the soldiers would run me through with their blades in front of all the partygoers, but . . . Mother always said the ways of this court were different. And perilous.

I shut my eyes and thought of her. On bright mornings, we would sit in the garden and bathe in the sunshine, and she would brush my hair and sing me folk songs. She let me watch her paint portraits and landscapes; whatever I asked of her, she could paint it. Some days, she'd ask for my thoughts—if a shade of green was too bright, if a person's pose looked natural. In every bit of her life, she made a place for me. She was even willing to give up whatever fear or grudge she had with this palace, all so we could be safe again.

"I need to find her," I told Lope, nodding. "He may be the only one who can help us."

Her face was severe, but her gray eyes seemed to smile. She had always looked at me like that—with the eyes of a lover. My heart ached; I tipped closer, hoping—

"You are exceptionally brave, my lady," she said.

Something invisible pricked my heart. *My lady*, still. How could someone write such poetry about me yet still refer to me so coldly? Had I been mistaken? Were her sweet words meant for another?

"Please let me stand beside you," Lope continued. "To keep you safe."

I pulled back from her, rubbing the warm place on my arm where her hand had once been. "I'm going to look like a fool up there, Lope. I won't ask that of you."

"I do not fear looking foolish," she said. "It's you I fear for."

Her protectiveness for me—was it out of love? Or merely duty?

"All right," I murmured.

Facing the party again, the bright decadence, the golden light that seemed to be emanating from the throne as if the

140

sun itself were sitting there—it was like I was facing my own future. Beneath the glow of the chandelier, the throne's silhouette was cast six times on the parquet, almost like the points of a compass or the halos artists would paint around the heads of the gods.

Like a needle through a pleat of silk, I pierced the crowd of nobles and stepped one foot onto the empty parquet, the sanctum around the throne.

Behind me, people gasped and whispered, a shocked hush settling over the court. I heard one woman tell me to get back in my place, but I could not. I would not.

I took another step toward the throne. Now some of the dancers had noticed. They halted their movements, glaring at me.

Another step. The dais was ten feet away now. I still could not quite see the king but in profile, thanks to the soldiers on either side of him. The soldier at his right shoulder, blocking my view, caught sight of me and gripped his rapier.

Oh, gods, I thought, *please help me, wherever you are.*

As I walked closer, the guard murmured something into the king's ear, and he leaned forward, turning to catch a glance—at *me*.

A dark eye. Pure white hair, bright as moonlight, resting in waves over his shoulders. The king tipped his head, whispering something back to the guard.

In a blink, the soldier was walking toward me. Lope

shoved herself in front of me, her arm barricading me from the man.

"Mademoiselle," he said, looking me in the eyes, "His Majesty requests an audience with you."

An icy wind swept through me. "He—*me?*"

He offered his arm to me, stepping between Lope and myself. "Right this way."

I reached around him. My pulse quickened as I saw the fear in Lope's eyes. "Please, let her come with me—"

"His Majesty's orders. Just you."

"If she needs me, I'll go with her," Lope said.

Now the courtiers' whispers had turned to murmurs and jeers.

"If you want to see the king," the soldier said, "do as His Majesty requests."

I wanted her beside me. I felt like half of myself without her. And seeing her so distressed anguished me. But this could be my final chance to find an answer as to my mother's whereabouts.

"I'll be right back," I promised Lope.

She withdrew her hand, standing back obediently. She even bowed her head to me, a servant following a courtier's orders.

Perhaps I *had* misjudged her tenderness toward me.

The soldier touched my back, guiding me ever closer to the king. All of the world seemed to fade. Somewhere far,

far away, the music played, dancers' shoes tapped against the floor, partygoers laughed.

When I looked at the king's face, my heart fell.

The man before me was only a few years older than I was—far too young to have known my mother, certainly, and far too young to be my father. But . . . I thought of the strange rumors I had heard in the marketplaces growing up, the whispered stories of the gods-blessed king. The king that had been blessed with eternal youth.

Was it a trick of some kind? His son or a double or . . .

But he looked like the paintings. His long nose, his proud smile, the dark brown of his eyes—the same shape and color as mine. His hair was white, but not like that of an older man—it was brighter, like the color of sparkling snow.

In a daze, I bent in a curtsy.

His gaze met with mine, his eyes widening. He touched a hand to his heart. "Ofelia?"

This impossible man, this being who resembled the faerie king from my storybooks, *knew my name.* "I must be dreaming," I whispered.

Of all things, the king laughed. "No, no, my dear, you aren't dreaming. But perhaps I am."

He extended a hand, not so that I might kiss his ring, but palm up, like he was asking for something. Like he wanted to hold my hand.

I tremulously reached out, laying my hand atop his. To

my relief, I hadn't mistaken the gesture; the king covered our hands, beaming up at me. "Gods above. You look just like Marisol."

Joy crackled through me like a firework. He knew her. Of course he did. That sanctuary I'd always dreamed of, where Mother and I could be protected from the Shadows—it felt a moment closer.

"How do you know me?" I asked. "How do you know my mother? Do you know where she is? I—I've been looking all over for her—"

"Answer me first," he said, slow and patient. "How is it you've come to my court?"

"Mother disappeared," I replied. "I came after her. My—my knight is over there, sire, and she protected me from the Shadows along the—"

He flinched, giving my hand a pat. "Please, child, don't speak of those creatures."

The denial cut through me. I never relished thinking of them, either, but they were the monsters he claimed to protect us from. They were our greatest threat. What was this act, as though they did not plague his own kingdom?

Still—I could not afford to argue with him. Finding Mother—finding her *safe*—that was all that mattered.

"Yes, sire," I said. "But you were saying about my mother?"

The king rose from his throne, standing a head taller than

me. He looked back at the soldier who had escorted me thus far. "Take us to the orangery. Let the celebration carry on while I speak with Mademoiselle Ofelia."

As the soldier walked before us, and the king gave me his arm, panic made my insides squeeze tight. Lope was standing among the nobles, one hand in her pocket, and her eyes firmly upon me. I wanted to ask for her to join us, to ask for her protection, or at the very least, her presence. But I feared too greatly saying something that would displease the king and keep me from my mother.

I didn't know him, didn't trust him, didn't even believe all of the stories about him. But he seemed kind enough. And he was my last link to Mother. So I let him sweep me out of the room.

In the hallway, I piped up, "Why the orangery, sire?"

"It's quiet there," he replied. "And I have much to tell you."

We walked quickly through halls, the evening light dazzling me and making me wince each time I passed a window. But I could not contain my questions until we had reached our destination. "Was Mother with you while you were gone? Is she somewhere in the palace?"

"She is well, I promise you." He smiled down at me. "I cannot tell if you have her curiosity or my stubbornness."

It startled me, how openly he spoke of being my blood. That he so easily accepted that I was his child.

"This is all so strange," I admitted softly. "Mother made me think I had no connection to this place at all. She hid everything, even her name, from me . . ."

He stopped in front of a narrow iron door. The guard stood against the nearby wall, a few paces away to give us privacy.

"She did not tell you, then," he asked, "that you were mine?"

His? All these years, he had been a character in my fairy tales, the king ruling an enchanted palace, someone I'd seen in drawings—pale imitations of the man before me. The sunlight set golden rays on his hair like a crown. I could scarcely believe that I was here, that the king stood before me, that he was my family, that *I* was a part of his marvelous story.

"Mother forbade all talk of Le Château," I said. "But I always asked; I always read books and asked for more stories and imagined living here."

King Léo lifted my hand and drew it to his lips. "My dear Ofelia—your heart has always called you to this place. And at last . . . you are home."

11

Ofelia

We entered the orangery, a large, bright room made of pale stone. The walls were lined with arches and paned windows. Evening sunlight added a shimmer of gold to all the plants—rose bushes, orchids, birds of paradise. There was row after row of orange trees, small and well manicured, each in its own little green planter box. The sweet perfume of orange blossoms filled the air. As I strolled beside the king between the rows of trees, I couldn't help but smile.

"It smells like my home," I said. "The nearby town has orange trees growing everywhere. The oranges taste awful, but their perfume is so magnificent."

The king nodded at me with a smile. "Yes, these are those very same trees, the variety from the south. A little testament to the many great beauties of my kingdom." He guided me through the stone room, past beautiful marble statues and flowering orange trees, until we reached a wooden bench with a red velvet cushion.

"This place is my little refuge," said the king. "The silence and the perfume . . . they bring me peace."

He sat down, and I placed myself beside him, careful not to touch his gold satin attire.

"This was Marisol's favorite room," said the king, his fingertips carefully brushing the leaves of an orange tree. He smiled, a distant, dreamy look in his eyes. "She would sketch here until sunset."

Once more, I longed to ask him to tell me outright where precisely she was, but he had brought me here. He had said he had much to tell me. I bit my tongue and let him speak.

"We wrote each other so many letters. Her words were so lovely. So true. I have kept her notes, after all these years . . ."

My efforts to be as cool and levelheaded as Lope were in vain. My lip trembled. I couldn't bear his reminiscing, not when it reminded me of the notes she would leave me in the morning: *Hard at work in my studio. Please try not to break anything.*

The king reached into his breast pocket and procured a lace handkerchief, holding it out to me.

"No, no," I said, "I cannot *weep* in front of a king. It's beneath you."

"You may weep in front of your father," he said, pressing the handkerchief into my hands. When he smiled, a dimple pressed into his right cheek, just like mine did.

Could it be so simple? To have lived with my mother as

148

the center of my universe in one moment, and in the next, to have lost her but to have gained a father?

I took a deep, shuddering breath of the warm air, fragrant with snapdragons and orange blossoms and roses. With his permission, I let tears fall.

"She came to the palace a few days ago," the king began. My head snapped up almost without my permission, desperate for answers. "She was asking for sanctuary from those creatures. And she told me about you." His thumb rose to brush against my chin. "A little treasure she kept for herself all these years. Beautiful. With eyes just like mine. And a head that is always in the clouds."

It made my stomach twist. She *did* say that about me. Her little treasure. Her cloud-bound daughter.

"The journey was hard on your mother," said the king. "When she arrived, she had a fever and a dreadful cough."

My hands flew over my mouth. "Gods above—is she all right?"

"Of course, dear." He gave my hand a reassuring pat. "I had my physician tend to her. He said the best option was that she stay at my residence by the sea for a while to heal."

I leapt to my feet. "Then I must go to her!"

I'd taken just one step when he caught me by the wrist. When I looked back at him, his eyes glimmered with pity.

"She is very ill, Ofelia."

"Then she needs me all the more." Already, I could see the

plan unfolding in my head. Lope and I, in a royal carriage, on a journey to the sea. I'd hold my mother again. I'd tend to her as she did me through all my childhood illnesses. And when she was well enough, perhaps Lope and I could stand on the shore together, watching the waves. "Where is this residence? I'll get a coach—"

"Ofelia." His voice was sterner now. "She is highly contagious and not fit for visitors."

"She wouldn't—she wouldn't accept that. She wouldn't want us to be apart for so long."

The king rose from his seat, his brow furrowing. It did not suit his face, so noble and pure and . . . *divine*. The face of a god, if we knew what they looked like. "Your mother is bedridden and weak. The physician would not even let me go with her. But she gave me a letter for you."

My body, clenched tight as the string of a bow, finally loosened. "She did?"

"Yes. I'll fetch it for you in the morning." Slowly, he guided me back to the bench, coaxing me to sit down again. "You'll be with her again in a fortnight, I swear it. But it would not do for you to also be stricken so ill. She would not want it."

Two weeks. Two weeks, after already waiting so long. I wanted her now. I wanted to feel the warmth of her pressed against my cheek, to smell the lilac perfume and linseed oil that bled into her gown.

"I've—It's been so long. I've faced so much to find her," I admitted softly. "Lope and I. New places and strangers and long walks and *monsters*. For so long I wanted an adventure and now I . . . I only want to *rest*."

"My poor child," the king murmured. I saw in his eyes a deep sympathy for me. "Of course. Whatever bedchamber you've been given here, it isn't good enough. I'll have you settled in the finest suites I have to offer. Tell me what you like, what foods, what books, what colors—I'll give you all that you wish and make for you a home that you've always dreamed of."

It was too much—too wonderful. Like someone had taken a seed from my mind and planted it, letting all my dreams bloom around me.

Lope would hear all of this and say, *It's too good to be true.*

But if the king was really blessed by the gods, if he had become holy . . . *couldn't* it all be true?

"Your Majesty," I said, shame making my cheeks flood with warmth, "might I—might I ask you a rude question?"

His eyebrows lifted and his cheek dimpled as he laughed. "We have many years of rude questions to catch up on, don't we?"

How easily he spoke of a future together. How seamlessly I seemed to fit into his life. He didn't know me. But he seemed to *want* to.

"The stories that say you were blessed by the gods," I said

151

softly. "I—I do not know which parts are stories and which parts are . . . are . . ." I bowed my head and picked my fingernails, even though Mother would have scolded me for doing so. "It seems impossible."

He tipped up my chin, making our eyes meet. Even with my doubts, he was so kind. "When I was not much older than you, I asked the gods to make me a great king. And they saw in me a great ruler for this land, so they blessed me with eternal life. They gave me this palace, and in my life, they've blessed me more and more. With *you*, for example." His eyes crinkled with a smile. "I always wanted a child, and all this time . . . you were out there."

The reminder was an unpleasant one. "Why *did* Mother keep me from you?"

The king sighed mournfully. "We were very young when we fell in love. Marisol found the pressures of courtly life to be too much. She wanted to live in the countryside. I agreed to let her be, to give her the peace that she wanted . . ." He trailed off before whispering, "If I'd only known she was with child."

Mother and I had our fair share of quarrels. And yes, I had tried to run away from her, tried to run to this very palace. But it unsettled me, the way she sounded like some villain, absconding with me. All these years, I'd had a father. A father who wanted me. *The king.* All these years, she *could* have taken us to Le Château. She could have taken us away from the Shadows. She could have called upon the king's aid the very day we were first attacked in the manor's garden. It didn't make sense.

The story my mother had given me had been so small, so sparse. I had been born fatherless and grew up in the countryside with a mother who preferred paintings to people.

In the king's story . . .

There was once a girl with royal blood, born of love, born loved by a king and an artist. A child raised in solitude, while her gods-blessed father waited in his golden palace for her to return home. . . .

I liked that story so much more.

What happened next?

"If it's all true," I murmured. "If—if you're my father . . . what does that make me?"

"You are my daughter. A princess by birthright. And when Marisol is home with us again, I will give you the crown you are due."

My eyes widened. Every last scrap of reality was fading away, leaving behind only a fairy tale. The one I had always wanted. "A princess? A crown?"

His Majesty squared his shoulders and leaned back, observing me with a proud smile on his lips. "It will suit you so well. Now, come. We have a party waiting for us, and I want to introduce you to everyone."

The ballroom was a golden blur. Courtiers pushed each other aside to greet me, to curtsy before me and kiss my hand. They marveled to each other that the king had found me. He had introduced me to everyone as *a miracle*.

For the first time in many days, I allowed myself to feel joy, unbridled and heady and thrilling. Music spun through the air. Decadent sweets were pressed into my hands. Young nobles tugged me onto the dance floor. We hopped and twirled our way through a gavotte, and my heart was flying . . . but my happiness wasn't quite complete. There was someone missing.

Across the dance floor, Lope waited, tall and pale like a column of moonlight. She stood at attention, her dark plait draped over one of her broad shoulders. Even from afar, her gaze was like an arrow, direct and arresting. And as if there were a cord tied to that arrow, I felt myself pulled toward her until I was in her arms again, my ear against her drumming heartbeat.

"Are you well?" she asked, drawing back, her hands firm and strong against my shoulders. Her finger carefully swept a curl out of my eyes, and my mind went blank as she did so. So many of my dreams had come true this night. What was one more? An imaginary world unfurled in my head, where her fingers would delicately stroke the length of my jaw—

"My lady?"

"Yes!" I burst out, though I could no longer remember the question.

A small notch formed in her brow. "The king, he—What is he like? Where did he take you?"

"He's kind and generous, and he really does know Mother!

He says she came here a few days ago and that she was ill and he sent her to the seaside to get better and I was upset that I'd have to wait so long but then he said—"

"Breathe," Lope reminded me.

I took a gasp of air and collapsed against her again with a bewildered, delirious laugh. "It's just incredible, Lope. I must tell you everything." With a glance back at the bright colors, the dancing courtiers, the king on his throne, engaged in a conversation with more strangers . . . it was so much, it made my mind grow muddled.

"Let's hide in the hallway," I said.

She led the way, keeping me tucked close behind her so that I was hidden just a little bit. We slipped through the crowd undetected. The guard at the door took one half-hearted glance at Lope before continuing his conversation with a young blond woman.

Hand in hand, we darted through the darkened corridors. Night had fallen so quickly. The candles on the wall were already lit, offering only small haloes of golden light here and there. Through the window at the end of the corridor, the half moon was waning.

We found a small window seat.

The seat was small, such that we were pressed knee-to-knee. I was uncertain of where I could settle my arms in such a way that wouldn't end up touching her. *How silly*, I thought. *I embrace her so easily, but sitting beside her on a bench, I feel like a nervous lover.*

I looked up at her, hoping for some sign that perhaps she felt as timid and affectionate as I did. But her face was so cold, except for the glimmer of fear in her eyes, near black in the darkness.

"The king said your mother was by the sea?" she prompted.

If my head was in the clouds, she was permanently wearing a pair of heavy iron boots, rooting her firmly to the ground. Often, I loved this about her. Yet sometimes I wished she'd join me in my dreaming, in my pleasant thoughts, for just a little while.

"Well, yes," I murmured. "His Majesty says his royal physician is with her. She is ill and is recovering at the king's seaside estate."

"El Palacio de Las Lantanas, then."

I startled. "How do you know?"

She lifted a shoulder. "I study maps quite a lot."

"Why?"

Lope folded her arms tight, turning away from my eyes. "For a few years I've been researching the path the Shadows have taken. If they have some sort of origin point. Or destination."

Another piece of herself she'd kept from me, just like the love poetry. She'd been doing research about these monsters for *years*. How many bits and pieces of her life did she keep tucked away, *locked* away from me like little jewels? Was it that she only shared the small, everyday things with me?

"What have you concluded?" I murmured.

"It's only a theory for now." She rubbed at the back of her neck, her brow bunched in thought. "I think of how storms are calm at their centers. And this palace, the *one* place they say is free of monsters. When I trace the path of the Shadows, it seems to me . . . it seems to me that they begin their journeys here. From this part of the kingdom, if not from the palace itself. The way that nobody speaks of the Shadows . . . I cannot tell if everyone is in denial or if they are keeping a secret."

Her familiar voice, gentle and quiet, helped remind me of the days before we reached safety. Of the darkness we'd seen. This palace was beautiful, yes. Maybe even gods-blessed. But that didn't explain the monsters lurking just beyond the gates, and my heart sank.

How I wished this fairy tale were simpler. That we could trust in this palace. That monsters did not gather close by. That Mother had been in this building after all, waiting for me.

"There's something else," she said.

I leaned closer, my heart pounding against my throat.

"Did you look at the king's feet?"

At once, I withdrew with an incredulous look. "Why would I—?"

"I saw it when he entered and when he returned with you. By candlelight, everyone in that room, we each had just one silhouette. But the king . . . he had six."

She seemed to be waiting for my reaction, but I had yet to understand. This was yet another day when I wished I'd been given a mind as sharp as hers.

"He casts six shadows on the ground?" I asked slowly.

"Yes!" she said. "Don't you find that odd? And they weren't just plain silhouettes." She rose, waving her hand in front of one of the sconces. A shadow of her hand passed back and forth against the wall. "They were *moving*, sliding just barely as he stood there, ebbing and flowing like tides, like living things!"

I felt torn, then. Her word was gold; it always had been. She never even exaggerated. But this sounded so . . . fantastical.

I remembered him sitting at the throne, shadows below him splayed out like the points of a star. Yet something in me doubted. His throne was ornate, his clothes more so, and the room crowded. Couldn't the shadows have been any manner of things?

On the other hand, not an hour ago he told me he'd been given eternal youth, and I believed him in a blink.

"How could that be?" I asked.

"I don't know. But this place, the darkness here, the Shadows' path throughout the years—your mother disappearing—it all seems connected somehow."

It did.

Mother had always said that this place was dangerous. But

it was so beautiful. She had said this place was cruel. But the king, he was so kind. . . .

Yet did any of that matter if my mother was not with me?

"The king forbade me from going to see my mother," I murmured.

Lope frowned. "How could he forbid such a thing? After all you've been through—"

"He says it's because she's too ill." My stomach began to ache with worry all over again. All the brightness and hope and happiness the king had thrown over me like stardust—it was fading away. Something ugly and dark was left in its absence. "I'm so frightened for her, Lo."

Lope's hands held tight to mine. "You will see her again soon," she said. Her eyes held an unbreakable promise.

My heart thrilled at her calloused fingers carefully cradling my hands. When she was so near, when she looked at me, I felt so safe. So certain.

Everything would be all right. Lope would make it so.

Her lips parted, but she seemed to reconsider whatever it was she wanted to whisper to me in that darkened alcove. My breath snagged in my throat as I waited. And my stare caught on her lips, rose gold in the candlelight. Her thumb swept in a slow, careful arc against my hand. I could no longer hold back; I swept her into my arms in an embrace.

I felt like a star, bursting with light, tucked safely within some darkness outside of time, outside of trouble. I always felt that way with her. Once more, I allowed myself to imagine her standing in the waves, the salty air tugging at her silvery hair. When she'd give me one of those rare smiles. And Mother would be there, and she'd be well, and she'd say, *You really love her, Ofelia.*

12

Lope

In these gilded halls,
I am no more than a ghost,
Heard but never heeded;
A girl without a name.

In the morning, Ofelia was summoned to breakfast with the king. I was not invited, but Ofelia steadfastly refused to be separated from me. The maids relented to her insistence that I join, and to my relief, they led us both out to the gardens.

We walked the gravel paths of the parterres, surrounded by swirling hedges and flowerbeds, until we were along the eastern facade of the palace. I was mid-stride when Ofelia gasped and caught my arm. My heart quickened, and I reached for the sword that wasn't there as I followed her gaze.

The breath left my lungs.

Before us, sloping gently into the horizon, the grand canal glowed in the morning light like a road made of gold. Set between us and the canal was a large white-and-gold fountain spraying plumes of water into the air. A dreamy mist hovered over the gardens and made it such that the forests of linden trees looked almost like green mountains in the distance.

No etching could capture so marvelous a view. And yet here it was, hidden away from the rest of the kingdom for only the nobility to enjoy.

I longed to stand there for hours, simply gaping at the majesty of these gardens, but my moment of peace was interrupted when the king called out for Ofelia.

He was in the same parterre, not far from where we stood. He sat at a small table covered in plates of fruit and pastries. Immediately, I glanced at his shadow—but today, a maid held a parasol over his head while he ate. There was only the silhouette of the table, the girl, and the parasol cast onto the gravel.

"Dearest!" cried the king as we approached. He rose to his feet to take Ofelia's hand. "Good morning. Did you sleep well?"

"Everything is perfect," she assured him softly.

Her new room was even more ostentatious than the last. A beautiful washroom with a marble tub, a large bed with a dozen down pillows, a daybed hidden behind curtains stitched with golden lilies, and a view directly into the marvelous gardens.

King Léo's eyes snapped to mine, as sudden and arresting as a clap of thunder. I'd never looked into the face of a king before. The illustrations I'd seen in books and the etching of his profile on our coins—they were nothing like this. He did not look like any human man I knew. The angles of his face were too sharp. His eyes were too piercing. His hair was the color of spider silk, silvery and strange, nothing like the white hair of the aged governess who'd raised me at the orphanage. Even his smile was wrong, like he knew some joke, some secret, that I did not.

This was the man the gods had chosen?

"Mademoiselle," he said, slick as oil, "you've brought me my daughter as requested. You are dismissed."

I stood, rooted to the spot, and Ofelia stepped between us, reaching back to cling to my hand. "No! No, this is Lope. My closest friend, my confidante, my guard—she is to remain at my side."

The king brought a blue porcelain teacup to his lips, his expression almost bored. "From which family do you hail, Mademoiselle Lope?"

He asked that question, but I knew he meant another: *You aren't nobility, are you?*

"I am one of the children who was trained to hunt Shadows—"

The king hushed me. I'd forgotten. He preferred to pretend the Shadows didn't exist. Even though I still bore a barely healed gash down the side of my face. Even though I had lived my entire life with the sole purpose of fighting them.

"I was trained to hunt *beasts* since I was small," I amended slowly. "A necessity, as our soldiers were—and remain—in other lands."

His Majesty set aside his tea, meeting me with a gaze that, I supposed, was meant to be warm. Something about him, about all of this, taking tea in this beautiful garden while monsters roamed just outside, made the hairs on the back of my neck rise.

"So you're an orphan," he said. "You've no peerage."

I stood steady against the blow I knew he had meant to inflict. I had heard it before: my accomplishments meant nothing. I was not born into one of the families that a king favored a thousand years ago. One of those great, gods-blessed families, like Ofelia's.

"No, sire," I replied, smiling as the courtiers did here, false as fool's gold. "I'm just a girl."

"Then why do you keep company with my daughter?"

This blow rang true, cutting me to the quick. This man was decidedly my enemy. But he spoke the truth. Who was I, a servant, to be clinging so to her mistress? To be so besotted?

"Father," interrupted Ofelia, her voice firm but upset, "Lope brought me safely to Le Château, despite the danger. Where I go, she will also go. You cannot deprive me of my mother and then deprive me of my companion!" She stopped her tirade just as her voice was growing more and more tearful.

The king waved at me. "Stand guard, then." He reached out a hand, and Ofelia carefully took it, sitting down beside him at the breakfast table. At his glare, I reluctantly stepped back a few paces, but kept Ofelia steadily in my view.

From his breast pocket, he procured an envelope for Ofelia. "You see?" he asked. "I do not wish to deprive you of your mother."

She gasped and tore it open. A tiny, pink seashell dropped onto her lap. She examined it, smiling, and then eagerly read the note. After a few seconds, a soft little sob burst forth. I ached, my fingers instinctually reaching for the handkerchief tucked in my pocket—but the king had already given her one.

"I told you she was at Lantanas," he said. "Why do you not believe me?"

Ofelia hunched over in her seat, her head bowed. "I—I just want to see her *now*. I want to embrace her again."

He held her hand in his. "You will, very soon. I know it is difficult being apart, but you must wait for her, as she says." Even from afar, his smile looked false to me. "I waited seventeen years to meet you."

She laughed, small and half-hearted.

"There's something else I'd like to show you," he said.

He lifted something over his head, something that glinted when the light hit it at just the right angle. Ofelia gasped, reaching out for it.

"Mother's locket!" she exclaimed, clicking it open.

My heart skipped. The ledger and now the locket. Had Her Ladyship really been here?

"She let me keep it while she is away," said the king. "This painting—this was the first time I ever saw your face. I know you've changed a lot, but . . . for a moment I could imagine it, if you had been raised at the palace. Your little footsteps scurrying through the hallways."

"Mother didn't let me run indoors at home," she said with a smile, and I remembered the last incident well—when she'd asked me to chase her around the manor, and she'd then run face-first into a wall. Apart from some blood and some bruising, she was all right, but Her Ladyship and I were mortified. It was only due to Ofelia's begging that I was allowed to enter the house again.

Soon, the king and Ofelia were eating together, chatting away about the past. About Ofelia's mother and her life at Le Château. About the king and all he wished for Ofelia.

One thing was plain: he intended for her to stay.

Night fell, and a great feast was held to celebrate Ofelia. In this strange palace, royal dinner was a strange affair, too. The king sat at a table with Ofelia at his side. The table overflowed with food, roasted pheasant, warm bread, bountiful vegetables, sugared fruits, wines, and cheeses from all over the kingdom. But no one else sat at the table. Instead, the courtiers watched the supper, quietly speaking to one another and ogling the table and their hosts as a quartet accompanied the affair.

Occasionally, as she spoke to her father, Ofelia would look at me, would point to me—but the king would always touch her hand and redirect her attention.

Unlike the nobility, I did not find enjoyment in watching the king eat.

It was suddenly too much. The smells. The sounds. The bodies of strangers pressed so close to me. The distance of Ofelia. I slipped out of the king's private dining chamber and into the corridor. All I needed was space. Just for a moment.

At night, the corridors were an odd dusky blue. It felt like I was walking through a dark sky. Instead of stars, candles floated in the shadows every now and again. I approached one of these lights—a tangle of candle flames.

It was a candelabrum in the shape of a woman, painted gold, her arms and her fingers molding and transforming into the candlesticks that bore the flames. The candles were decorated in crystals, and the woman's face was still and serene. Happy to be a decoration in the king's hallowed halls.

I tore my gaze away from the display, bile rising in my stomach.

The farther I walked, the more I glanced out the windows. The garden was so dim, lit only by a few torches. Each flickering flame was a potential Shadow. And something told me that even if I hadn't seen them, even if the king ignored them, there *were* Shadows roaming those allées.

If this palace was to be Ofelia's home, and my own, for the near future, I wanted to know it better than my own heartbeat.

I plunged deeper into the dark halls, passing paintings that looked faceless in the shadows of the night. When I found a small, simple candelabrum, sitting on a table, I lifted it up, using it to light my path.

The first thing illuminated was the painting above me. It was of a man riding a white horse, his sword held out, positioned perfectly behind the steed's head so that it resembled a unicorn. I raised the candelabrum farther, and my insides twisted at the face above me, watching over me—the king. And yet . . . and yet here, his hair was the same chestnut shade as Ofelia's. I tried to remember her stories, anything about why the king, a young man, would have white hair. She would have called it some mark of the gods, I thought. But there were other stories of hers—ghost stories, where those who had seen something truly frightening lost all the hue in their hair in one night. I canted my head, looking at the proud, haughty face of the young king, victorious in battle.

What was *he* afraid of?

Behind me, there was a soft murmur.

I whirled around, wielding the candelabrum like a blade. "Who's there?" I said.

The only faces around me were the paintings, dozens of paintings of the king. My heart was pounding in my throat. I glanced back in the direction from whence I'd come. Perhaps it had only been the chattering and the music from the king's dinner. But I was so far from the party now.

I took a shaky, steady breath. One voice within me, the colder one said, *You're a knight, damn you; stop trembling in your boots!* And the other voice said, *Perhaps in your fatigue you imagined a voice.*

Fairy tales and ghost stories. I needed to be vigilant for Ofelia. I turned to stride back toward the dinner party.

A note floated through the air, bright and faint, like fading sunlight.

I jolted to a stop. If the song lasted another second, another two . . . then it was real, I vowed.

And it did. But it wasn't just music.

There were words.

"Farewell, my love; farewell, my heart! Farewell, my hope!"

Once more, I spun back, holding out the candelabrum. The hall extended onward. The voice remained like a thin, silvery thread. . . .

I followed it. I kept one hand in my pocket, upon the hilt of the penknife.

The song continued, a lone voice raised high. No instruments supported the singer, this mystery woman. *Perhaps it is a courtier singing to herself in her bedroom*, I thought. But the music was imbued with such passion, such agony, that I couldn't ignore it.

Step-by-step, the voice became louder.

"Since we must serve the king, we must part forever," sang the woman.

Around another corner, I saw, for the first time in an eternity, people. Two men, standing guard outside a door. Black and gold in the light of my candelabrum.

The Hall of Illusions?

I treaded closer on silent steps. The beautiful, mournful voice continued, a little faint, still—but clearly coming from behind those guarded doors. When I was mere steps away, the knights finally saw me and startled.

The two knights crossed their halberds in front of me.

"You should be in bed," said the one with a mustache.

I frowned over his shoulder, as if I could see the singer behind the doors. "There's—there's someone in there. Can't you hear her?"

The one on the right with pale blond hair laughed, like I'd missed something obvious. "It's not real," he said.

I jabbed the candelabrum at the door. The song continued faintly within that room. "My senses are perfectly keen," I told the guards. "A woman is in there, in the Hall of Illusions." *And she sounds like she's in misery*, I didn't say.

"Yes, the Hall of *Illusions*," said the blond knight slowly. He snickered and shot his fellow a look. "Whatever is inside that room, whatever sounds or voices there may be, they're nothing more than illusions. More enchantments created by the gods."

"How do you know? Have you been within?"

"Only the king enters," said the knight on the left. He struck his halberd once against the floor. "Now on your way, girl."

I looked him in the eyes. For a moment, I granted myself a little fantasy, imagining that I had my rapier back in my hand. In a second I'd have the tip of my blade pressed into his jugular. I could sweep up his halberd and use it on his partner. I'd watch the haughty contempt in their eyes turn quickly into fear.

Such behavior was unwise. And I had no rapier, anyhow. To them, I was just a helpless, wandering girl. I took my leave.

As I walked back to the dining room, the strange song, the song that supposedly did not exist, grew fainter and fainter. Those guards may have thought me silly, but I was not a fool. If the hall was simply a room where false images and sounds could appear from nothing, why would the king conceal such a place? Everything in this palace was on proud display, framed in gold and held up to the light.

Something was in that chamber. Something he, the great, fearless king, wanted to *hide*.

13

Ofelia

After a day full of parties and more food than I'd dreamed of, I collapsed onto my new bed. My head was spinning, and all of the day's dancing didn't help.

Lope drifted into the room behind me like a ghost, quietly shutting the door. As soon as she did, I shot up, jumping off the bed and rifling through my bedside table. "Lope, I've hardly gotten to speak with you today! I'm sorry, I've just been rushed from one thing to the next!"

I removed the envelope with Mother's letter. But first I gently set aside the pale pink shell she'd included, no bigger than my littlest nail.

Crossing the bedroom, I placed the letter in Lope's hands.

"Here," I said. "Mother's note."

I stood behind her as she pored over the letter for the first time. I knew what it said:

My dearest Ofelia,

I write to you to assure you that I am safe and well. I shall feel better each day I spend here at Lantanas. His Majesty's staff take excellent care of me.

Sometimes the doctor permits me to sit and paint the waves. The colors here are so beautiful. I wish I could send them to you. This shell is the best I can do—its color made me think of you. This soft pink is just like that of the peonies in our garden back home. I love that you wanted all our flowers to be pink. It's like this color belongs to you now.

Until I hold you in my arms again, I know that the king will show you all the kindness a father ought to. Forgive me for not sharing our story sooner. It is difficult to speak of the past.

Soon, we will all be together. We can be a family at Le Château—how wonderful that shall be!

With a kiss,
Your Mother

The pen-strokes, the curves of the *M*, just like how she wrote them as she signed her paintings. The writing was *hers*. It wasn't the same as seeing her again, but all the same, holding this small part of her in this letter, it was a balm to the wounds of my sore, tired heart.

"She wants you to live here?" Lope murmured.

I nodded. "Yes, won't that be exciting?"

"She was so opposed to the thought only a few weeks ago."

"Things were different then," I said, taking the letter from her grasp. "Since then, she reunited with Father, and they've overcome whatever squabble they had, and when she is better, we'll all stay here. Safe from the Shadows, like we wanted!"

"But that was a lie," Lope said. "We *know* there are Shadows in this place, even if they don't speak of them here."

My hands flopped down to my sides. I had not seen a single monster, but I did not wish to vex Lope or make her think I doubted her. I did *not* doubt her. Even if each day without Shadows convinced me more of the king's assurance that we were safe here. "Well . . . we lived with Shadows at the manor. We endured them. You kept me safe. All I mean to say is that soon I'll be reunited with Mother." I pointed at her, and an idea sprang into my head. "And like you mentioned before—from here, you can continue your research into the origin of the Shadows. I bet they have more information than we could dream of!"

Lope leaned against a wall, folding her arms. Her silence and her stoic expression were grating against me.

"Why are you angry?" I asked.

Her eyebrows lifted. "I'm not angry."

"Something else, then. You're—you're unhappy. You're keeping something in."

How I wish she'd open her heart to me. That she'd finally confess whatever marvelous secret was doubtlessly hidden inside of her. Maybe it was her love! Maybe she'd finally give up on her stony exterior and would let it crumble away so she would fall at my feet and recite a thousand sonnets. I wanted it more than anything, to hold her close, to have her lips beside my ear, whispering poetry, and saying, *You, you, they were all about you.*

But Lope's gaze dropped. "A few hours ago, I . . . I heard something. I cannot explain it."

My heart leapt in my chest. Heard something? Had something frightened *Lope*? I sat upon the foot of my bed, my eyes wide. "What? What did you hear?"

She rubbed her temple. "It's going to sound mad."

"Tell me!" I exclaimed, anxiety rumbling within me from head to toe.

Lope sighed, her eyes closed. "While you were eating, I wandered the halls, and I heard . . . singing. A woman singing. I followed the voice, and it led me to the Hall of Illusions. As if some woman were behind those doors."

My heart skipped excitedly. "Were you able to go inside?"

"No. The door remained guarded. They said no one but the king could enter. They heard the singing, too, but they said that everything in that room was just an illusion. An enchantment, a trick played by the gods."

For some reason I couldn't quite place, gooseflesh tickled

my arms. I rubbed my skin and frowned at her. "Do you think there's another explanation?"

She combed her fingers through her black-and-silver hair. "If whatever lies within that room is so magical, so wondrous, why wouldn't the king share it, like every other marvel in this palace? There must be something within that he does not wish to show the court."

I thought about the father I was getting to know. The man who found joy in beauty and music and everything bright and loud. He wouldn't want to hide any splendor. But on the other hand, our first talk was in that quiet orangery. Despite the radiance to him, the golden effortlessness to him, his shoulders had sagged like he bore a great sorrow. He had held my hand so tightly, like he had needed me.

"Perhaps it's just a room he wants for himself," I said softly.

Lope pressed her lips, her brows drawn. I liked when I could look at her and see the machinery of her mind whirring like the inside of some magnificent clock. But gods, she must have been tired from all the thinking she did.

"It's . . . it's not as if there's some woman trapped in there," I said, making my voice sweet and light. "If she was trapped and unhappy or unsafe, she wouldn't be *singing*, would she?"

After a long moment, she finally admitted, "I have no argument, my lady, but . . . but something unsettles me about the king."

My brows rose. "I don't understand, he's . . . he's blessed by the gods—"

"They say that. Again and again," she murmured, her voice weak and tired. "But I've found that when someone shouts about how smart they are or how beautiful or perfect they are over and over again, it's because they're just the opposite."

It made sense. There was a play I'd read once about a man who touted how pious he was, over and over, only to be lascivious and cruel.

And yet . . .

"Lope he—he's so young. That must be proof he is favored by the gods. There can be no other explanation."

"If the gods could give you anything you'd ask for—of all the things you could ask, of all the people you could help, how could anyone noble and good ask for immortality? For *youth*?"

I gaped at her. "I—I've never wondered such a thing." It was, perhaps, an odd request for a king. In fairy tales, a king who'd been granted a wish would ask for wisdom. Unless he was a fool of a king.

"Well," I mumbled, "wouldn't you ask the same thing of the gods? *I* certainly don't want to grow old—"

"I do." She touched a trembling hand to her chest. "I did not get to see my friends grow old. I thought I would never live past sixteen! *That* is something I would wish for, at my most selfish—to die gently, wrinkled and gray and beautiful, with my beloved's hand in mine."

Her beloved. Was it me?

And then my thoughts snagged upon her other words—
she thought she'd die young.

It was not an unfounded fear. It felt like moments ago
that I was holding her in my arms, watching the pallor of
death creep over her lovely face. I squeezed my eyes shut.
No, I could not bear death, and *that* was why I would want
to be forever young. Forever safe from the clutches of such
darkness, such cold. If I had my way, I'd bless Lope with that
immortality, too. Perhaps *she* would be happy aging with
someone she loved, but even the thought of watching my
beloved fade away was too much for me to bear.

I could understand the king in the wish he'd chosen. To be
safe from death; to be forever twenty years old, the same age
when he was first crowned.

But if I lived at this palace, I'd grow older than he would.
Mother and I would age, and die, and he would be left behind.

Perhaps immortality was not such a wonderful gift, after
all.

"I admit we know very little about his character," I said. I
lifted the letter in my hand, giving it a little shake. "But Lo,
Mother clearly trusts him."

"Perhaps her note was forged."

I narrowed my eyes. "Forged? By whom?"

"Does the king have other letters from her? Or any of her
writings? A note or a request or something?"

I looked down at the handwriting. It was so clearly

Mother's. And she referred to our garden and the way I'd begged her to have a garden bursting with pink.

He'd kept their love letters, he'd said.

Was this letter only an imitation?

Lope stepped closer to where I sat, standing only a foot away from me. "This letter is the *only proof* we have that he's telling the truth," said Lope, her voice soft.

I was exhausted. By the doubting, by the way she was always in search of some enemy to save me from, even when I had yet to see any monsters here. All my life, Le Château was touted as the safest place in the country. The *only* place safe from Shadows. Everything in me rebelled against the thought that we had traveled here, had been through so much, only to not find that safety.

But I trusted her. She *had* saved me from Shadows, again and again, even while I slept soundly, carelessly, back at the manor. She risked her life while I dreamed.

It would be far easier to take the king at his word, yes . . . but Lope's instincts had never let me down.

"What are we to do, then?" I murmured.

I slipped off the bed and set aside the letter, letting my fingers graze over the seashell, over a silver mirror, over a new ruby necklace. I remembered sitting by the king's side in the sunshine and how he spoke so fondly of my mother. So reverently. He said they would sit by the canal together and that he could watch her sketching for hours.

When I was with her, I would forget that I was king at all, he'd said.

All of his beautiful words—could they really have been lies?

Then everything, all the beauty of Le Château, all the promise of Mother's safety and my marvelous, welcoming future—it would all shatter. I did not know if I could bear that.

And tomorrow, I'd have to act like nothing had changed.

"I cannot avoid the king, Lope," I said.

"No." Her eyes glinted. "But you can gather the truth about who he is. Not from him. From other courtiers. From exploring the palace, its paintings, its books. If we are trapped here, let us set a trap in return. Let us learn its secrets."

"Like the garden," I murmured. "With the guards and the way it's closed by night . . ."

She nodded. "I'll continue to search there. I have tracked the Shadows for years to this place—they must be somewhere on the grounds of Le Château, and I know that the king wouldn't dare let the Shadows inside to feast on his courtiers. I am *certain* their origin point is in the gardens. I feel their presence with every step I take. These creatures would have been born of the Underworld itself. If I can find Shadows out there, then I can find how it is they've entered our world."

The Underworld. Mother never read me stories of that place. I'd only heard whispers from the knights. That all the evil in the world came from that place. That the god that resided there, lord of all monsters, was so horrifying that a single glance from him or a word from his lips could make a grown man fall dead. That he was so unlike the gods, he must be some other kind of creature altogether. Something dark and powerful.

Creator of the Shadows.

I had avoided thinking of that place; I had hoped it a tale used to frighten naughty children into obedience.

"You think there's some . . . portal, or veil, to the Underworld? Here, in the palace?" I whispered.

"Everyone here believes the gods themselves touched this palace and blessed the king," Lope said softly. "Would it be so impossible for another god to have influenced this place?"

A shiver rushed down my back at the thought. "Please don't speak about this. It frightens me."

"You cannot look away from trouble forever," she said, her voice desperate and pleading. "This involves you, too. If the king forged that letter, it means that your mother is still missing!"

Tears burned in my eyes. "No. No, that's not the story that I want."

She clutched my hands in hers. Looking into her eyes again, the familiar, stormy gray, I remembered her looking so sweetly at me back home. So attentively. Why did she feel so far away now?

"My lady," she said, "seek the truth. If the king is trust-worthy, then we are safe. We're home."

"We're home," I repeated. It didn't sound quite right. Even a palace was just a hollow, heartless building if Mother wasn't there. But when Lope said it, *we're home*, like she and I were a home, the two of us—it soothed the ache in my heart, lifted it into hopefulness.

"No matter what, my lady," said Lope, her gaze firmly locked with mine. "I will protect you with everything that I am."

Her devotion. Her chivalry. It made my heart *sing*. My right hand carefully slipped out of hers, up the length of her arm, firm beneath her coat. I laid each finger delicately against her elbow. A gentle request I hope she'd understand. A question I hoped she'd answer.

When I looked up, her gaze was fixed upon my lips. My breath froze in my lungs. Her lashes were so long, like dusky shadows against her cheekbones. She bent close just a little bit. I tipped my head, and one of my curls swayed in front of my eye. Her cold fingertips tickled against my left cheek as she brushed it aside. Her every gesture was the epitome of tenderness.

A thrill rushed through me, bracing as a waterfall. So I wasn't a fool. She must feel the same; I wasn't overly confident to imagine that her poems had been about me—

Her shoulders squared, and with a deep breath, she stepped

back from me. "So then," she said, her voice measured, emotionless, "tomorrow we'll split up, that we may cover more ground. I'll investigate the gardens, and you'll investigate the palace."

By the names of all the faceless gods.

"Excellent plan, caballera," I said, smoothing the front of my skirts, willing my hands not to shake. "Would you please step out for a moment? I'll undress myself tonight."

She bowed and marched out of the room with the rigidity of a walking suit of armor. Once the door clicked shut behind her, I whirled around, leapt onto the large bed, and screamed into the nearest pillow.

14

Ofelia

Nights at Le Château were so strange. I'd get flashes of nightmares. Eerie shadows painting the moonlit walls. A tapping on my window, only to find it to be the branch of a small tree.

No matter how frustrated she made me, I slept better when Lope was beside me. She'd keep her back to me, modestly. Her black-and-silver plait coiled against the pillow. Sometimes her breaths would quicken, and I'd wonder, *What monsters does she fight, even in her dreams?* During one such nightmare, I laid my hand against her arm, covered in a starbright chemise, and her body loosened.

She was always like that. Always ready to fight.

If I found someplace beautiful, someplace peaceful to call home—would she be content with that, like I was? Or would I be asking a wolf to blunt its teeth and act like a housepet?

In the morning, her place in the bed was empty, except

for a small note in her writing, beautiful and scrawled, *The gardens*.

Perhaps if I proved to her that safety, that *peace* was something attainable here, that she could *rest* . . . perhaps she would be willing to stay with me. To call me hers.

I couldn't quite picture it, Lope accompanying me to a courtly dinner or gambling with me or enthusiastically attending a ball. Even when in her loveliest dress or court suit. The smile I gave her in my daydreams didn't fit.

My ladies-in-waiting soon appeared to dress me for the morning in linens and pale colors. They said I would be out in the garden today, where His Majesty had a surprise for me. After all of Lope's suspicions last night, and the mere idea that he'd forge a letter from Mother—I didn't know how to feel.

Outside, the king guided me down lanes of hedgerows, past groves of tall trees, beautiful rose gardens, statues, and ponds. The sun glowed warm against my face.

"I knew you would love these gardens like I do," said the king, squeezing my arm. "I am kept inside all day with dozens of meetings and tasks, but I cannot go a day without a walk outdoors."

We passed the bosquet dedicated to the god of life, and it was like a cloud of orange blossom perfume had floated by. I smiled dreamily.

"I used to spend hours in our library reading about Le Château," I said. "I would wish upon stars and eyelashes and dandelions that I would someday walk these allées."

The king chuckled and pressed a light kiss to the top of my hair. "And you, my love, are *my* dream come true."

As we strolled past the bosquets to the gods, I remembered Lope's charge to me, to seek out more information about the king and about this palace. I squeezed his arm and pointed to the bosquet that was fenced off—the one with nothing but a marble rotunda and a door within. "What is that area for, Father?"

Though I tried to stop, he continued our walk, batting a hand in the direction of the bosquet. "Just a place I go to gather my thoughts now and again. It's being redecorated. Someday it'll be pretty enough for you to visit."

We walked deeper into the labyrinth. In the back of my mind, I thought of Lope's observation. That birds did not sing in these gardens. I strained to hear birdsong. Instead, I heard music. Flutes, violins, a harpsichord, tambourines, coming somewhere from this garden.

"An orchestra in the garden," I murmured. "It's like something out of a fairy tale!"

"It's more than an orchestra, in fact."

We turned one more corner, and before us, a great group of courtiers was gathered in an area I hadn't yet seen—an oblong room, like a concert hall. And like some kind of theater, seats wrapped all around the space. The seats, however, were covered in plants, emerald green, like cushions of leaves instead of velvet.

Farther back, behind the nobles, was a vast wall of waterfalls, cascading over golden sculptures and real seashells. At the very top of this display, a man holding a staff conducted a group of musicians, each clad in gold as if to blend in to the display.

"Welcome to the ballroom," said the king with a proud grin.

My eyes went wide. "You mean we can dance? Out here?"

He gestured to a red-and-white marble floor laid in the gravel before us. "As much as you like. There is also a feast for you to sample and a great many young people who would like very much to know you better." He squeezed my hand with a bright smile. "You're the most sought-after girl in this court. Two young men have already asked me for your hand."

A wound in my heart pulsed. I could see a hand in mine, a hand that bore a ring and a promise and a future together. The white scars along her arm. The ink stains on her forefinger.

"I—I am not considering marriage just now," I admitted softly. That role of a lifelong companion was quite occupied, and I hoped it would only bloom and grow.

"Don't give it another thought." He nudged my chin, tipping my head so I'd look him in the eyes. His eyes, just like mine, crinkled up into a smile. "Enjoy yourself. This is all for you."

I curtsied in thanks. He patted my arm once more and

turned to stroll past courtiers standing by little tables, each of them bowing as he passed.

Something Lope had said filtered back through. *Six shadows, moving like they were alive.*

My eyes flickered to the gravel below his feet.

Six silhouettes, each in a different direction like points on a compass.

If it was a blessing, it was never remarked upon. Courtiers always kept their gazes lowered respectfully, but I doubted they were counting the shadows at the feet of their king or wondering what they could mean.

Was it a warning? Or simply a strange trick of the light?

A new song began. Lords and ladies and dukes and duchesses alike gathered on the marble, standing in a line. When I joined them, they clapped delightedly.

At once, a girl with long golden hair bounded to my side, dropping into a deep curtsy. "Your Highness," she said—though I had yet to be crowned—"could I have the pleasure of being your dance partner?"

"I suppose so," I said, "but my mother did not teach me many dances, Señorita . . . ?"

"Mademoiselle Madeleine des Hirondelles, Your Highness."

The title felt so strange and ill fitting for me. I laughed awkwardly. "Can I call you Madeleine, and you call me Ofelia?"

She dipped into her deep curtsy again. "As you wish. And as for dancing, Your—Ofelia—you have a great teacher in me. Just pretend to be my mirror."

Madeleine swept up my hands and pulled me into position. All the dancers had paired themselves into two lines, so Madeleine placed herself across from me.

The first song began, lively and bright. Madeleine swept her right arm through the air, so I did the same, a bit delayed compared to the other dancers in my row. She leapt, I leapt. She twirled, I twirled. She swept me nearer, until we were only a foot apart.

"You're an excellent pupil," she said to me.

I laughed and hurried to step back with the rest of the dancers. "Just wait until I've stumbled and knocked you over like a ninepin."

As I twirled in place, I could hear her chuckle. "It's an honor to be your ninepin, then!"

We reunited in the middle of the dance floor.

"This part's a little difficult," she hastily said. "Put your left hand behind your back—good." Madeleine slipped her right arm behind my back so she could hold my hand. She instructed me to do the same to her—with my other hand, I held the hand behind her back.

"We're like a knot," I remarked.

"Exactly. Now, we turn."

With our tangled arms, just like all the other dancers, we

spun in a slow circle. When I turned my head, Madeleine's eyes met mine, and my heartbeat quickened.

It was just a dance. But we were so close.

I closed my eyes for just a second. In my mind, the entire ballroom changed, cloaked in beautiful darkness with only spare candles glowing like starlight. And Lope was here, dancing with me, smiling down at me, dressed in a beautiful silver suit.

I didn't think you liked to dance, I would say.

She'd reply, *You never asked.*

"Ofelia?"

Madeleine's voice shocked me back into awareness.

Gods. I was standing in the middle of the dance floor, unmoving, while the other dancers carried on.

"I—excuse me—" I pulled away from her, running off the dance floor and onto the gravel, my face burning.

Footsteps pattered against the gravel. Madeleine. She touched my arm with a kind smile. "It's all right," she said. "Dancing is difficult for everyone the first time." She shook her head at me, something understanding in her eyes. "They say you grew up in the countryside? That you didn't even know the king was your father?"

"That's right," I murmured.

"You must feel rather lost."

I laughed bitterly. "I feel as though I'm drowning."

Her hand slid down my arm until her fingers wove with

mine. My body shivered involuntarily.

"Come with me," she said. "Some food and conversation will lift your spirits."

She pulled me over to a small table covered in marzipan pastries. I nibbled on a pastry while she asked a passing servant for sparkling wine.

Madeleine rested her head upon her folded hands like I'd seen Lope do when she played chess. "So, Ofelia, as a resident of Le Château, you must first learn how to be a good gossip," said Madeleine, a mischievous smile on her face. "Do you have any stories for me?"

My heart thrilled. This was the information I longed for; the sort of information Lope had asked me to uncover. And there was one question in particular that hadn't left me. *What had happened to the missing woman? The marvelous singer who vanished?*

"I—I heard something about a woman disappearing?" I asked faintly. "A singer, I think?"

A wide grin crossed her face. "Françoise, you mean?"

I nodded—though I couldn't fathom why a girl's disappearance would make her *smile*.

Madeleine scooted even closer to me, speaking in a low voice. "I know *all* the details," she said, her red lips parting in an eager grin. "You see, I am a dancer in the royal theater troupe, and we theater people, we all know one another's gossip. The palace has tried to keep this quiet, but I know the truth."

I leaned in, my eyes wide. "So who was this girl? What happened to her? Is she all right?"

Madeleine let out a loud laugh. "Oh, she's *more* than all right." She bit her lip as if trying to suppress a grin. "It's all a very sordid story, so you must promise not to say a word, all right?"

I mimed locking my lips with a key. She giggled and grabbed my arm.

"Françoise was a wonderful soprano," said Madeleine. "Not the best, we all knew. She had some issues with breath control and her vibrato wasn't very consistent. Anyhow. The important thing is that she was the king's favorite singer! He came to the opera every single night. Backstage we'd find flowers waiting, just for her, and we *knew* who they were from."

My brow furrowed. "My father . . . fancied her?"

"He's the king, you understand," she said, waving a hand, as if this explained things. But it sent cold seeping through my veins. Did he love so easily? How had he not mentioned Françoise? And . . . did his abiding love for my mother mean nothing at all?

While I stewed, Madeleine continued. "You could hear him in the halls humming arias. He was so happy; nobody had seen him like that in so long. The nature of their relationship was effectively an open secret among the company," she said. She jabbed her finger at the table, her eyes widening.

"But then, about a month ago, she just disappeared! We all found it very odd, but . . ."

Our glasses of sparkling wine were brought to us, and Madeleine briefly went quiet while they were set down. I took a tentative sip, my eyes locked upon her.

"We found a letter in her things," Madeleine whispered excitedly once the servants had walked away. "She'd been offered a starring role at an opera house in a country far north. But she hadn't told any of us. We don't think she even told the king." The blond girl raised her eyebrows. "I suspect they must have paid her *handsomely* if she was willing to set aside this palace and the king himself just for a leading role!"

My shoulders relaxed. "So . . . she hasn't disappeared?" I said softly. "She just . . . left the country?"

"Apparently so. She left without a trace. Her clothes were left behind, her possessions. I did some snooping with a group of singers and dancers when we found the letter inviting her away."

Another dark mystery put to bed. This young woman had not been snatched away by monsters or hidden away. Surely that meant that my mother was safe and sound, too, at Lantanas.

I patted Madeleine's hand. "I'm glad you told me this," I said softly.

Across this outdoor ballroom, I looked upon the king, sitting on his throne.

His gentle voice, his familiar eyes, the doting way he spoke of my mother. It was in Lope's nature to be suspicious. But perhaps there was no threat. Perhaps happiness could be found in this place. I clung to it, wherever it could be found.

Gods. There she was again. In my thoughts, at every turn.

I said farewell to Madeleine and strode past the dancers in their silks and the courtiers with their sparkling wines to settle into the chair beside the king.

"Is the event not to your liking, Ofelia?" the king asked.

I shook my head and absently plucked some flowers from one of the overflowing vases sitting beside me. "It's beautiful, everything. I'm just a dreadful dancer." I grinned playfully at him. "I've never seen *you* dance, Your Majesty."

He folded his hands in his lap, serenely watching the way the dancers moved in graceful unison. "I did, long ago," he said. "I haven't since my father passed."

My stomach sank. "Oh—forgive me, sire, I didn't know."

The king reached his hand across the arm of his chair. I gave him my hand in turn.

"That is why you are such a gift to me," he said, his thumb sweeping back and forth against the ruby ring on my finger. "You're the only family I have left."

My heart ached, like it was being torn in two. "How do you bear pain like that?"

He gestured to the party before him. "I surround myself with beauty. With happiness. Though I have seen darkness, the gods have blessed me mightily. I want for nothing."

When he turned back to me, there was a glimmer in his dark eyes. "So then, my darling. What is it *you* want? My only desire is to make you happy. Anything you ask for will be yours."

There was nothing. Or—it wasn't a *thing* I wanted. I wanted a moment. I wanted Lope, holding me, poetry spilling from her lips. I wanted her to kiss me and pledge to stay by my side, even at this palace. I wanted her to be so happy she forgot all her woes.

I plucked at the petals of the daisy in my hand, discarding them one by one into my lap. *She loves me a little. She loves me a lot. She loves me passionately. She loves me madly. She doesn't love me at all.* Again and again, until the final petal remained, the one declaring, *Not at all*, and I nearly growled in frustration. The king's voice interrupted me.

"Ah," he said knowingly. "There's a young man responsible for all of this."

I blinked and sat tall in my chair. "A young man?"

The king smiled. "I know lovesickness when I see it."

Oh, gods. If it was *that* obvious to the world and Lope still hadn't said anything . . . what did it all mean?

"There . . . there *is* a girl," I said.

He hummed in thought, his eyes searching the crowd. "Is it someone here? That girl, Madeleine, expressed her fondness for you. And over there is a young woman named Angelique—"

"Not someone here."

A servant passed close by, and I waved him over to gratefully take a glass of sparkling wine. I sipped on it and let the warmth and the bubbles rise in my cheeks.

"Whoever she is, I can certainly arrange a meeting if it would please you."

"We are, um, rather well acquainted already."

He raised a white eyebrow. "You don't mean that servant you brought with you?"

I wished the Underworld would split the earth apart and drag me away from this. "Father, it's . . . it's not all that important."

"It certainly is. How it vexes you!" He leaned closer, a friendly smile on his pale face. "I am not worried about her station. Hearts are mysterious things, are they not? Loving regardless of logic or reason."

I had reason. I had *plenty* of reasons. When I grew sorrowful and she laid her head against mine. The way she listened so intently to any of my troubles, no matter how trivial. She never dismissed my feelings. Even if my anxieties about my mother or my future or my story ideas were far less fearsome than the Shadows she faced every night. Lope always treated me as the most important person on Earth.

"Does she love you in return?"

I responded with a long sigh. She respected me, yes. But I was the daughter of the countess she served. Perhaps that respect was mandatory.

The dancers now danced in pairs, spinning around one another in slow circles as they gazed into one another's eyes.

"I once thought I knew," I murmured. "But she has never bared her feelings to me, and I'm not sure if it's because she's shy or because I'm mistaken, or perhaps she's waiting for *me*, or perhaps she wants to remain friends—"

"How long have you been fond of her?"

My cheeks burned. It was hard to describe. "We've known each other about five years. I've always loved her, but the way I felt about her, it . . . changed, recently. Like one day I was seeing her clearly when I never had before."

"And she was the one who accompanied you all the way to Le Château?"

"Yes." Yes—she must have loved me, at least then, risking so much on my behalf. With a twinge in my heart, I remembered holding her in the field just outside the palace, how pale she'd been, the shocking scarlet of the blood running down her face.

"If it's been so long," he said, "she has had a thousand opportunities to confess her love to you. Even if she was a coward, she could have written you a letter, could she not?"

I bristled. "She is no coward. She has nearly given her life for me."

"That is her role, as a knight."

How simple he made it sound. A king ruled. A painter painted. A knight fought to the death. But nothing was simple about Lope or my feelings for her. They were as tangled within me as the roots of a tree. An inseparable part of me.

The king gave my hand a gentle squeeze. "Perhaps it's for the best," he said. "Noble as your knight may be, it seems plain to me that she has no intention of offering you the affection that you so clearly deserve."

My heart split into sharp fragments. I didn't want to believe such a thing.

But his words . . . they echoed my own fears. They did not sound like lies.

Lies were wrapped in soft, beautiful cloaks. The truth was cold and harsh. And this one cut deeply.

The Lope I kept imagining in my head, she was just that, some character that I had created. The way I pictured her, courtly and swooning and reciting poetry to me in a rose-filled garden—that wasn't her. Lope was the girl whose back was always turned to me, ready to fight another battle. The one who never called me by my name, no matter how many times I asked.

Something was slipping out of my grasp; something I couldn't name.

A tear dripped down my cheek.

The king reached out, brushing it away with his thumb. I leaned into his hand. I wished it were Mother before me. I wished for her sensibility and for her embraces. But I was grateful, in this moment, not to be alone.

"Please remember, Ofelia," he said. "There are many young ladies at this court who would be honored to be in your company. Ladies who would not be so slow to assure you of their affections."

I wanted to let go. I wanted to drink until I was dizzy, to dance until my feet ached.

A ballroom in the middle of a monster-filled garden. Or simply a ballroom, music and beauty enjoyed unabashedly under the warm glow of the sun.

You cannot look away from trouble, Lope had said.

For one day, I turned from thoughts of her, and I danced.

15

Lope

The night is all I know.
It is an old friend with her blade upon my throat.
It is a warm blanket and a shroud.
When the cricket song dies, so, too, will I.

Each day, I went to the king's gardens, searching for what
I *knew* must be there: Shadows. The maps I'd drawn
indicated that the Shadows had come from Le Château, and
we had fought so many just beyond the gates. Besides all that,
I trusted my senses. When I walked the gardens, I found all
the things I had kept watch for at the countess's manor—
scratches in trees, the faint stench of smoke and rot, the lack
of any birdsong. I *wanted* to find a Shadow, to hold up its hide
to the king—if such a thing were possible—and say, *How do
you explain this?* But my searches were fruitless.

After several hours in the gardens and then in the library,

I finally returned to sleep, each night hoping dearly that I'd finally see Ofelia. We seemed never to cross paths, save for in the dead of night, when she'd rouse me from sleep as she crept in from a party, her hair mussed, her gait clumsy. She'd drop onto her bed and let out a contented sigh before falling fast asleep. I'd take comfort in her presence for a few moments before sleep overtook me, too.

And here I was, still, wandering the gardens in my endless search. Above the tall, neatly trimmed trees lining the horizon, evening light burned gold. I kept my hand against the hilt of the penknife in my pocket.

That second day, when the guard had stopped us in the garden, when we had gotten too close to some secret . . . she and I had been near a bosquet to the gods. The strange one—the one with only a door standing alone within a pavilion. I rounded a dozen twists and turns to find the bosquet, or any landmark, but I only came across rose gardens and groves, the canal, an obscene number of fountains . . . I'd lost my way. Again. I sighed and turned back onto the main gravel drive, following a long, skinny path flanked with trellises and hedges.

What I wouldn't give for someone beside me, to help me with my search. If Carlos were here . . .

Chevaleresse Beautemps back at the barracks had always warned me that wounds of the heart were very, very slow to heal. That some never did properly heal.

I tried to imagine Carlos beside me. What he'd say.

He would laugh. He'd lean his head against my shoulder and watch the setting sun above us. *The pain won't stop, but it'll change. And even so, you'll remember me. I am indelible.*

Then I smiled, in spite of myself.

No, I could hear him say, *I would never use the word* indelible. *But* unforgettable, *certainly.*

But the space by my side was still empty. My heart ached. With Ofelia gone, the only conversations I held were with ghosts.

A loud scream split the summer air. The voice of a man I didn't recognize.

With a flick of my hand, the penknife was drawn. To my right came the sound of crunching gravel, a hissing sound, and metal clanging against rocks. Sounds I knew.

At a run, I followed the direction of the voice, the dying sun casting strange shapes through the hedgerows. In a small grove near a row of marble statues, a knight was on his knees. And there, out of my nightmares, the sign I had been waiting for—three Shadows, taller than I was, surrounded him, their claws wrenching his arms and head backward. The man weakly tried to bat a rapier at the creatures, but when a Shadow's claws twisted and pierced through the gap in his armor at his shoulder, he let out a cry, his hand seizing and sending the blade clattering to the earth.

My chance.

I sprinted across the drive and first drove the penknife into the head of the Shadow inhaling the soldier's breath. The monster wailed and disappeared in a cloud of dark vapor, and the penknife fell. In the next blink, I had swept up the rapier. I reveled in the feeling—that I was complete again.

With their brother freshly killed, the two Shadows turned away from the man they'd chosen as their prey, dropping the crumpled form on the ground. I ran backward, luring them away from the man—or the body. Just as I'd hoped, the two of them bounded toward me, barreling on all fours, the shape of men, but the movement and swiftness of nightmares.

One leapt at me, and I twisted out of the way, heart racing. Half of me was thrilled by the hunt, and the rest was consumed by white-hot anger; utter loathing for the liars at Le Château who claimed these Shadows did not exist, and for these monsters, coming into our world and taking our lives away. Carlos. Other knights. Other children. Other innocents.

To my left, a Shadow cried, a hissing, rasping warning just before it swiped vicious claws at me. I dodged out of the way, sweeping my foot through the black vapor of its own legs as I moved. It collapsed to the earth. I had mere seconds before its legs would evanesce again. I surged to my feet and beat my boot as hard as I could into its head. It vanished with a soft crackling sound, like a dry leaf.

But I wasn't through.

After years of training, my senses had become attuned to the presence of Shadows. It was their earthy, smoky smell, and the faint scrape of their claws against the gravel drive. And something else, something inexplicable that let me *know* a Shadow was near. If I had been standing on the center of a clock's face, toward midnight, I would have *felt* the monster somewhere around seven o'clock.

Swift as a snake, without conscious thought, I took the rapier and twisted behind me to strike the Shadow perfectly through its gaping mouth. It groaned, a hellish death rattle, and then it, too, bled into smoke.

I wiped my brow and glanced about the grove for any signs of other straggling Shadows in the dusky light. Just like on that evening at the Bouchillon manor, Shadows had emerged before they were due.

The perimeter seemed clear. With the sword in hand, I strode back to the soldier, lying dazed on the ground. Thank the gods, not dead.

"Can you hear me?" I asked as I stepped closer.

"Yes." His voice came out in a hoarse whisper.

I offered the pale-faced man a hand.

He took it, groaning as he stood. Blood rolled down his temples in streams from where the Shadows had wrenched his head back. He wiped his forehead against the metal of his bracer and frowned at me. "You aren't a civilian, are you?" he asked, his voice still strained.

"Not quite." I kept my fingers tightly wrapped against the hilt of the rapier. "My company was hired by a noble family to keep them safe from the Shadows. It has been my charge since I was twelve."

"Gods above," he mumbled. "No wonder you know your way around that blade." The soldier reached out a gloved hand. "I'll be needing that back."

I reluctantly returned the rapier to its owner. He slipped it back into its scabbard and then tipped his head down toward a lane of hedges, bright with torchlight. "Come, I owe you my thanks. The beasts don't come near that spot. There's too much light."

Finally. Finally, someone who looked the Shadows in the eyes and acknowledged their existence. Finally, someone with a modicum of decency. I felt gratitude and kinship with him, as my fellow knight. Someone sensible, at last. In this new world of manners and dancing and lies, perhaps he would provide me with some truth.

Still, I swept up the penknife from the dirt.

The man laughed. "Very fair, Mademoiselle . . . ?"

"La Caballera Lope de la Rosa."

"Caballera de la Rosa." He bowed his bloodstained head to me. "Just Guillem will do. I'm only a soldier. I've served His Majesty for ten years now."

Ten years. Ten years of history in this place—of understanding the Shadows here.

With the knife still at my side, I followed at his heels. "You must know much about the Shadows."

"About the same as you do. No one knows much about them. Just how to kill them."

I shook my head, marching faster to keep up with his long strides. "No, there's more than that. I have been charting the paths they take. I have been counting them. They always came from the north—from this very area."

Guillem raised a brow at me. "What are you implying?"

My cheeks burned. "I—I don't know; I'm only asking a question. These creatures . . . they haven't been around forever. And sometimes they increase in number for no discernible reason."

The soldier sighed and stood beneath the shelter of a tall, burning torch. "Mark me, the king does not favor talk of such things—"

"Why does he not?"

"The king represents holiness and prosperity. He cannot be associated with the Shadows."

"But they are *here*! They are *on his grounds*!" My hands balled into fists; I wanted to grab a sword or run or do *something*. But this place, this ridiculous place, was all about restraint, even while chaos reigned outside.

I exhaled heavily. "Everyone dances around the truth here, and I'm asking you, soldier to soldier, to be honest with me. We have a common enemy." I pointed down the allée, back toward the scene of the attack. "For decades we soldiers have been bandaging a wound that will just keep bleeding unless we find a reason *why*. These monsters have been around since your childhood, haven't they?"

Guillem gave a stiff nod.

"I cannot allow another generation of children to grow up fearing them."

"Caballera," he said, his voice soft, exasperated, "if you swear on your life to repeat none of this, I will tell you everything I know."

I bowed low, offering my neck. "I swear it."

He tapped his hand against my shoulder, accepting my vow. "All right. They come at night, every night. They vanish by sunrise. I was hired in 1650. The queen mother's funeral was to be held at Le Château, and they needed more guards in the garden. The place was swarming with monsters then. They didn't let the courtiers outside at all." Guillem squeezed his eyes shut, like I did when I tried hard to remember. I wondered if his memories were painted in red, like mine.

"The past few months have been the hardest. There was a flood of them a couple of months ago. The king was out of sorts. He wouldn't let anyone into the garden. He had us patrolling round the clock. It was around the time that the king's favorite singer had fled the court. The king tried to keep things calm, but people were worried for her."

The singer. "Her name was . . . Françoise?" I asked, remembering what Eglantine had told Ofelia and me.

"That's right. She went missing, and we were suddenly patrolling the gardens night and day. If you ask me, it's almost like the king hoped he'd find her wandering the gardens instead of acknowledging that she'd left to be an opera diva."

"And since then?" I prompted.

He gestured back to where the Shadows had attacked him. "Well, *now*. Things have been unusually mad. Started around the time the Hall of Illusions appeared. The king demanded three soldiers in rotation to guard the new hall, even though we've been swarmed out here." Guillem nodded toward me. "We could always use another knight among our ranks. I can recommend you to the king."

A lump rose in my throat. I wanted nothing to do with *him*.

Besides, my head was spinning. My heart was yearning for quiet. For answers.

"No, thank you," I said, and a beautiful, honey-sweet thrill swept through me at the word—*no*. A decision, my decision, all my own.

How strange. Freedom, choice, used to be so impossible and so frightening, so *big*. For just a brief moment, I got to grip the reins of my life and pull in the direction I wanted to go.

It felt *good*.

With a final bow, I left him standing, speechless, in the golden circle of torchlight.

I had a suspicion about the king's favorite singer.

I barreled into the library, marching directly for the ledger that Eglantine had shown us. The last drops of orange sunlight trickled into the library, leaving only small pockets of warm, golden candlelight.

Bringing it to my desk, I flipped through the pages, past the reference of Ofelia's mother's arrival. And then further back in time, back and back. The rumors had mentioned that Françoise had vanished about a month ago. My finger ran down the column of names starting from the first day of the past month. I scanned each one.

LeNotre, Gonzales, Villiers, Moire . . .

Dozens of names, but no "Françoise de la Valliere."

I searched the list one more time. But I did not doubt my senses. My heart quickened.

Her departure had not been noted. She could have left in secret, I supposed, but the king's guards at every gate made that near impossible. The other possibility . . . she had truly vanished.

"Mademoiselle Lope?"

I whirled around at the sound of my name, my penknife already drawn.

Eglantine, the librarian. She had largely kept to herself each night I was here, busying herself with a novel or by tidying up her papers over at her desk.

She stood a few paces between me and the double doors now, a wry smile on her lips as she observed me. "I've been looking for my penknife," she said.

I breathed again. "My apologies, madam. I—I am not used to being defenseless."

"I understand." She kept her gaze upon the knife—which I had yet to relinquish. "This evening, I peeked at the books you studied so voraciously. I thought I'd find poetry and plays and sonnets, but no. Books about the king. Books about monsters. Books about the Underworld."

It sounded so absurd when all those things were strung together. She took a step closer. My mouth grew dry.

"Your friend is the daughter of this very king," Eglantine murmured. "I want you to tell me truthfully. Just one time, then I'll never speak of it again. I'll not tell a soul. What do you think of King Léo?"

I had been trained to preserve my life at all costs. I had been raised to be honorable and noble.

But above all, I had sworn to protect Ofelia.

"Why did you mention Lady Ofelia?" I asked. What sort of test was this?

"I want to know where your loyalty lies."

An older, more confident knight might have laughed at how boldly the librarian spoke to a trained soldier. But it was spoken with the candor I had been longing for since my arrival at Le Château.

So I answered truthfully.

"My loyalty lies with Ofelia," I said. "Not the king."

A smile spread across her face. "Then we have much to discuss."

16

Lope

The poets write so sweetly of the night,
But I prefer the daylit girl,
Safe upon the grass,
Making memories and making freckles
All for me to count.

Eglantine locked the library doors. We pushed together two tables, and she effortlessly fetched the entire stack of books I'd been poring over. After setting them on the table with a loud *thump*, she left and then returned with more documents: letters, leaflets, journals.

"There isn't a curious soul in this wretched palace," she muttered. "They're too afraid. Too afraid to seek answers or to push back against what the king calls the truth." She wagged a finger at me. "You're what I needed. A reader and a knight. Curious *and* brave."

"You . . . needed me?" I repeated.

She sat down, plucking a quill pen off the table and drawing open an empty book. "Yes, dear. But my story comes later. First, I want you to tell me all that *you* know."

For a moment, I was gripped by that very same fear she had described. Did the king have a spy hidden somewhere between the bookshelves? Was *Eglantine* to be trusted? And what did His Majesty do to those who doubted him?

"How do I know I can trust you?" I asked softly.

She raised a brow. "You've still got the knife, haven't you?"

I did.

"Then you're the one with the upper hand." Eglantine dipped her pen in the inkwell. "Go on."

I remained standing, resting my hip against the table. I wasn't sure where to start. "First," I murmured, "I've searched the ledger. I looked back through last month's record. I found no evidence that the singer, Françoise de la Valliere, ever left this place."

Eglantine nodded. "I noticed this as well, almost as soon as she'd disappeared. It was curious, almost as if it had been missed . . . but then when Mademoiselle Ofelia came to me with her mother having vanished under similar circumstances . . . I began to wonder if something darker was at play at this palace." Her gaze met mine. "Go on. What else have you found?"

For once someone wanted to hear my thoughts. My theories. All my efforts, finally heard. It was almost too good to be true.

"It is my belief," I said, "that all the Shadows plaguing our land come from one origin point. . . . If they are spawned in the Underworld, then they must have a way to enter this world. A door, or a portal." I watched Eglantine closely for her reaction to my next words. "I believe such a thing to be here, at Le Château. In the gardens. Where I was just attacked by Shadows that are said not to exist here."

She stopped scribbling down her notes with a deep sigh but said nothing. No shock, no surprise—her silence almost read as resignation.

"It's public knowledge, then?" I asked. "That there are Shadows in the gardens?"

Eglantine pursed her lips. "No, not public. But available for anyone who would choose to see, which the court does not. In the daylight, the nobility may roam the gardens, but when night falls . . . well, there are many parties to draw one's attention from such unpleasant things."

With a pang, I thought of Ofelia. How she would prefer a life like that. Dancing the nights away, surrounded by gilded treasures, sweet morsels, and joyful music.

While monsters bounded through the gardens, into the fields, farther and farther, to find lives to claim.

"Go on," urged Eglantine.

"It is my understanding," I continued softly, "that there have been more Shadows than ever before since the Hall of Illusions appeared. Before that, their numbers increased when the opera singer disappeared. And ten years earlier, they multiplied during the funeral for the queen mother. It seems too great a coincidence."

"Precisely," whispered Eglantine. The golden reflection of the candle flames made her spectacles gleam. She shakily removed her glasses from her face, setting them on her book. She wiped at her eyes, and I procured a handkerchief for her in an instant.

"There was one other time before that, too," she said. "Just before King Léo was crowned. We were at the old palace, then, the one before Le Château existed. The king's father and then his brother had both been claimed by the pox. Yet they couldn't even have a proper funeral because the monsters appeared mere days after. They were relentless. The royal knights had to fend off the creatures for three long months. . . . Then, a miracle occurred. The king told us that the gods had provided him with this palace out here in the countryside, a sanctuary. It was an answered prayer."

Eglantine's lip trembled. "I believed it. I believed in *this*. I was a child, then. And my mother had just gone missing. Growing up, I assumed that the Shadows must have—" Her voice broke, and she pressed the handkerchief to her mouth. After a moment, she collected herself and continued at a whisper. "But as I grew, I began to doubt."

She went silent for a moment, before continuing. "Before the Shadows ever appeared, before Le Château, before everything, King Léo hired my mother to help him with some secret project she could not name. She kissed me farewell, and said she'd be gone for a fortnight traveling with him. Yet the Shadows came, and only he returned."

"Sagesse?" I murmured. Eglantine's mother had changed her name, she'd said. She'd called herself *wisdom*. My mind had clung fast to this fact, this little bit of poetry.

Despite everything, fondness sparkled in her eyes. "That's right. That was her name."

Françoise. The countess. Eglantine's mother.

"What sort of work did your mother do?" I asked.

The candle flame whipped and flickered, like a moth beating its wings. The sudden movement startled me. Eglantine clutched her shawl against her heart. Her gaze was locked upon the flame.

"My mother was a favorite of the gods," said Eglantine. "She could pray to them, and they'd answer her. Every time. Sometimes she would read fortunes for a bit of coin or ask the gods to send blessings upon people in their times of trouble."

My heart leapt. I had only heard stories of people like that, favored people—people like the king. But I hadn't expected this, what courtiers called impossible. Eglantine had no title—her mother wasn't a noblewoman. She was ordinary.

Like me. And yet the gods heard her prayers.

Eglantine saw my shocked expression. "Yes, her abilities made her quite famous. In demand. But not well liked." Her mouth twisted into a bitter smile. "She was not of the . . . *status* that people expected for one so favored. The king's blessing was much better received."

"Then that's how the king was blessed?" I asked. "She interceded on his behalf?"

"I believe so. The gods did not listen to the king—or the prince, as he was at the time—before then. Only after my mother had disappeared did he become prosperous." She looked up at me, a determined set to her face. "So days ago when Lady Ofelia appeared, saying her mother had vanished in much the same way . . . And I never believed that Françoise de la Valliere would leave this court for another kingdom. Her friends are here, her career was here; she was a singer at the most splendid palace on the continent, and she had the favor of the king. It made no sense."

She pivoted in her chair, pointing at me. "So then. The king, shrouded by darkness that he adamantly denies. And a door to the Underworld. On *these* grounds that are supposed to be holy."

I rubbed my forehead in thought. "Why would the king allow a door like that to exist? Why would the *gods* allow for such a thing to exist?"

"One god would."

My blood ran cold. I gripped the table harder. "The king of the Underworld," I murmured. All I'd learned was slowly fitting together, piece by piece creating the skeletal remains of some hideous beast I'd thought was only fantasy. "King Léo hired your mother to speak to the gods. What if—what if he hired her to speak to . . . *him*?"

"It's possible."

"How?" The question felt foolish for an instant, before it suddenly thrilled me and sent my pulse galloping. "Can *anyone* communicate with the Shadow King? Can anyone ask him for his favor or—or create a door to his domain?"

Could *I*? Could I finally have the answers I'd been searching for my entire life?

Eglantine chose a volume from the pile of books on the desk, this one bound in stark contrast the others, with simple, plain leather. She placed it in my hands.

"I've kept it for thirty years. My mother's journal. She recorded nearly all her conversations with the gods."

I flipped through the delicate pages. *A supplication to the god of abundance—April 18th. A conversation with the god of forests. An answer from the god of the stars.* The book fell open to a threadbare bookmark, next to a page titled *A strange interaction with a new god.*

"Have you . . . have you tried to replicate these rituals?" I asked softly.

"I was unsuccessful." She slipped her glasses back onto her

face. "It seems whatever aptitude my mother possesses has skipped over me." Eglantine clutched the book. "Perhaps you will have more luck."

All my life I have offered to the gods and never received an answer. Yet here was a chance I had never expected, answers I desperately needed. I could not help but try, even to appeal to the monstrous god that haunted us all.

"I fear I'll have no more success than you've had," I warned her.

Eglantine pressed her lips in a sad smile. "Mademoiselle," she said, "I have looked in vain for my mother for thirty years. I don't know if this god has any answers. I don't know if this god will speak to *anyone*. But my mother . . . if she's alive somewhere, she'd be over eighty years old. I am running out of time. I am running out of hope." She extended a hand, laying it against my wrist. "I have given you the greatest treasure I have: knowledge. You are a knight. In this godsforsaken place, I have only seen *you* pursue justice and *truth*. I am begging you to help me find her. Or at least *try*."

"I shall," I said.

Despite her plea, she had seemed to expect my denial. At my words, she clapped a hand to her mouth, muffling a sob that seemed torn from her. Far away, bells clanged, making us both jump. The signal that the night's festivities were to begin. A siren's call to the ballroom.

Eglantine rose from the table, sniffling and gathering up

her books. "You should go," she said. "I don't want anyone to think we've been conspiring. The king hates private meetings."

I tucked the journal under my arm and carefully placed the penknife back on the table with a little click. When Eglantine caught sight of the blade, she laughed and said, "Wait! I do have something to repay you with."

She disappeared toward her desk, returning after a moment with something in her hands. When she set it on the tabletop, my eyes went round. A dagger, still in its sheath. I hungrily grabbed the weapon, unsheathing it. On either side of the handle, the guard was curved almost like a bow—a perfect parrying blade. After a world filled with riches and excess, I relished something so simple. The sharp blade glowed in the candlelight. With utter reverence, I hid the dagger within my coat.

"Better than a penknife," she said with a grin.

"Where did you get it?" I asked.

"The palace confiscates the nobles' weapons. I happen to have a key to such contraband." Eglantine nodded at the dagger. "Be careful. If our suspicions are correct . . . this is dangerous knowledge that we possess."

"What about you?"

The librarian grinned, lifting a heavy volume off the table with great ease. "I have lived in Le Château nearly my whole life, mademoiselle. I can handle myself."

"Very well." I bowed to her. "Thank you, Eglantine. For everything." I glanced at the library doors, back to where the "real world" lay. "I need to share all of this with Ofelia—"

"She's the king's daughter."

"She's my—" I faltered, because I did not know what to call her. *Beloved* was what I longed for.

"I know you trust her. I know you care for her. But any secret she slips would easily reach the ears of the king."

Ofelia was kind and delightful and gregarious. She was sweet and strong and impossible to talk out of a plan she had decided upon. For all these marvelous attributes, even I could admit, discretion was never her strongest suit. Still, keeping anything from her felt wrong.

"I just want her to be safe," I said.

She rested the heavy volume against her hip and turned to look at me, something piercing and sad in her eyes. "Then choose wisely what knowledge to share with her."

As I feared, Ofelia was not in her bedroom. I tucked Sagesse's book of gods under the mattress and knew I'd find her in the ballroom.

Through the darkened hallways, I followed the drifting sound of whining music and loud, raucous laughter. Already the hairs on the back of my neck stood on end as I prepared myself for the inevitable. Being around so many people. The way they unabashedly pointed and stared at me.

The doors to the ballroom were parted, allowing golden light to spill into the corridor. A single guard stood in the doorway, his halberd firmly planted on the floor.

"Name?" he asked me.

"Lope de la Rosa," I said. "I serve Lady Ofelia."

"If that is so, servant, why are you not with your lady?"

They never used to question me like this. I was always following just behind her. We were always side by side—now this guard completely doubted my place in her life.

His words, too, prodded a wound that I so often pretended did not hurt.

As much as I tried to forget it when she was braiding my hair or listening to me recite or spinning sweet stories for me, the difference in our stations had always been a great fracture between us both. Here at court, it was more like a canyon.

"Please—please have someone tell her that there is an urgent message waiting for her. Something she asked me to alert her of."

The soldier sighed. He took a step back, addressing one of his fellows hidden behind the corner of the doorway in the ballroom. A young man in the blue-and-gold livery of a palace servant crossed the room, slipping through the crowd of people. After a minute, Ofelia emerged, her scarlet skirts in her fists, and ran toward me with a grin.

"My lady—"

She reached past the guard in the doorway and grabbed

the sleeve of my coat, pulling me inside. In a whirl, she had us tucked away by a wall covered in equestrian portraits. All of the king.

Ofelia beamed up at me, her hands tangling with mine. Already, my heart was beating even faster than it had with the Shadows. Her cheeks were flushed bright pink. If I held my hand to her cheek, to feel its warmth, I thought it might feel like cradling sunshine itself.

Her beauty trapped all the breath in my lungs. Her dress was the same deep red as the roses in her hair. Her lips, too, were painted red, and around her neck was a necklace dripping rubies. Gray and black pearls were pinned in strands across the front of her bodice. She looked more elegant than I'd ever seen her.

"I hoped I would see you," she said. "You've become a phantom! I scarcely see you anymore."

My heart ached. *She longed to see me.* "Forgive me, my lady. I feel the same. I hope that you have not felt unsafe on your own while I have been researching—"

"Unsafe?" She laughed. "Heavens, no. I've been at the king's side. All I've been in danger of has been twisting an ankle while dancing."

My cruel mind whispered, *She does not need you.* I squared my shoulders and tried to maintain composure. "Then I am pleased, but . . ." I glanced about the ballroom, to the dancers in a thousand shades of red, crimson and scarlet and

222

vermillion, leaping and twirling like a bloody haze against my eyes. And the king, clad in gold, with his cold stare fast upon me.

"I need to speak with you in private," I whispered to her.

Ofelia's smile was doused in an instant. She released my hands and procured a fan from the pocket of her gown. It was black, painted with bright fireworks of red flowers. She fluttered her fan over her heart, that strangely restrained look still upon her face. "What sort of thing do you wish to speak about?" she asked primly. "Is it lovely? Or unpleasant?"

I swallowed a lump in my throat. "Well, unpleasant, but important—"

"Why must you worry yourself every single night? Why do all your thoughts gather around everything dark and wicked?"

A deep pain sliced through my chest, as though her words themselves had cut me. "I know it is distressing, but I only speak out of concern for you."

"Can it wait until the morning?"

"My lady, you are occupied most every morning—"

"No, *you* are occupied!" Ofelia snapped her fan shut and folded her arms. "When I rise, you are already gone. I do not even get to wish you a good morning."

"I am seeking the truth. In the gardens, in the library, and that is what—"

"I am doing what you asked of me. I listen for gossip, and

I gather up stories. I cannot do so with a dour expression, refusing to dance, refusing to participate!"

I flinched at the bite of her words. Perhaps she was anxious; perhaps so much mystery and doubt and all this chaos around her was making her irritable. I made my voice softer and sweeter. "I understand. Have you discovered anything, then?"

"His Majesty has no family left. He mentioned taking me to the Hall of Illusions someday, but I did not press the matter." She shrugged, letting her fan slap into her hand. "That is all. He is lonely."

Lonely. It seemed a paltry excuse for what I now knew. Three missing women. The sudden deaths of the king's father and brother. The Shadows, blooming into existence around the same time. All I wanted was to tell her this. To warn her. To *protect* her.

But there were a thousand eyes upon us. A thousand ears pricked up, hungry for more gossip.

"Please," I whispered, "I just need a minute to speak with you. But we must be alone. It's not safe."

"I don't want to leave the fête."

From behind her, a tall, slim figure appeared, carefully touching a hand against Ofelia's bare shoulder. My fingers itched for the dagger in my coat, until I saw who was standing behind her.

"Leave the fête?" said the king. "Oh no, you must stay.

There will be a fireworks show, and then some folk dancers from the south are going to perform for us."

"No, Your Majesty, I do not intend to leave," she said, smiling back at him. My heart ached. My lungs refused to fill.

King Léo's eyes met with mine. "Who is this vexing you, my pearl? The servant you mentioned?"

The servant. Was that all I was to her?

"Yes, this is Lope." She offered me a kind smile, melting away a bit of the frost between us. "All I want is for her to join me, yet"—her expression shuttered—"she does not seem to care for dancing." Ofelia looked at me quietly once she finished speaking, some question in her eyes.

I imagined myself among the nobles, performing their silly, regimented dances while a portal to the Underworld existed undisturbed in the gardens. Even if it would make Ofelia smile, the image felt so dissonant that it made me squirm. "I—I—"

"There are plenty of other ladies who would love to partner with you," the king interrupted, tipping her head forward to kiss her forehead. The king whispered something in her ear, and she shook her head adamantly.

Ofelia wiped a stray tear from her cheek, that strange, immovable smile still upon her face. "It's fine, Father. I just need a minute longer."

"As you wish." He wrapped his arm around her shoulders in a quasi-embrace. He raised a brow in my direction but did not even deign to look at me, only at Ofelia. "Doesn't my daughter look beautiful tonight, mademoiselle?"

She did. She was blossoming, thriving, glowing. My stomach tied itself in knots.

"Yes, Your Majesty," I said, my voice dry and hoarse.

He patted her back in a quick farewell and then reentered the crowd, back toward the throne.

I had completely destroyed the conversation, but I could not quite determine how to correct things. I meekly touched a hand to my heart. "Forgive me—truly, I did not mean to vex you—"

"Yes, you did." Her voice was so small, so defeated. "You came here to speak of monsters and villains and foes to battle. You don't listen when I tell you we are *safe*." She gazed up at me, her brown eyes a warm glow against the gold and red around us. "Give me a sweet word. Tell me something kind. You have poetry running in your veins. You always have!"

If only she knew the sort of nonsense I'd written about *her*. She wished for me to conjure beautiful words out of thin air. And what was I meant to say? My heart was beating the rhythm of the truth, and that is all I wanted to say to her, *Danger, Shadows, gods, deception*, but she wanted sweetness.

And now that she had asked for it, so suddenly, here in this ballroom, with beasts running wild outside . . . all my words dried up.

"I'm sorry," I breathed. "I—I can't."

Ofelia took a step back from me. There was a coldness in her eyes that convinced me, for the first time, that she really could be the king's daughter.

"Then good night, mademoiselle," she said. "I am going to dance until sunrise. I will try not to disturb you when I return."

She turned on her heel, her red skirts flaring like a rose in bloom, and then wove back into the crowd.

I'd not felt a pain like this before.

Claws against my arms, the nick of a sword upon my cheek, air burning as it left my lungs in a dying breath—

What a fool I was.

A worse fool, too, because I loved her still.

17

Ofelia

My head was pounding when I woke, and sunlight burned bright against my eyelids. I pried my head from my pillow. The rose petals had fallen from my hair and lay scattered about my sheets. Somehow, I'd managed to fall asleep in my gown.

"Lope?" I asked groggily. "Gods, I'm a mess. Can you—"

I paused. The daybed was empty, neatly made. A sigh loosed from my lips. I loathed the feeling that there was something invisible and amiss between us. Like a story left unfinished. Even though *she* was the one being so stubborn and gloomy. All I wanted was to embrace her and to hear her whisper, *All is well.*

I slipped out of my luxurious, soft bed. One of my feet was bare, and the other was covered in a yellow stocking, the garter still tied above my knee.

I glanced to the nightstand, where a small piece of paper

had been folded up. An elaborate *O* was scrawled on the top. I quirked an eyebrow as I flipped open the note.

> *Good morning—I did not wish to wake you.*
> *I am in the library all day. Please visit me when you have a moment. There is much I long to tell you.*
> *Forgive me. I was cold toward you last night. The truth is that I have difficulty finding words when I'm in front of you. My mind is a tangled web, as you know.*
> *You asked for it, so it is yours—something sweet:*
> *The light in your eyes puts the stars to shame.*
>
> *Lope*

It was as if all the strength I'd lost last night had returned, as if I were a dying plant, suddenly revived by cool rain. I pressed the note to my heart and twirled around the room. Those were the same sort of words she'd written about the girl she'd loved. The words I had prayed were about me.

I would keep my own love locked safe in my chest, for now—it wasn't fair of me, a noblewoman, the daughter of her employer, to make such a declaration to her. I wanted her to feel no obligation to me. *She* would be the one to lead our dance, when she felt safe and confident enough to unlatch her heart and let me see within.

I could picture it so clearly.

Lope would confess her love to me in the rose garden, and

we'd spend nights exploring the palace, experiencing all its wonders. Then, on quiet nights, we would read side by side in the library, nestled by a hearth fire.

I stood in front of a mirror, a little warped but still finer than any I'd seen in my life. My curls were in a haphazard pile on my head, sagging on one side, and my rouge had been smudged away. But I looked at my brown eyes the way she did. *They put the stars to shame.*

Those were not the words of someone uncaring.

Father had been wrong. Hers were the words of a girl with a tender heart, a heart tender with *love*.

Elation bubbled through me. I grinned and I couldn't stop giggling, even though I hadn't said a word. I held my hands against my burning cheeks, gazing into the mirror. Her words played in my head again and again, *Put the stars to shame, put the stars to shame.*

"Oh, I could kiss you now," I sighed.

And I would. As soon as I was presentable, I'd make my way to her.

After I pulled the braided rope to ring for my ladies-in-waiting, I noticed on the nearby clock that it was already three in the afternoon. I'd slept most of the day away—no wonder Lope had retreated to the library.

An eternity later, my two maids appeared and set about their work. As I sorted through the skirts and bodices in my wardrobe, I realized with a jolt that I didn't know what Lope's favorite color was. I would need to ask her immediately.

In the meantime, pink was never a poor decision.

My maids helped me into my gown and decorated my hair with pearl-tipped pins, and as they did so, they threw one another delighted little glances. I recognized those smiles.

"Is there intrigue in the palace today?" I asked hopefully.

"Yes!" cried Ainhoa, tying a string of pearls around my throat. "Oh, my lady, we are all dying of curiosity!"

I squeezed my hands together, grinning at my reflection. As if today couldn't be more divine. "Tell me everything!"

The taller maid, Estel, fetched me new stockings and a pair of shoes. "There's a *swarm* of courtiers in the hallway outside the Hall of Illusions. We couldn't figure out why— but it reminded me of that first night, when it appeared so suddenly. It *must* be something splendid."

My heartstrings tugged me toward Lope, toward the library, but my sense of curiosity was just too strong. And besides, I reasoned—it's on the way, isn't it? And Lope had wanted me to gather up secrets about Le Château.

Once I was dressed, Ainhoa, Estel, and I raced around one corridor and then another. The halls were so dark today— out the windows, heavy, black clouds blotted out the sun so completely that candles had already been lit. Around another corner, just as they said, we found a crowd surrounding the knights and the double doors. Courtiers stood on their toes, whispering, as they tried to get a better view.

I strode to the nearest nobleman, a boy about my age with a prim, silver suit.

"Pardon me," I said, "what has everyone so curious today?"

The boy whirled toward me, his mouth falling open. He hastily swept into a graceful bow. "Lady Ofelia! Forgive me, I—I know your father does not want us crowding by the hall just yet, as it is still incomplete—"

"Enough of that," I said, batting away his words. "I ask you because I shall burst if I don't find out what's causing all this commotion!"

He was pale, startled. I wondered if *I* was really the one causing such a reaction in him. "Well . . . if you will not tell His Majesty just yet—"

I gripped the satin sleeve of his jacket. "I am going to faint from excitement if you don't tell me immediately."

"We—we thought we heard a voice. Coming from the Hall of Illusions."

My eyes widened. "Someone's in there?"

The boy nodded, his voice trembling as he continued: "We think so. A few minutes ago we heard a woman. Then there was a man's voice, very soft."

It reminded me a bit of what Lope had said, about a woman singing in the hall. But a man *and* a woman speaking . . . If it was some sort of illusion, it didn't sound very interesting. Perhaps there *were* two real people within.

232

"That cannot be!" I said. "How did they get past the guards?"

He shrugged. "No one has seen a soul pass through those doors."

A hush swept through the crowd, and then I could hear it, too. A voice, desperate and scratchy, sobbing, as though she barely had any tears left.

Murmurs of confusion and concern swept through the crowd.

A person inside the Hall of Illusions? A person, hidden away, *weeping*?

It was a foolish thought. An impossible one, with how strictly the doors has been guarded.

My heart thrummed against my breast as I slipped through the crowd. When some people caught sight of me, they gasped and bowed. I ignored them, pressing on closer and closer to the painted-gold door, decorated with carved trees with soaring branches and roots that faded deep into an obsidian abyss.

Even the guards watching the doors had pressed closer, listening, frowning.

There it was again.

But this time the sound sent ice through my bloodstream.

I knew that voice better than my own heartbeat.

"Mother?" I called. It couldn't be; she was safe by the sea—but why was there a quiver in my voice?

There was one more whimper, so unmistakably hers.

I shot my hand out to grab the door handle, but the knights were too fast and crossed their halberds, barring the way.

From the Hall of Illusions came a loud shattering sound. The nobles behind me gasped and whispered. I leapt back. One of the guards frowned and reached for the door handle, but his partner snapped, "*Don't.*"

I stepped back from the door. The eyes of every noble were upon me. Some inched nearer, leaning as close as they dared to the door.

My maids flitted to my side. I leaned against Estel for support, wrapping my arms around her middle. I wished that she was Lope, that she could give me the comfort and the logic that I needed at a time like this, but an embrace would have to do.

"I—I swear it was my mother's voice," I murmured. "It's as if she's in there!"

"Well . . . it must be an illusion," Ainhoa said. "We know nothing else about that room besides its name."

The very idea made cold, invisible hands grip my stomach. I didn't know which I hoped for more—that my mother was only one door apart from me, or that she was safe at Lantanas and this was all some trick.

There were two loud claps: staves hitting the parquet. I knew the sound well by now, but it never ceased to make me jolt. The mutterings of the nobles went silent as death.

"Vive le roi!" called the first attendant.

"Long live the king!" echoed the lingering nobles.

"¡Que viva el rey!"

"Long live the king," I repeated.

His Majesty came in from the gardens, dressed in a deep purple suit embroidered with flowers and trees and peacocks.

"What a surprise to see so many members of my court gathered together like this," said the king. "I know you all are so very eager to see the frights and fantasies that the hall has to offer. But I assure you, friends, when the hall is truly prepared and suitable for the eyes of the public, you will be able to explore it at once. Until then, fear not if you hear strange sounds from within. The wonders of the gods are great. But they are not yet ready to be seen. We shall celebrate magnificently when they are."

The court kept their heads bowed, glancing among one another like naughty children caught misbehaving.

"In the meantime," said the king, "if marvels are what you seek, the royal theater troupe will be performing in the gardens in an hour."

The crowd around me moved like a current, nodding and bowing and murmuring thanks to the king. He strode up to me with a warm smile—but it faded when he caught sight of me. With a simple flick of his hand, he dismissed my ladies-in-waiting, who curtsied and fled the scene. How quickly he could make people disappear. "What troubles you, my darling?"

My heart was still quivering, as if Mother's voice were

echoing within my body still. "Father, I—I know it sounds mad, but I swear on my life . . . I swear I heard Mother's voice from within the Hall of Illusions."

His expression remained unreadable. He delicately placed his hands against the bare flesh of my arms. "I will tell you the truth of that room," he said. "It was a gift from the gods, but it is one that can bring heartache. In that room, you will see and hear things that seem utterly real. Depictions of what your heart is longing for the most. They're like phantoms. Or dreams."

Tears clung to my eyelashes. "Then I only heard her voice because . . . because I wished it so dearly?"

He nodded. "Perhaps your wish was so strong that you made the illusion appear for everyone to hear. But this is why I did not want to tell you about such a place," he said. "I knew it would only upset you while your mother is away recovering."

Only a door was between me and my mother. Even an image, even just the sound of her voice . . . I longed for it so deeply that my whole body ached. I wanted her to hold me again. I wanted to tell her all about Lope and my warring heart and all the confusing, twisting secrets of this palace. And I wanted her to smooth back my hair and whisper to me until I forgot everything sad.

"Please," I said, "please let me see her."

The king looked into my eyes, searching for something.

His thumbs brushed against my shoulders. "Do you know that I love you, Ofelia?"

The king had barely known me a fortnight. Still, he was so kind to me, so generous. He always asked me if I was happy or what wish he could grant. Perhaps the love of a family transcended time altogether; perhaps you just knew, right after meeting someone, that you could love them. Even Lope had said it—love is immortal.

"I know you do," I said.

He kissed my hand. "Then I will let you see this room. But you must remember—all that you see, all that you hear . . . it's a fantasy. None of it's real."

I threw my arms around him. "Thank you, Father!"

His Majesty laughed. His voice rumbled in his chest as he told the guards, "Let us enter, but no one else."

The two guards each pulled open a door.

My heart thrummed in my throat. The king offered me his arm, and I clung to it as tight as I could.

When we stepped through the doors, all the breath left my lungs.

The domed ceiling was made of black crystals, descending from above like jagged teeth. There were no beautiful paintings, no hanging chandeliers. The walls, too, were like the inside of a cave—dark stone swirled with gray. Lining the hall were silver candelabras with more crystals and lovely warm light. From the right side of the room, a dozen windows let in a sliver of light that gleamed magnificently across the other wall.

The leftmost wall was covered entirely in mirrors, clear and smooth as water and more perfect than I'd ever seen. I could not tear my eyes away.

"It's wonderful," I said.

"It is, isn't it? A shame I must keep it hidden." He parted from me, inspecting the craggy ceiling with his hands behind his back. "Perhaps I will have another one built." The king turned back toward me on his scarlet heels, gesturing to the mirror behind me. "Call for your mother."

I frowned. I looked into the mirror, pure as silver, at my reflection and the king's. It seemed mad. But I'd heard her. I knew I had.

I pressed my fingertips against the glass. "Mother?" I called. "Mother? It's me, Ofelia."

For a moment, I watched the mirror, watched as the king stepped closer to me.

Then slowly, another figure came into view.

My mother. Her image, standing behind my left shoulder. Her normally neatly coifed curls were in disarray, tumbling and loose. She was wearing her favorite dress, deep burgundy with accents in black. She'd wear it to any dinners she'd have with her painting clients.

She was perfect and so very real. I whirled back, my heart lifting, knowing that she was standing behind me—

No. Only the king was there.

I turned back to Mother—the image of my mother. *Just an illusion,* I told myself.

My hand trembled as I touched the glass. Her fingertips touched mine, but all I could feel was the cold, hard surface of the mirror.

"Mother, I miss you so much," I whispered.

She smiled at me, tremulous but true. Her hand quivered against the glass. "Oh, Ofelia, I love you. I love you more than anything."

"I love you, too." I glanced back at the king, who'd come closer, his hand soft against the space between my neck and my shoulder. "Heavens, she looks so real!"

Yet her eyes shimmered with tears. Her lips were pressed in a smile that didn't look quite right.

I pressed my palm deeper into the glass, as if I could touch hers. "She looks sad," I said, turning away briefly to look at the king. "I thought this was supposed to show me my heart's desire."

"These illusions are odd things. Even I do not understand them." He tucked a curl behind my ear. "Does it unsettle you, Ofelia? Should we leave now?"

"No!" cried Mother. As if she—or the illusion—could not bear the thought of being parted from me.

"Silence," the king said to the image. "You're frightening my daughter."

But Mother's eyes never left mine. She wordlessly touched the glass, drinking me in with that same desperate expression.

As if she wanted to step through the mirror to me.

"It looks so much like her," I said softly. But it only made me long for her more.

The king gently guided me away from the mirror. "Come, child. It does no good to linger here."

We swiftly left the strange room, and the thing that looked and sounded so much like my mother—it wept my name.

The guards shut the doors behind us, and I darted around a nearby corner, catching my breath upon a red-and-gold damask settee.

She was so lifelike. But so sad. It felt more like a curse from the gods than a blessing. *Look at what you are longing for.*

The king lightly took his place beside me on the settee. Without another word, I leaned into his embrace.

"Do not grow troubled," the king said, his voice sweet and golden as honey. "Your mother will be home from Lantanas in only a few days now. You won't need that ridiculous mirror."

I pressed my hand hard against my breastbone. "How I ache," I whispered. "Seeing her . . . I just miss her so dearly."

"It was all an illusion. Just a wonder by the gods. They don't intend to be cruel, but they don't truly understand us."

He sounded so calm. So used to this—*magic*. True, beautiful magic, the kind the gods used to make the world and all of us. The kind no human could wield or understand.

The gods gave him gift after gift—his youth, this palace, the mirrors.

But *this*. Nothing yet had convinced me as this had; this

utterly perfect facsimile of my mother, so close and so clear, as if I could walk right through to her. This was irrefutable proof. For anyone to have traces of such powerful magic so close to them . . . it could only mean that they were blessed.

And that meant . . . that all of Lope's concerns could be set aside. I had seen no beasts in the garden. There were no women trapped within the Hall of Illusions—only a bit of artifice, a bit of sparkle to show off the wonder of the gods.

Our days could be spent here, joyfully, in the daylit gardens. And our nights could be spent in this enchanted palace.

"I must go," I said. I had so much to tell Lope. "But thank you, Father. For all that you have done for me." I smiled. Now that I was past the initial shock, I was grateful for the lovely moment when I got to look into my mother's eyes again. "It was a sweet gift, seeing her."

"I have more for you yet," he replied with a smile. "Tonight will be the biggest fête of the year. Performers, fireworks, more delicacies than you can imagine . . . I want your heart to glow with happiness. To let all the court know how dear you are to me."

It sounded sublime. One of my most beautiful dreams, brought to life.

There was just one piece missing from my dream.

The beautiful knight who would whisper poetry in my ear.

The girl I loved.

18

Lope

God of darkness, god of the world below,
Heed the prayer of your nameless daughter.
Look upon her with your blank eyes.
Soften the cold stone of your heart.
Answer her pleas with your still mouth.

Iscarcely slept after my argument with Ofelia. I had tossed and turned, wishing I could pull my words back, that I could give her something beautiful instead.

She *deserved* beautiful things.

Yet the only peace offering I had for her was a single line of poetry.

I fled the bedroom quickly in the morning and spent most of the day in the library. I combed through Sagesse's journal, comparing her rituals to speak to each god. They followed the same pattern as any my prayers: a candle, a whisper, and something to sacrifice. In the entry for the Shadow King, the author had simply written, *He is eager to speak with me. I cannot tell if there is truth in what he says or what he promises.*

The first few times, I lit the candle, I said a prayer, I burned something—a rose from His Majesty's garden, a lock of my hair, an orange, which the tiny flame consumed with a greed that could only be supernatural—but this yielded nothing. My head ached from the attempts and my focus, and I turned my attention blearily toward the endless shelves and the dust motes drifting in the sunbeams.

Sunlight.

It didn't make for an inviting space for the king of Shadows. This king of the beasts that had defined my life, that had left me scarred, that had killed my friend. All there was to know about Shadows was this: they craved the dark, and they craved the air in our lungs.

Then that was what I would give this god.

One by one, I closed and latched each of the tall shutters letting light seep in from the garden. Only the barest gleam shone through the cracks of the shutters, and the light of my candle glowed confident and strong on the table I'd turned into a workbench.

I sat down in front of the candle, drawing the guidebook closer to me.

Scribbled in the margins of an entry, I found another note from Sagesse: *It seems the god of Shadows prefers there to be mirrors nearby when I speak to him.*

I patted myself down, as if I'd somehow be carrying a hand mirror for Ofelia to adjust her hair in. Instead, I fished everything out of my coat—a handkerchief, my journal, a stub of a pencil, and Eglantine's dagger. With a smile, I unsheathed it, watching the blade reflect the light and the pale silver of my eyes.

"I hope this'll do," I murmured. I placed the blade against a stack of books so that the candlelight glinted against it like a golden beam.

Then, if he was ruler of the Shadows, if he wanted my breath as they did . . .

When the Shadows took our breaths, they stole our lives, our stories from our bodies. I could not hand those over. But there was a way I could give him a part of myself. A bit of my heart, of my mind, my words upon a page.

From my journal I chose a poem about a summer night, one spent with Ofelia instead of on that wall. When I looked at the moon that night, it hadn't frightened me; it hadn't reminded me of my duty, of what the darkness brought. It had reminded me of a pearl, floating upon dark water.

It had been so very beautiful, so magical, that I had dared to share my very first poem with her.

My voice had trembled as I kept my eyes upon the page. My heart had beat so fast it ached, as if it were so frightened it wanted to flee from my ribs altogether. I hated and doubted each word of mine. And then, when I finished, when I finally had the courage to look up into Ofelia's marvelous eyes, I found *joy* there. *Pride*. She beamed brighter than the moon-light.

You're truly a poet, she had said. And then, even sweeter, *Could you read another one?*

In the present I rolled the poem into a scroll. Now it was a gift not for a girl but a god.

My voice was a reverent whisper: "King of Shadows. God of darkness and the Underworld."

I pictured him, far beneath my feet, far beneath this pal-ace, in the depths of the earth. A wicked, *monstrous* god. *That* was the one from whom I sought aid.

I had never claimed to be wise. When I wasn't following the orders of another, I listened only to my heart. And it was a foolish, impetuous thing.

"I call upon you, most humbly and most desperately," I continued. "I do not know if you will accept the prayer of a girl of common birth. From one who is favored by no god." I licked my lips, feeling the strangest sort of stage fright. "I do not ask for your favor. It is only the truth that I seek. Please . . . please answer me."

I touched the poem to the flame, which erupted, climbing up my arm and blazing into the air around me in a white blur. I yelled and staggered back, gasping as I desperately pried the coat off myself—but the fire was gone. The blue velvet bore no charring, not even the smell of ash. I stood there panting in shock, until I saw it.

The flame of the candle had gone black. It flicked back and forth, casting a sprawling, crooked silhouette upon the long table—like a man, stretched out and spiderlike. I covered my mouth. The creature bent its head, adorned with three thornlike spikes.

"What is your name?"

Its voice was like wind whistling through trees, like nails upon glass, like an ancient door slowly opening. My hand clutched my heart.

"I am Lope de la Rosa," I said. "I—I am from no household; I have no title—"

The figure's shoulders rose with a wheezing laugh. "Such things do not matter."

There was no malice in his voice, no irony. But what he said shocked me. And he—he was a *god*. He knew better than anyone. Better than a king.

Titles meant nothing.

"Is—is it not so that the gods blessed certain families?" I asked.

"I hear little from the world above. But I know the gods. They choose their playthings on a whim, set them in motion, and are back to their own devices."

Playthings of the gods. A chill ran through me. What else could he mean but humanity?

"Then," I said, "King Léo, fourteenth of his name—was he not blessed by the gods?"

The flame shook back and forth as he let out a sharp, cold laugh. "No gift comes freely, and certainly not from *them*. Léo is indebted to *me*."

My eyes widened. I leaned closer, gripping the table. "He entered a contract with you?"

"His tale intrigued me. His *ambitions* intrigued me." The projection upon the table fluttered its long fingers, making the flame sway left and right. "I find humans and their desires so fascinating. Is that why you have called upon me? Is there something *you* long for, Lope de la Rosa?"

Images flickered in my head like turning the pages of a beautiful book. Ocean waves, a shore I did not know, a grove of trees blooming pink, a cabin by a peaceful lake, Ofelia's lips parting in a radiant smile. The two of us, resting beneath the shade of a tree. A world without danger.

I shook my head, casting them away. "No, that is not why I have asked for your help. Your—your contract with the king. What were its terms?"

The creature took a deep, rattling breath. "He asked to live forever."

Just like the stories had said—but not quite. It was no blessing from the gods above. The king had made a bargain with the god of Shadows to buy his immortality.

"What price did he pay?" I asked. I knew the gods; I knew

that they dealt in exchanges. I could not even pray to them without an offering. Léo must have given something, *something*, to the king of Shadows.

A fist rapped against the library doors, jolting me out of my thoughts. One door handle jiggled, then the next. I swept up the dagger and tucked it into the pocket of my coat.

"Lope!" Ofelia called—as if she had leapt right out of my daydreams. "Lope, you won't believe what I just saw!"

With the ring of keys in hand, I staggered through the semidarkness to the library doors, hastily trying to and finally succeeding in unlocking them. Ofelia drew back the door, and bright light poured into the library, banishing my carefully cultivated darkness. I whirled back—but the candle had burned down to a lump of wax, and all that remained of the flame was a ribbon of smoke.

I swore under my breath and darted over to the table. I reached for my tinderbox with shaky hands and struck the flint again and again—

"Lope, what on earth are you doing?"

I dropped the tools and pointed to the candle. "I just spoke to the king of Shadows."

Not my most elegant words. But in the aftermath of the impossible, I felt like a child again, eager to express what had just occurred.

The color drained from her face. "What?! Lope, you couldn't possibly—you wouldn't *attempt* such a thing; you're too smart—"

"I did." I stepped through the darkness of the library into the beam of light coming from the corridor and swept her hands in mine. "I lit the candle, and I made a sacrifice—"

"*Why?*"

"I needed to know. I needed to ask about the king—"

She pressed a finger to my lips, her eyebrows furrowed. Then, she slowly moved her hands to cradle the sides of my face. "Come to my chambers," she said. "We must speak alone."

19

Ofelia

With Lope's hand in mine, I whirled into my bedroom. From my pocket, I procured the long golden key to my chamber and locked it, my hand trembling all the while.

Lope, Lope, fighter of Shadows, calling upon the king of monsters?!

I leaned back against the door and held my spinning head. Lope's cheeks were flushed, and her eyes gleamed in an almost hungry way, the way I'd seen when she was ready to dive into battle.

She was serious. Her plan to find Shadows in the king's garden—she wasn't going to give up on it. To the point where she was now *inviting* trouble.

"Lope, this must *end*!" I begged in a scratchy voice. "Gods, the *king of the Underworld*? Think of what he could have done! He is the creator of the Shadows. He could have killed you if he felt so inclined!"

"I do not fear such a thing."

It was as good as if she'd said, "I want to die." The very thought was like a spear through my chest, and I clutched at my heart like the wound was real. "*I* fear it, Lope! You fling yourself into the arms of death so carelessly! What is it *for*?"

"You," she said.

My bleeding heart was clawing at itself.

No. I didn't want that. I didn't want her in danger, I wanted her safe, I wanted her to *rest*. I wanted to dance in the king's ballroom and see her sitting in a chair beside my throne. If she wouldn't dance with me, at least she'd stop for one moment. Stop fighting, stop worrying . . . so I'd find some measure of peace in her lovely eyes.

"What you do," I said, voice trembling, "it isn't for me. Why do you keep looking for danger, looking for some sort of sadness where there isn't any? There need not always be some sort of tragedy, something to rescue me from."

With a sigh, Lope said, "I'm sorry. I cannot blot out such things, my lady."

"Stop calling me that." *My lady. My lady.* Such distance between us. Even during a conversation as important as this one. Even when I was *pleading* for her to show me her truest, deepest self.

Lope squeezed her eyes shut. "The . . . the Shadows and the missing women. I do not know how they are connected, but I do know that your father is a dangerous man."

"He's not," I insisted. I smiled, remembering the wonder I'd witnessed, the fact that by magic, by the enchantment of the gods, I'd seen my mother again. "He showed me the Hall of Illusions today, Lope, and do you know what I saw? Dozens and dozens of mirrors. And within was my heart's desire. I saw a vision of my mother. She looked so real. It was impossible. It was *magic*. The gods really did bless him."

Lope frantically shook her head. Her expression was a mirror of my own: desperate and pleading. "The god of Shadows says otherwise. He says that King Léo made a bargain with him!"

Confusion, shock, anger, tightened my muscles. "Lope, why would you trust the word of a *monster*? Surely he speaks in lies!"

"I believe him," she said, her knuckles turning white. "There have been three women in the king's circle who've gone missing: Françoise de la Valliere, Eglantine's mother, your own mother—and yes, I *know* it is said that she is in Lantanas, but—we only have *his* word of it. What if she ended up wherever the others did?"

My mother. Just when my anxieties about her were starting to heal, Lope was tearing open the wound. And for what? What did she gain from this constant search for trouble and danger?

"I cannot account for Eglantine's mother," I whispered, "but as for Françoise—she did not disappear. She received an opportunity to sing in an opera company in another kingdom! She left on her own accord—"

"Do you have proof of this?"

I dropped my hands to my sides. "Be reasonable! What other explanation could there be?"

"A violent one," said Lope coldly. "There is no record of Françoise leaving this palace. And as for my theory, there is precedent for violent disappearances. The king was second in line for the crown and his father and brother *happened* to pass at the same time—"

"Lope!"

My outburst made her freeze.

I rubbed my temple. *Why couldn't she let this go?* "I'm safe here at Le Château," I whispered. "I'm *happy* here. Can't you see how happy I've been? My family is here, and I know you do not care for the court life and the dancing—"

"This isn't about that; it's your *life* I fear for!"

"I am not in danger!"

"Just *hours* ago I battled Shadows out in the garden. I saved the life of another soldier. The monsters are *here*, Ofelia. Right beyond your window."

Hours ago? Shadows in the garden? Cold fear gripped my heart. But I had never seen such Shadows. And Lope . . . with each day, she was jumping at corners. Digging for secrets. More and more desperate for something that didn't seem to be there.

I had always feared for her. Feared that either the Shadows or the unbearable burden on her shoulders would claim her. But now I feared something else entirely: that this dogged pursuit of danger would pull her from me completely.

"I haven't seen any Shadows, Lope," I whispered, my voice trying to soothe and instead coming out raw.

Lope flinched, like my words had been cruel. Her shoulders sagged. "You don't believe me," she murmured.

The heartbreak in her eyes made me want to turn back time, to fix everything, to paint over the entire conversation in gold. "You're tired," I told her, soft and sweet. "You've been so brave. Fighting Shadows for *years*. And we've been traveling for so long. You've never once gotten to *rest*, Lope, and all this peril and bloodshed, it can affect you—"

"*Affect* me?" she breathed. As she blinked, her eyes were glossy, and my stomach plummeted within me. "So you think I saw nothing? You think I'm *mad*?"

"No, Lope, that's not what I—"

"I have protected you for five years," she said. "Please . . . don't you trust me?"

I clung to the bedpost for support. *Trust*, after all we'd been through. I was so tired of fighting. I was so tired of reaching out so desperately for her and her never taking my hand. "Lope, I have trusted you endlessly. Endlessly. I am asking you this one time to trust me, to come find *refuge* with me. I am inviting you into my heart, but you don't even let me into yours. You have written poems of love for me, you've loved me, and you've said nothing, for how long now? Years?"

The angry flush from her cheeks drained away in a second. "You," she said, her voice quaking, "you read my poems?"

Shame and horror made my whole body flood red-hot. No. No, no, no.

"It was an accident," I said through trembling lips. "I only took a little peek."

Lope dropped onto the bed, her eyes vacantly staring at the pale wall before her. "How long have you known?" she croaked.

Truth was the only balm I could offer. I hid part of my face behind the bedpost like a frightened child. "Since . . . since we first came here."

Her fingers trembled as they dug into the satin of her breeches. "Those were mine," she whispered. "Those were *mine*. My words, just for me. They're all I have."

Another lance to the heart. "All you have?" I asked in a small voice. "You have *me*. We could—we could forget all of this and start anew." I held out my hands for her, desperate for her to free herself from this dark haze of sorrow and let our love story play out. "Our feelings are out in the open now. We can put aside pretenses and just . . . be in love! Let everything else fall away."

She did not take my hands. She did not even look my way.

She'd never been like this. Acting like she didn't care for me.

I drew my hands back, holding them against the cold

spreading through my heart. "Lope, I'm truly sorry. I'm . . . I'm certain Father could appoint you as court poet if you wanted. If I talk to him, I'm certain he'll—"

"Your father is a wicked man," she said, her voice low and dark as storm clouds. "What intentions could he have, lavishing you with gifts and drawing your attention from anything monstrous?"

I flinched. "Is it so impossible to believe someone would love me?"

Lope trembled, wrapping her arms around her middle as if she were going to be sick. "Is that love? Someone who will wait on you and give you anything you want?"

"No! No, what I want is family and home and comfort and beauty!" I gestured at the glorious room around me, each golden ornament twinkling in the light from the window. "This is all I've ever desired, and my heart is broken to think that you don't want the same for me—"

"Five years," Lope spat. "Five years I have been at your side, and you have never *once* asked me what I wanted."

My heart lurched inside of me, something breaking apart. Had I really been so selfish? All this time—did she see me as a horrible, wicked friend?

"What *do* you want?" I could only ask, even if I was nearly too afraid to hear her answer.

Instead of looking at me, she closed her eyes, shaking her head. "I want you to believe me. I want to protect you. I want you to run away with me. We'll go by night."

Run away. Go.

She wanted to leave Le Château. She wanted me to go with her.

But I couldn't. Not after I'd fought so hard for this small piece of happiness. And not when she was asking me to cast it aside for what could only be suspicion or superstition.

"Is there nothing I can do to make you stay?" I asked.

Finally, her gray eyes climbed up to mine, but the agony in them made me freeze. "So that's it?" she murmured. "You're . . . you're going to *stay* here?"

No. No, I couldn't bear this; we couldn't be parted.

"Please don't leave," I whimpered, my shaking hands clasped tightly together. "I love you, I, I *ache* with how much I love you, and I want us to be together *here*. I will ask the king to give you a title, and we could marry—"

"Gods above, I don't care about a title," said Lope. Her voice was tired and frayed, like she had aged decades over the course of this one conversation. She rubbed her brow. "I don't care about any of this nonsense. How can you, *any* of you, dance over the Underworld? Take picnics in the same garden where Shadows roam? Your father made some bargain with the *king of Shadows*, and now they roam our world, killing freely. Because *he* lets them in, in exchange for immortality. I'm certain of it. *He* created a door."

This sounded like some dark fairy tale, not reality. Not

257

the man that I knew. "He wouldn't," I said soothingly. "Lope—the king may seem strange and aloof, but it's only because he's lonely, as I was at the manor! He's so kind to me, he wouldn't—he wouldn't do that—"

"While that portal remains, monsters enter our world. *Lives* are lost. People *will* die. Does that mean nothing to you?"

I frowned. "Of course I care. That is exactly why you are so important to everyone. We need the knights."

She exhaled, long and shaky. "I cannot ignore what I know, Ofelia. I cannot stay here and sit idly by, letting others be hurt."

I cannot stay here.

The silence stretched. I kept my gaze to the floor. I couldn't bear to see her eyes.

It was as if she hated me.

Hated everything about the palace that had brought me so much happiness.

Perhaps we were just too different.

Her battle would never ever end.

"You say that you cannot stay here," I repeated softly. I swallowed back tears and took as deep a breath as my aching lungs could manage. "If you are so unhappy here, perhaps you should just . . . just go."

"Is that an order, my lady?"

My mouth fell open at the ice in her tone. It was as if years of tenderness and warmth between us had been stripped away in less than an hour. "Lope!"

"Is that an order?" she repeated, her gaze pointed and direct as an arrow, daring me to look away.

Tears dripped down my chin. "You're breaking my heart," I whispered.

I waited for her to say something.

I waited for her to change her mind.

Instead, she rose, striding toward the wardrobe. The oak doors banged open as she grabbed her greatcoat and her tricorn.

She was slipping away. She was leaving. My worst nightmare was unfolding before my eyes.

"Don't go," I cried. "Don't go, please!"

For an agonizing moment, her eyes met mine. I could see her every emotion flickering there: hope, misery, fear, betrayal, resignation.

My darling poet, the girl whose words made my heart sing, said nothing, and slammed the door behind her.

20

Lope

Give me monsters. Give me gaping wounds.
Flay my flesh. Steal the breath from my lungs.
A pain I can ask for. A pain I can anticipate.
King of the Underworld, reach into my ribs,
Tear out my heart.
Feed it to your Shadows.

I strode out of Ofelia's bedroom and down the hall, my
pulse like thunderclaps in my ears.

Ofelia. Ofelia. Ofelia.

The strange, delicate balance between us had been shat-
tered, and now I was falling through open air.

I *couldn't* be angry at her, not at so sweet and so lovely
a girl, and yet I was. Rage pumped through my veins with
each thrum of my aching heart. My body felt like it was
buzzing, like I needed to run, run anywhere.

Had she always been like this? So naïve, so willing to overlook all darkness in favor of ignorant happiness? All these years I thought she was like the sun, but now . . . my eyes burned and my vision blurred.

I'd leave this palace. I'd leave the excess and the complicity and the wickedness behind and never look back.

I staggered against a wall, collapsing onto a nearby settee.

Emotion strangled me. Sorrow. Betrayal. Bitterness. Fury. Fear. Loneliness. They each gripped my throat and dug their talons into my brain. *Feel!* they commanded. I clawed my fingers against my skull.

How could she toss me aside like that?

Did she ever care for me at all?

We were supposed to be together, always. Her hair blowing in the wind as we rode on horseback to a new adventure. Her heart pressed against me as we faced life's troubles.

I wanted to be numb. I wanted to be a machine. I wanted to be a knight again.

My mind dug into the thought.

This was all Ofelia thought I could do. Being a knight. Destroying Shadows.

Perhaps it was.

So I'd do it. I'd fight these Shadows with every ounce of my being.

And the Shadows were in the gardens.

Ofelia and the king, they could carry on without looking

at the monsters prowling outside.

I could not allow it. I could not leave Le Château until the connection to the Underworld had been severed for good. I had to find the Shadows; I had to follow them. Their nexus *had* to be hidden somewhere in the gardens. The king would never let such beasts sully his sacred palace.

I leapt to my feet and put on my tricorn and my greatcoat, armor in their own regard. My right hand wrapped against the hilt of Eglantine's dagger, tucked safe in my pocket.

Instead of turning left toward the main palace gates, I turned right toward the gardens. Courtiers trickled back into the palace as the sun was starting to set. I pushed past them, ignoring their little cries of alarm.

I tore through the gardens. The sun was glowing merrily this late afternoon, almost mocking the misery within me.

My eyes roved about, snagging on any sign of a Shadow. A tree with claw marks. A patch of disturbed gravel. With Eglantine's blade in my hand, I marched through the allées of the labyrinth.

If a guard caught me, I did not care.

If a courtier glared at me, it did not matter.

Whatever came next—if I found this door, if I destroyed it or if I failed trying—I was certain that I'd be thrown out of the palace. After I acted, my stay at Le Château would end. My time to find the tear between worlds, to stitch it up somehow or to barricade it, was running short.

The Shadows seeped into our kingdom and romped so

freely through these gardens before slipping past the walls and off through our lands. Like wildfire moving too quickly to be contained. Consuming the breaths of hundreds, thousands, without a second thought.

The king had tossed a lit match into our world and turned his back as the flames devoured it.

My every footfall struck against the gravel. I ducked into bosquet after bosquet, looking for something, anything, that could possibly resemble a portal between worlds. All that I found were the wretched statues of the gods. They, too, were like the king, turning their faces from us and our problems.

Playthings of the gods, the Shadow King had called us.

I rocked to a halt in front of the Bosquet du Temple de l'Amour. I looked at the faceless goddess of love.

Misery seeped through the cracks of the stone growing around my heart.

How I longed for Ofelia. How I wanted her to bind up the very wounds that she had opened. I wanted to go to *her* for comfort, to tell her about the heartache *she'd* given me, and to feel her arms around me and hear her soothing words. An old instinct wanted me to defend her and call her blameless, but . . .

There was a fracture down the blank space where the goddess's face should have been.

Ofelia had chosen riches over me. Had chosen a stranger over me.

Our five years together.

Her kind words. My desperate poems. Every gentle embrace.

Had they meant nothing?

What lay before me now, if not a life with her?

I turned away from the goddess of love. I walked down the path and tried to banish the memory of when Ofelia had been by my side.

We'd walked this way, and we had passed another grove, one that was locked away—

Locked and guarded. My heart tightened like a fist. My feet were moving before I could even think. It was as though my body was magnetized now in the direction of that sealed-off area.

I turned a corner and found the locked bosquet. The large grille covered the opening between the two hedgerows. A soldier in silver armor stood with his back to me.

And there—behind the grate, beyond the guard—was that marble rotunda. The black, isolated door at its center was guarded on either side. From so far away, it was difficult to see properly—but the door almost seemed to undulate in the sunlight. Like King Léo's six silhouettes. Like the Shadows themselves.

Cold crept up the back of my neck, that old, familiar feeling. An instinct that had never let me down. Shadows were close by.

In the depths of my heart, I knew that this had to be the bosquet dedicated to the god of the Underworld. That Léo would keep it locked, hidden away, the barest gesture of respect to the god who blessed him with immortality.

And that strange, simple door.

All the evil in my life was because of that door.

I crept back from my view of the door, hiding in the shade of one of the hedges. My heart battered itself against my ribs. I was just a girl with a knife. What could be done?

My strategist's mind was racing—I'd subdue the knight by the grate, climb over, battle the other two guards. And then what? Was I meant to destroy a door between worlds with a dagger? With my fist? There were torches in this garden, but I couldn't carry one over the grate, and even if I did, could *fire* really be enough to rend asunder that which was made by the *divine*?

I was so close.

I was mere *paces* away from the source of so much sorrow. The place where nightmares and agony and pain were born.

And I could do nothing.

I stared at that door, screaming within, my heart thrashing, wishing I could call down a bolt of lightning to turn it to ash.

This feeling of helplessness disgusted me. I felt like a mouse, pinned against a wall, while the king, a lion, crept closer and closer to me, baring his teeth. No matter how brave that mouse was, no matter how boldly she stared down her foe, she was bound to die.

This was not a fairy tale that would end happily. It was a song in an undying loop, and I was stuck listening to it forever.

"You there!" called a man—a guard standing by the door. "What are you doing here?"

The soldier standing behind the grate turned, glowering at me. With one hand, he planted his halberd in the gravel, and with the other, he grasped the grille dividing us. "On your way, girl," he said in a low voice.

Another dismissal. But I would not hear it from him, this pawn of the king. I would not let him deny the monsters he guarded.

"Do you know what that door is?" I asked him coldly.

"I said *on your way*."

I took a step nearer, fury coursing through my veins. If I could not direct it toward that door, toward the king, this guard would do just as well.

"Do you know that you serve the man who brought Shadows into our world?" I spat. "That they come from that very door?"

The guard narrowed his eyes. He grabbed a thin metal whistle from around his neck and blew it. The sharp sound rang out through the gardens, and footsteps began to thunder close by.

Reeling, I ran toward the metal grille and started to scale it, my dagger still in my grasp. As soon as I lunged at the gate, the guard behind it staggered back, his eyes wide in alarm. My thoughts were fragments, *Run, fight, door, Shadows, escape—*

Arms wrapped around my middle and ripped me from the partition I scaled. I shouted with fury. Before my next breath, as I was in the air, I reached back with the knife and stabbed at the soldier behind me. The blade clanked uselessly against his plate armor. The force made the knife bounce from my hand.

In a blink, two soldiers held my arms. I shouted and kicked off the metal barrier, using all of my weight to fall backward onto the two men. They grunted as they struck the gravel.

I swept up my dagger and jumped to my feet. In the second afforded me, I ran, with no direction in mind.

Onward I ran, as the high-pitched whistle continued to blow. From an allée to my left, another guard appeared out of nowhere, a sword drawn. When he saw the dagger in my hand, he lunged at me, but I parried the blow with the dagger. With the moment I'd gained, I leapt backward. Then something sharp pressed into my spine.

"Yield," growled a stranger.

I didn't want to. I'd rather die—no. No, not that. Even though she wasn't here, even though she had told me to go, I knew Ofelia would weep, would plead for me to survive.

The blade dug a bit deeper into my coat. "Drop. Your. Blade," said the man.

Across from me, the other soldier had his sword pointed at me, too.

Hatred and sadness boiled inside my heart. My hand shook as, finger by finger, I let the dagger fall into the dust.

They dragged me down the gravel path, the door to the Underworld shrinking out of sight as they pulled me away. No matter how I fought, no matter how I kicked or shouted, these men were stronger. Without a word, without any fanfare, they took me to a back gate and tossed me out of the gardens, out of the bounds of Le Château.

I scrambled to my feet and grasped the black bars of the iron fence hidden among the hedges that extended like the walls of a fortress. I looked into the garden I could no longer reach.

The guards walked away, and to their backs, I shouted, "You are knights! Your duty is to fight the Shadows! You must put an end to this!"

Gravel crunched beneath their boots as they marched on, unfeeling, unthinking.

"Forget the king!" I bellowed. "Destroy the door, please, *please*, it's our last chance!"

But the soldiers disappeared within the twists and turns of the hedge maze. With a cry, I kicked the bars of the fence, which did little more than give a weak metallic *bang*.

It was as though my past, present, and future had slipped through my fingers all in one moment.

My entire life, I had fought and trained to be strong. To destroy the monsters that plagued our nightmares. To save everyone.

But I had not avenged Carlos. I had not ended the Shadows. I'd never see Ofelia again. A whole new life lay ahead of me, unknown and utterly blank.

And now the door, and any chance of stopping the Shadows, was firmly out of reach.

As anguish crept in around me like a dark haze, I clung once more to the bars of the fence, just to have something to grip tight to—even my dagger was gone. I watched my knuckles bulge against my pale skin. When tears threatened to rise, I swallowed them back like poison.

I had lost everything.

If I thought about it too much, I would crumble. I'd fall into a heap on the dirt. The strings around me, the ones I had twisted tighter and tighter over the course of my whole life . . . they'd snap if I contemplated for a second too long the gravity of all the ways I'd failed. And I'd collapse like a marionette, lifeless and bent wrong.

I could *not* think about the sorrow.

All that was left to do was survive.

I glanced to the heavens, not for divine aid but to follow the direction of the sun. I would go westward, back the way I'd come. I was just a body that needed to live. With heavy steps, I walked from the gate, from the palace. Shelter. Food.

Water. That was all that mattered.

The sky was painted orange, a warning flame, reminding me that regardless of who I was, pauper or princess or knight, in a few hours, the Shadows would come.

21

Ofelia

I sat on my bed, waiting for her. By the time I counted to one hundred, surely she would return. Surely she would not leave me alone, not after I had confessed to her, not after I had begged her to make a home here with me.

But when I had counted to one hundred a fifth time, fear froze my body rigid.

I had never shouted at her like that before. I had never seen such pain in her eyes. The grief and the guilt and regret of sharing the truth with her was like a repeated blow to my heart.

I tried to imagine myself through her eyes. Stubborn. Spoiled. Refusing to listen to her dearest friend, even after all we'd been through.

My mind was tangled in knots. I trusted Lope. I believed in her. She would only ever mean well. But I believed in the king, too. He had no reason to harm me or my mother. As for the Shadows, I could not explain them, but who could? And who could rightly pin their existence upon one man?

Pulling a pillow against my chest, I continued to stare at the double doors.

All these years, she had devoted herself to me. And even in Le Château, all her time, her hours in the garden, her fighting, her sword training, her journey here, her words, *they were all for me*. She deferred to me, even when I asked her to leave. But . . .

You have never once asked what I wanted.

The splinters of my heart pierced my chest. Tears dropped onto the white pillowcase. She was right. I had acted like only my desires had mattered. Like this was my story and mine alone. Now, all I wanted was to hear her story, every word of it, and to stand by and watch her carry it out.

But she'd left.

No—she was *leaving*.

I leapt off the bed and raced down the hallway, uncaring of my appearance, darting glances back and forth as if Lope would simply be hiding around a corner. My feet traced unerringly to where she had spent the most time lately. When I reached the library, I was relieved to find the door unlocked.

Eglantine was standing by the nearest table, gathering a stack of books. An old stub of a candle sat in a candlestick. Lope's poems had been on the table before, and a dagger, too—but they were gone.

"Have you seen Lope?" I asked her.

Her brow furrowed. "Not for a time, my lady."

I touched a trembling hand to my lips. Where would she go? Back to the manor? No, surely not. Her only memories there were sad and dark or memories of *me*—and she'd surely want to distance herself from those, too.

Perhaps she'd travel far, far away. As far away from me as she could.

The reality of it all made my vision list back and forth. *I will never see her again.*

"Do—do you know where she could have gone?" I asked the librarian.

She shook her head. "I haven't a clue. I didn't realize she'd left." She tilted her head, a question in her eyes—and the beginnings of worry. "Mademoiselle Ofelia, has Lope been gone long?"

Another dead end. I had nothing, no leads at all. I ignored her question, turning to stumble out of the library.

"Mademoiselle! Lady Ofelia, wait—!"

I didn't. I ran and watched candles flickering in the hallway, their flames warped by my tears.

I could send the king's soldiers after her. Men and their horses, north, south, east, west, until they found her, and then we—

A treacherous thought occurred to me.

Perhaps Lope did not want to be found. She had longed to see the world. She had longed for a peaceful life. A life away from her wall. Away from Le Château.

A happier life, away from me.

Lope deserved someone sweeter than me, someone kinder than me. Someone who listened to her. Who asked *her* opinions, who let *her* weep, who would hold *her* in her arms.

I dragged myself back down the corridor, gripping the molding of the wall like it was a tether back to my bedroom.

What a wretch I was. How horrid I was.

I loved her. I loved her smile when I'd tell a silly joke, and I loved the way she'd wrinkle her brow as she read a particularly riveting novel. I loved her weathered hands and her gentle voice. I loved how when I spoke, she left a beat of silence after my words, to truly think about what she was going to say. I loved her far more than I loved anything else.

Now all I wanted was for her to be happy. My heart was warring, longing for her presence again . . . but stronger than that was a painful pull. The desire to know that she was going somewhere sunlit and safe. That she'd find happiness. I wanted that even more than I wanted her hand in mine.

Let her be happy, I prayed, *though I never will be again.*

The rest of the day moved in a messy blur, like a streak of paint upon a canvas. Though I'd already slept, after the argument, and after the loss of the girl that I loved, I crawled back into bed, wrapping myself in darkness and warmth.

My ladies-in-waiting found me eventually and insisted in

soft tones that I *must* attend the ball tonight. At some point I must have acquiesced. In a long, slow blink, I was sitting on a throne again in a deep blue gown. Little crystal beads were sewn throughout, making it look like I was wearing the night itself.

The sound of the orchestra was muffled. The colors of the beautiful courtly costumes had faded. I stared with dead eyes, a crystal goblet of wine clasped in my hands. Even when I drank, I felt nothing.

"My dear?"

The voice in my ear made me jolt in my hard-backed chair, like I'd been woken from a dream. By the gods' mercy, I hadn't spilled my drink.

Beside me, the king smiled, almost sympathetically. "You seem distant," he said, soft enough for no one else to hear. "Are you unhappy?"

How plainly I wore my heartache. I sighed and set aside the tasteless wine. "I dismissed Lope from the court."

The king batted a hand through the air. "Then trouble yourself with her no longer! Your future is brighter without her."

I flinched and drew back into my chair, looking at him out of the corner of my eyes. Lope had claimed that he was responsible for the creation of monsters. For a bargain with the Shadow King. For the disappearance of several women. Perhaps even my mother.

Had he loved Mother? Or when she had left, had he so uncaringly rejoiced in the wake of her departure, too?

After he beckoned someone close, he reached for my hand. I gave it, but his skin was ice-cold.

Françoise and Mother, they'd both been close to the king. And now I was there, in his grasp, the daughter he so quickly declared that he loved.

Could there really be some sort of danger, like Lope supposed? My mind raced, picturing him slitting open the throats of women or drowning them or hiring someone else to do the crime. He was the king, after all. Who was there to make sure he obeyed the law? He *was* the law.

His thumb brushed against the back of my hand.

I glanced up. Standing there was my dancing partner from before, Madeleine, with her long golden hair cascading over her bare shoulders in beautiful ringlets. She dipped into a deep curtsey.

"Your Majesty," she said. She regarded me with a brilliant grin. The rouge on her cheeks and her lips made her look lovelier than any princess I'd seen in a painting. "Lady Ofelia, I am so blessed to be in your presence again." Her blue eyes flitted back toward the king. "Sire, with your permission, might I kiss your daughter's hand? She is so radiant tonight."

"You may," said the king, before I'd even opened my mouth.

Madeleine took a few careful steps closer, gently taking

my hand in hers. She pressed her lips to the back of my hand, then to my wrist, each kiss careful and soft.

I pulled my hands out of both of their grasps, setting them firmly in my lap. The ballroom was too much. The music was too high now, too loud. I could feel the eyes of the courtiers and the king upon me, making my skin bristle. Even my heart seemed to be echoing my thoughts, *Lope, Lope, Lope*.

"Mademoiselle des Hirondelles," said the king. "My daughter is feeling a little out of sorts tonight. Pray, would you take her for a dance? Or provide her with some company?"

I imagined it, standing on the dance floor again, moving stiffly and painfully as if I were a puppet, all for the king's enjoyment. No, I couldn't bear the sound, the dancing, the laughter, the people.

All I wanted was to be in my mother's arms again.

It struck me. I *could* see her again. In a fashion. Even if it was just an image, even if she was weeping . . . I'd feel less alone with her than I would here in this ballroom full of strangers.

"Might—might Mademoiselle Madeleine and I step out for a bit of privacy?" I asked the king in a low voice. If I was to leave this hall, he'd find it far more believable if I left with another.

He lifted a glass toward me with a smile. "Enjoy yourself. And return by midnight."

We passed through the crowd of courtiers, who continued their dancing, like tops set in motion, unable to stop. I thanked a hundredfold gods that the valet did not make some grand announcement that I was leaving the ballroom.

The valet shut the door behind us. As before, the faceless guards still watched over the ballroom door, and frightening as they were, I felt a little more at ease without their judging eyes upon me.

I tugged Madeleine down the hallway away from the guards.

"My lady, you honor me," she said, her thumb stroking the back of my hand.

Down the corridor to the right was my bedroom. To the left was the Hall of Illusions.

I halted in the middle, lifting the chain of pearls from around my neck and draping it over hers. She gasped and raised her hands to the precious necklace.

"Wait in my bedroom for me," I told her, my voice more shaky than romantic and confident, as I'd hoped. "I only want a quick walk in the halls before I see you. It helps me feel like myself."

A lie—no, a story. And in this palace, lies and promises and truths and stories gathered and mingled as much as the courtiers did.

"Pray, do not be long," she whispered. She blew me a kiss and then scampered away down the hall.

In the other direction, the corridor was lit by the occasional candelabrum or sconce, like a carpet of golden lights as I approached the only guarded door.

There was one guard there, small and slim but wearing the austere, faceless uniform of the most fearsome knights. His head was drooped slightly, and his grip on his spear was slipping. As I stood before him, he said nothing, only breathed. He remained to the side of the door, leaning against the frame—*sleeping*.

Thank you, thank you, thank you, I told the gods as I reached for the door handle.

The door groaned.

The knight gasped, sweeping up his spear and swinging it wildly. The rod smacked against my arm and I yelped in alarm. The figure in gold drew back, his head swiveling as he looked me up and down, and he let out a little squeak.

"Oh, heavens!" he yelped. "Lady Ofelia, I—I'm so sorry!"

Play the part. Tell the story.

My apology froze on my lips.

"As—as you should be!" I spat, sounding entirely like the nobles I had spent so much company in. "Do you know what you could have done? Should I tell my father, *the king*, about this?"

He dropped his spear and knelt on the floorboards with a loud clang, going so far as to press the golden forehead of his visor to the space between my stockinged feet. "Forgive me, my lady, I beg you!"

"You could have killed me," I said, touching a hand to my

chest. *Tears. I need tears.* I could make myself cry in dire circumstances, usually if I thought about something sad. Lonely children. Orphaned animals. My best friend and only love, gone forever.

That did the trick.

I embraced the lump in my throat and sniffed loudly. "Right when I found my family at last, you'd have taken it from me—"

"I did not mean any harm, my lady; oh, please forgive me! I'd do anything to fix this!"

There.

"Well," I said, followed by a long, beleaguered sigh, "the king let me enter this hall earlier today. I wish to visit again. Let me pass and give me a few minutes to recover from . . . all of this. Then I'll report to my father of your cooperation and valor."

"Absolutely," he whispered, scrambling to his feet, grabbing hold of the door handle and swinging it open. "Please, go in. I'll guard the door and see to it that you are disturbed by no one."

I curtsied to the boy. "Thank you, brave knight. And thank you for your service to our kingdom."

With my head held high, I glided into the dark room, the perfect image of a confident, powerful noblewoman. When the door shut behind me, I let out a long breath and held on to the nearest lampstand to keep from collapsing.

By night, the candles had been extinguished here. Only a small beam of yellow light from the torches in the garden illuminated the floor. A faint breeze sent a chill through the place and made a loose strand of hair flutter before my eyes. I followed the soft rush of wind to the end of the room. It was tucked subtly into the wall, but it was definitely there—another door, likely opening out to the gardens.

The wall of mirrors had been hidden behind white sheets. Why had it been covered? The king had seemed so uncaring about the illusions earlier.

With a trembling hand, I pulled a sheet from the wall, uncovering the first of many mirrors. But there were no figments in the mirror to greet me, just the lampstands behind me and my own pale reflection. I tugged each sheet and left them in a pile like snowdrifts, until every last mirror was uncovered.

Mother had been here before. I remembered it so clearly.

I slowly approached the glass, touching my fingers to it, my hand meeting my own reflection's. It was solid; it did not part like some strange veil. It was just a mirror. Only a mirror.

"Mother?" I called.

Silence.

I stepped back, looking about the room, shadowed and lonely and forgotten. In the depths of the night, all the magic seemed to have been drained from this place. All that remained was reality, cold and plain.

My stomach sank as I considered one more heartbreaking possibility.

What if I saw Lope in that mirror?

"Who are you?"

I whirled back to the mirrors. My vision doubled—no, the girl in the mirror before me wasn't another one of my reflections. She had blond hair. She wore a golden ballgown and had a pearl necklace around her throat.

"Who are *you*?" I breathed. What sort of trick was this? If the mirror meant to show me what I wanted to see, it must have been wrong. I'd never seen this woman in my life.

"My name is Françoise," she said, her voice soft and sad, like a funeral hymn. "Who are *you*?"

My heartbeat skipped. The singer. The girl who'd disappeared—who'd gone abroad? "Françoise? Are you Françoise de la Valliere?"

"Yes." She smiled, though tears sparkled in her blue eyes. "Has anyone been looking for me?"

I hugged my arms as a strange chill came over me. "I . . . not exactly. You, you left to go sing in an opera company abroad—"

"What?" Horror painted her pale face. "No, no! I would never; I would never leave my friends!"

The girl wasn't real. She was an illusion, just like the image of Mother had been. She had probably been that haunting voice Lope had heard. And yet, the sorrow in this girl's eyes was so real, so . . . painful. And why would the gods show her to *me*?

"What happened to you?" I asked.

"The king took me on a walk in the gardens—it was at night. I thought it was so strange, and then we kissed, and there was this door, and I woke up, and—" Her brow furrowed. "How is it you've come here? Only the king has visited before. And a time ago he brought—" Françoise's blue eyes went wide. "Are you Marisol's daughter?" When I nodded, she pressed her hands up against the glass. "Gods! You cannot be here. You must get away—"

"Let me see her," I begged, fisting my hands against the glass. "Please, I've come all this way to see my mother!"

"I'll fetch her, but then you must go. Go far away from this place." Her blue eyes shimmered with tears. She clenched her fists at her side. "You aren't safe here. Please don't stay one minute more than you must."

Her skirts fluttered as she turned on her heel and disappeared into nothingness. Once more, I was standing before the mirror all alone. I might have thought it to be a fantasy if not for the aching beat of my own heart.

You aren't safe, she'd said. From the *king*? What would the king do to me? To his own daughter?

After an agonizing moment, two faces appeared beside my reflection: Françoise's and my mother's. She ran to me.

I pressed my palm against the place where hers touched the glass.

"Darling, listen to me," she said, her tone the frightening, sincere one that she only used when she was truly afraid. I had heard it only twice before. "I am not an illusion. I mean this with all my heart: you must run away from this palace as soon as you can. The king means you harm. Françoise and I, a woman named Sagesse, and the king's family, we are all trapped here."

"Trapped?" My voice was softer than an echo. "In—in the mirror?"

"No, love." Her eyes shone, but she swallowed down her tears. "The king sent us to the Underworld."

The Underworld. Just like Lope had said.

I breathed heavy and hard, trying to piece together all I had learned.

"He—he said this mirror doesn't tell the truth," I said. "And you did not mention this before—"

"He told me he would *torture* you if I spoke. I was terrified for you. I—I didn't know what to do."

"Ofelia," Françoise said, "all that your Mother is saying is true. The king took me into the garden, and he pushed me through a door. Suddenly I was here."

"It was the same for me." Mother shook her head mournfully. "I'm so sorry you thought I'd forgotten you. I should have known that you would come after me. But now that the king knows you exist, now that he can call you his beloved, he will try to sacrifice you, too."

"Why would he do that?" I squeaked. "S-sacrifice—"

"It's a bargain with the king of Shadows, a trade—the lives of his loved ones for time on the throne."

My stomach lurched. It was just as Lope had warned.

She was right. About *everything*.

My mother banged her fist on the mirror, but it didn't tremble. "He'll do whatever it takes to keep that throne; Ofelia, don't think he won't—"

Her voice was drowned out by a whining sound to my left. The three of us turned. The door opened, and a tall figure appeared in the doorway, haloed from behind by golden light.

His six silhouettes seeped into the room.

I staggered backward into the mirror.

"Who is it?" asked Mother, her voice sharp and terrified. "Is it him?"

"Darling, why would you come here and frighten yourself like this?" asked the king in his soft, sweet voice. "I wanted this night to be perfect for you."

I wished I had a knife. I wished I had a sword. I wished I had Lope.

"Ofelia, run!" my mother screamed.

My head rang. My legs trembled. My palms grew dewy against the glass.

"They like to tell you what you long to hear," the king said, stepping closer, his hands behind his back like he did when we strolled through the corridors. His Majesty gestured to the women behind me. "You have always wanted to be a part of a fairy tale, and here they are, weaving one for you. Creating monsters out of thin air, stoking your fear—"

"Don't listen to him," Mother pleaded beside me. Her words were broken up with sobs. "Don't take another step closer to her, you *bastard*—"

My heart was crashing against my breast, louder than thunder and rooting me in place.

"The gods have a bit of a sense of humor, I've found," he continued, his voice smooth and utterly confident. It would be so easy to believe him. So easy to fall under his spell. "So often, they use this mirror to tease me. To shake my faith in them."

Mother slammed herself against the mirror, begging, "Please, Ofelia, *run!*"

Françoise inched closer to me, fear glistening in her eyes, too. "He told me he loved me, Ofelia," she entreated. "He threw me parties and lavished me with gifts. I set aside my friends and my family; I thought his favor was all that mattered in the world. But his sweet words meant nothing—he trapped me here—"

"Enough." The king held out his hands for mine. "This is why I didn't want you to come here alone," he said. "The mirrors can frighten as much as they delight. I didn't want you to feel afraid in this place. This palace is your home now. It's safe."

I wanted to believe him. I wanted to return to a world of glittering parties and men and women fawning over me.

But it was a lie. A lie Lope warned me of. I'd set aside everything else for this place, for the king's favor. My home. My loyalty. The girl I loved.

More than anything, I wanted her to hold me now. I wanted to be brave like her, and I wanted to be with her again, smelling her rose-and-smoke hair. The king was wrong. No place was safe if she wasn't there with me. No place was home if she wasn't there.

I raced away from the king, toward the back of the room and through the door to the garden. The night air was bracing and relieving; I gulped it down hungrily and dashed down the gravel path.

Anywhere, I thought, *go anywhere; get beyond these gates and go find her.*

To my left was the garden, stretching onward into darkness. I'd not been far beyond this path; I hadn't even been here long enough to explore a fraction of this beautiful garden.

At night, it was so different. Sharp angles, twisting branches. All the green in the world had turned black. The perfect place for Shadows to roam.

I didn't have time to search for an escape. I had to run and pray.

I bolted into the garden. Walls formed out of hedges. I ducked down one path, only for it to end abruptly. I darted down another, hoping for an exit, begging for some wall for me to scale, like on a night at the manor, long, long ago. How I'd jumped the wall and found Lope waiting for me on the other side.

Rounding one corner, I found another dead end, decorated with torches and a statue of a man screaming as he was swallowed up by the earth. I yelped and spun around, darting into the next corner. Empty, as well. I turned and found myself back at the statue, and then turned again, ducking through the winding, endless corridors of leaves.

Footsteps crunched on the gravel behind me. I dashed forward, passing groves of fragrant orange trees, the various bosquets dedicated to our faceless gods—

More footsteps. Faster now. Like metal grating against stone.

Gods, I begged, *gods, help me!*

I spun past a corner and jolted to a stop. In front of me was a tall iron fence. Behind it was another bosquet, surrounded by marble arches, with a small, domed temple of marble at its center. Four guards stood within, their silver uniforms illuminated by torchlight.

Guards. Servants of the king.

I whirled around but found myself face-to-metallic face with another soldier. He pinned my wrists together and yelled, "Over here!" to the other guards.

I screamed and kicked against him, my dancing shoes clanging against the metal of his shin guards. "Let me go, you *monster!*"

Behind me, the fence groaned open. Metallic arms grabbed me around my middle. I screamed and screamed, shouting the name of every courtier I knew—but nobody was coming.

Lope was long gone.

A third soldier used thick, rough rope to tie my wrists in front of me. Immediately, I tried to wriggle out, but any effort only made the bindings burn.

I frantically looked about the grove that had been locked away. There were no altars here, but in the middle of the temple was something else—a door. Its frame was made of stone, its middle made of twisted wood and vines. From afar, I could see both sides of the door. It made no sense, a gateway to nowhere. Then with a gasp, I remembered what Lope had told me. What the woman in the mirror had said.

There really was a door to the Underworld, right here in the palace gardens.

And that's where I would go.

I pulled against the soldier who kept his hands locked around my arms. Cold panic spread through me as he steadily moved me closer and closer to the door.

"No," I whispered, "no, please! Please, I don't want to die!"

"You won't die, Ofelia," said the king, strolling out of the shadows and closer to the rotunda. "You'll be reunited with your mother, just like you wanted."

How could he make it seem like this was some *gift* he was giving me?

I was on the final step of the rotunda now, only a few paces away from the strange door. Vines undulated across its surface like snakes, and black roses bloomed among them.

"Please," I begged, "please, I want to stay above—I want the sunshine. I want to live in your beautiful kingdom. I—I won't tell anyone. I'll leave the palace if you wish—"

"King of Shadows," said King Léo, addressing the door with a cold, firm voice, one ruler to another. "My payment to you. My own flesh and blood. My own child. Take my beloved Ofelia to your kingdom."

King Léo bent close to me, pressing a kiss to my forehead, his hand against the back of my head, holding me in place just as the soldiers did. His skin was cold and clammy, as loving as a kiss from a marble statue. From so close, I could see the gold chain of Mother's locket around his neck.

He must have stolen it from her, her last night in this world.

With a quick jerk of my hands, I grabbed the locket and yanked it as hard as I could. It broke, and I balled up the chain and clasped the locket tight in my hands.

The king drew back, frowning. "Spoiled thing," he muttered. His gaze locked with mine. He grasped the door handle behind me.

"I don't understand," I asked, panic constricting my voice. "Why would you call me your daughter? Why would you be so kind to me if all along, you were just going to—to—"

His hand lightly caressed the side of my face. "You *are* my daughter, Ofelia. And I love you dearly. Otherwise, none of this would make a difference."

The door opened with a soft *click*.

Wind roared; there was the rustling of leaves, a horrid howling sound, and then the men around me began to scream—all except for the king.

The knights released my arm, shrieking and falling to the pavilion floor. A massive Shadow sat astride one, ripping the helm from his face and wrapping its long claws around the boy's throat. Shadow after Shadow poured from the doorway, swarming and draining the breath from the knights around us.

Ungloved fingers grasped my arm. I took one final, horrified glimpse at the king.

"I love you," he said.

And then he shoved me through the open doorway.

22

Lope

Misery, why do you follow behind me,

A Shadow,

A carrion bird?

Wait, wait still.

Your turn will come.

I am not yet done.

With the last pearl earring I had, I purchased a night and a meal in an inn, and sunshine spilling across my face woke me—something that was once a rarity for me. I used to spend my time sleeping through the best hours of the day. Now, I was able to see all the beauty of daytime. To feel warmth upon my skin.

Everything, even sunshine, made me think of her. My heart was heavy as a stone within my ribs.

I sat up in the bed, weary but grateful for its lumpy

mattress and itchy blanket. This was the inn's finest room, and I luxuriated in it: its dingy walls, its shutters that did not close all the way, the armoire with a crack down one of its doors. From below gently wafted the smells of eggs and bacon and warm bread. As quick as I could, I plaited my hair, dressed, leapt into a pair of boots, and barreled downstairs.

The common room was cheerful and sunny, with men and women chatting at round tables and playing cards. A true warmth, unlike Le Château's constructed merriment. I settled onto a barstool, my fingers drumming against the swirling grain of the wooden bar. As I was trained to do, I listened.

"The Deschamps just had a baby, have you heard?" asked a woman to her friend behind me.

"Oh, how lovely! Cynthia is healthy, I hope . . ."

"My husband and I just returned from a trip to the mountains," said a man. "The air is so clean there, and the blossoming trees at this time of year . . . it was delightful."

"I've always wanted to go there."

"Mademoiselle? Señorita?"

I winced, my fist clenching tight, and glanced up.

A pretty girl stood behind the counter, her skin freckled and glowing with health, her eyes bright and hopeful, her smile beautiful and genuine. My heart skipped.

"Something to drink?" asked the girl. "Or eat?" When I did not answer, she leaned close, frowning. "Are you all right?"

There was no malice in her eyes. No secret intent. This was not the court, with its whispering and careful insults and deceit. Nor was it the battlefield, where a monster could creep behind me and take me by the throat if I did not listen carefully enough.

This was the world now. My world. One where strangers didn't know who I was, that I was a knight, that I was a poet. I was someone worthy of dignity and kindness simply as I was.

"I—I'm fine," I mumbled. "I am hungry, though. I'll take anything you have."

"Right away, señorita." She dipped in a curtsey—a curtsey for *me*—and vanished into an adjacent room that smelled of smoke, herbs, and salt.

I folded my fingers on the bar and tried to ignore the constant wish to talk to Ofelia. That I could untangle my thoughts with her help. That she could have awoken by my side and would be sitting beside me, bouncing with energy and rambling about the day she would plan for us.

No. I'd never see her again. If I'd been brave enough to declare my love for her sooner, maybe things would have been different, but . . . that wasn't my present. I had no one to guide my future.

No one but me. Nameless, with no connections, no family.

The world was open to me.

I could take my horse and go southwest. I could see those mountains the man had spoken of. I could see foreign cities. Lands I'd only seen in books.

Without Ofelia, those places would be less bright. Less beautiful. Hollower.

But I'd still get to see them. And I had a heart full of words that could finally be put to use, describing more than just the moonlight on the fields beyond the manor's walls. The more I imagined it, the more it felt right; the more it seemed true.

The young barmaid set a cup of tea before me, as well as a plate covered in a thick piece of bread, cured ham, and slices of cheese. I ate with fervor.

"You must be off to Le Château," said the girl.

I stopped eating. Those words, that place, would always be a throbbing wound in my heart. "I just left, actually."

Her brows raised. "Really? Gods. Nobody wants to leave that place."

My hands shook as I reached for my teacup. Despite the delicacy, despite the baths I'd taken at the palace, somehow, there was always dirt under my fingernails. "I think I'm immune to its charms," I muttered as I drank my tea.

The barmaid laughed, and I lifted my head again. She smirked—not like she found my comment foolish, but like there was some common joke between us.

"What is it?" I asked.

"The people in these parts," she said, "we're more like you. We see the palace for what it is. Gold, painted over refuse."

My eyes grew round. "You don't . . . you don't call it blessed?"

She quickly glanced over my shoulder, looking at the

295

other guests, perhaps deciding if there was anyone she'd mind overhearing. But she leaned closer to me across the bar. "The king crows about how the gods built that palace for him," she whispered. "But my grandfather was one of the builders."

I blinked. "I—human builders?"

She nodded, her face turning grave. "Thousands of them. The king wanted the palace built quickly. He hired as many men as he could. They worked hard, too hard. Hundreds died. Some were crushed under stones and their bodies were just left there."

"Gods," I hissed. This was worse than I could have dreamed—and yet, it was exactly what I would have thought. The Shadow King had blessed the king with immortality. He had not mentioned the palace at all.

Of course. What was called a gift from the gods was only a veneer over more darkness and death.

"The water channeled for his fountains brought a drought in our village for months," she continued. "We had to craft a new waterway."

"And—and decades have passed, and nobody has spoken up?" I asked.

"The king claims that the gods are on his side. That he was chosen by them." She carefully drew back. "Those who challenge the king challenge the very gods themselves. It is not so simple. And His Majesty . . . he holds so much power."

She glanced out the sunlit window. "The king provides our villages with knights to vanquish the Shadows that come at night. He handsomely paid those left behind from the palace's construction. We are not fooled. But we will accept his bribe, even so."

Someone hollered, "Marie!" from the kitchen.

She showed me an apologetic smile. "I have to go tend to some baguettes." Marie curtsied. "I'm glad you were able to get away from that place, señorita."

She slipped into the kitchen, leaving me there at the bar.

I was right.

I was right.

The king did not care for any life but his own. For a palace, for his image, he'd let hundreds die and waved off the idea with a few gold coins and a flick of his hand. He was so powerful that decades had passed, and this had been kept secret.

Hundreds had vanished. No wonder three women were so easy for him to disappear.

And Ofelia—

How could she be safe within the king's grasp?

I dragged myself back up the stairs. With a click, I locked the door to my room behind me and slumped onto the bed, unmoored once again.

For a time, I had fooled myself into thinking I was a hero. Into thinking that I could save Ofelia or at least save *someone* from the Shadows that plagued our world.

But who was I? A lone girl without even a sword.

My stomach lurched. No matter my determination, the world would turn just the same. Kings would rule. Wicked men would be rewarded. Shadows would fester through the kingdom and kill children. Make orphans. And necessitate the creation of more and more knights like me.

I considered it again. Breaking back into those gardens, once again wrestling my way to that door. Perhaps some guards would fall to my prowess. A cost to save the lives of many. But how, *how*, could I keep the beasts from entering this world? A door created by a god could not be so easily sealed.

I sat up in bed.

I knew of one being who could close such a door. I knew of one *more powerful than a king*.

In a blink, I had leapt out of bed and placed a candle on the vanity with its small metal mirror. With my tinderbox, I lit the flame, then I closed the shutters, covering them with a blanket until the only light in the room came from the flickering candlelight. From within my satchel of all my worldly possessions, I found my journal and flipped past poems.

My last one for her. I had compared her kindness to the caress of petals against my fingertips.

I would write another one. Just for her—someday.

All the breath in my lungs was trapped within me, heavy as a breastplate. I sat in front of the mirror and looked my reflection in the eyes.

We have survived so much, you and I, I thought. I was grateful for the scar on my face; proof that I'd escaped death. Proud of my lips, capable of speaking sharply and sweetly. The eyes that had seen horrors and beauty and had wept and endured all of it.

I set the poem into the flame.

"King of Shadows," I whispered among the crackling of the flames. "God of darkness and the Underworld."

Once again, the flame bloomed into a white column; I drew my hand back just in time. When the strange, heatless fire shrank again, the flame turned black as ink. The long shadow it cast spread and twisted until it splayed upon the nearest wall. The tip of the Shadow King's horns touched the ceiling.

The creature—the god—bowed its head like a tree snapping in a strong wind. It steepled its long fingers together. "Lope de la Rosa," he said, his voice just as soft as before but strangely . . . *warm*.

"How did you know it was me?" I asked.

"I have come to know you by your poems. Their longing and their desperation and their beauty. You have sent me many. I thank you. I am a great admirer of your art."

The whole conversation felt so odd, so impossible, halfway between a nightmare and a dream. "You—I never sent you other poems, just one—"

"'To any god who will listen.'" It was my own voice he echoed back at me, cracked and fervent. It was my same prayer, night after night after night, a cry into the darkness. *Will anybody listen?*

"Oh," I whispered.

He laughed, a low, rattling sound. "I was not what you expected, was I?"

Certainly not a giant Shadow with a taste for poetry.

"Well, I—I am grateful that you like my words—"

"The girl you wrote those lovely words for"—the voice interrupted, his silhouette creeping across the floor, as if the god was standing behind me—"who was she? Did she never receive any of your poems?"

My heart shuddered.

"She read some. She read them too soon. I wanted to share them with her someday, but . . ." My words faded off into nothingness. I folded my arms around my middle, gazing into the flame. "Her name is Ofelia de Bouchillon—or Ofelia de Forestier."

"Ofelia?"

The recognition in his voice made ice pool in my veins. "Do you know her, sire?"

He curled in on himself and then, in a blink, the silhouette on the wall before me—it was *hers*. Her short, full figure, her curly hair, her hand reaching out. I knocked the chair backward, pressing my palm against the shadow of her hand upon the wall.

"Ofelia!" I cried, tears leaping into my eyes. "Ofelia, I don't understand—"

Her silhouette flickered and then grew, unfolding like the wings of a butterfly until the former appearance of the Shadow King returned. Without thinking, I swept a hairbrush off the vanity, throwing it at his shadow. "Bring her *back*!"

"My dear poet," said the king, his voice pitying and mournful. "Why are you unhappy? It was only her image. I thought you would like to see her. I did not intend to upset you."

"Have—have you seen her?" I asked, angry tears spilling down my cheeks. "Please speak true to me—I fear for her. You are a god; you know more than I do. Please tell me if she is well."

"She is safe here. If she asks for anything, I will provide it to her. She will not die or grow old—"

"'Here,'" I repeated, my heart louder than musket fire. "*Where* in the thousandfold names is *here*?"

"In my kingdom. The realm below."

I sank onto the floor, my hands over my mouth. *The Underworld. The Underworld.*

"That's impossible," I breathed. "How could she have entered—"

But I remembered. The reason I had called upon the Shadow King in the first place.

If there was a door in the garden that let Shadows *out* . . . surely it could let mortals *in*.

And I had *left her there*.

"How can she return to our world?" I begged.

"She cannot. She was given to me as a part of your king's bargain. Regardless, I cannot form doors from my realm. Only your kind can. And only the god-favored one, Sagesse, was ever able to."

Sagesse. Eglantine's mother.

"She's alive?" I asked.

"In a manner of speaking. Time does not pass here."

That was all I needed to hear. "What can I do to bring Ofelia back? I will bargain for her. I will give you anything."

The Shadow King touched a spindly finger to where his chin would be. "Would you take her place?"

"Yes," I said. Despite her unkindness, despite our quarrel, despite her stubbornness, nothing made her deserving of a life drenched in darkness. She belonged in the sun.

"What a marvelous ballad that would be," said the Shadow King with a sigh. He soundlessly clapped his hands together, and the candle wavered with the movement. "Sagesse knows how to perform the rite that will bring you here. You may speak to her in the Hall of Mirrors."

"Hall of Mirrors?"

The god tipped his head like he'd misheard. "I created it recently. A punishment for your foolish king. A room where he can see the faces and hear the screams of those he sacrificed."

A Hall of Mirrors. A room where the king could see Sagesse and—and Ofelia's mother.

Ofelia had spoken of a place in our last words together. About the Hall of Illusions and a vision of her mother . . . that hall that the king kept hidden away, as if it was full of his shame—

"Your candle is dying, Lope de la Rosa," said the Shadow King, his form flickering.

"Wait," I said. "Wait—I need to know. Is there a way I can stop your Shadows from coming into our world?"

The Shadow King seemed to loom larger. "No. I have my reasons for their existence."

Chills erupted across my back. I wanted to rage at him, to beg it all to end—but he held Ofelia's life and her freedom in his hand. My fists clenched at my sides.

The Shadow King touched his hand to his head and swept in an impossibly low bow, nearly bending in two. "Until we meet again."

I swept my coat off the end of the bed. My world had been turned inside out. I was heeding the words of a Shadow. I longed to return to that horrible golden palace. I was disobeying Ofelia's orders. I was commanding *myself*.

Come storms, come crowns, come gods themselves. With all my blood and all my strength, I would bring her home.

"King of Shadows," I said, my voice confident and firm, "tell Ofelia to wait for me."

23

Ofelia

When I lifted my spinning head, I was instantly aware of the strange, gritty sand clinging to my arms and my hands. My feet were bare except for my stockings—my shoes must have fallen off during my descent. I was lying on my side, and a short distance from me, Mother's locket lay in the muck. I swept it up and cleaned up the front with my thumb, revealing the *M* for *Marisol*. Without thinking, without feeling, I hid it in my pocket and wiped my hands on my skirts. My hands were nearly white in the odd light from behind me.

I turned and found the moon—no, a massive, white crystal, glowing from within, from where it was suspended high, high above in a black void. Little white and purple crystals glittered around it like stars. And beneath them, pulsing slightly, back and forth, was a body of black water, extending far beyond what I could see.

Remembrance struck me like a blow.

I had been running through the gardens.

I had been running from my father.

"*Ofelia, beloved of the king,*" came a whispering voice from behind me.

My heart plummeted as I slowly turned. Standing on the beach was a Shadow. But it wore long black robes and a crown on its brow: a simple band of gold, with four long, threadlike spikes.

A king. A king made of darkness.

A scream was caught in my throat.

"Do not be afraid," said the creature in that same everywhere-at-once whisper.

I couldn't run. I remained frozen, the waves behind me murmuring, my heartbeat crashing in my ear, the figure in front of me holding out a hand.

"Please come here," it said.

"Are you—are you the god of this place?" I asked, my voice faint as a breeze. "The lord over the Shadows?"

Its fingers, long and clawed like a Shadow's, curled into a fist.

"I am their maker," said the creature. "Their father."

It was all as Lope had said. The monsters plaguing our world had come from the depths, had poured out of the gardens of Le Château . . .

This god was responsible for my nightmares, for my pain,

for the scars on Mother's arms, for Lope's lifetime spent fighting monsters, for the deaths of thousands.

I didn't dare take a step closer. I wrapped my chilled arms around myself, taking a quick glance up to the heavens—to the place from which I'd fallen. Above me was nothing but a black abyss, peppered by those white and purple crystals.

The cold within me spread up my shoulders and down my spine. I inched back, closer to the black water. "Please send me back to my world," I whispered. I frantically shook my head, my breaths gathering in my chest like sharp icicles. "I didn't ask to come here. The king—the king pushed me through a door; I didn't want—"

"He gave you to me."

Deep in my memory, I could hear King Léo's voice echo, *King of Shadows . . . Take my beloved Ofelia to your kingdom.*

"I—I am not his to give! I don't belong to anyone!" Frightened tears dribbled down my cheeks. "Please, I want to go home!"

"Only a mortal who crafts a door between worlds can open it on either side. I am trapped here below as much as you are." He glided closer—he had no legs. His dark robes melted into the dark earth, like he was part of it—or like the world and this god were one. "The bargain was made. What's done is done. You belong to me and this world now."

He reached out to me, his long fingers unfurling. "Ofelia," he said, his whispering, inhuman voice freezing me in place.

"I must touch your hand, only for a moment."

His long, cold fingers wrapped around my wrist. I stood there numbly.

There was nothing more I could do. No other way I could fight.

My story was finished.

I was bound here forever.

"I'll not hurt you as your king did," said the monster. His other hand lightly brushed the skin of my palm.

With him standing so close, I could now see that this creature, this god, *did* have a face. It shifted, sometimes with a long nose, sometimes with a small one, sometimes with a jagged line of a mouth, other times with soft lips. But always, his eyes remained glowing white embers.

His forehead bunched. His shoulders rose and fell, and he let out a mournful sigh.

"A pity," he muttered.

"What?" I asked.

His eyes met with mine. "He did not love you." He released me and snapped his fingers. I flinched—but nothing happened. And then—movement.

Far behind the king of Shadows, the black beach led up to dark hills, dotted by what looked like stars. And on the tallest of those hills was a long, stone staircase, with someone, a human, quickly descending.

The god caught me staring and glanced at me. "Her name

307

is Marisol. She was sent here, like yourself."

Mother.

I gathered up my skirts, covered in mud and sand, and sprinted across the beach, through the dark grass.

"Ofelia!" she cried.

"Mother!"

I had traveled so far. I had missed her for so long. For many horrible days, I feared she was gone forever. This fate of hers was even worse. But we were together again.

She threw her arms around me, and once again I was enfolded in the smell of lilacs and oranges. I wept, laying my face against her heart, her fingers curling in my hair, her chest heaving with sobs of her own.

"She is your daughter? The one you feared for?" asked the monster.

Mother's voice came out small and choked, "*Yes.*"

She let out another sob, and my chest ached like someone was twisting my heart in their hands. Mother pulled back from me, sweeping a strand of hair from my eyes.

"I'm so sorry," I whimpered. "You are only here because of me. If I hadn't begged you to go to the palace—"

Mother silenced me with a kiss to my forehead followed by another tight embrace. "You are so brave, my love. You faced monsters just to find me again." She took my hand. "Come, I'll take you to the others."

"Wait," said the king of Shadows, his voice like the

rushing of the waves behind us. He slipped soundlessly closer to us, moving like a cloud across the sky.

My mother wrapped her arms around me. "Leave her be!"

"I'll not hurt her," he said again.

He knelt onto the ground, the darkness in his robes blending with the black earth, and took my foot in his hands. His brow furrowed. "The other mortals came here with coverings on their feet. You do not have any. Why is this?"

"Shoes, you mean?" I murmured.

"Shoes," he repeated thoughtfully. "Why don't you have them?"

I laughed softly—as strange as it was, as much as looking at the god made my insides turn, he spoke in an almost childlike way. "I—I think they fell off," I said.

Mother tugged on my arm. "Please," she said. "I have not seen my daughter in so long. I wish to speak with her—alone. I beg you."

"Only a moment more." He let out a long, slow breath, and out of the black nothingness around us, the ends of my pale stockings were covered up by new shoes, identical to the ones mother wore. These, however, were made of black glass. They sparkled in the dim light, and when he set my foot back to the earth, I realized how very comfortable the shoes were.

"There," he said.

"Thank you," I replied, barely above a whisper.

He inclined his golden-crowned head, like he was a

gentleman greeting a lady. "You're welcome, Ofelia."

I stared at the creature's face, vacant and changing and so much like the monsters that had nearly killed me and Lope not long ago. It was not difficult to imagine this beast opening its jaws and letting out the horrible, rasping scream that haunted my nightmares.

Lope had faced these Shadows. She'd risked her life every night at the palace, if only to protect me. Now she was gone. Now I would never see her again.

I'd at least make her proud. Even if she would never know. I wanted to be brave because she'd taught me how.

I held out my hand toward him. Mother gasped and grabbed at my arm, pulling me back from the creature. "We—we'll be off now, Your Majesty—"

"What is your name?" I asked him.

A ripple ran through him, and he bent his head away from me. A crack formed in his face where a mouth should have been. "We gods do not have names," he groaned. "The beloved of King Léo call me the king of Shadows. Or the creature. The monster. The beast."

"Why do you not have a name?"

The god twisted his head back toward me, his whole body at a tilt. "We gods cannot be known. That is the way of things."

Amid the fear beating in my throat, there was a pang of sadness in my middle. "That sounds very lonely," I said.

He did not speak.

Mother's fingers wove between mine, prompting me to look at her. Her blue eyes were as clear and beautiful as I remembered them. She was here. She was real. "Come with me, darling," she said. "There is much I must tell you."

I glanced back over my shoulder toward the beach. The nameless god had vanished.

"Can he just appear and reappear as he likes?" I whispered.

"Ignore that creature," said my mother, guiding me up a stone staircase carved into a black hill. "He'll pester you with questions and torment you with the past."

We stopped at the top of the staircase. All around us was tall, black grass, brushing up against my knees. Affixed to black bushes were small, glowing sparks, like fireflies or stars, growing from the leaves. It was beautiful, yes, but twisted— like the world through the fog of a dream.

Mother's hand squeezed mine. When I turned to look at her fully, tears glittered in her eyes.

"Let me just have one moment," she said. "One moment to have you to myself."

Her hand pressed against my cheek. She looked at me, and I took her in, too—her beauty, her warm eyes, and the way she was smiling, despite her tears.

I nestled my head against her heart, fitting myself perfectly into her embrace. "You were right about that palace. About the king. I should have listened to you—"

She hushed me and pulled me onto a bench made of glossy black stone. She rested her chin atop my head, slowly brushing her fingers through my hair. "I should have told you the truth sooner. I was so scared. That is why I ran away. That is why I changed my name. I never imagined that Léo would hurt either of us—it was the palace and its secrets that I did not trust."

I shivered at the sound of his name. "Did you ever love him?"

"I did. I thought I did. But he was the king. He held incredible power over me. He could command of me anything he wanted. Even if the king was kind, even if he was more romantic than my husband was. His crown always loomed over us."

Her words twisted in my middle. A girl, ordered about by a king. Commanded to do this, to go here, to say that. To love, if told to do so.

I thought of Lope.

She would have done anything for me. And she had.

I was the king's daughter. I was just like him.

I wished I'd had the chance to be different. To show Lope the respect she deserved. To listen to her better. To be slow to speak. To look darkness in the eye rather than paint it over with gold.

As my thoughts gathered like storm clouds, Mother continued in a soft voice: "Luc made a comment in public about how close the king and I were. In a blink he was serving in His Majesty's army, stationed at the front lines, and then he was gone." She began to rock me, and for once in my life, I didn't mind the way she treated me like a little girl. "Eventually I was brave enough to leave. I could feel you fluttering inside me, and I knew I could not protect you there."

Mother pressed a kiss to my forehead, dampened by her tears. "You deserved so much better. I'm sorry."

I wrapped my arms around her. "I couldn't even dream of a better mother." From within the pocket of my gown, I withdrew the locket, showing it to her. "The clasp is broken," I said. "But it's back where it belongs."

Flipping open the latch, I looked at the painting of the two of us. Side by side, pressing close together, us against the world, just like we were now.

"Marisol?" came a man's voice, warm and light.

Mother swept up the locket and rose to her feet. At the sight of the man before me, my heart lurched—he had the same dark eyes, the same proud nose, the same sharp features as King Léo. But he was smaller, and his long, curly hair was dark brown, neatly kept even in this strange, empty place. When he saw me, the color drained from his cheeks.

"Oh, gods," he said. "He couldn't have—his own daughter?"

Mother nodded and helped me up, pivoting me toward the stranger. "I'm afraid so. This is Ofelia, your—your niece."

My eyebrows rose. "I have an uncle?"

The man reached out a hand. I offered my own, and he gave my knuckles a light kiss. "I wasn't wearing a hat when I was sent down here, so in lieu of that . . ." He gracefully spun his hand from the top of his head in a low bow. "Philippe, Duke of Lierre. Léo's big brother." Philippe batted his hand at the air. "Of course, just 'Philippe' will do. As my dear brother has demonstrated in this grand game of the gods, titles and stations are all quite purposeless in the end."

"You—you were first in line for the throne?" I murmured.

"Quite unfortunately." He gestured behind him, where a lane of dark gravel led to topiaries of black and silver, including an archway made of leaves. "Come, I'll introduce you to the others."

The others. In the mirror I'd seen Françoise, and I had heard that this same fate had befallen Eglantine's mother. . . . Who else was here? How many people had the king sacrificed? How many lives had he extinguished?

Beyond the archway, Philippe guided us through a massive garden. If the palace gardens were a loud declaration of the glory of the king, this was just its echo. Low hedges were carved into elaborate swirls. Fountains only trickled, with no figures atop them, just stones stacked into towers. Beds of flowers bloomed gray from stem to petal.

In an alcove, as motionless and dour as statues, were three women and one man. I recognized one of the

314

women—Françoise, from the mirror. She was sitting beside a pond, lazily dragging her finger through the black water. When she glanced up at me, her lips pressed together. Like she was holding back tears.

"I'm so sorry," she said. "We were too late to help you."

I shook my head. "It was my fault."

"It was no one's fault but Léo's," Philippe said firmly. He gave my shoulder a squeeze and guided my gaze toward a couple sitting on a stone bench.

The man was about my mother's age, with my same auburn hair, tied into a queue. His coat and breeches were plain black but finely made. Sitting beside him on a bench was a woman probably twenty years his senior, with blond hair that was closer to white now. Their clutched hands and their closeness on that bench—it was an ageless, strong love. One that outlasted the Underworld.

Philippe gestured to the couple with an open hand. "My mother, Caroline, and my father, King Augustin."

With a pang, I remembered the king's story—his family's deaths, and how tragic they had been for him. How lonely he had been without them.

All a lie.

The couple looked up at me, their eyes mournful but kind.

Philippe touched my shoulder. "This is Ofelia. Marisol's daughter. And . . . and Léo's, too."

The queen mother leapt up and swept me into a hug. I

almost startled back, but her embrace was so warm, and my mother's steady presence at my side calmed me. The queen mother—my grandmother—gently pulled back to look at me, cooing over me and telling me how beautiful I was, how sorry she was, before pulling me back in. She hugged me so close, like she'd always known me.

Her husband, the old king, stood close by, smiling at me. "Forgive her enthusiasm," he said softly. "You're our first grandchild."

The queen drew back, cradling my face in her hands. "How could he let you go? How could he do this to you? Oh, I could strangle him!"

"Let me go first," piped up Philippe.

"No, no, we've all agreed. Should the day ever come, I throw the first strike." A young woman who had been sitting by the fountain approached us. She wore a very old gown, in deep reds and greens, and a pair of spectacles on her nose. Her dark blond hair rested in a loose plait against her shoulder. When she reached out a hand to greet me, an array of bracelets clattered on her wrist. "Sagesse Lavoie."

I shook her hand but frowned. Her name was familiar, but I couldn't quite place it. "Are you my family, too?"

"No," said Sagesse. Her voice was scratchy and raw, like she hadn't used it in a very long time. "But I ought to explain to you how we all came to be here. What binds us."

"That creature, the god—he said we were all the king's

316

beloved," I recalled. "And Lope said something about a . . . sacrifice?"

"Yes." Sagesse sat on the edge of the fountain, her head at a tilt as she watched me. Something about her eyes seemed so familiar. "Many years ago, Prince Léo came to me, asking for help in speaking to the gods. It is easier for me than most to hear their voices. On occasion, they'll even answer my pleas. The god who lives here? He is very talkative.

"Léo asked that I help him talk to *this* god, the king of Shadows. The prince wanted more than anything to be king, and to be king forever. He promised me a title, a place in his court, *security*, if I were to speak on his behalf. And I did. The god made a proposition: Léo would sit on the throne, ever young—but for a steep price. For every ten years he wished to reign, he would need to give the Shadow King the life of a person he loved with all his heart. He accepted the deal. Thanks to me, he got his door to reach the Underworld. And for his first sacrifice?" The bracelets on her arms jingled as Sagesse pointed to herself.

My brow furrowed. "He loved you?"

She threw her head back with a one-beat laugh. "Gods, no. He thought he could get away by sacrificing anyone. And I knew too much. At least he was punished for trying to fool the king of Shadows. But it was only a wound to his vanity. Turning his hair white."

Sagesse nodded to the old king and Philippe. "Next, Léo

317

gave up his father and then his brother. He truly loved them. And the sacrifices worked. He reigned and did not grow old. After twenty years, when it was time again, he sacrificed his mother."

Queen Caroline lifted her head. Her cheeks were stained with tears.

"I was next," Françoise spoke up. She met my eyes, worry making her brow wrinkle. "What year was it when you were . . . up there? I do not know how long I've been down here."

"It—it was 1660," I replied. How did time pass here? In this black abyss, in this world run by a chaotic god, did days last centuries? Did years last merely seconds? Even if I found some way to reunite with Lope . . . would she be gone from me by the time I returned?

Her brows rose. "But . . . it was the year 1660 when he sent me here! It was June then—"

"It is only autumn, now," I said.

"It's odd," Philippe muttered. "Françoise's sacrifice worked for Léo. There was love in his heart somehow. He *did* care for Françoise . . . but then he didn't need another sacrifice. Not for another ten years."

Mother's face was cold and still. "He just . . . cast me aside because I was there. A convenient extra sacrifice, strolling into his home . . ." Her eyes were glassy as they fell upon me. "He had what he needed. He could have let you go."

"It—it didn't work anyhow," I said, my voice soft, almost apologetic. "The king of Shadows said that Father—Léo—did not love me."

My voice broke on the last word. I couldn't understand it. How could I still long for his approval, his love, when I knew now what a monster he was? He was nothing more than a painted mask of a kind man, a father. But a father nonetheless. The only one I'd ever had. Someone who *should* have loved me.

Mother's hand around mine helped ground me.

"He won't stop," I murmured. "He'll send more and more people down here and let out more and more Shadows, and it will go on forever, because no one can stop him. No one *will* stop him. Everyone believes he's blessed by the gods."

"Easier to say the gods blessed him than to admit the ugly truth. Making a bargain with the king of the Underworld." Sagesse folded her arms tight and dug the toe of her shoe into the gray dirt. "The bastard didn't even pay me."

"Are we the only people here?" I asked.

"I'm afraid so, my dear," said Philippe.

I looked to each of them, their gray faces, their weary eyes, the utter, painful quiet of this place. Gone were the brilliant reds and violets and greens of the king's garden. Gone was the beautiful rosy pink of Lope's lips. There was no birdsong, no music, no dancing. It was as still as death, here below. Drained of life as it was drained of color.

I looked to the horizon, this world that was now my home forever. Beyond the dark, grassy hills around us, a tall castle stood like a beam of silver light atop a cliffside. Its edges were straight, and every tower was topped with spikes, as if the entire building were made of arrows.

"Is that where he lives?" I asked. "The king of Shadows?"

"Yes," said Sagesse. "Sometimes he summons us there. He asks us to tell him stories."

My eyebrows pressed together. "Stories?"

Mother nodded. "We don't know why. But he wants to hear about the world above. Everything, down to the smallest detail. We have to sit there, trembling in his presence, retelling our lives. . . . I think he enjoys seeing us cower before him."

I thought of the two kings I'd met—one beautiful and cruel and the other frightening and odd and . . . childlike.

If the Shadow King liked stories, I could weave them with ease. Stories were like heartbeats, reliable and steady. I knew the shape of a good fairy tale so well, it was like following a well-trodden path back home.

Perhaps with my stories, with all the bravery I could muster, I could soften whatever stony heart lay inside him. If he made a bargain with my father, surely he would listen to me when I petitioned him for our freedom.

I began to walk across the stone-paved garden, onward toward the palace, white as moonlight.

"Ofelia!" Mother called, chasing after my heels.

"I want to speak to him," I said, my stride unbroken.

"He's—he's wicked, Ofelia. He created the Shadows. He's not *human*, you can't just—"

"I can't give up," I said to her, pausing to throw her a glare—but tears had sprung into my eyes. "Maybe it's hopeless, maybe I'm helpless, but I will claw my way out of this place if I must. For all of us. I have to be brave; I have to be brave for . . ."

I couldn't say her name. Her smiles, so rare and so satisfying when they were won. Her hand so firm around mine. Her gentle, patient spirit. The way her fearless demeanor would melt away to a sweet blush when I gave her a compliment. The wrinkle in her forehead when she concentrated. Her faithfulness, no matter how stubborn I was. That beautiful, endless faithfulness.

With trembling hands, I swept the few tears from my cheeks and walked on. Behind me, Mother's footsteps clicked and crunched against the stone path.

"You don't need to come," I murmured.

"I want to," she said.

After a few steps in silence, I let my right hand drop to my side, my fingers apart, inviting.

She held my hand, just like on our morning strolls. Instead of forests and meadows around us, there were dark plains as far as the eye could see. The cold air rustled the plants and made our skirts sway, but her palm was so warm against mine. The callus from forever holding her paintbrush was still there.

The king had banished us below.

He had dragged us into his story. But our tale would not end here.

24

Ofelia

The Shadow King's castle loomed over us upon the silvery cliff face. Mother and I entered and wove through the palace's dark hallways, where amber-colored crystals glowed on the black walls and strange small sparks drifted through the air like fireflies.

Le Château was light and sunshine and gold. This place was its inverse. The walls of this castle seemed to close in on me like I was trapped in a cave. Even so, I was mesmerized by the lights floating through the corridors, little stars in a world made of the night sky.

There were no chandeliers, no paintings, no tapestries. There were no servants, either, but sometimes in the little halos of light formed by the sconces, there'd be a flicker of movement—a Shadow slipping down the hallway.

The corridor gradually sloped upward, a long, winding ramp that was sometimes missing its walls altogether. I looked to my right as the wall broke to see that false moon once more, shining brilliantly over sparkling water.

We climbed higher and higher until we stood on a massive balcony. In one corner was a large pane of glass, like a dark mirror. Very faintly behind the glass was another room, with stone walls and ceilings and silver candelabras. The other side of the Hall of Illusions, I supposed. There were stone benches along the railed perimeter of the balcony, and across from the mirror was a tall, white door. It soared to the ceiling of the palace, easily the height of four men.

My hands trembled. I squeezed them tight against the fabric of my gown to try to calm myself. Then I knocked upon the door.

"Enter," came a voice, slithering and gentle, but somehow loud enough that Mother and I both leapt in alarm.

I slipped into the room with Mother following behind me.

It was nothing like I imagined. The room was surprisingly bright, with marble floors and towering walls that were covered not in plaster or wood but thousands and thousands of books—not a blank inch of wall to be found. There was a black chaise longue decorated with fluffy white bundles, like clouds. There were three tables with various items meticulously set out and sorted. Gold rings, gold coins, a locket, a book, a small, skinny bone. A sword, sheet music, a pair of golden dancing shoes, a pomegranate. Dozens of strange items with no common theme to them.

At the far end of the circular chamber, the Shadow King sat at an enormous desk white as bone, sifting through papers as though he were a clerk or barrister and not a dark god. He lifted his head, his white eyes flaring like flickering candles at the sight of us. Mother curtsied and I followed suit.

"Marisol," he said slowly. "Ofelia. I did not call for you."

"No, sire," I replied, standing tall, calling on the confidence that Lope would have wanted me to have. "I wished to have an audience with you." With a glance at Mother, with a scheme and worry in my heart, I said, "Alone."

Mother's eyes widened, but the Shadow King said, "Very well. Marisol, wait outside while I speak with Ofelia."

She whirled toward the king. "Sire, please—"

"Ofelia has made her choice." The king nodded toward my mother. "She will return to you soon."

I squeezed Mother's hand. "It's all right," I promised her at a whisper. "I need to do this on my own."

She sighed, shot me one of her "we'll talk about this later" glares, and she then exited the king's chamber.

My glass shoes clicked against the white marble as I crossed toward the chaise longue and what appeared to be the small clouds covering it. I placed my hand against one, and it was just as soft as it looked, a bit like the white fur stole Mother wore in the winter.

"Do you like them?"

I gasped at the suddenness of the voice to my right. The

Shadow King stood at the far end of the room, watching me carefully.

Cradling one of the clouds, I held it to my chest to help suppress my galloping heartbeat. "They're—they're very pretty. What are they, exactly?"

The little white sparks of its eyes dimmed somewhat. "Pillows, I thought they were called."

Pillows. In such a place, in the palace of a king of darkness, why would he want *pillows*?

"Oh!" I said. "Well, they do seem a bit like pillows. But they . . . need to be covered by a bit of fabric." I held the white mass in my hands again, inspecting it. "It looks more like a cloud than anything."

"A cloud," he repeated. When I glanced at him again, he was holding a black stick and touched it to a long white scroll. "Tell me what a cloud is."

Every time I attempted to look at him, my stomach roiled. In my mind, I could only see him unhinging his jaw and snuffing out my life like all the other monsters would have done.

"I—I—A cloud looks very similar to this," I said, holding the ball of fluff with my head bowed. "But they hang in the sky, high above."

There was a gentle scratching sound as his pen poked at the scroll. "I see," he said. "Can you release that cloud, then?"

I drew back my hands. Slowly, it floated into the air, as did the other ones, lifting up to the domed, white ceiling of the room. It was so strange and marvelous that it gave me an odd comfort. I forgot, just for a moment, that I was in a monster's library.

"Why did you seek an audience with me, Ofelia?" asked the Shadow King.

I folded my hands tight, holding them against my thrumming heart. "Your Majesty," I said softly, "I've come to ask for our release from this world."

The white lights of his eyes turned cold. "Ah," he said, setting down his pen. "I told you, child. It is impossible. Only *your* kind can create a door. And our friend, Sagesse—she has attempted this to no avail. Such doors can only be made in the world above."

I frown. "You are certain?"

"Doors are outside my domain. Whatever magic allows mortals to send their prayers and offerings to us gods, it is one-way. So it has always been." The Shadow King gestured with his long, wispy fingers toward the tables of oddities.

"These are offerings?" I asked, approaching one table carefully.

He moved silently, like the heavy creeping of fog. He was beside me in a moment, running his smokelike hand over the treasures. His white eyes became half-moons, almost as if he were smiling. "Generous gifts," he said in his whispering, slithering voice. "Stories, dozens of stories. Little glimpses of your world above. I always want more."

The Shadow King lifted a small ceramic figurine depicting a couple dancing. He brought it closer to me. "They are called dancers, aren't they?"

His voice was so hopeful and small. It startled me, how mild he could be. "Yes," I answered softly.

"But this does not move," he continued. "What is the purpose of this object?"

The knot in my chest from standing beside this monster, this giant Shadow, began to loosen slightly. He spoke like a child, asking to understand the world for the first time.

"I think it's only decoration," I said. "Humans . . . humans sometimes keep objects in their homes just because they're beautiful. Or because they inspire memories."

His white eyes sparkled. "Fascinating!" He glanced around his chamber. "Where should I put this 'decoration'?"

It was almost like a strange dream, how light and happy he was in this cold, dark world. "I—I suppose it'd look nice on your desk," I offered.

The king swept over to the white desk, setting the painted figure on one side—then the other. He turned it, hemming and hawing as he went.

"Is there nothing you can do for us, Your Majesty?" I asked softly. "You are a god; nothing is impossible for you. Please, if you like humans so much, won't you show us some mercy and release us?"

He turned away from his desk, his eyes piercing me. "It cannot be done, Ofelia. No matter how you beg or cajole. Your king made his bargain. His door is closed."

The sharpness of his tone made me flinch back, prepared for him to move and strike me, to take my breath. But the Shadow King simply returned behind his desk and back to his papers.

"It's . . . it's over, then?" I asked softly. "We're truly trapped?"

He tilted his head, farther and farther than what was natural for a human. He said nothing for a moment, almost like an animal watching its prey. Then he said, "I want to hear the story of your life, Ofelia. From beginning to end."

Beginning . . . to end. The implication pierced my heart. My mouth felt dry and thick as cotton. I couldn't save any of us. We were down here for who knew how long. Frozen in time.

Would I be the same, unendingly young until time itself was just a memory to me?

Could I truly be trapped here for eternity?

The Shadow King lifted a hand, and a white chair evanesced up from the marble. "Sit," he said. "Tell me about your life in the world above."

I supposed I had no choice. I was too tired to fight back, too heartsick to resist. Still, to relive the life that was now lost to me felt like salt in my wounds.

The new shoes he'd given me clinked musically as I approached and sat across from him.

This is my existence now.

Stories had always been a source of comfort for me. I could control how they'd end. I could watch different emotions dance across Lope's face as I wove a tale for her. The happiness, devastation, and laughter my tales had wrung from her.

"Go on," coaxed the Shadow King.

I imagined it was Lope I was telling my story to. That she was here, listening as carefully as she always had. Her eyes gleaming, like I was telling her the most interesting thing she'd ever heard.

"I don't know my story anymore," I murmured. "A few days ago, I thought my mother had one name, that *I* had the de Bouchillon name. Now . . . my name is the least of what's changed . . ." My voice petered out.

The Shadow King leaned forward, as if prompting me.

"My mother vanished," I began, "and in my attempt to find her, I learned that she was keeping so many secrets from me. That she had been in love with the king. That she had . . . That the king was my *father*. All I wanted was a family, for us to be together and to move past the lies and the secrets, but . . . my father is a wicked man."

When I tried to sum up the whole of my life, it sounded so small, so pathetic, so tangled.

"I don't really know who I am anymore," I said.

My life was *through*. My story had ended. And its ending had been full of lies. Daughter of Mirabelle, daughter of Marisol, daughter of the king, daughter of a monster. Lope's friend, Lope's beloved, then the girl who broke Lope's heart.

Could growth or even *hope* be possible in a place like this?

Glancing up at the monster, my heart hammered quicker, and I balled my fists tight. The Shadow King was the ruler of this place. He'd not done anything to harm us, true, but even looking at him made my skin prickle. I needed to do what he asked. I needed to tell him a story.

"Once upon a time," I said softly. The king of Shadows sat taller, the embers of his eyes twinkling like stars.

"There was a girl who was faithful to me ever since my childhood. She played with me. Laughed at my silly jokes. At night she fought to protect me from the monsters outside my walls. And sometimes, when she found a moment, she liked to write." My throat grew tight. "Her name was Lope, a name she picked because it was a poet's name. She composed beautiful poems, and sometimes she shared them with me. Little gifts of words. And one day I asked her to come away with me to a palace, a wondrous but dangerous place. She forsook everything and nearly gave her life for me. Still, I didn't see it—I didn't see that she loved me."

With every word, it was growing harder to breathe. Harder to see, with the tears fogging my vision.

"How does the story end?" he asked, his voice light with wonder.

I squeezed my eyes shut. Thinking about her, about this girl I loved so, was enough to make me ache. "I broke her heart. And then I was sent here. And she, she's still up there. Which is better, I suppose. But I miss her so. I wish I could apologize to her. I wish she could know that I really do love her."

I shook my head, wishing that were enough to erase my thoughts. They were too painful. "It's not a very good story, I suppose, if it has no ending."

"Tell me another?"

It was a request, not an order, hopeful and gentle. The kindness in his voice made me lift my gaze, only to recoil again. He still looked *fearsome*. Like a man's shadow come to life, but bent at the wrong angles and with piercing white pinpricks for eyes. Something about him, something unnamable, made me unable to look.

"Is it all right if it's a pretend story?" I asked him. "It hurts to talk about my life. Now that it's over." If it was. If I was truly . . . *dead*.

"Any story," he said.

I cleared my throat and closed my eyes. My life was filled with dozens of storybooks that I'd read aloud to Lope at night, cuddled under blankets when the nights grew cold. And of course, the ones I made up for us, to playact or just to see her eyes widen with surprise at each new twist and turn.

I told him the story of the two girls who flew to a foreign land on a giant bird. Of the knight who rescued a princess with nothing but a rose. Of a castle made of snow and the heartbroken prince who lived inside. Story after story, and after a few, the Shadow King stopped taking notes on his scroll and simply sat, his hand against what could have been his cheek, his pinprick eyes ever on me.

After a seventh story, my voice was growing hoarse. I leaned back in the chair, daring myself to look him in his eyes. "All right," I said. "Now I'd like to hear *your* story."

He blinked and lifted his head, as if he'd been woken from a dream. "I have not been asked that before." He bowed his head and wove his long fingers together. "No one has wanted *my* story before."

The sadness in his voice was startling. If he had been a human, I would have reached out and touched his hand. But I was too afraid to do so. Instead, I said, "I imagine the story of a god must be very interesting, sire."

His eyes seemed to shine a little bit brighter.

And he told me his story.

"Long ago, before Earth was made, the gods were. I was the youngest of them. We were given roles to carry out in the creation of the world. One to give it light, one to grow the plants, one to carve out rivers and oceans, on and on.

"The other gods finished their tasks, creating the world,

creating the animals, creating man, and, satisfied with their work, prepared to enter their Kingdom Above to stay and to rest.

"'What can I make for this world?' I asked them.

"The gods scowled and recoiled from me. They found me ugly and frightening. 'You have no place in this world,' they said, 'so we will give you one of your own.' And the gods gave me this world below. It was cold and dark and desolate, even more so than what you see today.

"Though it had been many years since I walked on the earth, I remembered bits of what the world looked like. I remembered the moon and the stars and the sea. Sometimes, on a very rare occasion, a mortal would rip open a door between worlds and speak to me. I relished these moments. Relished the sound of another voice and the chance to hear tales of the world above. I am a god, and so I do what all gods do: I create. I tried to create a world for myself out of the pieces I heard about the world above us, the world you came from. I created animals of my own, and I created my own being, the beings you call Shadows. They are my messengers, and when a door opens between worlds, they slip through and gather stories for me. When they return, they whisper the stories they've captured on the breaths of humans. It is the only way I can hear about the world above. In addition to the seven of you."

For a moment, I pitied him. Forgotten, feared, and then

exiled to this place. Exiled from the gods' own kingdom. But his final words gave me pause.

"You ask your Shadows to give you stories?"

"Yes."

I frowned. A great coldness was seeping through me. "They . . . they *kill* people. They steal the breath from our lungs. They tried to kill me, tried to kill Lope!"

"When your kind die, they go to the Kingdom Above to live with the gods in peace and happiness." He strode to the bookshelves and stroked the books' spines. "I know the lives of your kind. I know the sorrow you endure. Perhaps the end of a life is not as tragic as you may think."

"Yes it is!" I marched over to his side, glancing at the books that held his attention. On the spine of one was the word *Noémie*. On another *Victoire*. On a third *Jordi*.

I gasped, covering my mouth. The beautiful, jewel-colored books around me now meant something so different. Each one a life. Each one a life stolen by Shadows, whispered into the ear of the Shadow King, stored forever in these books.

The bookshelves went up and up and up. I spun to take in the whole room. So many, lining every wall. Looking at all the books and the names on their spines, I thought of how close Lope came to becoming one of these stories. And how her friend Carlos must be here somewhere.

"There's a book I want," I murmured, my heart thundering in my ears. "Show me the one for Carlos. Carlos . . .

de la Vega, I think it was?"

The Shadow King stretched out a hand, pointing to a book shelved high, high above me. It loosened itself off the shelf and plummeted down, right toward me. I yelped and leapt backward, but the king of Shadows intercepted it and then held it out to me. I snatched it from his grasp.

The book was dark blue like a sapphire. *Carlos* was written in gold on the spine and the cover. And I wondered, *What would my book look like?*

I could not let his story go unread. I did not have the chance to know this boy, this boy Lope adored, when he lived on the grounds of my own home.

I opened the cover and stood, reading his story. Every page I turned a moment of his life, passing by. He was an orphan. He had a sister, but she was adopted by another family. He spent a few years training to be a knight before he joined the mercenary company my mother had hired.

And I saw Lope's name.

There was a girl named Lope, Carlos said in his account. *I was assigned to be her mentor, and I chose her as my new family from the start. She was not very good at saying so, but I knew she loved me fiercely. She gave me extra rations. She played chess with ferocity. She listened to me cry over my lost sister. She taught me how to read. She laughed at my jokes. She was my best friend. Out of everything, I miss her most of all, more than sunrises or crickets singing or chocolate religieuses. I hope she lives a long, joyful life.*

Tears dripped onto the pages, and I closed the book fast before I could do it any damage. How I wished I could send this book to Lope. I turned to face the Shadow King, who watched me silently with his head at a tilt.

My hand shook as I held the book aloft. "He was just a boy," I said, my voice trembling, my jaw clenched. "He had so much life to live. He had friends, people who loved him— you *stole* that from him." I pointed at the bookshelves. "From all of them!"

He just . . . stared at me. Saying nothing.

"You want to know so much about humans," I whispered. "Can you even *fathom* what it's like to lose someone you love?"

"I cannot," he said.

"Have you not felt *love*?"

The lights of his eyes dimmed. "I have not."

"Do . . . do you feel nothing when your Shadows die?" I whispered. "I—I've seen them disappear."

"They reform in the darkness. It takes time, but no, they do not die."

"So you don't understand," I whispered. "You don't understand that when you take a person away, you are ripping the heart from the chests of their family, their friends . . . the world, it stops turning, and meaning and light and hope, they just . . . fall away."

"You've told me your story, Ofelia," said the Shadow

King. "Nobody you loved has died."

"*I* am the one who has died," I spat. "Thanks to you, I am trapped here below. I will never ever see sunlight again. Or walk through a field of flowers. Or taste fresh fruit. And—" I had to stop to catch my breath, trying and failing again and again. The most painful loss I could not speak. In my mind, I pictured Lope beside me, offering me a handkerchief, that sweet, concerned little notch in her brow. The words were wrenched from me as more tears fell. "I'll never see my beloved again."

"That isn't so."

I lifted my head, frowning. "Are you mocking my pain?"

"No," said the Shadow King, his voice soft and, somehow, a little mischievous. It felt absurd in the face of what I had just told him, and rage began to bubble up inside me. "Tell me, little Ofelia, what is it called when one human withholds truth from another one?"

"A lie?" I snarled.

"Not that." His eyes sparkled. "A secret?"

I scrubbed away tears with the heel of my hand. "What are you talking about?"

"Before you came to speak with me," he said, "I received a sacrifice." He lifted a paper from his desk. "A beautiful poem." He glanced down at it and read, "'*How gentle is her spirit. How tender is her heart. Her words are like the soft glow of morning light. And her kindness is delicate and sweet, like drops of spring rain . . .*'"

My heart skipped.

"*Lope*," I breathed, her name sounding like a grateful prayer.

"She gave me a message for you," he said. "She intends to come here. She asked you to wait for her."

Hope, bright as the dawn, burned inside my chest, like my heart had finally returned to me.

"She will meet you at the mirror," he said, and without a backward glance, I sprinted out of the study.

25

Lope

Things the darkness has stolen from me:
The colors of the world.
Birdsong.
Childhood.
The laughter of my friend.

Once again, I stood before the golden gates of Le Château Enchanté.

Gravel crunched. An unfamiliar knight approached, staring at me through the golden bars of the fence. The guard's
eyes were pink-rimmed with exhaustion—a look I knew
well.

"You're no noble," he said, just by the look of me.

"I know the registrar," I replied, my head held high.
"Madame Eglantine. She . . . called upon me. She will vouch
for me."

He hummed, looking me up and down—but did not seem to recognize me or see any threat to me. "Wait here," he said.

Through the bars of the fence, I gazed upon this splendid palace, gleaming in the morning light. Dozens of windows on an exterior of red brick and white marble. The roofs made of deep blue slate, crowned with gold shining bright white in the dawn. With the shape of the building, a long hall with two sprawling wings on either side, it was almost as if the palace were reaching for me.

Before, I'd been its guest, its inferior, meekly entering its magnificent halls.

Now it was only another beast to slay.

Eglantine briskly strode down the drive from the palace. She wore a black gown and kept a purple shawl wrapped around her shoulders, just in time for the first winds of autumn. Seeing her, my only connection to this place now, made my body loosen with relief.

Side by side, Eglantine and the guard stood across from me at the gate.

"Do you know this girl?" the guard asked.

The librarian didn't smile, but she bowed her head to me. "Mademoiselle, I'm so pleased you got my letter. Come in, come in."

She waved at the guard, and with a shrug, he signaled to the soldier in the tower to let the gate part. I slipped through as soon as it opened the smallest fraction.

With a bow, I said, "Good morning, madame."

"Good morning, good morning, come this way." She grabbed my forearm and pulled me away, off into some sort of cloakroom, with unpolished boots and riding gloves and shoes to be re-cobbled.

Eglantine shut us in the small room, lit only by the sunshine filtering through the cracks in the door.

"What in the name of the gods are you doing here?" she hissed.

"Your mother," I said, not waiting a moment, "your mother—she should be in the Hall of Illusions. The Shadow King said she'd be there—"

"The Hall of Illusions?" She narrowed her eyes at me. "She's in there? *Alive?* What do you mean?"

"I spoke to the Shadow King," I said breathlessly. "The Hall of Illusions, it serves as a window to the Underworld. And within that window, we will find Ofelia and your mother. They are *both* trapped in the Underworld."

She covered her mouth. "Gods, I'm a fool."

The heartbreak in her voice startled me. "Why?"

"The king said—he said Ofelia had run off with a lover. I thought he meant *you.* He's claimed he's so heartbroken that he won't leave his chambers, and I *believed* him. It seemed like . . . something Ofelia would do."

I forcefully pushed down the anger that had risen at the thought of the king tarnishing Ofelia's name. There were more important things at stake right now.

"That doesn't matter." I gripped her hands. "Thank you for getting me through the gates. Now I need to get into the Hall of Illusions."

She furrowed her brows, deep in thought. "The palace is crawling with guards. There have been Shadows sighted *inside* the palace. Nobles are frantic; five knights have already died—it'll be difficult to sneak in."

Five knights. Five more needless casualties.

And, I thought coldly, five absent places.

When Guillem, the knight I'd rescued in the garden, heard I now wanted to serve as one of the king's knights, he was relieved. He led me into a room lined with gold-plated greaves on the floor, breastplates on the wall, and swords that hung by each of them. From a table, he chose a helmet and held it up in front of my face. "Looks about the right size."

He helped me into both legs of my greaves. It took me a moment to adjust to the weight; back at the manor, we rarely wore metal armor like this, except for the occasional breastplate. Fighting a Shadow required speed above all else, and while this heavy golden armor looked beautiful, it would slow me significantly. Next, he fit me into the breastplate and gauntlets, and after fastening them all into place, like bolting me inside some metal coffin, he placed the helm over my head. Its chin jutted out, the gap between my neck and the helm just enough that I had some empty space to breathe, as there was no mouth on the mask. I saw the world through the slits of the mask and realized that for now, no one could see the scar along my cheek. No one could recognize me. I was invisible.

Best of all, once again, I had a beautiful, shining sword at my hip.

As I made my way toward the Hall of Illusions, the palace was buzzing with activity, preparing for a fête as though nothing had changed. Servants carried vases of flowers the size of dinner plates, gilded instruments, and trays heaped with white cakes. Far down another corridor, servants' gossip accompanied the tuning of the instruments.

It was chaos. I was nearly to the hall now, but how could I sneak in with so many witnesses?

The door at the end of the hall opened, and the king emerged, clothed in blinding white with a long fur cape trailing behind him. Two young women in white dresses carried the train of his cloak, their gazes lowered and their cheeks rosy. I stepped quickly to the side of the hallway, standing at attention.

Another soldier on the other side of the hall saluted as the king passed.

With each confident step, His Majesty grew closer to me.

There were deep wrinkles around his eyes and mouth now, as if he'd aged thirty years in just a few days—not even the powder he now wore on his face could conceal them. I could not help but imagine this was some sort of divine retribution. If the Shadow King had blessed him with youth, perhaps he could curse him just as easily.

King Léo's eyes, the eyes he gave Ofelia, fell on me. A shiver darted down my back. Sweat gathered on my neck beneath the heavy armor.

Salute, damn it, I begged myself. *He's not looking at you. He doesn't know who you are.*

But he *did*, I could feel it. His agelessness, the way he so easily hid the truth of the palace and its construction, his door to the Underworld . . . What other dark powers did he have? Could he see the contents of my heart, or hear my vicious thoughts?

I snapped into a salute, my gaze upon him.

May you rot, I thought. *May you decay. May vermin consume you.*

He turned his face from me and stared ahead. It was so easy for him to pass, to stroll right by me, as if I didn't loathe him more than any creature on this earth. More than any Shadow.

My hand trembled against my sword.

I could plunge it through his back.

It would be so easy.

But then what? A dead king would bring me no closer to the girl I'd lost. The girl I loved.

When the last inch of his white cape slipped around the

corner, I slackened with relief.

After he left, I ducked around the corner and strode down the corridor, left and right and left, to the Hall of Illusions. Courtiers did not even glance at me as I passed on the fringes of the hallways, all of them clothed in white just like the king had asked.

I approached the corridor wherein was housed the Hall of Illusions. To my surprise, there was someone standing there, a woman shouting at the golden-armored knight before her. She had a book pressed to her chest.

Eglantine.

"I'm here on important research for the king!" she insisted.

"Madame, the king made his wishes very clear. No one is to enter the hall."

"But—but he means to start restorations on it, and he requested a list of artists to commission, and I have a book of names right here!" she insisted, holding up her book. "I only mean to take some notes!"

"Shouldn't you be preparing for the fête?" he asked.

Eglantine opened her mouth, but I neared the two and interrupted her, saying, "Soldier, I've just left my post at the king's hallway and was instructed to come here next. I was told you're being sent to guard the ballroom with the others." When he said nothing, I thought of Ofelia, and how, when she was in doubt, she would add more details to her story. "I'm a new recruit. Came from the countryside. Trained in special combat with Shadows. I hear they are a particular problem in this part of the palace, along with strange noises. Is that true?"

"Yes." The soldier's voice quavered.

"I'll take it from here." I saluted the knight and, after a beat, he saluted me and then left.

"Mademoiselle . . . ?" murmured Eglantine.

I took one cursory sweep of the corridor—no onlookers, no Shadows—and swept the helmet off my head. Shaking out the hair that had begun to stick to my face, I felt I could finally breathe for the first time in hours.

Eglantine beamed at me. "Excellent work."

"Let's hurry."

The two of us slipped through the double doors. I set my helmet aside on the parquet and frowned at the room before us—dark and strangely empty. The walls here were more like that of a cavern than those of a palace. Stepping forward a little farther, I could see the vast wall of mirrors—and a pale figure standing in the glass.

I gasped and put a hand to my sword, but Eglantine raced past me, pressing her hands to the glass.

"Maman!" she cried.

The woman standing before Eglantine in the mirror looked much like her but younger, with her dark blond hair in a long plait. She, too, wore spectacles, and several golden bracelets on her wrists.

"You're so beautiful," said the woman—Sagesse. Her voice caught with tears as she pressed her hands against her daughter's, as though she could push herself through the glass to her.

Then, in the panel of a mirror to her right, a faint shape appeared. Its edges grew more defined as the silhouette grew closer and closer, and then I saw her, the light in her eyes, the joyful tears, the bright smile she wore just for me, and I had never felt such an equal blend of agony and joy all at once. "Ofelia," I gasped.

Ofelia, Ofelia, my beautiful one, my sunlit girl, trapped forever in a world of monsters and darkness.

Had I only seen her yesterday? It felt like an eternity had passed. I drank her in like I was dying of thirst.

Her fingertips pressed against the glass, pressed up where mine were. Her chest heaved as if she had been running. I searched her for any scrapes or bruises, but apart from her cheeks, red and shining with tears, she looked the same as she had when we'd parted. I longed to brush her cheeks dry, to kiss her face until she'd cry no more.

"I love you," I said, declared, vowed, promised, pledged. The words that had echoed in my heart for years finally rang out like bells celebrating a homecoming.

"I love you so much," she said, the most beautiful refrain to the most beautiful song. Her fingers caressed the glass. "And I'm so sorry. Lope, I'm so sorry. I've been awful to you.

Horrid and selfish. I should never have been so thoughtless toward you. I never should have doubted you. I should have listened to you." She leaned her forehead against the glass, sniffling. "You were right about everything. I'm a fool. And a worse fool for how I've treated you for all these years. Like you were only a servant. You're not, Lope, you're an artist and a hero and my dearest friend, and anything else you want to be. You're—you're everything to me. And I . . . I shouldn't have read your poems, either. I'm so sorry."

My sweet, gentle girl. I never should have doubted her kindness. Not even this wretched palace could tarnish her golden heart. "I forgive you. Of course I forgive you." I touched my brow to the mirror, too, and for a moment imagined it was just the two of us there, without Eglantine or Sagesse. That there wasn't a sheet of glass between us. That I could feel her warm skin against mine.

"I'm going to rescue you," I said, "and when I do, I'll write a hundred poems for you. For your eyes alone."

She drew back, and my heart dropped at the alarm in her face.

"You mustn't come here." Her voice was choked and meek. "You cannot come for me. You must run; get as far from this place as you can, before the king hurts you—"

"I don't care," I said. "I'll fight. I'll fight for you, and I'll win. I won't stop until you're safe."

"Please. Please, I couldn't bear it if something happened to you. You were right. The palace is dangerous. The king even more so. *Please*, Lope." Her forefinger stroked the glass, right over my cheek. Her eyes shimmered with tears. "You spent your whole life saving me. Let me save you. Just this once."

"And I've spent my whole life obeying orders," I said. "No longer. I'm coming for you. No matter what it takes."

She didn't speak. Her long lashes fluttered, dripping more tears on her cheeks. Her lip trembled. "All right," she whispered. "Let me know what I can do to help."

"You intend to come below?"

The voice was Sagesse's, acerbic and surprised. Her brows were raised as if in a challenge.

"Yes," I said.

"Lope," said Ofelia, "your theories were correct—there *is* a door in the gardens. That strange, isolated doorway we saw near the bosquets of the gods. But it is locked behind a fence, and when I was taken there, the king had his guards all about."

"I tried to break in once before. The guards intercepted me, I—"

"You could create your *own* door," said Sagesse.

My heart leapt. "But—the king hired you for your power to speak with the gods," I said. "I don't have the gift that you do."

"There is only a ritual to be performed. Anyone can do it, if they know how. Yes, it would be *helpful* if you had some prior fortune in communicating with the gods—"

"But you have!" said Ofelia. "The Shadow King, he knows you. He has heard your prayers. He has read your poetry."

She was right. I *had* bent the ear of a god.

"When we open this door," I asked, "will Shadows come through?"

"Yes," Ofelia and Sagesse said in one voice. My throat tightened. Ofelia knew these doors very well. It was thanks to the king that she'd been banished through one.

Sagesse continued, "When you make this door, when the Shadow King welcomes you, he will guarantee safety only for the person who opens the door and the person he'd bargained with. This is why Léo may open the door unharmed. And why I was not attacked by the Shadows."

Eglantine drew closer to the mirror, her fingers trembling. "If we do this, if we open this door, can we let you through?"

Sagesse simply shook her head. "I cannot say. But it's our only chance."

"There must be some way for us to help you," I said. "The King Below—he likes bargains?"

"Yes."

"Good. Then I'll make one with him. Something good enough that he'll free the lot of you."

Sagesse pressed her lips into a thin line. "I admire your certainty, child. But bending the will of a god is no easy task. First, the door." She looked back at her daughter, the first glimpse of warmth appearing in her eyes. "Lope will need your help, Eglantine. It's better to have a second person close at hand. You'll need to be in a dark place where you can concentrate. Light a candle to help attract the attention of the Shadow King. Make a line on the ground where you want the door to be—a line in your own blood. And the person who creates the door, they must prepare something to sacrifice. Something cherished. A body part or some sort of ability will do, as long as it's deeply precious. Place a symbol of the sacrifice on the line of blood."

Ofelia's hand covered her mouth. She was growing quite pale.

Sagesse nodded. "King Léo, for instance, gave up his dancing."

Any sacrifice, I'd make. I'd do it for her. "What next?" I asked.

"Write down an oath to the Shadow King, that in exchange for passage into his world, you'll give him whatever you've promised him. Mark it with the blood of the person who will enter the Underworld and burn the note. Speak to the king of Shadows and beg him to let you come here." Her hand curled into a fist. "I will speak to him here, too, to encourage him to let you in."

"I'll do it," interjected Ofelia, squaring her shoulders. "I've told him about Lope. About our story. And I want to help you, even in the smallest way."

My stomach turned at the thought of her speaking to some monster on my behalf, but the conviction in her eyes was unshakable. She smiled at me. My heart fluttered.

"Lope," she said, her eyes never falling from mine, "there's something else I want you to know."

Whisper to me everything;
Whisper me the world.
Let's lie side by side like always
And tell me every story of your heart!

"The Shadows," she continued, "they act as messengers for the Shadow King. It's not just breaths they steal. They take stories." She ran her lip under her teeth. "The stories are bound into books. And I read Carlos's book. He loved you, Lope. And he knew that you loved him, too."

An invisible blow beat against my chest, like a Shadow knocking me down. The ache of missing him burned in my stomach. I could not make sense of the despair and the relief warring through me. His voice, his own words, but in some storybook, made at the behest of a monster-king.

I wished he were here with me. I wished he could have known Ofelia as I did. I wished he could have known *me* as I was now.

But I had not loved Carlos in vain. Nor would I love Ofelia in vain.

This time, I would save my loved one. I'd save her from the dark, faraway grasp of the Underworld.

"Thank you," I said.

"Please be careful," she whispered.

A warm fire was beginning to kindle in my chest. She loved me. She'd said it, and it was true.

I was worth being loved.

"I'll be with you soon," I vowed.

She nodded. "I know you will."

To the king, the best place for a door to the Underworld was a garden. A garden where no one could enter.

For Eglantine and myself, we chose a room that no one cared to enter.

The courtiers cared more for the king and his parties than for books. So the library became our haven.

We shut and locked the tall doors, moved aside tables, and cleared a spot on the wooden floor between two bookshelves in the far reaches of the room. With Eglantine's help, I unfastened myself from the metal trap of the armor encasing me, and, in my waistcoat, chemise, and breeches, finally felt like myself again. The boots I kept, sturdy leather and easy to run in, except for the protective metal plates atop.

Eglantine's hands trembled as she placed a candlestick on the floor before us.

"I've never . . . I've never successfully spoken with the

Shadow King before," she whispered. As if he could hear us now. Perhaps he could.

When I looked at her, Eglantine's gaze was miles off into the distance. "For years I searched for Mother. I hoped for so long that she was alive. And all this time, she was so close to me. Just behind a door." She raised her head, a long silver-blond coil of hair falling before her dark eyes. "I'm so close."

I carefully touched her arm. "I intend to go alone, Eglantine."

She frowned. "What? No, not when my mother is so near!"

"We do not know what it will be like below. The presence of Shadows is guaranteed. Even if the Shadow King has promised us safe passage . . . I think it is wise if you stay behind. In case something should happen. I am fast, and more importantly, I have years of experience with the Shadows."

She shut her eyes, exhaling, her shoulders drooping in defeat. "Promise me you'll bring me my mother?"

I pressed my fist to my heart. "I promise."

"Good." She nodded. "Then let's create a door. First, we'll need a line of your blood."

I drew my sword and gave a little swipe across my ring fingertip. I winced at the pain and then pressed my hand to the floor, painting a streak of red across the wood.

"Have you thought about what you mean to sacrifice?" she asked.

How casual it seemed. How simple.

At first, I thought to give up an eye or my tongue. Both of these I relied on to keep those I loved safe. I thought, too, of giving up my poetry. But if I did that, if I saw Ofelia again, I'd scarcely be able to breathe. My words were how I understood the world. All of existence would become gray. Meaningless. And none of it would be for me.

There was another ability of mine. One I never asked for but was assigned, just because of my birth. But something I deeply cherished, nonetheless.

My fighting. I could give him an arm, or my hand, or—I stopped myself. The king had given up his dancing, yes. But he bore no evidence of any sacrifice, not even a scratch or a missing finger.

I laid my sword in the line of blood.

"Take my ability to fight," I said.

Eglantine frowned. "Are you sure that's wise?"

No. No, I wasn't sure. I didn't know how I could shield Ofelia from harm without my skills, my training. I didn't know who I'd be without it.

"Even if the Shadows disobey, even if they pursue me, I still have my speed," I said. "I can run for my life if I must." My fingers balled into fists against the knees of my breeches. "But I'll not leave until I've made my deal with the King Below."

She nodded slowly. "Very well." Procuring a quill, ink, and paper, she said, "I assume you can write, if you named yourself after a poet."

"Yes."

"Write the first promise, the one that opens the door. Mark it with your blood, like Mother said."

I did, and with my fingertip bleeding still, I slid the drop of blood beneath my name like a flourish.

Eglantine read over the letter to herself, nodded, and then took a deep breath.

"I hope this works," she admitted.

I grimaced. "Me too."

In a slow, soothing voice, like reciting a lullaby, I read the words of my letter.

Something prickled within me, the same feeling as if I were being watched. A chill danced across my back. The flame of the candle waved back and forth. Eglantine gasped.

"Please," I said, "answer our call."

The sword rattled against the wooden floor. Gooseflesh crept up my arms.

I set the corner of the paper in the flame, and it was consumed in a bright flash that soared to the ceiling, fire and smoke pluming into the air, blinding my vision. I blinked, and a dark figure loomed amid the white smoke. I gasped, reaching for the sword—but it was gone. Instead, I threw my arm in front of Eglantine.

But it wasn't a Shadow. It wasn't a monster at all.

It was a door. Shining black like ebony, tall and pointed at the top. It was encrusted with silver spirals and delicately spotted with drops of ruby-like red stars.

"You did it," whispered Eglantine.

My pulse bounded. Yes. Yes, I'd done it, and now I was one step closer to Ofelia. One step closer to the happy ending of our story.

"When I open it," I said, "Shadows will come out."

"They'll not harm us, she said—"

"No, they won't." I pointed behind us to the library doors. "But they'll escape into the palace. They'll look for someone to kill." Cold lanced at my heart and stiffened my muscles. The king's door had released Shadows into the world. Perhaps the same Shadows I'd fought back at the manor. And now I would do what he had done. Sending more beasts into the world. Into a building filled with innocents.

I gritted my teeth and pulled myself to my feet. "Close the door fast behind me," I muttered. "Let as few as possible come through."

"I'll do my best."

I helped her stand, and her hand squeezed against my arm.

"I'll be at the door, waiting for your return," she said. "Good fortune to you, Lope de la Rosa."

I bowed to her. She startled. No one had done that before, I supposed; not to her. She was from no great family. But her help, her companionship, her guidance—it was more noble than any of the courtiers here.

Slowly, tremulously, I curled my hand around the door's handle.

26

Lope

Those who are brave
Fight past their limit;
Those who are brave
Press on through the final tears they have to shed.

With one sharp pull, the door was open. There was the horrible, grating, keening sound of Shadows as they pushed past us like storm winds. My head was spinning, my legs were trembling, but every second I lingered in the doorway, I let another Shadow through.

I lunged through the door and heard Eglantine slam it shut behind me. I whirled on my heel, and there it was, closed, with a shining golden doorknob. And behind me, the Underworld lay beyond—where there was only blackness, thicker than darkness, pure *nothing*.

Something slithered around my feet. I gasped and gaped

down at a dozen Shadows, their claws clutching at the fabric of my breeches. My hand flew to my hip—but my sword was not there.

I turned back to the monsters, crawling, grasping, but not yet opening their mouths. Not yet trying to kill. Fear paralyzed me. I'd never felt so useless before. So naked. Without a sword, who was I? If not a knight, who was I?

I moved to bat them away with a blow of my arm—I was trained to fight, even without my sword—but my arms were slow, useless. Like they wouldn't obey me.

It was true then. All of my combat skills—gone.

Still the Shadows undulated around my feet. I shut my eyes and listened to my haggard breaths and my pounding heart.

You're doing this for her, I chanted. *Whatever it takes, it'll be worth it for her.*

Opening my eyes again, I glanced about me, my hands fisted so that I would have the fortitude not to look at the monsters.

My eyes were growing accustomed to the darkness. I stood atop a tall spiral staircase. Below, plains and hills of black grass extended all around me, and even the moon looked desolate, casting long white beams over an inky ocean below. It was a strange moon, glowing and misshapen. A crystal. More crystals, bright purple, gleamed in the dark expanse above the water. This world was only an echo of the one above. A darker, sadder one.

Ofelia. Find Ofelia.

My feet slowly trudged forward, down the stairs, pushing through the swamp of creatures surrounding me. They clung to me still, following my every step.

"Leave me," I spat.

They hissed, that awful sound that made me shudder in spite of myself, but followed me still.

"Fine," I muttered. "This is your world, isn't it? If you're to follow me, can you at least take me to Ofelia?"

The Shadows didn't move. I wasn't their master, I supposed.

Their master. What had Ofelia said?

That the Shadows were messengers for the Shadow King.

I needed to find him first if I intended to bargain for Ofelia. If I could send him a message, I could follow his creatures, his heralds, right to him.

"I have a message to be delivered to the king of Shadows," I told the crowd gathered all around me.

They did not so much as whisper.

I sighed, dropping my hands to my sides. "Tell him Lope de la Rosa wishes to have an audience with him."

Silence, still. If they didn't want a message, what did they want?

Stories, Ofelia had said. They didn't just take breath, they took stories.

I had no strength, but I had my poetry still.

I did not memorize my poems, but after so many nights on the wall, watching, listening to the night, doing nothing but waiting for monsters, I'd gotten quite good at creating new poems and then letting them die in my memory. Verses and words, detached, disjointed, sewn back together in my head just because they sounded lovely as a whole.

I wasn't a real poet, in my mind, not like the poet I named myself after or any of the greats. Meter and rhyme took effort for me. But poetry was, at its core, playing with words. Like how Ofelia wove her stories, adding twists and turns, new characters and new surprises. Ideas to be strung together like pearls side by side on a strand. I couldn't explain how I knew the way they fit together. Something deep in my chest told me so.

I closed my eyes and pretended to be back on the wall. Thinking moony thoughts of Ofelia, and Carlos saying, *You're dreaming of someone, aren't you?*

Yes. Yes, I was always thinking of her.

"*A girl in love,*" I whispered.

"*She sings a song no one will hear,*
She bears a wound no one will see.
She places her neck upon an altar
And draws the knife herself.
She pleads to the gods for mercy,

She pleads to the skies for courage,
A thousand Shadows she battles a night,
And none compares with the monster of her mind,
Drawing her to what she cannot have."

My voice shook. My poem wasn't done. My story wasn't through.

"No more.
She will brave your monsters,
Your Shadows,
Your claws,
And she will proclaim the love
She's kept silent for far too long."

Upon opening my eyes, wet with tears, I found that the Shadows had retreated a few paces, watching with their empty faces, tilted as if to hear me better. Then, like leaves swept up by a gust of wind, they moved together in one wave, winding through the tall grass. They streamed forward, down the steps, in the direction of the moon—east, then, if there was an east here.

I chased after them, my feet thankfully still nimble despite the sacrifice I'd made.

The farther I ran, the more I could see before me. The beam of moonlight ahead disguised a tall white spire on a hill. A castle of sorts, as high as Le Château was wide. It looked like a knife, piercing the blackness of night above.

The Shadows led me to the castle, which was just as dark and filled with Shadows as the rest of this meager excuse of a world. The other monsters turned their faceless heads toward me but did not move, did not lunge, did not try to kill me. Even so, with each Shadow I saw, I remembered my training. I remembered Carlos. I remembered how close to dying I had been.

If not for Ofelia.

"Take me to her," I whispered, praying, not to any gods but to these monsters below. I prayed that she would not be harmed. That in the hour since I'd seen her in the mirror, she looked the same, that her heart still beat.

I would rescue her. This would all be over soon.

The darkness of the castle faded as I climbed a winding staircase. Brilliant white moonlight streamed in from a great gap in the castle walls, like it'd been blown away by cannon fire. Something in the sky caught my eye—large, puffy clouds, floating in the air, where I was certain there'd been none before. They shone brightly, even where they did not rest in moonlight. Like clusters of stars.

"Lope!"

My heart seemed to leap out of my chest. I whipped toward the sound, the dearest sound in the world. At the top of this great white set of stairs stood my love, resplendent in the moonlight that crowned her auburn hair with silver. Her tears sparkled like crystals. Her smile shone down upon me, and I would have rested there forever, if not for the ache in my chest begging me to go to her.

"Ofelia."

It was only a whisper, only an exhausted, exhilarated little murmur of delight. Part of me couldn't believe she was really here. Or that she'd want me.

But now she was racing down the stairs toward me.

I bounded toward her, letting Shadows slip past, parting around us.

We met on the landing of the stairs, and she threw her arms around me and—

And I kissed her.

I kissed her.

I kissed her.

My head spun. I pulled back and looked into her eyes, at the fondness there. After everything, fool that I was, I was still breathless at the thought that she cared for me, too.

Then Ofelia's hands cupped my face, drawing me closer still.

In a moment to breathe, she whispered, "Don't let go," and so I didn't.

Her lips brushed my scar. Her fingers tucked a long, errant curl behind my ear, and her lips met mine again, sweeter and more fervent than any poem I could try to write.

Give me a thousand more moments like this. Give me a thousand words to try to piece together the wonder of having her in my arms, feeling her heart crash against mine, her fingers clutching my waist.

"What's this?" said a strange, groaning voice.

Every bit of my soldier's instincts flooded into me, and in a flash, I stepped in front of Ofelia and reached for the sword at my hip. My hand grasped at empty air, and my heart dropped at the reminder.

Standing at the top of the stairs was the Shadow King, just as I had seen him in the library. But what I thought before were horns were actually the golden spikes of a thin crown. And here, face-to-face, his eyes blazed like two white flames. He was flanked at either side by Eglantine's mother and Mirabelle de Bouchillon. More prisoners of this Shadow King.

"Lope de la Rosa," he said, drawling my name, as if he savored every syllable. "My favorite poet. Welcome to my kingdom."

He, who had created the Shadows. Who had bargained with Léo. Who accepted *lives* as payment. I imagined plunging my sword into his chest and escaping with Ofelia, with everyone. Fighting had always been my solution before. But now I was powerless. Except for my words. Except for my poetry.

"Release Ofelia," I demanded. "Release everyone!"

I blinked, and the monster now stood an inch away from

us, its neck craned so that the void of its face was close to mine. It had the same hoarse, shuddering breath as the Shadows. Ofelia yelped and clung to me.

"What did you do, Ofelia, when you greeted this girl? Your mouths touched."

There was a moment of silence.

Ofelia glanced back at me, her round face pleasantly pink with a blush. "We kissed, Your Majesty. It's how we show affection to the person we love most in the world. And you see, this girl . . . she's the girl I love most."

Her fingers wove with mine. I felt as if my heart might fly out of my chest and back to the world above.

"Ah," said the monster, understanding something. "You love each other very much, then."

"Yes," we said in one voice. We smiled. For a moment or two, I forgot that I was in another world, a world without light. I had everything I needed, with her hand in mine.

Almost.

"I've come here to make a deal with you," I told the Shadow King. "I want to take Ofelia and her mother back above." I glanced over his shoulder, spying Eglantine's mother as she and Ofelia's mother both descended the stairs. "I intend to take Sagesse with me, too."

"One can be more easily arranged than the other," said the Shadow King, slow and thoughtful. He pointed a long finger at Sagesse. "I have preserved all the king's sacrifices. Time does not march forward here. But should Sagesse return to the world above, all the years gone from her time would return to her. She would be, I believe, eighty-three years old."

Sagesse's face remained stony; undeterred.

"On the other hand," said the king, "Ofelia and Marisol would age only by a few days. Nothing noticeable at all." His long fingers curled into a fist. "Even so, you would have to offer me a rare prize indeed in exchange for such a treasure."

"What kind of prize?" I asked.

"For a chance at immortality, for an everlasting throne, King Léo was willing to trade away the people he loved most in this world."

"I have no one left," I said. "You already possess the one I love more than anything."

Ofelia wrapped her arms around my middle and pressed her cheek against my heart. Like when we used to rest against each other in the manor's gardens. Like things were normal, even just a little bit.

"I gave you my power to fight so that I could come here," I told him. "What more do you want from me?"

Ofelia lurched in my grip, looking up at me with wide eyes. "What?!"

I nodded and brushed a curl from her forehead. "I gave him my sword and my ability to wield it. But for you I'd give anything. Do anything. Don't you see? I've reached into the Underworld for you."

"I know." She blinked, tears sparkling against her lashes. "But the world is dangerous, Lope, and now you must live in it defenseless?"

"I do not live in it at all if you're not there," I whispered. My hand cupped against her cheek. "Soon we'll be together, back in the daylight, and we'll find a place where we no longer have to fear monsters or men. I won't need a sword anymore."

She nodded, chewing on her lip. She didn't quite believe me.

"What, then, will you give me?" asked the Shadow King. "It must be a treasure equal to three souls."

Before, he'd asked for lives. And King Léo happily provided, but . . .

The king.

My eyes widened. "I'll give you King Léo. The prideful man who thinks he can use you like some servant."

Sagesse grinned wickedly. Ofelia's mother gasped.

The Shadow King cocked his head at me, and though I couldn't read the white flames of his eyes, there was something satisfied in them at my offering. Something vindictively pleased.

"That seems a suitable trade." He extended his hand. "If you bring me King Léo alive, I will in turn allow you to take three sacrifices to the world above. Are we agreed?"

Ofelia tugged on my sleeve. Worry wrinkled her brow.

"How will you do it?" she whispered. "He's a *king*. He's surrounded by guards. He's untouchable."

I wished to look at her forever.

My thumb brushed against her cheek. It grew warm under my touch.

She loved me. This, *this* was what it meant to be happy.

I would have done anything to keep her forever.

"I may not have a sword," I said, "but I'm clever. I infiltrated the palace to find you today." I swept my fingertip against the bridge of her nose and delighted at how it made her smile. "Nothing will be impossible for us."

Ofelia stood on her toes and kissed me again. My head swirled and my heart batted and I didn't want anything else in the world, just her arms fastened around my middle forever.

Sagesse approached me, her head held high like a queen's. She laid a hand against my arm. After decades in the Below, I imagined that her skin would be cold. But it was as warm as anyone's.

She slipped a gold bracelet off her arm and onto mine. "Give this to my daughter until I see her again . . . in case . . . in case your mission should prove too great," she said. The seer turned back toward the Shadow King. "Sire, you were able to create a mirror that showed the king this world. I humbly ask that you make one more mirror, a smaller one, so that my daughter can see me when she pleases."

He cocked his head. "What will you give me for it?"

Ofelia balled her fists. "Sagesse has given you everything already," she snapped. "Her stories, her life, her years. All she wants is a way to see her daughter more. Is that so horrible? Can't you be generous, just for once?"

"I can be," he said, almost defensively. "But, dear Ofelia, what good is a bargain of mine if I give treasures away to mortals with no price?"

"It's something humans do," she replied. The fearlessness in her voice was like a perfect, harmonizing note within me. It made my blood sing with delight. "Humans give without asking for anything in return."

"Why?" asked the monster.

"Kindness," she replied. As if it was a concept this beast should understand. Ofelia swept Sagesse's hands in hers. "Please, sire. You are powerful. You've created this palace and the moon and those clouds. It would be easy for you to make such a trinket for Sagesse."

The Shadow King pulled his hand close to his heart, tightening his grasp into a fist. Then, when he unfurled his long fingers, two silver mirrors lay within, each about the size of my hand, with small, thin handles. He offered them to Sagesse.

She took them in her hands and curtsied before the monster. "Thank you, sire."

"That was very kind," Ofelia noted.

"Creating mirrors is a simple thing." His neck twisted, his head bending toward me. His eyes, two white stars, focused unwaveringly on mine.

Sagesse pressed one of the little hand mirrors into my grasp. "Please give this to Eglantine," she said. Her eyes crinkled behind her spectacles. "I look forward to seeing her again."

"You will," I vowed, and kept the mirror firmly in my left hand. With my right hand, I grasped the hand of the Shadow King.

"Our bargain is struck," I said.

He bent low, his cold voice slithering into my ear. "If you try to trick or betray me . . . there will be punishment."

I blinked, and suddenly I was pressed up against the door through which I'd entered this world. The castle was gone, the Shadows were gone, Sagesse and Mirabelle and Ofelia— all back in that castle, hidden in the moonbeam far beyond where I could see.

Part of me wished I had been given the chance to wish Ofelia farewell.

But perhaps this was better. After all, this was no goodbye.

We'd be together—just as soon as I captured the king.

27

Lope

How beautiful the song of my blade through the air!
How lovely it is to accompany such music.
How sweet to be the hand that can hold the pen
That can change a page to a poem.

I stumbled out of the darkness, into the library, and shut the door behind me—thankfully, no Shadows had followed me. Steps hurried toward me, clacking against the parquet until Eglantine stood in front of me.

"Are you all right?" she asked breathlessly. She frowned. "Where is my mother? And Ofelia?"

"I made a bargain with the Shadow King," I said. "I'll not get what I bargained for until I've delivered what I owe him." I rested against the door, my chest heaving, and held out the mirror to her. "As for your mother, you have this to speak with her."

Eglantine snatched the mirror, looking into it with a furrowed brow.

"Be warned. The people in the Underworld are trapped in time. If they return above, they'll age the years they spent below. And your mother—she could grow so old to be past her living years." I noticed the bracelet on my wrist and remembered. I tugged it off my arm and held it out for her. "She wanted you to have this, too. To remember her by."

Eglantine slipped on the bracelet and cradled the mirror in her hands. "Mother!" she said, her voice cracked and desperate. "Mother, are you there?!"

"Yes, love, yes."

The voice, the same one I'd heard minutes ago, came from the mirror. Craning my neck, I could see Sagesse's face in the little oval of perfect glass. It was just like the Hall of Illusions, in miniature.

"I will be reunited with you soon, my love," said Sagesse, "if you help Lope succeed in her task."

Eglantine glanced at me, her forehead furrowed. "What did you offer the king of Shadows for Ofelia's and my mother's freedom?"

I tightened my fists at my sides. "I will give him King Léo. Alive."

Eglantine's mouth hung open. "You—you're not serious."

"She is," said Sagesse.

Eglantine gaped at her mother's reflection. "How in the

name of the bloody Underworld are we supposed to capture the king and send him below?!"

"Where is your door located? The one to the Underworld?"

"It's in the palace library," I said.

Sagesse hummed a thoughtful tone. "Léo's not the literary type. You need to think of something that will bring him into the library."

I wracked my brain to think of what could bait a king. He had everything he wanted and more. Even so, he wasn't content. He was always throwing parties. Always surrounded by his courtiers. Telling them stories, telling them lies about his godliness. It was their love he wanted more than anything. Their attention. Their worship.

"Where is the king now?" I asked Eglantine.

"At his fête." She lifted a finger, remembering. "You were inside the door for about three days. He claims the party is to 'lift his spirits' after his beloved daughter vanished."

"Then we shall have to remind him that I'm right where he left me!"

I glanced down at the mirror. Only half of Sagesse's face showed now, and on the left portion of the silver mirror, Ofelia had squished herself into view. "You could use me! Use my voice!"

"Use this mirror, you mean?"

"Yes!" Her one visible eye sparkled with mischief. "He

wants everyone to believe he's perfect, untouchable, absolutely blessed. He tried so hard to silence any rumors about the Hall of Illusions or the Shadows or—"

"What happened to you," I said. "He told the court you had run away with me."

Ofelia huffed. "The man is an *ass*."

My heart sang, hearing her curse.

Her eyes creased in the corners with a smile. "Well, if I've run away, I'm about to give my father a pleasant surprise."

Eglantine was hidden away in the library, lying in wait, holding on to the mirror. I, meanwhile, marched straight toward the ballroom, once more dressed in the guise of a palace guard. All around me, swanlike courtiers swam past, attired all in white for another night of parties.

At the ballroom doors, I stood before a gold-clad knight and bowed before him.

"I have . . . surprising news that must be relayed to the king," I said, doing my best to lace my voice with the utmost gravity. "Lady Ofelia has returned to the palace."

The knight lowered his head, his helm shielding me from any sign of emotion on his face. But his voice betrayed him, stunned and urgent. "What? How? Where is she?"

"She's closed herself into the library. She says she won't come out until the king comes to visit her."

The knight huffed a loud sigh. "Take me to her, then."

My heart skipped. That wasn't our plan. "Well—can you not fetch the king? She won't leave the library until she gets what she wants. I've tried—"

"I'll not go disrupting the king on the merits of rumors alone."

Very well. I'd let them follow me, but no matter what, I could not open the door for the knight.

With all the other courtiers gone into the fête, the corridors were empty. I stopped in front of the double doors of the library, gesturing to them. The knight leaned forward and jiggled the golden door handle but found the doors would not budge.

"Father?" called Ofelia from within. The sound of her voice rekindled the flame in me that fueled my every step. "Father, is that you?"

The knight's eyes widened behind the visor. "No, Your Highness. I'm Edouard, a knight serving His Majesty—"

"I shall not open this door until my father comes to see me," she snapped. The authority with which she spoke was truly remarkable.

"I'll try to calm her down," I told the knight. "Will you please send for the king?"

The knight nodded, defeated, and raced toward the ballroom.

I sighed, leaning against the door. "They're gone."

"Good." From within the library, I could hear Ofelia sigh.

"I confess I'll be glad when all this adventuring is over. I once longed to be the hero of a story, but I never imagined it would be so exhausting," she admitted. Then her voice turned more somber. "I'm sorry for all of this. If I hadn't dragged you to Le Château to begin with—"

"You gave me the greatest adventure of my life," I told her. "I never thought I'd see *any* of the world beyond the manor."

"You deserve the world, Lope."

I believed her.

After all we'd endured, after proving how capable and clever and fierce we were, we deserved to call the world ours.

"We can go see it together," I said. "Somewhere peaceful. A valley, perhaps. A cottage tucked in a meadow."

Her light, pretty laugh rang out. "Well, then, maybe I have enough energy left in me for another adventure or two. If you're there with me."

"It's where I'll always be." I smiled now, thinking of how she tried to send me away, how we thought we could ever be parted. No. We were bound together, and not just by the countess or our shared birthday or our love of literature. We would never be separated again. I vowed it.

Footsteps sounded at the end of the corridor. One set, by the sound of it.

The king had come alone.

My pulse quickened, and my stomach seemed to somersault into my throat. This was it. I was now to trap the king.

Thoughts whirred in my head. When I succeeded, when Ofelia and I were together again and back in the world above, what excuse would we give as to the disappearance of the king?

It did not matter. I did not care who would ask for his whereabouts. I'd take Ofelia far from this wretched palace.

His Majesty strode down the corridor, stopping in front of me. He was dressed all in gold, with his startlingly white hair draped artfully over his shoulders. Up close, the new lines around his eyes and his mouth were all the more pronounced. There were little age spots on his forehead, poorly covered up by powder.

"A soldier said he heard my daughter calling for me in the library," said the king.

"Yes, Father," Ofelia cried from behind the door.

The king's pupils shrank. The color drained from his face. He looked at me and then at the door. He lunged for the door handle, tugging at it with both hands, but the door did not yield. His cheeks growing redder and redder with exertion, the king glared at me over his shoulder.

"You're dismissed," he said.

"No!"

He flinched at Ofelia's command. I bit down on my lip to hold back my smile.

"I'll let you in, Father," she said. "But Lope will come, too. After all, she knows what it is you've done to me."

Once more, his dark eyes met with mine, narrowing with recognition as I removed my helm. For the first time, looking at him, I felt more powerful than he. I felt like I had more strength. More knowledge. For just a moment, *I* was more worthy of his crown than he was.

The lock clicked.

With a rough push, the king burst into the library, marching forward. Using all the stealth I'd been trained to possess, I silently closed and locked the door behind us. On the floor to my right, a few feet away, the hand mirror lay. Eglantine left it there—she must have hidden herself away when she heard the king approaching. I swept it up and hid it behind my back.

Glancing about the library, King Léo turned on his heel, scowling at me. "Where is she?"

"You know very well where I am, Father. Where you put me. Where you put all of us."

My determination soared at the rage that shook Ofelia's voice.

The king narrowed his eyes at me, the only source of the sound. "What sort of trick is this?"

I withdrew the mirror from behind my back and showed it to him. He gasped, staggering back.

"Oh, Father, you look horrible," Ofelia said. I could almost picture how fury would have painted her eyes dark. "How did you explain your appearance to the court? Did you say that your skin had aged from worry? Or that you'd been blessed again? Some other lie?"

He squared his shoulders—and then began to walk back the way we'd come.

"You're dead," he said. "I do not fear you."

My heart skipped. He was leaving. No, no, I needed to draw him closer to the portal. I stepped backward, closer to the aisle where it was hidden away. "Wait!" I called out to him. I brandished the mirror. "You may not fear the dead, but the court—when they see their beloved Ofelia, when they hear her voice, they'll know what you've done." I held my arms wide as he looked back at me over his shoulder. "I'm no more than a servant, and one look at your many shadows was enough for me to know what kind of man you truly are. You are not blessed. You're a serpent. A selfish wretch."

He turned fully toward me. He looked like the illustrations of wolves in Ofelia's fairy tales, hungry, ready to pounce.

"I suppose you want the mirror, then," I said, holding it out to him.

He quirked an eyebrow, taking slow, measured steps toward me. "What would you like for it? A title? A girl? Would you like that scar removed from your face?"

Yes, I thought. *Come get me.*

"What would I like?" I hesitated, as if drawing out the thought while I stepped backward, closer and closer to the door's hiding place. "You'll have to find out."

With that, I darted into the bookshelves, around one corner and past another. I could hear his footsteps behind me, always. After another turn, I stood before the black door with its metal handle, the door that had grown from my own blood.

Something grabbed the back of my hair.

I cried out. The unseen force behind me threw me onto my knees, sending the mirror skittering across the wooden floorboards.

The king loomed over me, pulling me onto my back, his knee pressed hard into my ribs, his hands wrapped tight around my throat.

"Do you know what becomes of those who defy me?" he hissed, his thumbs pressing into my windpipe. His dark eyes were flat as stone. "You do not know. Because those who defy me *are not found*."

Kick, I begged my legs, but no—thanks to the sacrifice, it was as if they'd forgotten how.

Scrape, I begged my hands, but no—they, too, refused to move.

"My servants will come and sweep you up like refuse," he hissed. "Your body will be tossed in a river. Or perhaps I'll feed you to my dogs."

When a Shadow stood above me, taking the breath from my lungs, it did so thoughtlessly. It did it out of servitude to its master, a king deep, deep under the earth.

This man, this king, was taking my breath and watching me with satisfaction in his eyes.

I choked. He did not flinch.

My body jerked beneath him involuntarily, and he pushed back harder.

He wanted to see the death in my eyes.

"What a useless knight you were," he spat.

Darkness lingered on the outskirts of my vision, and I was screaming in my head, my cries permeating throughout the whole world—

That screaming I heard. It was Ofelia's, too. She was calling out my name.

There was a loud thump, muffled and painful, like the final beat of my heart.

The hands loosened from my throat.

The king slumped to the floor.

Eglantine stood above me, chest heaving, a large book still held aloft. Among the spinning world, I could read the title of the volume that had taken down the king: *His Majesty's Innumerable Victories*.

He groaned but was stirring still. I glanced at the mirror— it was empty. Ofelia had vanished.

"Are you all right?" asked Eglantine, heaving with breath. She offered me a hand, and with every inch of me quaking, I slowly stood.

It felt like the pull of the earth had been magnified ten-fold. All my years of training, the strength I fought so hard to gain—all gone. "I'm alive," I said softly, my voice rough and hoarse. Standing on my feet again, I heard Eglantine call my name. I looked up in time to catch a penknife in its sheath.

I smiled at the familiar blade, whipping it from its sheath. I approached the king, kneeling and pressing the blade to his jugular. With my other hand, I grabbed the back of his snow-white hair, holding him in place as his eyes struggled to focus on mine. He sneered—but there was real fear in his eyes. I knew it well.

"I have the power of the gods on my side, *girl*," he growled. "One word from me and they'll turn you to ash."

How that would have left me bowing and pleading only a few weeks ago.

Now I smiled. "Call them," I said.

His confident look flickered for a second. "You cannot harm me. I was granted immortality."

"Immortality, perhaps. Invincibility?" With a bit more pressure, a drop of blood rolled down the king's throat and dribbled down his golden clothing. *"Perhaps not."* The simple act was enough to leave my arm burning with pain. I gritted my teeth. I took a deep breath. "Shall I put your immortality to the test, *sire?*"

"What do you want?" he snapped.

The answer was immediate, like oil catching fire. "I want

Ofelia," I whispered. "And I want you to *rot*."

Before he could speak, I said, "Eglantine, are you willing to come below with me?"

"Yes," she said.

I nodded at her, this librarian, my ally. "Open the door."

"Door?" The king's eyes focused behind me on the isolated black door standing not far from where I knelt. His pupils became pinpricks. He started to struggle against me, his movements sluggish and weak, but I held his hair tighter and kept the blade firm against his throat.

"You have nothing to fear, Your Majesty," I said coldly. "You are favored by the gods, aren't you? I should think you are good friends with the god of the Underworld."

"Guards!" he bellowed. "Guards!"

Eglantine dashed to the door to the Underworld, glaring at the king as she held the doorknob. "You. You sacrificed my mother for your *vanity*," she hissed.

We had no time. I jerked the king to his feet, my blade still at his throat. "Get ready," I told her.

He continued to scream. Footsteps began to resound like drums in the corridor. I felt a pang of regret for what we were about to do, releasing more beasts into this world.

Eglantine threw open the door to darkness. Shadows came flooding out, slipping past the three of us, through the library, out into the palace. More screams came from the corridor, men in *agony*.

Wading through currents of Shadows, I pushed King Léo through the door, and in a blink, Eglantine enfolded herself behind me in the cold and the dark of the Underworld.

With one hand, I closed the door behind us.

28

Ofelia

It was happening again.

She was dying again.

I raced down the spiral steps, out into the gray garden beyond. There were hedges like in the palace gardens, but all through these grounds were high-pitched whistles, the roaring of beasts, low, shuddering sounds—animals but not quite.

Sprinting down the straight path, I saw the Shadow King standing there at the end, taking notes on his scroll. Behind iron fences, Shadows of all sizes fluttered and slithered and crawled within their pens. One took on the appearance of a horse with its jaws opened, far too wide, and its eyes pure white and utterly frightening.

The god sensed my presence, turning his bright eyes upon me. "Ofelia?"

I clung to the black, silky fabric of his sleeves. "He's killing her," I rasped. "King Léo, he's killing Lope!"

"I'm sorry, child." His words were soft and true but utterly useless to me.

I glared up at him, my hands tightening into fists. "We can't let this happen! You're a *god*, can't you help me?!"

"I do not have that sort of power, Ofelia."

All my strength was sapped away, and I fell to the stones of the path, clutching his robes and sobbing. "Please, please save her!" I begged. "I'll give you anything, my blood, my heart, my life, any of it; it's yours, just spare her!"

I could see her face so clearly in my mind: her blue lips, her closing eyes. That awful gurgling sound as she lost her breath again.

She died for me. Just as she always said she would. She came to the Underworld for me. And then she gave her life, fighting for mine.

I wept so profusely that I could barely breathe. When I tried to imagine a world where Lope, beautiful, valiant, marvelous Lope, was gone, every inch of my body grew ice-cold with grief . . . and with rage.

A hoarse scream tore its way out of my throat. Cursed be the gods who turned their faces from us, cursed be the king who'd taken her from me, and cursed be the Shadow King who treated us like prizes he'd won in a game.

But his arms wrapped around me.

His limbs were crooked and bony. He held me too gently, like he was afraid he'd break me.

I sobbed into his robes, and his hand gently passed over and over against my hair.

"When you saw her," said the Shadow King, "when you kissed her—I had not seen a human smile, not like that before. When you were together, there was such brightness in your eyes. I have heard of that feeling. Joy, it's called?"

I nodded, my throat burning from my cries and from every ragged breath that scraped against my lungs.

"And that was love, when you stood side by side, when you kept reaching for her hand." The monster brushed his fingers through my hair again. "We gods do not know how to love. It is a human invention, you know. And it was so beautiful to . . ."

His voice trailed off. Somewhere to my right was a soft, slithering sound. When I lifted my head, I saw a little Shadow, its head cocked at me.

"We have guests," said the Shadow King. "King Léo, a woman, and—and a girl."

Lope. Please. I sat up straight, still clinging to his robes. "Take me to them."

He snapped his long fingers.

Suddenly, the menagerie was gone, and we were on a grassy plain. A few steps from us, Lope stood, very pale, with a heavy band of bruises around her throat. Eglantine was to her left, and the king was in her grasp, a blade pressed against his neck.

Peace, gratitude, and utter joy washed over me in a flood, and it felt as if my heart could finally beat again. I darted toward Lope, slamming into her and burying my head against her heart.

"Oh, gods," I sobbed. "I thought you were dead!"

"I promised I'd come for you." She kissed my hair. My pulse raced. I couldn't believe she finally touched me like that, looked at me like that—that I could hold tight to her and speak my love to her at last.

I drew back just so I could look into her eyes again, see the vitality in them. The prettiest gray, like the feathers of a dove. I cradled her face between my hands, my thumbs brushing her soft, warm cheeks. "I want to look at you for a thousand years," I said, my voice pinched.

A grin spread across her normally solemn face. "Then I will live a thousand years for you."

The Shadow King drifted close, grabbing King Léo by the throat. His eyes flew open, and he gasped, clutching at the hand coiled around his neck.

"No!" he choked. "We—had—a—deal!"

"I have a deal with her," said the Shadow King, pointing to Lope. "Lope de la Rosa. And you have broken your deal many, many times."

Lope bowed at the sound of her name. "Sire," she said, looking to the Shadow King. I perked up. I recognized that tone of her voice, one I rarely heard—it said she had something up her sleeve. "There's something I found curious. All this time, King Léo said that it was the gods above that had blessed him. That they had gifted him with youth and prosperity . . . in fact, he *never* mentioned you."

The Shadow King hissed, throwing Léo onto the grass. From the blackness around him, Shadows rose, wrapping around the king's legs, his arms, his neck, holding him in place before us, lifting up the king as if he were a painting on the wall. His eyes were round with fear—and with vicious hate.

"Loathsome mortal," growled the Shadow King. "I want you to see those you sacrificed so that you could sit upon your throne. See the ones you loved and know how they hate you. Let them *show you*."

Once more, the Shadow King snapped his fingers. Thin clouds of black smoke arose, and from them stepped the others: King Augustin, Prince Philippe, the queen mother, Françoise, Sagesse, and my mother. She ran to me, sweeping me into her arms.

Sagesse caught sight of her daughter. She covered her mouth.

Eglantine threw down her knife and ran, throwing her arms around her mother, who could now have been mistaken for her sister.

"I missed you every day," Eglantine said, her voice thick.

Sagesse hushed her and rocked her in her embrace, back and forth, like she was still a young girl. "I never ever forgot you, my Eglantine." They spoke for a moment, weeping, embracing, laughing. And then, after a few more heartbeats, Sagesse whispered something in her daughter's ear, and Eglantine released Sagesse from her hold, a smirk crossing the librarian's face.

Sagesse turned to approach the king, her head held high. Her eyes narrowed at him. "*You.*" Sagesse growled the word.

She promptly rammed her fist into his stomach. He let out a loud cry. She spat in his face.

"I missed my daughter's life," she said. "You *wasted* all my years because you thought I'd be a suitable payment. Bastard." Sagesse spun on her heel, her eyes gleaming with tears and fury. "Are you going to kill him?" she asked the god.

"No," said the Shadow King. "There is no death here. He'll stay here, preserved." He lifted a finger. "On the other hand, it was by my power that I kept him young above. And, Lope, you say he never credited me for this. Never thanked me for it."

In a blink, the Shadow King was standing at Léo's shoulder, his hand around the king's jaw. "I think instead you shall age, Léo, age and decay, but never die. I'll build you a hall just like the other one, a hall of mirrors, where you may forever look at yourself . . ."

Fear glimmered in Léo's eyes, but he clenched his jaw. "The gods will not stand for such treatment of their chosen king!"

The Shadow King's face split in a wide, crooked smile.

"The gods have never cared about you."

The monsters clinging to King Léo hissed delightedly, their claws digging deeper into his flesh. Blood stained his gold brocade and satin.

"I'll send him away," said the king of Shadows to us all, "if you'd like to bid him farewell."

King Augustin turned his back. His son did the same, and the queen mother, trembling with tears, hid her face against her husband's shoulder.

Françoise shook her head and stood at my side, holding tight to my hand. "I never want to see you again," she whispered to him.

Sagesse waved her hand in a strange symbol. "May your every moment be agony," she said—a promise. A curse. Eglantine held her mother's arm, smiling triumphantly.

I had no words. And neither did my mother. The king was my father, but only in the barest sense of the word. He didn't want me. He didn't love me. He was a liar, a coward, a foul mockery of a father and a king.

Lope took a stride closer to him. I wanted to reach out, to pull her back, to protect her—but her head was held high. She grinned, looking him fearlessly in the eyes. "Long live the king."

He spat in her face. She laughed.

Rage thundered through me; an inarticulate sound of fury ripped from my throat as I made to claw at him, but

Mother and Françoise held me back.

"Please," said Mother to the Shadow King. "Take him away from here."

With another *snap*, Léo and the Shadows that had bound him were gone. A memory that would never touch us again. As Lope cleaned her face, I marched over to her, pulling her back into my embrace where she belonged.

"You're unbelievable," I said, muffled against her shoulder. "And perfect."

Her ribcage reverberated with the sound of her laugh. She wound her arms around my middle, both of us pressed close, warm and glowing like embers.

"Your Majesty?" Lope called to the Shadow King. "With King Léo gone, what will become of the door he made?"

"It is useless now. No one can open it, from your world or from mine."

She exhaled, almost as if she didn't believe him, and she held me even closer. "How—how many other doors remain? That allow Shadows into the world above?"

"Just your own, Lope de la Rosa."

"Then the Shadows—"

"They will stay here with me and with the king's beloved."

A beautiful, relieved smile crossed her lips.

The Shadow King twisted his head toward my mother. "Now then. The bargain is complete. Three of you may return to the world above. Ofelia, Marisol, Sagesse—would you like to say goodbye to the others?"

King Augustin, Queen Caroline, Philippe, Françoise. They had showed me such kindness and warmth, even in this cold, desolate place. And they'd remain here forever. All of these people doomed by the greed of the king.

My father had sacrificed them all to get what he wanted.

I could not be like him.

A plan began to bloom in my mind.

"You're concentrating," Lope murmured. "You're going to bite your lip raw."

"I have an idea," I said. "We must talk a little farther from the others."

I asked the others for ten more minutes. Though I knew time moved strangely here, that above seconds or days or years could pass in such time, I needed just a moment in private.

A moment to gently break the heart of my beloved.

She followed me to the beach. I pulled her down to sit side by side with me, the waves before us, the crystalline moon above us.

"Whatever your plan is," said Lope, "I'll gladly partake."

Her loyalty made my heart soar—and then sink as I thought of the pain I would soon cause her. I squeezed her hand tight and hated the words forming on my tongue. "I can't go above with you."

"What?"

Her voice broke in two. I dared to meet her gaze, but the despair there made me crumble. Tears spilled from my eyes, and she hastily brushed them aside.

"You—you don't have to go with me, if you don't want to," Lope whispered. "I can go my way, and you can go yours—"

"I love you," I said, pressing a kiss to her cheek. "I *want* to go with you. But what I want . . . it's not the only important thing." I pointed to the others far behind us. "They have been trapped here forever. Separated from time, separated from their loved ones. They don't deserve this. So I will make a trade with the Shadow King. I will stay here, and he will release *all* of them to the world above."

"Then I'll stay here with you."

I clenched my eyes shut. I knew she'd say such a thing. Dependable, beautiful Lope.

"Listen to me," I whispered, and she was utterly silent, even though her eyes were burning. "I meant what I said. You deserve the world, my love. You deserve to go out and see it."

"I don't want it." She shook her head, tears tumbling down her cheeks. "I don't want the world. Just you."

I hushed her again, cupping her cheek in my hand. She canted her head, kissing my palm.

"I am all you've ever known," I said, "and all this time, I've been your mistress. I don't want to be that anymore. I don't want to order you about." My finger carefully traced a strand of hair, placing it back behind her ear. "I don't have a title or money or gifts, but I want to give you this choice. I want you to decide for yourself if I am all that you want. Go. See the world above. Drink in all its beauty. Write ten thousand poems."

"And if I decide that it's you that I want?"

I laughed at the certainty in her voice, and then ached, because I had never felt so confident before that somebody loved me. And I was about to lose that love.

"In a year's time," I said, "if you choose me, I'll be here. I'll be yours. This world below will pale in comparison to the one above, but it'll be ours. But please, Lope. Give yourself a chance. Go and live. And not for me—for yourself." I wrapped my arms around her waist and desperately tried to hold back tears. "I just want you to know how much I love you."

"I know it," she whispered. "But do not ask me to leave you like you did before—"

"I ask nothing of you." I bowed her head close to mine and pressed a kiss to her brow. "It's your choice. You get to decide what you want."

Lope slowly drew back from me. She gazed at the giant crystal, suspended over the smooth obsidian waters. A small smile flitted across her lips—fond and nostalgic.

"I want . . . another moment," she said. "We have been

running and fighting for so, so long. All I want right now is to sit on this shore with you, for just a little longer."

We rested next to each other, watching the dark waves lap over themselves. The seafoam was like lace and would cling to the sparkling sand for a moment before it faded away.

We listened to the waters, like rushing winds or the sound of a lullaby.

"This used to be my dream," said Lope. She delicately fit her hand in mine. "I'd lie on a beach somewhere, and you'd be there, too."

"Do you want to lie down?"

She smiled, bending close to nestle her head against mine. "It is difficult to tell you what I want. All the silly things my heart aches for."

"They're not silly," I promised her. I tucked her hair behind her ears and cradled her face, admiring the white and purple reflections against the steel gray of her eyes. "May I speak honestly with you?"

"Yes." Lope pressed a kiss on my forehead. "Titles and stations and pretenses. Can we let them all fall away?"

"Please."

She kissed my temple and my cheekbone and the corner of my mouth. I wanted to melt into her touch, to let her sweep me away like the tide.

"I—I am afraid of saying the wrong thing," I murmured. "For so long, I was used to . . . how things were before. I'm frightened that my old self, or perhaps my true self, will burst forth, and I'll say something hurtful to you and not know it. Or that you won't feel safe enough to tell me something." I swallowed a lump in my throat. "In truth I . . . I simply have no idea what I'm doing. I want to love you well. I want to give you all that you deserve."

Lope carefully tipped my chin toward hers, and another kiss from her made the worries in my mind fizzle away for a moment.

"Here's my truth," she said, her words tickling my lips. "I am utterly clueless when it comes to love."

I laughed, soft and sad. "I wish we could start over."

"I don't. We have come so far. We have earned our scars. We have changed. I loved you before. I love you now. And I wager I'll love the person you'll become, too."

I shook my head at her. "You deserve someone perfect."

"Isn't that for me to decide?"

My cheeks grew warm. "Well, yes."

"Then I want someone imperfect. So we can grieve at our own weaknesses. And perhaps strengthen each other, too." She tipped her head, her dark hair falling in a beautiful wave down her shoulder. "Will you accept me, then? Will you look at my flaws and love me anyway?"

"Gods, yes." I grabbed the lapels of her coat and pulled her close for a deeper kiss.

After another and another, she slowly reclined on her elbows until she rested her head in my lap. When I brushed the hair from her brow, her eyes drooped shut. She looked more serene than I'd ever imagined.

She felt that way with me.

"There," she whispered. "This is my dream."

For so long, Lope had been watching over me. Constant vigilance, constant fear. To see her be so still and so at peace was a sweeter gift than I could imagine. Divorced of the pain and the fear, she was simply a girl. A beautiful girl, who I loved.

I wanted days and days like that for her. I wanted her to rest under millions of stars or on a gently rocking boat or in a meadow in some distant forest.

But like all moments, this one had to end.

"I'll go," she said. "And I'll miss you every day."

Together, we left that shore.

I prayed one day we'd see another.

Just before we joined the group waiting for us, Lope drew me into an embrace—and then whispered in my ear.

"The girl I love,
Worth more than a thousand crowns,
Than all the kingdoms,
Beyond precious
Is the one my soul calls its own.
You are my own,
My own,
Let my heartbeat ever call it so."

A poem. A poem just for me.

"Thank you," I breathed.

We parted from our embrace, and she kissed me again, brief but firm. "I will write to you," she said. "I will burn letters to you and send them here below. And the Shadow King—he could share your messages with me when I pray."

I traced my finger along her cheekbone. "I wanted you to experience a life *away* from me."

"And I think that's nonsense." She smiled. "Some distance, I can allow. But I cannot live as though you do not exist. We have spent so many years choosing our words carefully and hiding our hearts. If I am to leave you, even for a moment, I will reach for you, no matter what. I want to hear all your thoughts, even when I cannot see you." Her shoulders sagged, and she sighed, making a lock of hair on her forehead flutter. "I think that's the most forthright I've ever been."

I squeezed her hand. "I quite like it."

Hand in hand, we approached the king of Shadows.

"Are you ready to return?" he asked in his sweet, soft voice, nothing like how a monster's voice should be.

"Not quite," I said. "I would like to make a bargain with you."

Mother's eyes widened. My grandmother gasped and whispered anxiously with her husband, the old king.

"You have me very curious," said the god.

"I want you to release *all* of the king's beloved back into the world where they belong," I said.

"What?" whispered Philippe. Hope glimmered in his brown eyes.

The Shadow King tilted his head and wrung his long fingers together. "Why would I do such a thing?" he asked. "I'd be left here . . . alone. With no new stories of the world above."

I gave Lope's hand a final squeeze before I took a shaky step closer to him. "I'll stay here. I'll be your storyteller. Forever."

Mother gripped my arm so tight, I thought she'd break it. "Ofelia, no!"

The god's eyes narrowed. "One soul, only to lose six? It is not an equal bargain."

What did he want? He wanted to understand humanity. He wanted to know our stories. He wanted to know about our emotions, about joy, about love . . .

I had nothing to give. Nothing to give but love.

"King of Shadows," I said, with all the authority of a princess, "if you free these souls, I will tell you stories. And I will prove to you that human love is real. Not some selfish thing like the king made it out to be. I'll tell you all I know about the world above. You have heard my stories once before. You know they are spectacular indeed."

His eyes brightened like a flaring candle.

Mother stood in front of me. "I'll stay in her place."

I clung to her arm, glaring at her. "Mother, no—"

"You are my daughter," she snapped. "It is *my* duty to protect *you*—"

"This is what it means to grow up," I replied. "Instead of reading stories, I can write one now." I nodded to the Shadow King. "You have my proposal."

"I accept your bargain," said the king of Shadows.

Mother's arms fastened around me. "Then I'll stay with you, too."

He snapped his fingers—but nothing changed. Nothing felt different. Though I'd accepted the price I'd pay, I let out a long sigh.

The bargain was made. They were free.

I turned to Françoise and all of my family. "It isn't right, what's happened to you," I said. I looked at them, some smiling, some with tears in their eyes—some with both. "I cannot undo what King Léo did. But you deserve *life*."

"You are nothing like the king," said Françoise. She curtsied deeply to me. "You are as brave as you are good."

The others approached me, keeping their gazes shied from the god watching over us.

"Bless you, my child," said the queen mother, kissing me farewell.

King Augustin embraced me, and so did his son.

Sagesse crossed the dark grass toward me, her daughter's hand in hers. She reached into the pocket of her gown and held out the small, magical hand mirror.

"Since I am with my Eglantine again," she said, "you can use this to speak with your love, even while you are apart."

I pressed the mirror against my heart. "Thank you," I said.

She was right. I could see Lope still, even for a few minutes each day. We could continue to speak. Like Lope had said, it would only do us good to stay in correspondence with each other.

Lope stood close by. With her bruised neck and her tangled hair and her scar and the scabbard at her hip empty.

I remembered—she'd given up her strength to open the door to me.

"Sire?" I murmured.

"Yes, child?" asked the Shadow King, kneeling so he could look me in the eyes. His were brilliant white, like snowflakes suspended against a dark sky.

"I don't have anything to give you," I said, "but I ask most humbly that, when you send my Lope back into the world above, you give her back her strength, so that she can protect herself from unkind people. And the Shadows that are still above—I don't want them in the world, bothering her or anyone else."

"I will call on them to return through Lope's door. I no longer need Shadows in your world," he said, his thumb brushing my cheek. "I have you here, to tell me a thousand stories. There are so many things I want you to teach me."

Another good thing to come of this. How swiftly, how easily, he could rid the world of his monsters. The world would become bright again, like everyone was waking from the same nightmare.

"Of course," I told him. "I have so many stories for you."

His eyes sparkled with his smile. "Then I will return Lope's strength to her, as well as this gift." He pinched his fingers together and drew them in a line. Out of the darkness, a thin, shining sword appeared, reflective from tip to hilt, as though it had been made of melted mirrors. He offered the sword to Lope. "To my favorite poet. A god's blessing."

Lope knelt in the grass before us and accepted the blade. She curled her hands around it gently and looked up at the Shadow King.

"Thank you, sire," she said. She admired the shining sword. "It is a treasure. But I pray I will never have to wield it."

The Shadow King's eyes glinted. "You can use it as . . . what's the word? Decoration? For memories and beauty."

There was not quite forgiveness in her gaze but something settled. She gave him a nod and a small smile, and then turned to me.

She lifted her head, beaming up at me, and in her fond, warm gaze, I felt like I was standing in a sunbeam.

"I love you." Her gray eyes shone with tears, brimming with an adoration that I wanted to fall into forever. "A thousand cities, a thousand mountains, a thousand kingdoms won't change that. I'll come back. I'll come back with a thousand new poems for you."

My own tears began to fall as I dropped onto the grass in front of her, and Lope took the chance to anchor herself to my sleeve, pull me close, and press her lips to mine. I tangled my fingers into her braid as I held her to me. If I kissed her long enough, kissed her deeply enough, perhaps this moment would never end.

The ones the king had sacrificed ascended the slow, spiraling staircase back to the door Lope and Eglantine had made. Mother stayed behind with me, her arm around my shoulders.

Lope was the last one, finally rising from the grass only when I gently pulled her to her feet. She gave me one last kiss, and then our hands slowly slipped from each other's grasp.

She climbed the winding staircase, up onto the landing far, far above. She stood in the doorway, a rectangle of beautiful, amber light—what was now the last place through which Shadows could enter our world. As she gazed at me from above, hundreds of monsters scurried past her, pouring down the stairs like someone had spilled a giant inkwell. Just as the Shadow King had promised. Finally, they became fewer and fewer, drop by drop, scampering through the tall grasses or disappearing into the hills of this vast world below.

Lope and I looked at each other through the doorway, so, so far away.

I imagined her running carefree through a sunlit world. Her smile when she'd see a mountain for the very first time. Her hands slipping gently through sand or the turquoise waters of the ocean.

I didn't regret my choice. Not for an instant.

The door between worlds shut like the cover of a book.

EPILOGUE
Lope

I opened a door to darkness,
Wherein I'd find
My sweet, sunlit heart.

When I opened the door to the Underworld, the air
that greeted me was warm and gentle. No Shadows
slid past my ankles, just as the Shadow King had promised.
I could see nothing through the doorway but a black abyss,
yet the faintest smell of orange blossoms made my heart feel
at home again.

I wished farewell to Sagesse and to Eglantine. I took one
last glance about the library, at the bright colors, at the glow
of the sunshine, *real* sunshine against the books.

A light waited for me below.

I set one foot into the void, landing against a sturdy
surface—the top of a staircase, I remembered.

I would descend these steps to the Underworld. And with Ofelia by my side, I would forever call this place my home.

I shut the door behind me.

The golden light of the library shrank, folding smaller and smaller like a piece of paper—until it was gone.

The gravity of it struck me. I clung tight to my leather satchel, filled with every remnant I could bring with me from my travels. Flowers pressed between pages of sonnets. My book of sketches—small, meager things, my rudimentary attempts to capture the majesty of a mountain or the peacefulness of a cabin by the lake. And my own journals were filled to bursting, musing about the beauty I beheld, trying to fit every ounce of it onto a page, so that Ofelia might experience it with me.

With trembling breaths, I felt my way down the steps, a thin onyx railing serving as my guide. We had spoken so often with the use of the mirror. Our bond had changed, breaking and reforging and learning and growing.

Yet I'd not held her hand in a year. I'd not felt her breath upon my neck. I longed for the days when I'd wake up beside her and the faint scent of roses and orange blossoms from the perfume in her hair would fill the air between us.

I knew her; I trusted her, but even so, doubt whispered poison in my ear, *What if she doesn't want you?*

The dazzling light drew me away from my brooding. Somewhere in my descent, I'd passed some invisible barrier,

I'd slipped into some different world, where the sky was golden, like twilight in summer. I stopped in shock, gazing out at the land before me.

To my left were dozens and dozens of cherry blossom trees, just like the ones I'd seen on my journey. They were surrounded by fields of flowers of all colors, and a path wound through them all, leading to—to a bed, right there in the middle of the orchard, covered in blooms, vines twining around the wood frame.

Ahead of me was a range of lilac mountains, capped with snow. But they did not look to be made of stone—their texture was soft and loose. Like brushstrokes, as if someone had painted the mountains into being.

And on my right, a still, calm lake was like a pool of gold, reflecting the sky. The lake was ringed with pink sand, and far, far away, I could see three small figures in bright clothing.

Ofelia. One of them had to be Ofelia.

I could not contain all the hope and the happiness within me. Gripping tight to the railing, I called to the trio below, "Ofelia!"

One figure scrambled to their feet and shielded their eyes against the sunlight. Then her bright, joyful cry rang out through the whole world, and she was tearing across the flowery plains.

As fast as I could, I bounded down the stairs. At the very

bottom, the earth beneath my feet was not black stone as before, but soft soil. Before me were vast fields of lavender, just like the ones I'd seen in the southeast, except these grew so wildly, so freely, all the way up to my waist. I breathed in the soft, sweet perfume and touched my fingertips to a lavender sprig—it was real. A little damp, delicate, full of life. Such beauty, all in this place that had been so dark, so cold.

"Lope!"

In the distance, there she was, wading among the lavender blossoms. With the light behind her, I could not see her face, just her silhouette, outlined in gold like she had become a goddess in my absence. She wore a wreath of flowers in her hair, all of them gleaming in the light—golden blooms that crowned her and fell, draping throughout her curls.

We raced toward each other, and then, at long last, I held her fast in my arms. Amid her crying and her delighted laughter, she pulled back from me, kissing my hair, my brow, my cheeks, my lips.

"You came back," she whispered, tears glowing in her eyes.

If the gods had faces, they'd look like hers. A brilliant smile that made my heart stop. Her soft, pink lips that I wanted to *worship*. The constellation of freckles across her cheeks and shoulders, and those eyes, those warm, brown eyes that made me feel like I was the most important being in the universe. The place of the goddess of love must have been usurped by

Ofelia, who radiated warmth and affection like sunlight.

I pressed my forehead to hers. "I could not live with my heart so far away."

Her thumbs delicately brushed my cheeks. "I hope you found happiness up there. That's all I wanted; I wanted you to be happy—"

I interrupted her with a kiss. The way her breath faltered in a soft gasp against my lips made starlight sweep through me. "I am the happiest creature, above or below."

She stood on her toes, clutching the lapels of my coat before gracing me with another kiss. "We'll call it a tie."

For a moment, we lost ourselves in quiet, in our closeness, in whispers and smiles.

Somewhere, the stillness was interrupted by a barking dog.

Ofelia laughed as I raised an eyebrow.

"Is there a *dog* in the Underworld?" I asked her.

She grinned, taking my hand. "Come, there's so much to show you."

I followed in her wake through the fragrant fields. "So much has changed in this world. . . . How can it be?"

"Soleil always had a talent for creating things," Ofelia said over her shoulder. "He just needed the guidance of someone who remembers what it's like above! And your letters, your poems, they helped us tremendously!"

Soleil? I hadn't a clue who that could have been; the only others below were Marisol and the Shadow King. Had he made a bargain with some other poor soul in my absence?

"It's so perfect, Lo," she continued. "Whatever Mother wants to paint, he and I help craft it for her. We can change the landscape whenever we feel like it."

We stepped out of the fields and onto the beach made of pink sand. Not far from us, Ofelia's mother was painting the portrait of a blond man sitting in front of her. Resting on his lap was a strange dog that seemed to be made of black vapor. Another smaller one, also seemingly made of shadow, was curled up on the sand beside Marisol.

Before I could ask about this, Ofelia loudly declared my presence. Marisol set aside her brush and palette and bent down, letting the not-quite-dog leap into her arms. The blond man in a cerulean suit rose from a stone bench, and the two ambled toward us.

Marisol had changed in small ways—she wore her dark hair loosely and bore an easy smile on her face. Over her buttercup-yellow gown she wore her artist's apron, covered in smudges of paint.

"Caballera de la Rosa," she said in greeting.

"Just Lope, please, madam."

Her eyes crinkled warmly. "I am happy to see you again, Lope. My daughter spoke so often of you. For you to choose a life down here, to give up the world above . . ."

I wove my fingers with Ofelia's. "It's an easy choice," I said. I cast a quick glance at the stranger to her right but couldn't help but focus on the odd-looking dog in the countess's arms. "What . . . what *is* that?"

"It's a Shadow," said Ofelia, leaning forward to scratch behind its floppy ears. It lolled its black tongue and kicked its back foot as she petted him. "Soleil said they came to him asking for new forms, too. To change like the world has."

The man extended a hand—but I paused. Where I thought his hair had been blond, it was now auburn, the same color as Ofelia's. Perhaps it was a trick of this new world; perhaps my mind was addled with fatigue from all my journeying. I cautiously accepted his handshake. His eyes, to my great surprise, were the color of amethysts.

"What a delight it is to see you again," he said with a white-toothed grin.

My brow furrowed. "Again, sir?"

He winked. "I looked a bit different last we met. But rest assured, I have not changed. You are still my favorite poet."

His voice was faintly, faintly familiar—but softer, smoother, not whispered. Only one person—one *being*—called me their favorite poet.

My hand flopped to my side. "You're the—the Shadow King?"

"He goes by Soleil now," said Ofelia.

The king of Shadows, now named after the sun. In the light, his face kept changing—his nose would be small or large, his eyes would be bright blue or deep black, his jaw was sharp and square one second and round and smooth the next, and his skin shifted between different shades of warm brown tones.

"How can this be?" I whispered.

Soleil looked fondly at Ofelia. "My two friends. Most especially Ofelia. She remembers the world so vividly. The way she describes it is marvelous." Ofelia's pink skirts bloomed as she curtsied. He reached into his breast pocket, passing me a piece of paper. "And these! The poems you sent us inspired our work!"

I unfolded the page and found verses in my own hand. Vaguely, I remembered this poem, describing the line of the mountains jutting into the sky. As Ofelia had asked, I had fed it to the candle flame, as I would a sacrifice. The poems were not consumed or absorbed, then, but sent, preserved, to the king himself.

But there was one poem I had prepared for my reunion with Ofelia. I dug through my bag and pressed it into her hands.

"I owe you a poem," I said to her. "I owe you a hundred."

She folded the paper with a demure smile. "Nonsense. You may share your art with me when you feel ready to do so."

"I'm ready."

Ofelia grinned, flipping the paper open and reading it over. The words had been repeating themselves in my head over and over for weeks now. I bent close to her, my arms around her and my lips beside her ear as I read them aloud:

"I have seen the ice-peaked mountains,
The floating city,
The forest filled with flowers,
And yet as far as I've been,
As far as I've seen,
Nothing, nothing,
Is as beautiful as you."

She laughed a little sob and then kissed me, pressing me close in a tight embrace. "Oh, I have missed you so!"

"I'll not part from you again," I said. "I promise."

We soon remembered that we were standing there kissing and swooning before both Ofelia's mother *and* the king of this realm. We parted, collecting ourselves—but tears rolled down Soleil's face. The Shadow dog whimpered and wiggled in Marisol's arms until she shifted the creature into the arms of the god. Soleil smiled a little bit as he pressed his creation against his heart. But there was heartbreak in his eyes.

"Soleil?" Ofelia asked. "What's wrong?"

"I asked you to teach me about love," he said, his voice pinched with emotion. "I wanted to learn how to be a human, and I—what a fool I've been."

Marisol stepped closer to him, her hand against his shoulder. She looked him in the eyes not like a cowering subject, but as one friend to another. "What do you mean, dear?"

He set down the dog and let it scurry back to its napping spot on the beach. Soleil wiped at his eyes, his lips trembling.

A bit speechless, I offered the god my handkerchief, which he accepted with profuse gratitude.

"Sacrifice," he said tearfully. "*That* is what love is. Ofelia, you were willing to stay here below so no one else was trapped. Marisol, you sacrificed the sun and life and freedom, so that you could be here with your daughter."

Marisol wrapped an arm around Ofelia, beaming down at her. I could only imagine the strength of the bond they had formed over this long year together.

"And Lope," he continued, "you had the chance to live in the world above, to go anywhere . . . but you gave that up. You gave that up so you could see Ofelia again." He clutched his hands to his breast. "I have kept you for myself. I am—I am no human, try as I might to fool myself otherwise—"

"You're more human than so many," said Ofelia. "Far more than my . . . than my father."

"Exactly." Soleil shut his eyes, as if remembering something painful. "I . . . I do not wish to be alone. I fear it. But hoarding you for my own, when you could be above, feeling real air and real sunlight upon your face . . ."

The twilit king seemed to come to some conclusion. He placed his hand against Ofelia's cheek. "You're free to leave," he said. "All of you."

My heart skipped.

Ofelia was shaking her head. "No. No, I won't leave you, you'll be here all alone—"

"I have my Shadows," he murmured. He gestured around him. "This whole world is thanks to you. It's not the same; *I'm* not the same." The god pressed a kiss to her forehead. "I will be all right, dear one."

Marisol's hands were clasped together as in supplication. "Are . . . are you certain about this, my lord?"

Soleil nodded, even as tears fell. His blue-green-golden eyes aligned with mine. "My heart, it *aches*. How do you bear the pain?"

"The pain you feel—that is love," I said. "True love changes you. It leaves a mark upon you. Even if no one can see it."

He was quiet for a moment, sliding his hand over the place where his heart should have been. His shoulder shuddered with breath. "Then . . . maybe I am human after all."

The god bent down, meeting Ofelia eye to eye. A proud, brilliant smile brightened his face like sunshine. "Oh, Ofelia," he said, his thumb brushing her freckled cheek. "You have fulfilled your promise to me. You have taught me how to love, just as you said you would. What a beautiful curse! What a tragic gift!"

Ofelia threw her arms around him, weeping. "I don't know what to do! I cannot bear to leave you, and yet—"

"Your world calls to you, my dear one," he said.

"But—but I will miss you so," she whimpered.

An idea struck me. The same solution we'd had when

Ofelia and I had been separated. I reached into my satchel and procured the small hand mirror.

"Sire," I said softly. I held out the mirror, which glittered in the golden light. "We could continue to communicate, just as Ofelia and I did."

Ofelia gasped and rooted around in the pocket of her gown until she procured her own small hand mirror. She curled Soleil's fingers around it. "Take it," she said, "and we shall speak often."

He beamed down at Ofelia.

Her mother approached, wrapping her arm around her daughter's shoulders. "And there's no reason we couldn't come visit you again, my friend."

Soleil pressed the mirror to his chest. "Would you really? Would you speak to me, would you remember me, would you think of me?"

Ofelia stood on her toes and kissed the warm human face of the god. "I promise," she said. "And why should we be the only ones to know about you? We will tell others about you, about the great and kind god of stories, Soleil."

The man, once the king of Shadows, grinned as he bowed deeply to Ofelia. "Until we meet again. I am grateful to have been a part of your story, dearest Ofelia."

She squeezed his hand, her nose wrinkled. "The story's not done yet."

He neared the two of us, lifting Ofelia's hand and placing

it in my own. His eyes crinkled in the corners. "Indeed it is not," he said.

We bade farewell to the god and his new world.

The countess ascended the staircase, and Ofelia's fingers curled against my arm, a perfect fit.

Standing there at the foot of the stairs, she looked into my eyes, her smile pressing dimples into her rosy cheeks. "How sweet it is," she said, "to be with my home once more."

Pressing a kiss to her brow, I whispered, "Come with me into the light, my heart."

And I led her above into the dazzling daylight.

ACKNOWLEDGMENTS

Dear reader, thanks for reading my acknowledgments!

If you are an aspiring writer, I send you all my love and encouragement. This book is proof that your creative dreams can come true. Even if those books are very, very stubborn.

If you're a friend looking for your name, *thank you* for all you've done for me as an author and as a friend. And if you for some reason don't see your name, please forgive my deadline brain. I love you and am grateful.

If you're someone who needs to read acknowledgments so that you have one hundred percent completed a book, high-five yourself, because you are almost done!

Now on to the specifics. Thanks first to my family, Mom, Dad, Myles, Cosette, and Mr. Bingley. Thank you especially to Mom for making and delivering soup to me during my wild deadline days, and Dad for his endless book cheerleading and book mailing. I am so blessed by all of you. Myles, you are my favorite trash can of the sea.

Thank you to the independent bookstores who have supported me so fiercely and have been kind and generous beyond measure. A special shout-out to my St. Louis–area independent bookstores and my friends there: Emily Hall Schroen and the entire Main Street Books crew (including baby Alexander), my friends at the Novel Neighbor (hi Stephanie, Kassie, and Haley!), and my friends at Left Bank Books (thank you, Shane).

Thanks again to all those at Harper who brought this book to life, especially to Clare Vaughn, for her endless email answering and patience, and to Stephanie Guerdan, whose editorial vision and advocacy for this book means the world. Hugs to my lovely agent, Jordan Hamessley, who has fought so hard for this book. It makes me feel . . . sentimental!

Thank you to those who read this book and loved it from the beginning: Eliza Unseth, Lyndall Clipstone, Lucy M., Marcella, and Allison Saft.

Thank you to all the influencers, bloggers, readers, and booksellers who have enjoyed and shared my stories!

Hugs to Becca, Jake, Emily B., Jenni, Little Sarah, Brittany, Trisha, Dorian, Monica, Deke, Tania, Amna, and all my French family!

Emily Bain Murphy: Thank you, my dear friend and older sister. You are such a blessing to me. Hugs as well to

Liv, the aquarium expert, and Cecilia and James, *Overcooked!* master chefs.

Esme Symes-Smith: Thank you for always being there for my book release days, my victories, and my "books are hard" days. You are a wonderful friend, and I'm so lucky to know you.

Thank you to those at Château d'Orquevaux for your hospitality and inspiration.

Thank you to Shelly, my massage therapist, for keeping my arms and hands in working order!

Thank you to my university professors for your cheer-leading and kindness.

And to April and Alex, who said I didn't have to pay for Indian food if I put them in the acknowledgments. But also, for your sweetness and hospitality—my time in NYC was such a blessing, and I'm so grateful to you.